THE DAUGHTERS OF WINSTON BARNETT

DARA GIRARD

ISBN 13: 978-1949764369

THE DAUGHTERS OF WINSTON BARNETT

ILORI PRESS BOOKS, LLC

P.O. Box 10332

Silver Spring, MD 20914

www.iloripressbooks.com

Table for Two

Gaining Interest

Careless Rapture

Dangerous Curves

Familiar Stranger

It Happened One Wedding

Unexpected Pleasure

Midnight Promise

Sweet Temptation

Always and Forever

Truly Yours

Say Yes

Clifton Sisters

The Sapphire Pendant

The Amber Stone

The Emerald Ring

Fortune Brothers

A Tempting Proposal

A Seductive Arrangement

Novels

Promise Me

Honest Betrayal

The Daughters of Winston Barnett

Remember My Name

Illusive Flame

Winterwood Lane

Collections

The Lady Next Door and Other Stories

Five Holiday Tales

Lost and Found

10 Holiday Stories

School Days: Five Story Collection

Holiday Hearts

To my parents.

ACKNOWLEDGMENTS

First I would like to thank Jane Austen and Sholem Aleichem for creating stories that have inspired, entertained, united and delighted generations. I also want to acknowledge and thank Sheldon Harnick and Jerry Brock whose music and lyrics from the musical *Fiddler on the Roof* continues to resonant in the hearts and minds of millions. Special thanks to Deborah Silberman for her keen eye and continued encouragement and Tom for keeping Debbie happy. Lastly, my dearest appreciation goes to the numerous individuals who have helped me along this journey. Your support and belief in me is a treasure I will never forget. Without your guidance, generosity and encouragement I would never have been able to follow my dreams.

"Life is a dream for the wise, a game for the fool, a comedy for the rich, a tragedy for the poor."

Sholem Aleichem

~

*"One half of the world cannot understand the pleasures of
the other."*

Jane Austen

~

"Many rivers to cross."

Jimmy Cliff

CHAPTER 1

She should have burned the letter.

Janet Barnett stared at the white paper clutched in her father's large brown fist and sighed. If she had the chance to do it all over again, she would have read Valerie's letter, memorized its contents, and then tossed it in the fireplace. Instead, she'd left it on the desk in her bedroom where one of her four sisters had found it.

Now she sat before her father, a tall, lean figure with a voice that could shake the rafters (although a gentle breeze could also produce the same effect because the old house was in desperate need of repair), listening to how she'd disappointed them. Her father loomed above her as though she was part of his congregation and he was standing at the pulpit leading a sermon. As one of the deacons in their evangelical church, he was well-versed in that task.

"Do you want to break your mother's heart?" he asked.

Janet glanced at the quiet figure sitting in the chair beside him with eyes that could be both innocent and shrewd but now looked near tears. It was a rhetorical question so Janet knew it wise not to answer. Her mother's heart was a delicate organ she'd damaged many times before. She'd bruised it when she'd announced she wanted to be an artist, she'd cracked it when she'd said she wanted to study at the university and now at twenty-two she threatened to shatter it completely.

Her father tossed the paper on the side table. "Do I not provide for you? Is my home not grand enough? Didn't I work two jobs so that you can live this way?" He raised his hands, his palms held out for her to see the calluses marring the surface. "To think the day would come that a *dawta* of mine would insult mi this way," he said, his Jamaican accent growing thick as his anger grew.

"It's not like that," Janet said.

"Then why do you want to leave me?" He looked at her as though she'd threatened to remove a vital organ. She belonged to him and the thought of her moving out was a violation, a shame he could not bear. She could imagine the gossip that would spread like a dense fog throughout Hamsford. Hamsford was a small city with a large Jamaican community nestled so close to the tip of Southern Maryland, it could fall into the Atlantic Ocean. But although it was small in size, the gossip was always big.

"Did you hear about Brother Barnett's daughter?" Sister So-and-So would say. Mr. Barnett was never called Deacon because he was averse to titles that put him above others. "She want to leave."

"Why would she do dat?" Sister Busybody would reply.

"Dem let her go to university. It's given her funny ideas."

Sister Busybody would lift her chin in disdain. "I never let mine do dat."

"Yes, that was their first big mistake."

"No, not their first. Dem have five daughters you know. A sensible couple wouldda had at least one boy."

"Yes, you're right. But I blame de girl too. You'd think she'd have more sense after the scandal."

"Janet!" Her father's words cut through her thoughts. "Are you listening to me?"

"Yes," she said with a little more force than she meant to. She cleared her throat with a tinge of guilt. "Of course I'm listening."

He made a sweeping gesture of the room as though it were a grand palace, instead of a cramped space. "Why do you want to leave the safety of your home?"

But Janet knew the silent question he'd never ask: *Why do you want to leave me?* And she didn't know how to answer him because her emotions were so mixed. She admired and resented him; loved and despised him, or rather his control over her life. He was both her protector and her jailor, but she could not make him understand that. She'd wanted to escape his rule since she was seven. At seven she'd imagined a tornado had swept her family away, at twelve she'd been adopted by another family, and now she knew that if she didn't move out they would drive her mad.

A smug smile touched his lips. "Just as I thought. You cannot find an answer."

"That's not it."

"How can you even think about leaving this house after what happened?"

Janet felt her insides grow cold. "That was over a year ago."

"Do you think shame goes away? Do you think despair disappears? I don't care if twenty years pass. You'll leave this house under only one condition."

She shook her head wanting to scream, but she kept her voice low. "Daddy, it's time that I—"

Her father lifted a finger and waved it at her and she inwardly groaned knowing the words that would come next. "There's only *one* time to leave this house," he said, his Jamaican patois punctuating his otherwise perfect English dialect. "And that's when you are married. A *dawta* should move from her *fadda's* house into the house of her husband's. That is God's will. And in my house we will serve the Lord."

"But—"

"I am not an inflexible man." He clasped his hands behind his back. "I have considered your need for independence. I'm not an unreasonable man, am I?"

Janet waited recognizing another question that sought no answer.

"Didn't I allow you to live in the dormitory at the university? Didn't I?" he repeated demanding a response.

"Yes."

"Exactly. I gave you your wish. You wanted to live on your own with your friend. And you promised that you would be good. And you promised that you would be safe."

"I was."

"Yet after a year you were back at home and your friend was—"

"Yes," Janet cut in. "I know." She looked away no longer able to face him or the truth of his words. He was right. She'd been allowed to go out into the world, but had come home under a cloud of disgrace. Although she couldn't forget the incident she still remembered the sweet taste of freedom. But she hadn't known how short it would last. How one phone call would be the beginning of the end.

CHAPTER 2

"Janet, please come and get me."

"Ramani! Where have you been?" Janet glanced at her watch. It was ten minutes after midnight. She'd been unable to study wondering where her friend and roommate was. "I've been up all night worried and I have an exam tomorrow."

"Just come and get me."

Janet's anger was quickly replaced with fear. "Where are you?"

Ramani told her the location then quickly hung up before Janet could ask more questions. Such as *How had she ended up so far off campus? Why did she need a ride home? What had kept her out so late?* These questions assaulted her as she changed into a pair of jeans and a shirt. They'd only been in the dorm eight weeks and Janet was still getting used to the pace. But she loved it. Her dorm room was everything she'd hoped it would be and it included a large window and a view of the trees and manicured lawn. Ramani wasn't the neatest of roommates, but Janet didn't mind how her books littered the floor or that her bed was usually left unmade. For the first time in her life Janet was able to hang a picture on the wall —a Mondrian—and have a small sculpture of a dancer on her side table. In her father's house such things were considered idols and false gods. Ramani listened to music she couldn't listen to at home. They both had fun filling their tiny fridge with ice cream and frozen dinners. When they'd first tasted nachos, they'd giggled like children. There were no rules or restrictions. They'd been able to eat what they wanted, when they wanted. Janet could study late at the library and return home without answering to anyone. Her father's shadow didn't loom over her.

But Janet was already beginning to wonder if the freedom was too much as she sped down fraternity row. She turned down an empty street unsure if she'd gotten the directions right. Janet parked and looked around, but didn't see anyone. She started her car again then saw a figure illuminated under a flickering streetlight. Janet turned off her car and walked across the street, hoping the person wouldn't be too drunk to give directions. "Excuse me," she called out then halted when the figure lifted its head. It was Ramani.

But not the Ramani she knew. This Ramani had one eye swollen shut, her long dark hair hung in disarray, her dress torn and one shoe missing. Janet ran over to her.

"What happened?"

Ramani limped towards her. "Just take me away from here."

Janet grabbed her friend's arm then let go when she winced. "You're hurt. We have to go to the campus police," she said, surveying the damage the muggers had done.

"No."

Janet gently took Ramani's hand and guided her to the car. She smelled of booze and cigarettes, but Janet knew her friend didn't indulge in either. "Then I'm taking you to the hospital."

"No, I just want to go to sleep."

"But Ramani."

"I said no. Take me home." Ramani edged her way into the car with a grimace then slammed the door closed.

Janet looked at her feeling helpless then got into the driver's seat. "We'll report this in the morning," she said as she started the ignition. "You know it's not safe to leave a party this late. At least you still have your handbag so the thief didn't get what he wanted."

"Yes, he did."

"He took your wallet?"

Ramani laughed bitterly. "Janet, I wasn't robbed. I was raped."

Janet nearly swerved into the sidewalk. She quickly got control of the steering wheel then looked at her friend outraged. "Then you *have* to go to the police. You—"

"And let this get back to my parents? No. Just take me home. I'll be okay. I need you to do this for me. Please."

It was the pleading that silenced her. Ramani was her oldest and dearest friend. She would do anything for her and she knew Ramani would do the same. They'd become fast friends in elementary school and by middle school they'd been inseparable. Most of Janet's friends were kids of immigrants or immigrants themselves. Her friend Sarah Chou's father never spoke English. Vajra always swapped her roti and beans for Janet's fried plantain. But no matter which country they came from they had this in common—the fathers ruled the house and the mothers ruled the kitchen. Daughters were to get married while sons achieved and made money.

Whether Asian, African or Indian another rule was universal —honor your parents and obey and live by the rules of the 'old country'. The consequence of disobedience was real. They'd had a friend who'd been blinded by acid when she'd flirted with a married man; another whose brother had been disowned because he wouldn't take over his father's business.

However, Ramani was different. She straddled both worlds with skill, showing one face to her parents and another to her friends. She was the only daughter of three children and was confident and beautiful. Her parents owned a stand in the downtown marketplace and another fruitful office supply business. Many of the East Indians mingled with the West Indians and the Maliks were popular with everyone. They invited Janet into their lives as if she were family. Although she could never spend the night, Janet used to watch Mrs. Malik make samosas and remembered the smell of spices like turmeric, cinnamon and curry. In turn, Ramani would visit her and help in the garden.

After high school, several of their friends went in different directions. Vajra entered into an arranged marriage and now lived in Colorado. Sarah moved away to attend a college on the West Coast because she had family there ready to support her.

But Ramani and Janet knew their parents would never allow them to travel far from home, so they both were thrilled to be admitted to the nearby university, which was an hour away. Following a year of commuting, they convinced their parents to let them live in the dorm during their sophomore year. Both fathers inspected the surroundings and once they learned that it was an all female dorm with no alcohol allowed, they gave their permission. Janet immediately dove into her studies and now that she lived on campus attended sports events, plays and theatrical programs. Ramani explored the night life. Janet warned her friend to be careful, but Ramani reminded her that Janet didn't need to worry because there were no rules to break.

For the first time, their life without rules scared Janet. She felt lost. She led her friend to their dorm room wishing she knew someone who could tell her what to do.

"I need a shower," Ramani said kicking off her remaining

shoe. She went into the bathroom and closed the door.

Janet waited to hear the water running then picked up the phone. She began to dial then disconnected. Ramani was right. If she got the police involved then her parents would find out and they wouldn't be sympathetic. They'd see her as damaged goods. They would ask why she was out so late. They would blame her. But they didn't need to know. She could take Ramani to the health center on campus or the ER and because she was of legal age no one needed to be called. But Janet knew she couldn't force her friend to do anything. She set the phone down and began to clear up Ramani's side of the room, putting the books in a pile on her desk and folding back her bed sheets. When Ramani emerged from the bathroom and saw what Janet had done she smiled. "Thanks for coming to get me."

"Any time."

Ramani got into bed and buried herself under the covers. Janet sat on a chair unable to sleep. She stared at her notes but saw nothing.

"Janet?"

"Yes?"

"Don't worry about me. I'll be fine."

But she wasn't. Soon Ramani was disappearing for days and Janet didn't feel like she had a roommate. When Ramani did show up she smelled of beer.

"School is suppose to be fun," she said when Janet chided her and told her to focus on her studies. "This is our freedom."

"You can be too free."

"Really? I don't think so. Freedom is my right. Life, liberty and the pursuit of happiness and I'm happy."

"But your parents—."

"I'm an American. If they'd wanted me to be Indian then they should have had me there. Besides, what they don't know won't hurt them. Now what do you think of my skirt?"

"It's too short."

"For an artist you're such a fucking prude."

Janet winced not used to her friend swearing. "You never thought so before."

In high school Ramani understood why Janet had to wear shorts or skirts past her knees and never show bare arms or feet. But she hadn't felt out of place with her friends like Sasha who always kept her head covered or Virginia who could never wear shorts or a swimsuit because a woman showing her thighs was considered indecent. They all agreed Ramani was the luckiest because she could wear anything and show off her midriff when she wore a sari.

Ramani shrugged. "Things change."

"They can't change this much. You never attend mosque. You eat meat all the time, even though you promised your father you'd at least eat three vegetarian meals a week. And your clothes—"

"Who are you? My mom? We came here to escape all that. What about you? You're looking at nude drawings and drawing naked people all the time."

"For school."

"I heard you listening to a reggae song the other day that would have your father screaming and—"

Janet held up her hands. In her father's house she was allowed to listen to classical, gospel, opera, some easy listening and country (country music mentioned God enough to please her father) but absolutely no rock, pop or reggae. "Okay I admit that I'm not perfect but I'm not throwing away all that I've been taught. Ramani, you have to have limits. We promised to look out for each other."

"I can look out for myself."

Janet didn't believe her, but knew nothing she said could change Ramani's mind. She invited her to a meeting at the International Student Association or the ISA as it was sometimes

called, which was held every month in the Student Union building. But the meeting had the opposite effect. Ramani distanced
herself from Janet even more and slowly became a stranger.

"What are you doing?" Janet demanded when Ramani
returned back to the dorm around eleven p.m.

"I'm seeing someone."

Janet paused, realizing the significance. Janet wasn't allowed
to date, not even a man in the church, unless the intent of
marriage was made public. She also knew that Ramani wasn't
allowed to date without her family's approval. "What's his name?"

"Ian."

"He's white?"

Ramani grinned. "You have something against white guys?"

Janet folded her arms.

"He's got a friend and when I showed him your picture, he
thought you were cute."

Janet let her arms fall. "I'm not interested."

"I hope you know that men were created for a lot more than
sketching," Ramani said, tapping a recent drawing Janet had on
her desk.

Janet chewed her bottom lip uncertain. "You really like him?"

"What are you? My father?"

"I hate when you compare me to him."

"Then stop asking so many fucking questions."

Janet sighed not wanting to argue. "If he's important to you I'd
like to meet him."

"Fine. Meet us tomorrow for lunch in the Student Union.
Let's say twelve-thirty. I'm sure you'll like him as much as I do."

Janet hated him on sight. He had dirty hands and a lecherous
glare, greasy hair and clothes that hadn't seen a washing machine
in a while. But Janet could have ignored his appearance if he'd
treated her friend with more dignity. Instead, he kept squeezing
her butt and brushing his hand against her breasts. To Janet's

relief he didn't last long. Soon Ramani was seeing someone else. Janet was never formally introduced but she eventually knew more about him than she'd wanted to when she walked in on them one afternoon.

They were both naked in Ramani's bed, humping like rabbits. He was calling her 'Beauty' and she was calling him 'Beast' and the name suited him. He was hairy everywhere. Janet's artistic gaze looked on in wonder. She never knew hair could cover a man's entire backside.

Ramani saw her and waved. "Just give us a few more minutes. Okay?"

Janet backed out of the room and closed the door. She leaned against the wall trying not to imagine what was happening inside. She failed. After ten minutes passed, Janet knocked on the door.

"Just a couple more minutes."

She waited five more minutes then pounded on the door. "Beauty! You're about to deal with an angry Bitch if you don't open this door right now," Janet said surprised by her own words and level of anger. She heard footsteps then the door swung open. Ramani tied the belt of her robe. She clicked her tongue. "Such language. What would your Daddy say?"

Janet pushed past her and set her backpack on her desk. The Beast held out his hand to her. "Hi I'm—"

Janet waved him away. "I'm sure you're a nice guy, but your name doesn't matter."

He kissed Ramani then left.

Ramani shut the door. "You didn't have to be rude."

Janet unzipped her bag.

Ramani walked over to her bed. "Sorry about that. Next time I'll leave a note or something on the door." She rested a hand on her hip. "Don't look at me like that. It's not like I'm pure anymore." She flashed a cynical smile. "I'm soiled goods remember?"

"No, you're not," Janet said thinking about the rape Ramani

wouldn't talk about. "I can't say I agree with what you're doing, but at least have some standards."

"I've got standards. Did you see the size of his dick?"

"I don't care how well endowed he is. That's not enough."

Ramani laughed. "Then your standards are too high."

Janet scowled. "That's not what I meant. Ramani, don't do this. I know you're hurting. You need to see a counselor."

"I'm fine. I'm just having fun. I can't help if my fun is different than yours. I don't want to try ice skating. I don't want to go to different restaurants and try different foods."

"You used to."

She shrugged. "Life is to be lived and I'm planning to live it to the fullest."

And she did. She got drunk, had sex, and ate junk food. And as Janet saw the friend she loved slip away from her, her worry increased. Perhaps Ramani was right and she was a prude. What was wrong with tasting the temptations of life? The Amish had their Rumpspringa right? This was Ramani's turn to experiment. To be a little wild. But why did it feel wrong somehow?

"Tell her parents," Marisa Espinoza said when Janet shared her fears with her friends at the ISA. She was also an art student and had green streaks in her dark black hair and a ring in her aquiline nose.

"Do you want her to get killed?" another student said.

"I don't see another choice."

"I say let her be," a third student said with disdain. "She's become one of them. American women are selfish and shameless. They don't care about anyone but themselves. There is no sense of loyalty or duty."

Janet shook her head. "Ramani isn't like that. She's a good caring person."

"Is she thinking about her family's name every time she spreads her legs?"

"It's not like that."

"How many boyfriends has she had this semester alone? Four?"

Janet folded her arms. "She's just confused."

"She's selfish, but she's not alone. Look at the TV. You see women talking about sleeping with other women's husbands without a grain of guilt, of cheating on their own men, of driving drunk with their children in the backseat. If that's freedom they can keep it. My husband knows that if he lays a hand on me, my father and brother will slice him to bits."

Janet wanted to argue, but at that moment the bell rang and they dispersed.

She sat alone feeling miserable, then something fell into her lap. She looked down at the shiny foil packets in her lap.

"If she won't let you help her there's nothing you can do," Marisa said.

Janet held up one of the objects.

"You know what it is, right?"

"Either really flat candy or a condom."

Marisa smiled. "Yes, either way, tell her to use these."

But Ramani only laughed. "Thanks, I've got my own supply. But *you* could put them to good use."

Janet felt relieved when winter break came. She avoided most of her family's question about dorm life and enjoyed the holidays. Fortunately, when Ramani returned to campus she was more like her old self. She went with Janet to basketball games and paid more attention to her studies. Janet's spirit lifted when Ramani didn't introduce her to a 'special' someone. They laughed as they used to and watched their favorite shows while munching on pizza and popcorn. Ramani's junk food habit hadn't diminished and she gained weight, but Janet didn't say anything because her friend was happy. Janet was certain everything was back to normal. In one night that hope was shattered.

CHAPTER 3

Janet never suspected anything when her phone rang. She was in the middle of trying to memorize classic artists and their famous works.

"I'm in the stairwell," Ramani said when Janet answered her phone. "I need your help."

Janet found her friend on the second level doubled over in pain. She hurried down the stairs. "What's wrong?"

"I feel so sick," Ramani gasped. "I think it's something I ate."

"Why didn't you take the elevator?"

"It was taking too long."

"Let's go to the health center."

"No, I just want to lie down. Get me to our room."

They had three more floors to go, but Janet knew it was useless mentioning it. She took Ramani's arm. "When we get you upstairs, I'll decide then."

They slowly climbed, Ramani gripping the railing as if it was the only thing to keep her up right.

"I think you should rest," Janet said.

"I can make it," Ramani replied through gritted teeth. Sweat gleamed on her forehead and her face was flushed, but Janet knew she was determined. When Ramani could no longer stand, she made it the rest of the way by crawling on her knees. Once they reached their floor Janet helped her up and ushered her into the room.

Janet led her over to her bed. She gripped Janet and panted. "No, no I don't want to mess up any of the sheets. Take me to the bathroom."

Janet's concern grew. "I could get you a bucket if you think you'll be sick."

"Please Janet."

"Let me get a doctor," she begged as she pushed open the bathroom door.

"It's the cramps that are killing me." Her nails bit into Janet's arm then relaxed. "Oh. Good. They're going now." She eased down on the toilet seat and rested her head back. She unzipped her coat. "Could you make me a bath?"

"Do you know what you ate? Do you want me to get you some seltzer water or Pepto Bismol?"

"No, I just need to get in a bath."

"Fine," Janet said grateful for something to do. She turned on the water, checked the temperature then put the stopper in. She thought of adding bath bubbles but rejected the idea. As the tub filled she turned to her friend whose eyes were now shut.

"Let me help you with your coat," she said removing it for her.

Ramani looked at her, her hazel eyes bright with tears. "Janet, please forgive me," she said in a choked voice.

"What are you talking about? I don't need to forgive you. Come on. Get undressed. The bath is almost ready." When Ramani didn't move Janet helped her out of her sweatshirt then unbuttoned her blouse. "Have you forgotten it's spring? Why are you wearing so many layers?"

"I didn't mean for any of this to happen," she said in a small voice.

"Of course you didn't. Don't worry." She unbuttoned Ramani's top and tossed it away. She looked at her friend's face then she looked down and froze. She suddenly understood why Ramani had been wearing bulky clothes lately and the weight gain she'd attributed to lots of junk food. She'd come up with a number of reasons, but never this.

Ramani nodded to the bath. "The tub is going to overflow."

Janet snapped out of her paralysis and turned off the faucet. She took a deep breath then turned. *This wasn't happening.* "Why didn't you tell me?"

Ramani rested a hand on her swollen belly. "What would you have said?"

"I don't know," Janet said, her mind reeling. *How could Ramani be pregnant? What would happen now?*

Ramani gripped her hands into fists. "Shit, here comes another one."

"Don't tense up like that. You're supposed to breathe."

"What the hell do you know about this?"

"About as much as you do. Getting knocked up doesn't suddenly make you an expert."

Ramani released a breath. "You're right. I'm sorry." She stood and a rush of water fell from between her legs. "Fuck."

Janet forced herself to breathe. *It was really happening. Her friend was having a baby. Now.* "Your water just broke?"

Ramani pulled off her skirt and panties. "Well, I didn't just wet myself."

Janet stared at the evident swell of her friend's stomach, feeling foolish that she'd never noticed it. "Let me help you into the tub."

Once Ramani was settled Janet got a pillow from her bed and

put it behind her head. Ramani sighed with pleasure. "That's better."

"I should call—"

Ramani stretched out her hand to her. "Don't leave me."

"We can have the ambulance here in no time."

"No one can know about this. And I can't bear to do this by myself."

Janet sat on the rim of the tub, resigned. She grabbed Ramani's hand still hoping she would open her eyes and realize it all was a nightmare. "I won't leave you. No matter what happens, I'll never leave you, but we need to—"

Ramani grimaced. "I feel like I have to push."

"Then do it."

She bore down then relaxed and looked up at Janet. "Can you see anything?"

Janet peered down. "Not really."

"Look harder."

"I can't look any harder and don't even think about asking me to put my head under the water."

Ramani held out her hand again. "Get me a face towel."

"Why?"

"Because I don't want anyone to hear me scream."

Janet handed Ramani the towel. She bit into it as she bore down again. She rested her head back and looked hopeful. "Anything?"

"I think I see some hair."

"You're not sure?"

"Check it yourself."

Ramani tentatively felt between her legs. "Yes, that's the head. It'll be over soon."

But it wasn't. Ten minutes later they'd both lost patience. "Why the fuck is this taking so long?"

"I don't know," Janet said worried. "Grip your knees. Yes, that's it. Keep pushing. Something's happening... I see a head."

Ramani closed her eyes exhausted. "Good. Help me get it out."

"It's coming. You're making progress."

Ramani slapped the water with the flat of her hand. "I don't care about progress. I want it out! Be my God damn forceps!"

Janet stripped down to her panties and bra, jumped in the tub and gripped the baby's head. "Why did you have to do this in the tub?" she asked sweat dripping down her forehead.

"I saw a woman do it on TV. She made it look easy."

"You shouldn't believe everything you see on TV."

Ramani laughed then her face changed into a grimace.

"Yes, push, push it's coming!"

"Get it out!"

"Keep going. You're doing great."

"Stop being so cheerful."

"You're doing it. It's almost there."

"It hurts like ahhh..." She bit into her towel, her face red.

"It's out," Janet said as the baby slid into her arms. She lifted the baby out of the water and cleared its mouth with her finger. She turned it over and patted its back until it let out a cry. She said a silent prayer. "It's a girl."

"Shit!"

Janet ignored the outburst. "What are you going to call her?"

"I'm not calling her anything."

Janet handed Ramani the baby. "Rest her against your chest so that she can feel your heartbeat. That will help her stop crying."

"Where are you going?" Ramani asked when Janet climbed out of the tub.

Janet dried herself off with a towel. "I need a shoestring to tie off the umbilical cord. No don't get up. You're not done yet."

"What do you mean?"

"There's the afterbirth."

"How do you know all this stuff?"

Janet winked. "I didn't sleep through Sex Ed and I took First Aid during freshman year."

"I can't believe your father let you go to Sex Ed."

"I forged his signature," Janet said then exited. She grabbed a shoestring from one of her sneakers then looked around for something to wrap the baby in. She snatched a large beach towel off the top shelf in her closet.

"I have something for—" Her words died away when she saw Ramani holding the baby under the water.

Janet dropped everything and yanked the baby away. "Are you crazy?" Janet checked to make sure the baby was still breathing. It was.

"I have to get rid of it."

"No way."

"I have to," Ramani said in a frantic voice. "My life is ruined if anyone finds out. Do you care about this thing more than me?"

"You can't kill her."

Ramani met her eyes. "It's been done before."

Janet stared back. "No."

"Either she dies or I do. You know what will happen."

Janet did, but she didn't want to think about it now. "I'll take care of it."

"What are you going to do?"

"I don't know."

"You can put her in the dumpster downstairs."

Janet ignored her. She changed then wrapped the baby up tight, emptied out her sports bag and put the baby inside. She left without saying goodbye. Luckily Janet knew that an unwanted baby could be dropped off at a hospital—no questions asked. That was exactly what she did.

When she returned an hour later, Ramani didn't ask what she'd done with the baby and Janet didn't tell her. Three weeks later, summer break came and they drove home. "No one can ever know," Ramani said. "Promise me. No matter what happens this will always be our secret."

"I promise."

But secrets were hard to keep in Hamsford.

CHAPTER 4

Rumors of Ramani's drinking and partying began to surface but one day it reached the boiling point. Janet received a text message on her cell phone (a model so old it still had an antenna) from Ramani's cousin, Darika. Janet rarely received phone or text messages because her father always checked so the sight of it shocked her. Darika's words shocked her even more: *Ur n trble. They know.*

Janet didn't breathe as she stared down at the message. *What did they know?*

Seconds later her father barged into her bedroom. He snatched the phone from her hands. "Downstairs! Now!"

When Janet walked into the family room she saw Ramani and her parents. Janet sat next to her friend who avoided her eyes. She looked over at her parents. "What's going on?"

Her question started a firestorm of rage and accusations. Someone had sent a photo of Ramani dancing at a party to her brother and her father had seen it. Janet listened to the shouting inwardly calm—they didn't know about the baby.

"You promised you'd look out for each other," Mr. Barnett said.

"Why did you let her go out? You should have stopped her!" Mr. Malik said.

The accusations and reprimands continued for the next hour until the Maliks left, splitting their families for good. Janet's freedom was gone. A week later Ramani went on a trip to India and was never heard from again.

~

"Are you sure you want to do this?" Frederick Durand asked his friend as they looked down over the city of Hamsford. He was unimpressed but tried to be objective.

Jeffrey Farmer nodded with a sense of satisfaction. "Yes, I'm going to finish what my father started. With your help of course."

"You'll always have it."

"This is a chance for a new beginning for both of us."

"I don't plan to move here."

"At least you're staying for a while, that will make a difference."

Frederick shrugged, not wanting to dampen his friend's enthusiasm. "So you're really going to move into that place?" he said glancing at the house behind them.

Jeffrey grinned. "I know it's the size of an outhouse compared to your place, but I like it." He turned his attention back to the town. "I know it's not London, New York or Vancouver but this is home to me. And I bet you'll learn to like it here."

"Then you'd lose."

Jeffrey laughed. "No, I won't. Just you wait. You'll change your mind."

"Why?"

"Because Hamsford is like no other place on earth."

~

JANET COULDN'T LEAVE. She wouldn't let her. Mrs. Barnett stared at her daughter unsure of who she was anymore. Janet wasn't as beautiful as her sister, Beverly, but she had an arresting face. Dark brows and high cheekbones and eyes that hinted at the Arawak Indian heritage she'd gotten from her father. Mrs. Barnett sighed. She didn't understand her daughter's need to be away from family. But Janet had always been different from the rest. Even as a child there had been a willful streak that frightened her. She'd seen that same streak in Ramani, too.

What was so special about this independence people always talked about? She didn't agree with children staying out all hours of the night at age sixteen just because they had a driver's license. Or with parents kicking a child out at eighteen or twenty with no stability of home. She'd never been alone in her life. Solitude wasn't even an option, not that she ever sought it. She had stayed in the same room with her older sister until she was married. Family meant everything to her and she felt rich in it. Why couldn't her daughter see how lucky she was?

Janet felt her mother's shrewd gaze and tried not to shudder. She felt like a bird forced back into a cage. It had been a year since the scandal. She hadn't returned to the dorm or school, she had stayed home and helped around the house and the community. But it was time to leave. She couldn't stand another year of her father's booming voice, her mother's whiny replies, and her sisters' arguments. Then there were the constant visitors. At times she felt as though she lived in a hotel with a revolving door. The moment one person left another would enter. There was Uncle Treton, a lecherous old man with grabby hands who'd stayed for three months. Cousin Merleen, who wept for no apparent reason, and Aunty Mindy, a vain woman who did only two things: spend hours preening herself in the bathroom, and taking the largest portions at mealtime, all the while, stating that she "Hoped she was not a burden to the family."

But the Barnetts were generous people and beyond family obligations, they also opened their home to visiting church brethren. More often than not, more than one person came and when families visited, people filled their living room, at times spilling into their modest-sized kitchen, until she could imagine hearing the walls expand. Everyone would gather and talk, all at once, carrying on three or four conversations simultaneously.

She couldn't stand another year with the lack of privacy—one could not eat alone or close her bedroom door. Her parents didn't understand her need for solitude. The Barnetts were a family that did everything together. They ate together, prayed together, and holidayed together. There was no such thing as doing something alone.

Years ago her younger sister, Francine, woke up in an empty house and she'd thought the Rapture had come and she'd been left behind. She'd wept uncontrollably for days. Janet would have jumped for joy.

Her father waved the paper. "I'm going to tell Brother Williams about this."

Janet reached for the paper then snatched her hand back. "No, please don't," she said with a note of panic. She didn't want her friend Valerie to get into trouble. "All the blame is mine."

Her father tapped the paper. "So *you* want to get Beverly involved in this stupid scheme of yours?"

To him it was a scheme, to her an escape plan. "I thought if we were together—."

"You'd take care of her as you did Ramani?"

A searing pain ripped through her. "That wasn't my fault."

"No, but it happened anyway."

Janet blinked back tears determined not to cry. "I've been out of school for a year. I've now resumed my studies and—."

"You can finish them from home."

A slow seething anger began to rise within her and Janet fought to suppress it. She knew that a daughter should love her father and forgive him any faults. But what Janet feared most wasn't the wavering of her faith; it was that the small burning kernel of hatred that, at times, took her unawares, would grow and settle. If she didn't leave her father's house soon she feared it would take hold her of her completely and seize her body and soul. But she knew she was fighting a battle she could not win.

She had failed. That's what they wanted to remind her. That's what they'd never let her forget. But she needed a second chance.

Janet knew it when several weeks ago her father had refused to allow her to accept a trophy for winning first prize in an art show.

"What is that?" he'd said when she'd shown him the large prize.

"I won," she said holding up the trophy with both hands so everyone could see. She then cradled it close. "I'm going to put in on my desk."

"No you won't."

She paused. "What?"

"Do you think you're better than your sisters?" He pointed at the trophy as though it was something evil. "That is a symbol of pride and I don't want it in my house. You can throw it away or give it away. I don't care, but I don't want it in my house. You don't have much to be proud of now, do you?"

That's when she'd looked at her father and for the first time hatred festered like an acid wound, Ramani's tragedy still lingering.

Mrs. Barnett spoke up. "Oh Winston don't be so harsh. Let her—."

He shot his wife a look, stunned that she'd contradict him. "I said no."

Janet donated her beloved trophy to a charity and that same day she wrote to her best friend, Valerie, asking her how to convince her older sister Beverly to move out with her. She knew the risk. Her parents blamed her for Ramani's behavior, but she still had to get out and she knew Beverly would make a perfect roommate. She hoped that if they moved out together and did not live in the dorm, her parents wouldn't worry as much. The letter her father now had was Valerie's reply.

"It was just an idea. I thought you would be pleased if we stayed together."

"Pleased?" His voice cracked with surprise. "Pleased to lose two jewels in my crown instead of one?"

"If you don't trust me with Beverly, I could live on my own and—"

"Absolutely not."

"You'll get murdered," her mother said.

Janet sighed. "I won't get murdered."

"And you'll be lonely. A woman shouldn't live alone. It's unnatural." By now tears glistened in her eyes but still didn't fall.

In Hamsford, for the females who were members of their church, a woman eighteen and older was only one of two things: married or unmarried. And those who were unmarried tried to change their status as soon as possible. Her mother leapt to her feet and retrieved the newspaper from the couch. She opened it then shoved an article in Janet's face. "This woman was raped in her own bedroom."

Janet shook her head. "I won't get raped or murdered. God watches over unmarried women as much as the married ones."

Her father frowned. "He watches over his unmarried women by keeping them in their father's house." He clasped his hands together and lowered his head in regret. "I blame your school for this. What is wrong with our home? Do I ask anything from you? Do I ask for any money from you? I pay the mortgage and electricity. Do you think the water runs itself?"

"Daddy, I am grateful for all that you've done, but—"

He held up his hand. "No, there's no discussion. You will stay in this house until you are married."

Janet threw up her hands exasperated. "Who am I to marry?"

"In God's time the right man will come. You are still young."

And suffocating. Even if she looked at the local male population as a means of escape, her choices were few. Her small town did not boast a variety of eligible men. And to be considered eligible a man had to past the J.C.E Test: Jamaican (by birth or heritage), in the Church, and Employed. Most viable possibilities had left Hamsford to attend universities in other states and married women there—to the shame of their parents who strongly believed there were only two types of women: those in the church and those in the world.

Everyone knew a woman in the church was better than a woman in the world. The privileged few of their particular church (there were other churches, but they didn't count) were quick to discuss the 'fallen angel' who claimed the world as his playground. Not that Janet looked forward to marriage. The thought of moving from obeying her father's rules to those of her husband held little joy.

Janet leaned forward hoping to make her parents see reason. "I've always been a good girl. I've done well in my studies and I try to do all that is right. Can't you trust me?"

"This is not about trust. You are meant to stay home."

"But—"

Her father sliced his hand through the air in a dismissive gesture. "This conversation is over." He turned away ready to end the discussion. "Never talk 'bout it again."

Janet jumped to her feet frustration making her voice tremble. "Daddy, if you'd only listen!"

He slowly turned around. "You dare raise your voice to mi?"

"No," she said, her voice faltering when she realized her error. "I just—"

"Do I not have ears? I heard you and now you will listen to me. I said you will stay home and that's final." He waved his fist to the ceiling and the rafters shook as his voice continued to rise, causing the tears in her mother's eyes to fall. Soon the late winter sun that shone bright through the blinds felt like it had been swallowed up by thunderclouds. "Do you want everyone to think that my home is a place my daughters flee?" He placed a hand on his chest as though his heart would fall out. "That my home is so distasteful that they would prefer to put their lives at risk than stay? Is that what you want?" His voice fell to a whisper. "Is that how you want to honor me? How you want to honor our family name?"

Janet lowered her gaze. "No."

"Then it's finished. You'll stay home."

She sank back into her seat, the weight of defeat making her legs numb.

"Janet?"

She made a motion that could be misinterpreted as a nod. It satisfied Mr. Barnett who smiled at his wife in triumph.

"Good." He tore up the letter as though ridding its evil contents from existence. "You tell your friend not to send any more letters like this or you won't receive them at all." He threw the remnants in the wastebasket then cupped her face, forcing her to look at him. His thick fingers felt rough against her skin, although he tried to be gentle. "I know you are a good girl and I want you to continue to be." He patted her on the shoulder then left the room.

Janet glared at the wastebasket feeling as though her dreams were as useless and scattered as the letter.

Mrs. Barnett took the seat next to Janet. She was a petite woman with sharp eyes and an even sharper will, which she kept well concealed behind a quiet demeanor. She took Janet's hands and squeezed them. "We want the best for you and we know what that is. You want us to trust you, but you must trust us first."

Her mother's lack of understanding only made Janet's frustration grow. "I won't do anything to shame you or Daddy. I'm smart and—"

"Evil doesn't care about how smart you are. We know the dangers of this world. Please, I know that you are learning strange things at the university, but do not be tempted by the world's lies, they always sound sweet and delicious as a succulent fruit. But the moment you consume it you begin to die because the fruit is poisonous. Just like the one hanging from a certain tree we know."

"But Dee-dee—" Janet began using the endearing term they called their mother to separate her from the other mother figures they'd had in their lives.

Her mother didn't allow her to continue. "You are like a moth drawn to a flame, but you will get your wings singed when you get too close."

Janet knew she was smarter than a moth, but thought it best not to argue.

Mrs. Barnett took her silence as a sign that she'd reached her and patted Janet's hand, her mind quickly turning to other important issues. "Now let me see what we'll have for dinner tonight."

Janet waited to hear her mother's footsteps disappear down the hall before she raced over to the wastebasket to retrieve her letter. With some tape she could repair it. Not only had Valerie given her ideas, but she'd also described her spring holiday detailing all the sights and sounds Janet was eager to one day experience herself.

"Mi haffi empty dat," a flat voice said above her.

Janet jumped back startled and looked up at Mrs. Lind, a second cousin from Jamaica currently living with them, who helped with household duties. Her face was as flat as her tone with beady dark eyes and a mouth that looked as though it had been cut into her face with a crooked knife. She moved like a shadow, with skin just as dark, and wore dresses that hung on her skinny frame as loosely as wet sheets draped on a clothesline.

"It's barely full," Janet said.

Mrs. Lind's expression and tone didn't change. "I was told fi empty it."

"I'll do it later."

"Now."

Janet balled her hands into fists. She couldn't even go through the wastebasket privately. She took a deep breath, resisting the urge to upturn the contents of the wastebasket over Mrs. Lind's head, and stood. "Fine." Resigned she dropped what parts of the letter she'd been able to gather and stormed out. In the corridor she heard footsteps scurry up the stairs like large rats leaving a kitchen feast and knew what to do next.

CHAPTER 5

Janet was a problem. Mr. Barnett closed his study door, pleased with the privacy it gave him. Unlike his wife he understood the benefits of solitude. He'd slept three to a bed growing up and as a young man had lived with various relatives who'd allowed him little time to himself.

He walked around the study, restless. He had to get his daughter to understand how right he was. He knew the ways of the world and she didn't. He knew that men did two things with beautiful things—possessed or destroyed them. He had to protect his possessions. He'd once had a man want his younger daughter Trudy when she was twelve. The man had been attracted to her dark skin and light eyes and had offered him a price. Mr. Barnett had refused him, but had started to see how men looked at his daughters with lust in their eyes. But he brushed his worry aside, the man was an African anyway and he'd never surrender one of his daughters to them.

Mr. Barnett finally sat. The crisis was over. Janet would stay home and he'd make sure she knew why.

Janet found her younger sisters, Maxine and Trudy, in their bedroom pretending to read. She stood in the doorway and watched Maxine read her algebra book upside down and Trudy the dictionary. "Who was in my room?" she asked.

They looked up. "What?"

She folded her arms. "You can play innocent with Dee-dee and Daddy, but not with me."

Maxine shook her head, looking younger than her fifteen years, her hair twisted in ringlets around her face. "I don't know what you're talking about."

"Me neither," Trudy added. Although a year older than Maxine she tended to follow her sister's lead.

Janet nodded. "I see." She turned.

"Was he really angry?" Maxine asked.

Janet stopped. "About what?"

A guilty pause filled the air. When Janet turned, Maxine looked ashamed. "I couldn't help it," she admitted. "When I saw that letter on your desk I told Trudy. I didn't expect Daddy to hear us." She tossed her book aside and leaned forward eager for details. "What's he going to do?"

"Nothing."

"He'll think of something," Francine said eagerly joining them. As the middle child Francine felt adept at accurately reading the habits and behaviors of everyone in the family. She pushed up her glasses and clasped her book of verse tight to her chest. Had she a keen mind her plain features could have been over looked, but her pedantic manner only emphasized them.

"Yes," Trudy said. "He'll probably have the pastor come up with a sermon with you as the example."

Maxine grabbed a book and stood on her bed. She lowered her voice in an attempt to imitate the pastor's deep baritone. "I heard a story that will make you know that the Evil One can tempt even the most righteous among us."

Janet frowned. "Quiet, Daddy might hear you."

Maxine continued unconcerned. "I heard that some of you young ladies have taken a sip from the waters of sin. But though those waters taste sweet there will be a bitter sting!"

Trudy lifted her hand as she'd seen the church sisters do. "Amen."

Janet snatched the book from Maxine. "That's enough."

Maxine fell down laughing. "I bet that's how it'll be."

Trudy began to stand. "Let me try."

Janet flashed a malicious grin. "If you want to be an actress perhaps I should tell Daddy about your ambition."

The two girls quickly sobered. To Mr. Barnett being an actress was a step down from prostitution (since prostitution at least had the distinction of being one of the oldest professions).

"Stay out of my room," Janet warned them then walked down the hall.

Francine followed. "There's really no point you know. A tree must grow where it is planted until God uproots it."

Janet rolled her eyes. "Goodbye, Francine."

Francine shrugged and headed downstairs.

Janet entered her room, flopped down on the bed and stared up at the ceiling where she'd posted a picture of Edvard Munch's *The Scream* to remind her that she wasn't alone. Her high school diploma gathered dust under her bed and she knew her college degree would meet the same fate if she continued to live under her father's roof and she didn't want that to happen. She wanted to put it in a frame and hang it on the wall. Was she too proud? Was that really her flaw? She heard a light tap on her door and wanted to grumble 'Go away' until she heard her sister Beverly's gentle voice ask, "Can I come in?" as she peered her head inside.

Janet absently gestured to a chair.

Beverly gingerly crossed the room and sat. "How angry was he?"

Janet threw an arm over her eyes. "He nearly turned purple." She heard a little snicker and frowned. "It's not funny."

Beverly covered her mouth. "I'm sorry. It's just that you're the only one that can make him turn that color."

"I'll put that on my resume of talents."

Beverly touched her arm. "I'm really sorry."

"Me too." Janet sat up and bit her lip thoughtful. "I will wear him down eventually."

Beverly stared at her stunned. "You mean you'll risk his anger again? Do you *want* to be punished? Wasn't what happened with Ramani enough to convince you that home is a place of safety?"

"No." Janet shook her head suddenly weary. "You don't understand."

She lightly touched her hand. "How can I when you never talk about it?"

"I know," Janet said, but she couldn't talk about it.

"Father's anger isn't worth the risk."

"What choice do I have? I think about what happened every day, but it wasn't all bad. Sometimes Ramani and I had fun. Clean fun," she clarified when Beverly frowned. "I have to live my own life. I can't stay here forever."

"You won't live here forever. You'll get married some day.'

"I can't wait that long."

"Not everyone will end up like Valerie."

Janet's dear friend Valerie was an example of a woman's worse fate: over thirty and still without any prospects. "This isn't about Valerie. Or Ramani. Or Daddy or anyone. It's about me. I want to move out. I have to."

"But what's so wrong with living here?"

Janet stared at her sister amazed, wanting to reach out and shake her. But Beverly's question was as innocent as her nature.

She was pure in both heart and mind. Her exquisite features did not make her vain and she was kind to everyone. At times Janet envied her sister's trusting nature and kind heart. She felt so far from the virtues her sister had. "I wish I knew how you can stand it."

"Stand what?"

"We're grown women being treated like children. Wouldn't you like to eat dinner when you want to? Be able to close your bedroom door? Not have to eat with everyone all the time?"

Beverly shrugged. "I don't mind it."

That was the problem. No one else in the family minded except her. At times Janet truly thought she'd been born into the wrong family. Although Beverly worked 'in the world' as a secretary, she was content with their sheltered existence. The church they attended, Full Gospel Apostolic Church was a moderately conservative church. But while some of the members were allowing their young people more allowances, the Barnetts remained staunchly conservative. No make-up. No cutting of their hair. No loud jewelry.

Restricted activities —most of them centered on the church. They could wear jeans. It took only one fierce winter for Mrs. Barnett to convince her husband to make that concession. However, all jeans or pants had to be one size larger so they wouldn't cling.

Janet knew that there was a greater world out there and that she could navigate it.

She had only recently been able to convince her father to get a computer, but *without* internet access. Fortunately, they could gain access to the internet either at school or at their local library. At home they had email access by using a special machine usually reserved for senior citizens since some were not yet familiar with all the new technology.

Janet used it frequently to correspond with family, especially her favorite Aunt Bernice. Her father distrusted the computer just as he did too much education, which he felt polluted the pure spirit by introducing dissatisfaction and encouraging change. In spite of living in America for over twenty-five years, there were still many American customs her parents didn't understand. Their lack of exposure, compounded by their strict religious beliefs, kept them from changing with the times.

But Janet didn't see the world that way and was certain that if she could open Beverly's eyes to the opportunities then she would leave with her. They could have the life she'd hoped to share with Ramani. "But there's so much we could do." Her voice shook. "Oh, Bev, please just think about it. I can get around Dee-dee and Daddy somehow, but I can't live on my own and we'd make great roommates."

Beverly wrapped her arms around herself unsure. "I don't know."

"Just think about it. Please."

Beverly looked at her sister for a moment then nodded. "I'll think about it. I know it means a lot to you."

Janet hugged her. "Thank you."

Beverly patted her sister as she would a happy child then pulled away. "So what are you going to do now?"

She bit her lip. "I don't know, but I'll come up with something. Right now Daddy doesn't ever want to discuss it again."

CHAPTER 6

"In my day," Mr. Barnett said to his captive audience at dinner that evening, "back inna Jamaica a girl was happy to stay home. She stayed until her father approved the right man for her to marry."

Mrs. Barnett nodded. "As it should be."

"Girls didn't go racing off on their own without thought. A girl from a good family listened to her parents."

"Daddy," Janet said straining for patience. "I don't want to dishonor anyone. I just want to—"

Mr. Barnett waved his fork at her. "I said we will not discuss it."

"Right."

"If you would prefer to struggle out in the world nothing can be said."

"Daddy I won't—"

He set his fork down. "Didn't I say not to discuss it? Why are you determined to bring up a topic I don't wish to discuss?"

Janet lowered her head. Her father could stick to a topic like a curry stain on a white shirt.

"I don't know why you're determined to talk about leaving us and going out on your own. Why do you want to drag your poor sister along on your foolish plans? Why do you want to live this fairy tale you've imagine?"

"It's not a fairy tale. Other girls—"

He pointed at her. "Not another word out of you. I said I don't want to discuss it."

Janet sighed and glanced around the table desperate for someone to introduce another topic.

Francine spoke up. "I heard Sister Agnes' niece has a bun in the oven."

"When did she get married?" Mrs. Barnett asked.

"She isn't."

Mr. Barnett threw up his hands. "Lord God! You see what can happen to you? Do you want that kind of news to fall on my ears?"

"No," Janet said, giving Francine a swift kick under the table and making a quick slicing motion against her neck.

She winced and returned to her meal.

"Baby, baby, baby," Mr. Barnett said. "Inna this country all I see everywhere is a young girl with a baby and no man. That's what these girls have. If they'd stayed in their father's home they wouldn't be like that."

"That wouldn't happen to me," Janet said.

"No, it won't because you're staying here."

A moment of brief silence followed then Mr. Barnett opened his mouth again, fortunately Mrs. Lind came to the rescue as she set steamed calaloo, a green leaf vegetable similar to kale, on the table. She had prepared their favorite foods: steamed green bananas, cornmeal dumplings and her special dish of smoked mackerel. The beguiling aroma provided a reminder of home. "Mi hear Jeffrey Framer has returned home," she said.

"Good," Mr. Barnett said. "Even those who go out into the world know that it is best to return home."

"I wonder why he came back," Janet said eager to keep the new topic alive.

"There's only one reason," Mrs. Barnett said with a look of anticipation.

"What?"

"To get married."

Janet frowned. "How do you know that?"

She turned to Mrs. Lind. "He didn't come home with a woman, did he?"

"No," Mrs. Lind said. "Him still single. He just bought the Westland property."

Mrs. Barnett clapped her hands together as though someone had offered her a grand gift. "He's single and settling. This is perfect."

Janet furrowed her brows. "I don't understand."

"That only shows how young you are." She stood. "When a young man with a good education returns home to settle he only wants one thing." She pushed in her chair. "To find a good woman in the church." Her gaze fell on each of her daughters. "And I'm going to make sure that his selection is one of you."

"Where are you going?" Mr. Barnett called after his wife as she hurried out of the room.

"To make grata cake. It's Sister Daniels' favorite." This was a favorite sweet snack, made out of shredded coconut and lots of sugar.

Mr. Barnett frowned. "Why bake anything? That woman salivates if you open the refrigerator. Besides she doesn't need any more cake," he said referring to her rotund figure.

"No," Maxine said with a sly grin. "But mother needs more information about Jeffrey Farmer and Sister Daniel will have it."

"I don't approve of a man going after degree after degree," Mr.

Barnett said. "But he comes from a good family." He jerked his chin towards Janet. "You used to be good friends if I remember correctly."

Janet shook her head then glanced at her sister. "No, that was Beverly."

Mr. Barnett turned to his other daughter. "Is that right?"

Beverly kept her head lowered. "Yes," she said in a quiet voice. "But that was a long time ago."

~

"My mother's already been over to see him," Valerie Williams told Janet a few days later as they walked the neighborhood. They lived in Old Hamsford, which was affectionately called "Little Jamaica" because of the large concentration of Jamaican immigrants who had decided to live there. The Barnetts and Williams, along with most of the residents of Old Hamsford, loved the fact that they could walk to anywhere they needed. They did their shopping by walking to the market and they could walk to the park, library and especially church.

The cold grip of winter had released its hold allowing the warmth of spring to breakthrough. The dirty snow melted along the roadside while red and pink buds highlighted the bare trees. Valerie wore a simple lime green wrap coat and a pair of sturdy brown boots. A kind, intelligent, and sensible woman she had only two major flaws: a homely face and advanced years.

Janet had known Valerie all her life, but more as an acquaintance than a friend because of their age difference. But all that changed last year when Valerie helped Janet through her grief and became her closest friend and confidant.

"I don't know why he came back," Janet said. "He returned briefly to attend his father's funeral, but left just as quickly. Not that I blame him."

"The official story is that he came back to complete his father's work—building the new wing of the Hamsford's Public Library and dedicating it to him. But I think there's more to it."

"Why?"

"Because he bought a house."

That was no surprise. The Farmers were always buying something. They were the opposite of their surname. They'd never farmed anything, but owned a lot of property and made it their duty to acquire more. The Farmers and Williams were part of Old Hamsford's founding families who settled in the area in the early part of the last century. Sympathetic Quakers, earlier residents of the area had helped them get land. One individual, Mr. Delaney, developed a friendship with Thomas Cornelius Farmer, Jeffrey's great-grandfather, and purchased a large amount of land and sold it to him. In those days, blacks could not get loans from the banks.

Mr. Farmer then built one hundred single family homes and sold or rented them, at reasonable prices, to the blacks and whites living in the area at the time. The Williams did the same, but on a smaller scale. Initially, there were many migrant workers, primarily African American, living in Hamsford, but a majority left with the Quakers and Jamaicans (of all stripes and cultures) began moving in. And the Farmers continued to build. They were the real estate moguls in the region. Their wealth had grown from single rental homes in Hamsford, into a sprawling real estate empire that included apartment complexes and businesses.

By the time Jeffrey and his sisters inherited the estate they owned more than one thousand apartments and townhouses throughout the Mid-Atlantic under Farmer and Son Realtors, a profitable hotel in Ocean City, and a lakeside house just outside of Hamsford. Jeffrey's father had been one of the early investors in Maryland Central Bank in 1987 and now owned around half a million shares. After his death Jeffrey had taken over his position on the Board of Directors.

Jeffrey was the eldest and only son, and held the responsibility of securing an education and making sure his family's millions doubled.

"His family already owns one of the largest estates in the area," Janet said. "why would he need another?"

"Why would any man need his own house?" When Janet didn't readily reply, Valerie helped her. "To start a family."

"If I had the money to buy my own house, I'd shout just to hear my own echo."

"He's following the path set for him. This is what his father wanted, but I'm also certain he's leaving his options open."

Janet shook her head. "He shouldn't have come back."

"Don't feel sorry for him. He has everything. Youth, education, money."

"I can't see much use for them here."

A sly smile touched Valerie's lips. "Well, it isn't all bad."

"What do you mean?"

"Can't you guess?"

Janet stopped walking and rested her hands on her hips. "Would I be asking if I could?"

Valerie looped her arm through Janet's and began walking again. "Jeffrey's presence certainly widens our options."

Janet blinked then understood. "Oh no. Not you too!"

"Why not me? I know I'm older than he is and not as good looking, but that doesn't make me any less ambitious."

"Some men like older women and your looks are fine. That's not what I meant. I just thought—"

Valerie laughed with a little sadness. "Poor Janet. I make a poor substitute for Ramani, don't I?"

Janet suddenly felt guilty. "No," she said quickly. "You're perfect just the way you are."

Valerie raised a knowing brow, but didn't contradict her. "Not everyone is as adventurous as you Janet and it's wrong to expect them to be."

"I know." Janet glanced up at a slowly moving cloud eager to change the subject.

Valerie patted Janet's arm. "I'm sorry about the letter."

"It's not your fault. I forgot to hide it. I'm glad you enjoyed your holiday."

"My parents weren't too pleased. They'd hoped this particular Brother we met at one of the three churches we visited there would have taken interest. It's humiliating to be offered up like a prized pig and turned down."

"Anyone who turns you down *is* a pig." Janet kissed her friend on the cheek. "But his loss is my gain."

"They even offered him a car in the deal."

Janet burst into laughter then quickly sobered when her friend didn't smile. Her good humor turned to outrage. "That's ridiculous."

"What's truly ridiculous is that he decided to buy the car from them."

Janet narrowed her eyes. "Are you certain you're not exaggerating the truth a little?"

Valerie sniffed. "At the expense of my pride? Hardly."

"You wouldn't have to deal with that if you—"

Valerie pointed at her, her tone firm. "Don't even ask me."

Janet let her shoulders drop. "It was just a thought."

"Then erase it from your mind."

"If I had half your money I would be out of here faster than you could say Hallelujah."

"The money isn't mine. I'm unmarried and my father feels he needs to protect me."

"The right man will come along."

"I hope it's soon. What about you? Do you think the right man will come?"

Janet hesitated. She hadn't thought about it much. "I honestly don't think there's a man I could love more than my art. With my art I feel completely myself—alive, powerful and free. I don't think I'd ever feel that way with a man. And I won't settle for anything less than the deepest most passionate connection."

"You might."

Janet shook her head. "I don't think marriage saves a woman from anything."

"It saves her from loneliness," Valerie said in a quiet voice.

Janet didn't feel lonely so she didn't know how to respond. She looked away instead.

Valerie halted. "Oh no." She grabbed Janet's hands and dragged her to a nearby bush.

"What is it?"

"I just saw Mother Shea."

Mother Sheridan, better known as Mother Shea, was the Seer of the church. At age eleven she'd saved her parent's lives by warning them not to travel that day. When the route they were to take was destroyed by a bridge collapse young Shea was heralded as a Seer, one who receives visions from God. However, as she grew up, her visions became less about warnings and predictions and more about obligations. Two weeks ago she'd been told that Brother Jeremiah was to donate three hundred dollars to the church, which he did promptly. She was a striking figure known for her extravagant hats. She had one hat in particular, which she only wore on certain occasions. It had so many feathers one thought that at any moment a bird would peek its head out and chirp. Mother Shea could afford such luxuries because she had found it very profitable to accept payment for her visions.

Janet clasped her shirt in panic. "Do you think she saw us?"

Valerie shook her head. "No, I don't think so."

"Do you think she's coming this way?"

"I don't know."

"Go on. Look."

"I'm afraid to."

"Then I'll look." Janet peeked her head out and saw Mother Shea in the distance. "No, she didn't see us."

Valerie rose cautiously. "She's wearing that awful hat. That means she's on an official call."

"I wonder what she's up to."

"You'll soon find out. She's heading towards your house."

CHAPTER 7

Her feet were killing her. As Mother Shea made her way up the long driveway she recalled how vanity was a sin and could also be painful. She promised herself to never again become victim to it by buying a pair of shoes that were too small just because she liked the color. She hobbled up the walkway and glanced up to see the two younger Barnetts at the window, but they did not see her. They were too busy watching their high school boys' track team jog past. She turned and saw two of the boys slow their jog to a walk, looking to catch the girls' attention.

"Go your ways!" she shouted at them. They quickly picked up their pace and ran ahead. Mother Shea then looked up at the window and said, "Where is your mother?"

"In the kitchen," Maxine said unable to hide her disappointment that their fun had been cut short.

"Thank you," she said, but doubted her answer had been heard before Trudy shut the window. Mother Shea shook her head, she sensed trouble, but she hadn't come about them, and continued to make her way around the back.

"Sister Barnett," she called tapping on the back door and peering through the window.

Mrs. Barnett glanced up from what she was doing and opened the door with a smile. "This is a surprise."

The scent of fresh spices greeted her as she entered the kitchen. "Yes." Mother Shea forced a smile as her pinched toes reminded her that if she didn't find relief soon she wouldn't remain upright. She hobbled over to a padded chair and fell into it. She slipped her shoes off relieved, although the throbbing continued.

"How are things with you?" Mrs. Barnett asked, wiping flour from her hands.

"I'm still here, Thank God. I always say things can't be too bad if I'm still breathing."

"Yes." Mrs. Barnett hesitated then asked, "So what brings you here?"

"I have news for you."

Mrs. Barnett's brows shot up. "Really?" She pulled out a chair and sat in front of her.

"Yes, the best news a mother could ever hope for." She stared at a large pitcher of ice-cold sorrel juice, a delicacy for those from the Caribbean. Its bright red color gleamed against the white tiles of the kitchen.

"My throat is a bit parched."

Mrs. Barnett got up and poured the juice then waited. Mother Shea took a long swallow then set the cup down. "Your husband makes the best sorrel juice around."

"Thank you."

"I wish—"

"No, disrespect, but you said you have good news for me?"

"Yes." When Mother Shea lifted the glass again Mrs. Barnett closed her eyes and prayed for patience. At last the glass was empty and Mother Shea set it down satisfied. "I had a vision last night. But before I had this vision I bumped into Brother Jerome at the grocery store."

"Yes, and—?"

"He spoke to me about your Beverly. He said she has touched his heart and he would like to ask for her hand in marriage, but he wanted to ask my opinion first. She has been in his sight for a long time. I told him that I would wait and see what the Lord tells me. Well last night the answer came." She lifted her glass. "My throat still feels a bit scratchy."

Mrs. Barnett poured her some more sorrel juice, quietly reciting one of the Ten Commandments: Thou shalt not kill.

Mother Shea took a long swallow then said, "And the answer was clear." She lifted her glass again.

Mrs. Barnett gripped the handle of the pitcher. "And the answer was—" she prodded.

Mother Shea set the glass down with a click. "That your Beverly is to marry Brother Jerome. This morning when I told him about my vision he said he'd speak to Brother Barnett right away."

Mrs. Barnett nearly dropped the pitcher unable to believe her ears. "Are you sure?" she whispered. "Brother Jerome wants to marry my little Beverly?"

"Yes."

Mrs. Barnett clasped her hands together and glanced up at the ceiling. "Praise God." She knew it was un-Christian to be so aware of social distinction but she couldn't help it. No matter how she fasted and prayed the desire and envy never left her. She'd been raised lower middle class and had been sensitive to the slights and limitations of her background (the second hand clothes, the lack of education) and desperately wanted better for her daughters.

"Hmm." Mother Shea sniffed the air. "Is that rum cake you're making? Lord knows I've always thought your baking is the best in the area."

Mrs. Barnett stood, taking yet another hint. Mother Shea never left a house empty handed. She cut a big slice and wrapped it in foil.

"God bless you." Mother Shea slipped the cake in her bag. "Just think of the blessing. Brother Jerome is already very established and now he's come into some valuable property. Your daughter will be well provided for and never want for anything."

Mrs. Barnett already knew of Brother Jerome's good fortune from the women in her prayer group. But she had never thought of him as marriage material for one of her daughters. "It's all I could have ever hoped for," she said excited then she sobered. "However, there may be one problem."

"I can't think of one."

"Winston."

"What about him?"

"He's never liked Brother Jerome."

"That's fine because he doesn't have to marry him. He only has to shake his hand and give his daughter away. Besides this marriage is appointed of God. It was in my vision. God is never wrong."

"I will talk to him."

"And if you can't convince him, Brother Jerome certainly will." Mother Shea stood and winced. "And you don't have to worry about thanking me; Brother Jerome has thanked me handsomely. I am just pleased that God uses me this way and I was able to give you such wonderful news."

"Are you all right?" Mrs. Barnett asked seeing her limping.

"I am paying the price for my own foolishness. Good day."

"Good day." Mrs. Barnett watched Mother Shea go then returned to her cooking. There was a lot that needed to be done, but first she had to go into town to buy a package of Winston's favorite ginger tea.

~

"WHAT WAS MOTHER SHEA DOING HERE?" Janet asked her mother the moment Mrs. Barnett returned from her errands. She stood in the kitchen and watched her mother prepare a tray with growing concern.

"Never you mind."

"But she was wearing *that hat*. I saw her. She only wears that on special visits."

"Yes, I know."

"Is it bad news?"

"Would I be setting this tray if it were?"

Janet studied the tray where her mother had placed a thick slice of Jamaican spice bun, which she had made the day before, fresh goat cheese, and ginger tea. "No, but you usually set this kind of tray when you want to convince Daddy of something."

"Perhaps," Mrs. Barnett said without looking up at her daughter. She arranged the items on the tray.

Janet pressed her hands together as though in prayer. "Dee-dee, I'm begging you."

Mrs. Barnett flashed a secretive smile. "You'll find out soon enough," she said then picked up the tray and left the kitchen.

Moments later Mrs. Barnett knocked on the door to her husband's study then entered. "I brought you something to eat."

Mr. Barnett looked up from his desk and smiled in greeting. "Thank you, darling," he said pushing his papers aside to make room for the tray. He lifted the tea and took a sip then briefly shut his eyes in pleasure. "Delicious."

Mrs. Barnett sat primly and watched him, as though her husband's comfort was her greatest concern. "I'm glad you like it."

She glanced around the room at the row of books and maps that crowded the wooden bookshelves lining the study. Although Mr. Barnett was not a strident advocate of formal education he had a healthy appreciation for knowledge. As a self-made man, it had been the books he'd read in the libraries where he'd spent his time in-between jobs that had transformed him from a Jamaican office clerk into an American businessman.

He'd had a hard life in Jamaica. He hadn't been poor but certainly not middle class. He had worked a variety of jobs—cutting sugar cane, packing in a fish cannery, and digging in a bauxite mine, the job he hated most. The promise of a new life and a chance to better himself was why he'd immigrated to America. Although it hadn't been easy, his hard work had provided a level of income that suited him and he knew that, in time, he would make more. Anything was possible in America while back home his station in life had been stamped in stone from birth.

He remembered loving a girl who he'd wanted to marry, but once her family found out which parish he was from, which school he'd attended and his family's name they immediately put a stop to it.

Of all the elements of the British occupation in Jamaica he hated most was the continuation of the class system. In American and more importantly in Hamsford, the society was more fluid and he planned to reach the top one day.

While his accounting business, Barnett's Accounting Firm, wasn't making him rich, it met his family's obligations and allowed him the honor of sending money 'back home' to help needy relatives. It also put him on the elevated income level of Hamsford's middle class. He knew how far he'd come, although his wife didn't always seem to remember.

"How has your day been?" he asked her, the tea having put him in a chatty mood.

"Fine, thank you." She shifted in her chair. "I had a visitor."

"Who?" He took a bite of the bun, which lifted his mood even higher.

"Do you like the bun? I made it without fruit this time."

"It's perfect as always. Who came by?"

"Mother Shea."

He stopped chewing and swallowed as though the bun and cheese had turned to chalk. "What did she want? Did she come to empty our pockets?"

"No, I wish you wouldn't speak that way."

"How can I not speak that way? The moment that woman opens her mouth someone ends up paying for God's favor."

"She has a gift."

"I do not deny that. I only question what her gift truly is."

"I hope you don't speak like this in public."

"Of course not. I leave sensible discussions for you." He leaned back and folded his arms pensive. "So what did she say?"

"She had some wonderful news."

"What was the news?" He took a sip of his tea.

"Brother Jerome is to marry Beverly. Mother Shea saw it in a vision."

Mr. Barnett nearly spit out his tea. "Brother Jerome? Perhaps she should go back to sleep and dream again."

"Winston, this is no time to jest."

"I am not jesting. I can't give my daughter to that man. His hands are as soft as guava jelly and I've never trusted a man with soft hands. It means he's averse to working."

"But he is rich."

"By the sweat of your brow ye shall eat."

"Not all men are meant to labor. King Solomon probably had soft hands and he had God's favor. He was also wise."

Mr. Barnett pointed at her. "Which brings me to my second point—"

"No," Mrs. Barnett quickly interrupted. "He may not be a

clever man, but he is Jamaican, a member of our church and rich." She leaned forward resting her hands on the desk her eyes bright with promise. "Imagine what he can provide for Beverly."

"You speak about money, but is his soul rich? What currency comes from his heart? Gold or pennies? He's a vain and pompous man. I want a Godly man for my daughter. One who will lead her into the ways that are right."

"Every man has his faults. You are not here to judge them. He is a good man overall. And Beverly is too pure to ever be led astray. She will be good for him."

"Yes, but—"

"Your tea is getting cold."

He took another sip.

"I understand your concerns," Mrs. Barnett said in a soothing voice as she pushed his plate of bun and cheese closer to him. "But you cannot deny that Mother Shea has a gift of sight and she asked nothing of us, so there is no hidden agenda."

"Yes, but—"

"Don't forget your snack."

He took a bite of the bun and cheese.

"We cannot pretend anymore Winston."

"What do you mean?"

"The money. I know you try to provide for all of us and Beverly contributes, but money is still tight."

"I can provide for my family."

"How much have you sent home? Didn't you help your sister with a new roof? Your brother begged you to help him start a chicken farm that failed. You can pretend to them that you're some rich American, but I know the truth. Beverly's marriage will be a financial relief for us. And we'll have only four daughters to look after instead of five."

"I know Dee, but—"

"When we first came to this country you had so many dreams."

Yes, he remembered those dreams. Their American journey had started in New York. His wife had grown up in the country and had to adjust to city life, but he was a city man at heart having grown up in Kingston and Montego Bay. But both had found New York a hard adjustment. They hated the stark, cold brick buildings, large tenements, high rise apartments and public housing. The winters were cold and dreary, chilling them until they felt their skin had been ripped from their bones; the spring was wet and unpredictable with little greenery to announce the changing season; summers were too short and sweltering; and autumn was an unwelcome reminder that winter was on its way.

And his wife hated the isolation. The church they attended was a welcome relief, but didn't help to eradicate the sight of the rats, the roaches, the dirt, the crime and the dark one bedroom basement apartment they could afford as she looked after two little girls under five.

They'd moved to Hamsford because of its location near the water, the Jamaican community and the large evangelical church they now attended. Tourists helped keep Hamsford viable. Word had grown about their annual Carnival and access to Maryland crabs, Caribbean dishes and entertainment. And as business grew around him, his business grew as well, although it was slow.

"They're still possible," he said wanting his wife to be patient.

She released a weary sigh. "And they're getting old like we are. We're no longer young. You can't work this hard forever."

"I know money is tight—"

"It's always been tight," she said with bitterness.

"But it will improve."

"When?"

"In time. God will bless us."

"He has blessed us. Open your eyes, because with all your concerns you are forgetting one thing."

Mr. Barnett lifted his tea doubtful. "What?"

"With Beverly married Janet will have no one to run away with."

Mr. Barnett stopped with the tea cup halfway to his mouth then slowly set it down as his expression cleared with understanding. "You are right."

She nodded. "I know."

He clasped his hands together pleased. "I will give my consent right away."

OUTSIDE THE STUDY door Maxine and Trudy tried to listen in. "Can you hear what they're saying?" Trudy asked.

"Barely. Shut up."

"I was just asking."

"Well don't."

"If you two would stop talking you might hear something," Janet said.

Francine added, "Eavesdropping is a waste of time. We'll find out everything anyway."

"Then why are you here?" Maxine challenged.

"I'm here to supervise."

"I didn't know you could have four eyes and still be blind as a bat."

"Don't be rude," Janet said as Francine adjusted her glasses.

"She doesn't have to act like such a know-it-all."

"Apologize."

Maxine rolled her eyes then looked at Francine. "I'm sorry. You're free to supervise as long as you keep your big mouth shut." She turned back to the door.

"They're talking too low," Trudy said disappointed. "Oh, quick, I think she's coming."

The door swung open and Mrs. Barnett appeared. She didn't question why her daughters were gathered in the hallway, her mind was too preoccupied with the upcoming wedding. "Where is Beverly?" she asked.

"She went into town," Francine said. "but she'll be back soon."

"Why did Mother Shea come?" Janet asked, this time hoping to get a response.

She wasn't disappointed. Mrs. Barnett rested her hands on her daughter's shoulder her eyes brimming with tears of joy. "She had a vision."

Maxine frowned. "She always has visions. What does it have to do with us?"

Mrs. Barnett turned to her youngest daughter and pinched her cheek. "It will change our lives. For this was the most wonderful vision a mother could ever hope for."

"Dee-dee," Janet said her patience quickly unraveling. "What was the vision?"

Mrs. Barnett began to reply then heard the front door open and pushed past her daughters to greet Beverly in the foyer. She enveloped her in a big hug. "Oh, I have wonderful news for you."

Startled, Beverly awkwardly hugged her back. "I'm glad to hear it."

"Which you will hear after dinner," Mr. Barnett said, coming out of his office. He pushed past his daughters, gave his wife a peck on the cheek then grabbed his jacket. "I will be back."

Mrs. Barnett eagerly helped him straighten his jacket so that he would make the best impression possible. "You'll see him now?"

"Yes," he said then walked out the door.

Janet fell to her knees and stared up at her mother. "I'm

begging you with all that is holy and good; please tell me what is going on."

"Get off your knees," Mrs. Barnett scolded. "You shouldn't make such a mockery of a sacred position." She tapped her chin. "I must go see if Mrs. Lind is ready with dinner," she said then hurried to the kitchen.

Janet crumpled to the floor and groaned.

Beverly fell to her side in distress. "Are you all right?"

"I have a horrible feeling."

"Do you think you'll be sick? Francine go get a bucket."

Janet sat up. "I'm not going to be sick." She stared at her sisters' worried faces. "Really. Don't you see what's happening?"

They shook their heads.

Janet took a deep breath and spoke slowly as though addressing people who spoke a foreign tongue. "Mother Shea came to visit today and now our parents are happy." She paused. "Doesn't that concern you a little?"

Maxine shrugged. "I'm curious, but what's there to worry about?"

Francine pushed up her glasses. "You should take pride in our parents' joy."

Beverly rested a gentle hand on Janet's arm. "Get up. There's nothing that can be that horrible."

Janet let her shoulders slump then stood. "Perhaps you're

right. I'm probably over dramatizing things."

Beverly nodded. "Exactly."

Although the Barnett daughters pretended not to worry all through dinner, it was difficult because their father wasn't home yet, and rarely, if ever, missed dinner time. They pretended not to worry as they sat anxiously waiting in the family room that night. But when their father finally returned home, they peppered him with questions.

Overwhelmed, Mr. Barnett held up his hands to stop the barrage. "Enough. I will let you all know what your mother and I have been up to." He sat down in his favorite leather recliner. "Everything is all set." He fell silent, leaving a dramatic pause and watched their faces then said, "There's going to be a wedding."

"Whose?" Janet said in a hoarse voice, the only one bold enough to ask.

"Beverly's." Mrs. Barnett cupped Beverly's face in her hands. "You are going to marry Brother Jerome."

Janet leaped to her feet. "Brother Jerome! You can't be serious."

"Do you think this is a barnyard?" Mr. Barnett demanded. "Keep your voice down."

"I'm sorry."

"Now wish your sister joy," Mrs. Barnett said. "She is to be a rich woman."

The three other Barnett sisters offered subdued congratulations, but Janet could not. "But he's old," she said in protest.

Mrs. Barnett sent her a stern look. "He's not that old."

"He's older than Daddy."

"Not quite."

"And aside from that the man's a f—"

Mr. Barnett stared at her in outrage. "Do you want to be struck down dead? You are not to call anyone a fool."

"Not everyone is meant to be a scholar, Janet," Mrs. Barnett added.

"But I think—"

Mr. Barnett raised his hand for silence. "If I want to hear opinions, *I* will offer them." His hand fell to his side. "How dare you question my decision. Am I not the head of this household? Have I not been given the duty to care for all of you? Do you think I've acted hastily without thought? Is that the kind of father I am?"

"No."

"Then why would you insult me?"

Janet briefly shut her eyes in regret. "I meant no disrespect, but we all know that Mother Shea—"

Mrs. Barnett put a finger to her lips. "Shhh, you do not want to invite trouble. While we may have seen and heard certain things, we must never deny her gift and she asked nothing of us. This is God's will and a blessing for us. You may not like him, but you are not the one who is going to be his wife." She looked at Beverly. "How do you feel, my dear?"

Beverly held her hands tightly in her lap and smiled. "Honored. Of course I will be Brother Jerome's wife." She hugged her mother then walked over and hugged her father.

Janet stared at the scene in paralyzed disbelief. "All right," she said in a pious tone. "I will offer no more opinions. However, may I ask one question?"

Mr. Barnett nodded. "Certainly."

"How much did Brother Jerome pay Mother Shea to have this vision?"

Her sisters gasped; her mother shut her eyes and moaned while her father leapt to his feet with rage. "Go to your room and don't show your face until morning."

Janet raced out of the room then fell on her bed and cried. She wept that her sister would marry a man she despised and that she'd lost her only chance of freedom. She felt herself go cold inside. She knew it was better to go numb than to feed into her rage. She squeezed her eyes shut and whispered in a desperate plea, "Dear God, don't let me hate him."

"You're too passionate, Janet," a quiet voice said from the doorway.

Janet stiffened hoping her sister hadn't heard her words.

"That is why you'll always be hurt."

Janet wiped her eyes with the back of her hand and sniffed, releasing her tension. She turned to see Beverly and shook her head. "But you can't marry him. You *can't.*"

Beverly sat down beside her sister and smiled. "But I will. No, don't argue. Just listen. Did you see their faces? Did you see their happiness? That is what I can give them. After all they have done for us I can honor them this way and the wishes of the Lord."

"You think the vision was real?"

"Mother Shea saved her parents' lives and she's saved the lives of others. You can't ignore her gift. And if her gift says I should marry Brother Jerome then I will."

"I know you don't love him, but do you even like him?"

Beverly shrugged nonchalant. "He's established. Decent."

"Pompous, proud—"

"Janet."

"I'm sorry."

"You can learn to like anyone and even love them in time."

"How much time? Centuries?"

Beverly shook her head. "You're not being serious."

"Don't you want something more?"

"Misery comes from wanting things to be different than they are. Here in Hamsford my prospects are slim. I accept that. You have dreams and ambitions but they only make you unhappy. You're always striving to change things instead of accepting things. I am content. I don't expect much and this is a blessing. This is my destiny." She placed a finger over Janet's lips stopping her from speaking. "I know that you had your heart set on moving out, but I've thought of another idea."

"What?"

"After I'm married you can come and live with me. I'm sure Daddy would agree to that."

Janet plastered on a smile in order not to cringe. She'd rather pluck out her own eyes than live in the same house as Brother Jerome, but she knew her sister meant well. "You're sweet. Why can't I be as good as you?"

"Just see the best of situations instead of being so quick to judge. You'll find that life is full of happiness and you'll be more content."

Janet held her sister's hands. "Good and wise. If I didn't love you, I'd be jealous. You're perfect."

"I'm far from perfect." Beverly bit her lip. "Is it wrong to admit that I'm a little scared?"

"No, that's human." Janet drew her knees to her chest. "I suppose I'll have to be nicer to Brother Jerome now."

"Definitely. Be polite."

Janet stared up at the picture of the screaming image on her ceiling, inwardly feeling the emotion it portrayed. "I'll try my best."

"You'll have to try very hard."

Janet looked at her sister. "Why?"

"Because he's having dinner with us tomorrow."

BROTHER PETER JEROME arrived promptly for dinner the next day. That was to be expected because he was a man who prided himself on his punctuality and consideration of others. According to Mrs. Barnett's wishes, Mrs. Lind had prepared a sumptuous bowl of seafood rice consisting of freshwater crab meat, oysters,

mussels, and shrimp seasoned with tomatoes, onions and corian-
der. There was also okra stew seasoned with beef jerky, garlic and
other aromatic spices, steamed tilapia and cornbread.
Throughout dinner, Brother Jerome boasted about his punctuality. He was a very fine, slender figure of a man with a long delicate nose, slim lips and smooth skin that belied his age. He
vehemently denied coloring his hair, although all the men in his
family grayed by thirty-five, and he was several years past
that mark.

He fancied himself a well-educated man because he had a
Master's degree. He also fancied himself a cultured man because
he was a second generation Jamaican-American and thought he
knew more about the American culture than anyone foreign born
ever could. Throughout dinner—when he wasn't pausing for
breath or food—he praised the Barnett's taste in clothing, food,
home decor and their fine looking, well-behaved Christian daughters and told them of how blessed he felt to soon be one of the
family.

"We're happy too," Mrs. Barnett said too excited to eat.

"It was time for me to finally settle down. It is my duty to help
my fellow man and I feel privileged to release you of the burden
of one of your daughters."

Janet cut into her tilapia with a smooth, quick motion. "I
think our father and mother would prefer to see us as blessings
rather than burdens Brother Jerome."

He blinked. "Yes, of course. I meant it more figuratively than
literally."

Janet opened her mouth to inquire 'How so?' but received a
warning look from her parents and a pleading one from Beverly
and relented. "I am sorry. I misunderstood."

"That's okay. Not everyone can grasp the subtleties in
conversation."

Janet gritted her teeth and stabbed her fish nearly cracking her plate.

"When will you hold the engagement announcement?" Maxine said eager to attend a celebratory event. It had been a long time since the family had attended any.

"In three weeks. I've already started making the arrangements. I plan to hold it in the ballroom of the Wellshire Mansion and hire a classical string ensemble and the Red Mango Catering Company," he said, looking pleased with the family's surprised expressions. He'd wanted to impress them with the expense of his arrangements and had succeeded. Status and prestige were a currency in Hamsford and he wanted to flaunt his. "Nothing less for my intended." He smiled at Beverly.

Francine smiled in approval, while Maxine and Trudy immediately began discussing what they would wear. Throughout the rest of dinner, Mr. and Mrs. Barnett thanked both God and Brother Jerome numerous times for their blessing. Janet concentrated on her dinner, wishing to be elsewhere.

JANET FOUND comfort in her studies and was going over her homework when her father appeared in the doorway and said, "Come with me to the market," before turning away.

Janet knew not to question him and shut her books and followed him to the front door. He waited for her as she put on her shoes and jacket then opened the door to the bright sunlight that had wiped away all signs of winter. "We'll walk," he said.

The scent of rain and remnants of a downpour hung in the air and glistened in the grass and on the budding trees. The sun cast a misty haze over the sidewalk and several of the small stone buildings that stood as a reminder of the settlement by the Quakers. The poorer residents lived on the outskirts of Old Hamsford in box houses like those built after World War II. Closer to town, the majority of detached homes were two-story structures—some brightly colored surrounded by fanciful gardens. Janet walked quietly by her father, avoiding the mud and puddles.

After a few blocks her father said, "We are alike in many ways. Had you been a boy—" He stopped then shoved his hands in his coat pockets. "I, too, dreamed of a better life. That is why I came to America. I had dreams, Janet, just like you, but I made mistakes. Mistakes I wouldn't have made had I listened to others, or sought counsel. You do not have to like Brother Jerome, but you must respect him. And me."

Janet looped her arm through his. "Daddy, I do respect you. I respect no other man more." *Please don't force me to stop.*

"Not even Pastor Wainwright?"

"Not even him. Sometimes I wish..." She let her words fall away knowing she could never say what she wanted to: That sometimes she wished she'd been born the boy he'd wanted, then there would never be a separation between them. They would talk as equals and she could venture out on her own with his approval. They could talk and discuss freely, but that couldn't be, and no amount of wishing would change that. She loved her father and didn't want that feeling to ever leave her. "Daddy, I don't mean to hurt you and I am sorry if what I do causes you pain."

"I just want you to understand that I know how you feel."

Janet forced a smile, knowing that he couldn't. "Yes."

"You must be patient."

How patient? She wanted to ask. He'd been patiently waiting for things to happen in his own life. The day he'd be able to afford a grand house, buy a brand new car, eat in a fine restaurant. But every year remained the same. Even though Mr. Barnett had been to college, he had earned his accounting degree by attending night school for years, money was always tight.

"I will try," Janet said hoping to reassure him.

He stopped at the edge of the street and faced the town. Only a busy four-lane road separated their safe community from the more boisterous downtown. The main crossroads, Main and State streets, resembled any town center, but boasted businesses reflecting their heritage. There was Carib's Restaurant, Dominique's Tailor and Dress Shop, Raj's Curry Shop, Mr. Pinky's Jerk Chicken Stand and The Red Apple, a grocery store that carried food imported from the Caribbean.

"I was in the world once. Not long, but I was tempted briefly." Mr. Barnett looked down at his daughter beseeching her to hear him. In truth he'd been more than tempted; he'd succumbed to his baser nature. He'd only briefly shared his past with his family, but they never knew the full truth. He'd been reckless as a youth. His nickname had been Wild Winston and he'd lived up to it. He drank, danced and smoked—sometimes ganja, sometimes something stronger. Then there were the women. Just the thought of a big breasted woman could fill him with lust. Still could, if he wasn't careful. After he'd returned to the church he'd become strict and disciplined. He was determined that his daughters wouldn't get caught by the kind of man he used to be.

He knew the thoughts of men. Girls in the church had been a favorite of his and his mates. They were pure and virginal—at least most of them—and easy conquests. As long as he kept his daughters safe and close to home they'd never be one of them. "I know you see things on that campus of yours and in this town, but you must remember that their ways are not our ways. You can be among them, but you'll never be one of them. Our traditions keep you safe. Do I make myself clear?"

"Yes."

Mr. Barnett patted Janet's hand and his mouth spread into a grin. "Good girl," he said then they crossed the street.

People crowded Pembrose Place, a large indoor market in the middle of town, which was a favorite gathering spot for most of

Hamsford's residents. The deep guttural beat of reggae and hip-hop from several speakers blasted above the crowd, and mingled with vendors shouting out the latest prices and the best fish catch of the day. The scent of food drifted through the halls: boiled corn, ackee and saltfish, roti, cornbread, and spiced Jamaican patties. People bought them along with imported drinks among the sound of old talk, new gossip and bartering. This was the order of the day at the market.

Mr. Barnett stopped at Mr. Beecham's vegetable and fruit stand. Mr. Beecham didn't have a memorable face; he boasted only a medium build and thick heavy brows, although his hair was thinning. He was not a member of their church, or any church for that matter, but he was a Jamaican and always had the best selection of organically grown fruits and vegetables, so Mr. Barnett was a faithful customer.

As a boy, Mr. Beecham had grown up working on his father's farm, and while he had never had the opportunity to go to school and study agriculture, he always had interesting creations by growing hybrid vegetables and fruits. Mr. Barnett was about to ask him a question when a voice cut through the crowd. They turned to see a large spiral hat coming towards them.

"What's this peeny thing you give me?" Mother Shea said approaching them. She placed a tomato on the table.

Mr. Beecher sighed, use to Mother Shea's demands. "Is there something wrong?"

"You don't see it's too small?"

"When you buy in bulk the sizes will differ."

"I asked for a bag of tomatoes. Not a bag of peas."

Mr. Beecher grabbed another bigger tomato and handed it to her. "Is that better?"

"Yes, thank you. I truly appreciate your help. You know how I hate to complain."

He reached for the other tomato, but Mother Shea grabbed it

first. "I'm sure no one will want this one, it looks a bit damaged and I'd hate for it to spoil." She nodded to Mr. Barnett and Janet then walked off.

Mr. Beecher shook his head. "How come I always lose money when that woman's around?"

"You wouldn't be the first," Mr. Barnett said then asked him about his potatoes.

Janet took the opportunity to wander around the market. She slowed her walk when she spotted the Maliks' market stand. She saw Ramani's cousin, Darika, working and walked over to her not knowing what she would say, but still feeling compelled to go. When Darika saw her, she glanced around then motioned Janet closer.

"I'm not supposed to talk to you."

"I know," Janet said. "Did you find out anything?"

Darika shook her head.

"Darika!" Mr. Malik said coming from behind the back.

She jumped and returned to work. Mr. Malik walked past Janet as if she didn't exist.

Janet licked her lips. "I hope one day you'll understand," she pleaded to the man she'd known most of her life.

Mr. Malik began folding a piece of fabric.

"Janet!" Mr. Barnett called. She turned and rushed over to her father. He yanked her closer to him. "What were you doing?"

"I just—"

Her explanation was cut short when someone called his name. They turned and saw Brother Jeremiah making his way through the crowd as if no one else existed. That proved easy for him because he was built like a brick building and people stayed out his way for fear of injury. "I have a question," he said brushing Janet aside once he reached them.

Janet took no offense. Except for Mother Shea, the men in their church did not see women as important when it came to making decisions. And she felt proud that people listened to her father's advice.

Mr. Barnett nodded. "Yes, Brother Jeremiah."

"I have a real big problem," Brother Jeremiah gently pulled Mr. Barnett aside. "I made a large contribution to the church, expecting to get money from one of my customers," Brother Jeremiah said referring to his home repair business. "But he's refusing to pay me, and I don't know what to do."

"How much does he owe you?"

"Well, you see, because of some hard times he was having, plus he and his wife have three little children and she's expecting their fourth, I agreed to do some things for him, and—"

"How much does he owe you?" Mr. Barnett interrupted not wanting to suffer through one of Brother Jeremiah's long, detailed stories.

He muttered something.

"I didn't hear you. Speak up."

"Twenty-five hundred dollars," he said a little louder.

"What? How—?"

"We agreed that he would pay me back, weekly, but as I told you, with a baby on the way, and..." He shrugged his massive shoulders, helpless. "I need the money. If Bessie finds out, she gon' kill me!" Brother Jeremiahs' wife Bessie had the look and texture of a cornflake—light brown and brittle—but despite her appearance she could put the fear of God in anyone, and would surely give her husband a month of tongue lashings, if he did not find a solution.

Brother Jeremiah wiped his forehead with a worn handkerchief. "What should I do? I need that money by the end of the month. Laud God help me!"

Mr. Barnett gave his friend a reassuring pat on the shoulder sensing his distress. "Let me think it over and I'll call you this evening."

"Thank you." He turned like a startled deer when he heard his wife call him. "I'll wait for your call," he said before disappearing in the crowd.

Mr. Barnett made his purchases then he and Janet headed for home. He didn't speak most of the way then said, "What do you think of Brother Jeremiah's troubles?"

Janet hid a smile used to her father's sly way of asking her advice. "Daddy, you've always followed the ways of Solomon. Doesn't he talk about seeking counsel? Shouldn't Brother Jeremiah seek out a financial counselor to help him know how to work with customers such as this one —now and in the future?"

"Hmm. Yes, I think you're right. I thought the same." Her father placed his hand on her shoulder, with just enough pressure to make her wince. "What did I tell you about the Maliks?" he asked in the same neutral tone.

Janet swallowed. "I was just saying hello."

He tightened his grip. "That wasn't my question."

"You told me not to talk or visit them."

"So why did I see you over there?"

"I have no excuse."

He didn't speak for a few moments then said, "I forgive you. Tonight we'll watch *The Harder They Come.*"

Janet resisted the urge to roll her eyes. Her father always had them watch the Jimmy Cliff classic movie about a young Jamaican corrupted by city life and the church woman, who loves him, leaves the church and sleeps with him, but then is betrayed. Janet didn't mind watching the movie because she loved the soundtrack and it was the only time they were allowed to listen to reggae.

"Okay," she said.

He halted and forced her to face him, his dark eyes piercing. "And don't disobey me again."

CHAPTER 9

A bright red cardinal swooped down to grab an abandoned French fry only to be beaten by a squirrel. This event went unnoticed by Janet who sat on a concrete bench outside the Student Union building, staring at her grade.

"You look like you want to fly," a familiar voice said.

Janet looked up and saw Marisa. She waved her paper. "I got an A."

"I'm glad." She hesitated. "We weren't sure you'd come back."

"I wasn't sure either, but I had to finish what I started." And going to school was freeing.

It didn't matter that her parents didn't care about her grades, or that her sisters didn't understand her ambition. Here she didn't have to placate some man; she could freely express her opinions without censure. Art was her passion. She'd discovered it at age three when she'd first plopped her hands in wet paint and spread bright colors all over a sheet of paper. The messy wildness of that experience intrigued her. And as her talent grew, she felt and enjoyed the exhilarating power of creating images—of taking what was in her mind or in front of her and transferring it onto a surface. Her parents found her hobby harmless because initially she primarily did paint-by-numbers of simple scenes and sketches of people's faces, which she kept in her closet, but they didn't know her hidden passion—abstraction and surrealism.

"Here. My professor also liked this." She opened up her portfolio and showed her friend a sketch she had done of her mother and Mrs. Lind in the kitchen.

"Amazing," Marisa said then a gush of wind swept past scattering Janet's drawings. "Quick before they blow away!"

The two women scrambled to catch them as people strolled past. Janet tucked what she could away and Marisa rushed back to her breathless. "Did you see him?" she asked handing Janet the rest of her work.

"Who?"

"That black guy. My God how could you have missed him?" She swung her head around trying to find him again.

"What's so special about him?"

"He's one of the most gorgeous men I've ever seen and he helped me get your pictures." She giggled. "He actually thought they were mine, but I wasn't going to take the credit so I pointed you out."

"Oh," Janet said with little interest. "Well, thank him for me, if you see him again."

"I'll certainly try," Marisa said with a cunning grin.

Errol Seabright was an ordinary man with a long face and heavyset body. Nothing exciting happened to him. Money was tight, but fortunately the women were loose so he was never bored. He thought life was good. He sat out on the twelve foot wooden terrace that wrapped around the cut stone building he helped manage with his sister Sigonya. The house sat on the rolling hills of Hanover near Montego Bay and offered him an enviable view of the lush vegetation including the banana, grapefruit, and tangerine trees and the sea in the distance.

He liked his work and the opportunity it gave him to look after his Aunt who used to be a housekeeper when the owners had lived there. Now the place was rented to visitors. Life was calm with few surprises until a letter came through the mail one day. He stared at it with amazement then jumped up from his seat on the porch and called through the screen door.

"Sigonya!"

"What?"

"Come quick!"

A thin rail of a woman with thick braids pulled back with a scarf appeared at the screen door but didn't come out. "What is it?"

"We get a wedding invitation!"

"From who?"

"Peter Jerome."

"The mayor's grandson found himself a wife?"

"Yes."

She stepped outside and snatched the invitation from him. "Let mi see for miself. I never thought dat I would live long enough to see him get married."

"He's a man."

"I know but dat bwoy weird."

"How you mean?"

"Remember when he'd come visit for summer holidays? How stiff and stuck up he was. Just cause him family have a toilet inside the house instead of outside."

Errol kissed his teeth. "We all do the same ting in it."

"Exactly, but that family was always that way. Always tinking dem better than others."

Errol sat down and rocked back in his chair. "We going?"

Sigonya smiled at her brother. "Of course. Dis is a show we haffi see."

~

"WHAT ARE YOU WEARING?" Mrs. Barnett demanded when she saw Janet come down the steps.

Janet glanced down. "My dress for the engagement party."

Mrs. Barnett waved her away. "Go back upstairs and change into your blue dress."

"Why?"

"Because Jeffrey Framer is going to be there and I learned from a reliable source that he favors the color blue."

"But I don't have a blue dress."

"You have the one Grandma Lucy sent you three years ago."

Janet gasped in horror. "But I hate—"

"I don't care." Mrs. Barnett shoved her back up the stairs.

"Dee-dee, please—"

"Do you want me to go get your father? Go change."

Janet passed Maxine and Trudy in the hallway. Both girls tried to hide their giggles as she headed to her room.

Moments later Janet emerged wearing a blue dress with enough ruffles to make her resemble a life-size carnation. Mrs. Barnett beamed when she saw her. "That's much better," she said walking around her. "Now you are to do only two things tonight: Smile and keep your mouth shut. The moment you feel like opening it, put food inside. Is that understood?"

Janet nodded.

Maxine bounded down the stairs then spun around in her yellow dress. "How do I look?"

"Beautiful as always," Mrs. Barnett said. "If only you were a little older."

"I'll be sixteen soon."

"Yes, but not old enough. Trudy let me see you. Yes, that's lovely and Francine." She looked at her middle child and controlled a wince. The dress was attractive, but did nothing to help her face. "You'll do. And of course Beverly." She looked at her eldest daughter then touched her chest speechless. Brother Jerome had sent Beverly an expensive, full-length, green sheath dress with delicate lace trim, and sewn-on sequins down the side. She looked like a rich woman. "You are perfect as always."

WHEN JANET ENTERED THE BALLROOM, she nearly ran out in horror. A sea of blue dresses choked the room. All unmarried women between the ages of eighteen to sixty-eight had adorned themselves in blue. And the ladies from Janet's church stood out like an oak tree in a rose bed. All their dresses reached below their knees and elbows. While some of their gowns were stylish and elegant they were no match for the women whose outfits displayed a lot more flesh. Janet wanted to disappear into the coat closet. Mrs. Barnett saw the look of dismay on her daughter's face and said brightly, "Never mind. Your dress looks the best and you're prettier than them anyway. Jezebels," she muttered under her breath as one young woman in a strapless dress sauntered past. "He's still a man of God and won't be swayed by them. He'll want a good woman in the church."

Janet offered her mother a strained smile then saw Valerie off to the side. She raced over to her. Although her friend also wore blue, it was subtle and very classy. Janet hugged herself as though she were trying to squeeze tight enough to make herself disappear. "It's so humiliating."

"At least you're not alone in your humiliation."

"You're only wearing a hint of blue. I'm drowning in it. No

one could tell the difference between me and a blueberry. I'm not even interested in Jeffrey Farmer."

"Just wait until you see him. You might change your mind. Wait... I think I see him now."

Valerie wasn't the only one. Soon a rustling of gossip filled the air as all eyes turned to the entrance. Jeffrey Farmers' sisters, Karen and Tanya, entered first. They were a very distinguished pair who would have caught people's attention even if they did not have an eligible brother. Both women had nut brown skin and attractive figures, but their similarities ended there. Karen was not a beautiful woman, but her arrogance gave the impression that she was. This illusion was furthered by her money and status in the community. Tanya was better looking, but didn't know it so she ate up compliments like a vulture living on crumbs.

Jeffrey walked in behind them. He'd been given all the good looks in the family, and the humility. He had an easy going nature and an ability to light up a room just by entering it. His smile fell on the first person he met—Sister Daniels. She returned the expression then crumpled to the floor in a faint. Sister Daniels' collapse caused a commotion briefly redirecting people's attention from the last person to enter.

"Just as handsome as I remembered," Valerie said of Jeffrey.

"Who is that man with him?" Janet said, noticing his companion.

"I don't know. He's certainly not from around here."

Within moments their mothers raced up to the two young women, unaware that Francine was following close behind because she had nothing better to do. Sister Williams said in an excited tone, "Do you see that other man?"

"It's hard not to," Janet said intrigued. He was the tallest and most handsome man in the room. She couldn't help but stare.

"He's rich and he's Jeffrey's closest friend. He is going to help with the construction. His name is Frederick Durand and he's *an Original.*"

"From the Continent," Francine added.

Mrs. Barnett sent her middle daughter a cutting glance. "Where else do Originals come from, silly girl?"

"I wonder which part?" Valerie asked studying the stranger's fine, handsome features.

"His parents are West African and it's rumored that his wealth is twice that of the Farmers. In the hundreds of millions," Sister Williams added.

"Pity he doesn't past the JCE test," Janet added, still unable to remove her gaze. She admired his air of authority and compelling presence that penetrated the crowded room. He was a new and refreshing sight. She wondered how she could finagle an introduction.

Mrs. Barnett grabbed Janet's hand determined to put her matchmaking plans into action. "He's not important."

Half of the crowd agreed with her and quickly dismissed Frederick Durand because of his background—an Original and either a Methodist, Anglican or Muslim, because most Originals were—which was a pity because he was so rich. They could accept him if he was Anglican, but the fact that he hailed from the continent was too much of a difference for most of them to overlook.

Soon the other half dismissed him because of his conduct. He hardly spoke. When he did—or rather was forced to—his replies were short and curt. He never smiled and stationed himself against the wall as though he'd entered a leper colony and was afraid of infection. Gossip quickly spread about the Original's bad behavior.

"Look at him keeping to himself away from our girls," one guest said.

"You have to be careful around them," her friend replied.

"I don't trust dem at all," a third admitted. "My Gloria knew a friend of hers who married one, went home to his country and found out she was his sixth wife! It took her three years to save enough money to come back to America."

"Her parents let her marry?"

"She met him at the college and didn't ask permission."

Mr. Barnett overheard the conversation and spoke up. "That's why children always should."

"Hm," the first woman said casting a look at the newcomer. "I know he's close to the Farmers, but I wonder why he came at all."

"I'm glad he's here," her fourteen year old daughter said in a dreamy voice. "He's *gorgeous*."

The women gasped and the girl's mother boxed her ears, told her to go and the conversation changed to something else.

Mrs. Barnett didn't care about the gossip. She kept Janet at her side until she could find an opportunity to put her plan into action. "You must reacquaint yourself with Jeffrey before you lose your chance." She searched the room then seized an opportunity and shoved Janet into Jeffrey's path; fortunately he stopped himself before he crashed into her.

"Excuse me," Janet stammered.

He smiled. "It's my fault. There are a lot of people here. I have to watch where I'm going."

She held out her hand. Through the corner of her eye she could see her mother making a face in horror, but ignored her. "I'm Janet Barnett. You may not remember me..."

Jeffrey vigorously shook her hand and his smile grew. "Of course I remember you. And your sister Beverly and your other sisters..." he faltered.

"Francine, Trudy and Maxine."

He nodded. "Yes, they must be all grown up now."

"Not quite." At that moment she saw her sister, Francine, talking to an older woman who looked as though she was ready to fall asleep. Then her gaze fell on Maxine and Trudy who were flirting with two musicians from the ensemble who were taking a break. One of them, a good looking young man with an athletic build, was showing Maxine how to hold his violin and bow in a manner that put their bodies very close together.

"So is everyone doing well?" Jeffrey said.

Janet snapped back to their conversation. "Yes."

"Your mother and father are in good health?"

"Yes, excellent," she said seeing her father's loaded plate as he sat at a table with several other men. She didn't dare look at her mother. "Thank you." She cleared her throat. "I am sorry about your loss."

An expression of sadness skittered across his face. "It was very kind how the community came together to honor my father."

"We all loved and admired him."

"That is why I'm finishing his project and dedicating a wing to him. We plan to have a big event to celebrate."

She looked past him. "We?"

"Yes, my friend Frederick and I." He snapped his fingers. "I should introduce you. You two would like each other." He turned.

Janet's heart began to race at the thought of speaking to the stranger, but then she saw her father's watchful gaze and knew it wouldn't be a good idea. She seized Jeffrey's arm and turned him back to her. "Perhaps another time."

He blinked confused by her hesitation but nodded. "Okay."

"Wonderful," she said feeling silly.

"So what have you been up to?"

"I'm studying Art History at the university. I plan to maybe work at a museum or teach."

"Good for you." Jeffrey glanced up when someone called his name and motioned him over.

"You're popular," Janet said feeling his hesitation.

"Yes," he said with a shade of regret that was instantly replaced by a grin. "Perhaps we could talk longer a little later."

"Thank you." She backed away. "I'd like that."

He tugged one of the ruffles of her sleeve. "Nice dress," he said then left.

Janet suddenly remembered the ugly dress she wore and covered her eyes wanting to melt into the floor.

"What did you say?" her mother demanded once Jeffrey had gone.

Janet let her hand fall. "I talked about our family and his father."

"That's all?"

"There wasn't time. I thought you didn't want me to say much."

"Don't be irritating. You know when it's the proper time to talk."

"He's not interested in me."

"Then be more interesting," Mrs. Barnett said.

"Without opening my mouth?"

"Just smile and listen. A man always finds a pretty woman interesting. If you stay silent long enough he'll convince himself you're beautiful." The mention of beautiful things turned Mrs. Barnett's thoughts to her eldest daughter. "Now I must go find Beverly."

Mrs. Barnett found Beverly surrounded by people offering congratulations. Brother Jerome stood at her side his hand resting on her shoulder as though he'd glued it there.

Mother Shea came up behind her. "I am so happy that I played a role in this union. Not a big part mind, just a little one. Just think. It was my dream that made this certain and I helped spread the good news. But, as you all know, I am not one to put myself forward to receive praise. My gift is from God. I know my place, and that although small, my part in this blessing will be remembered."

Mrs. Barnett nodded. "Yes, of course."

"Has Mrs. Lind made her batch of doilies this year?" Mother Shea asked. Mrs. Lind was known for making intricately crocheted and embroidered doilies using finely woven cotton, or silk thread.

"Not yet."

"Oh, how I love her doilies. I have a place that will be perfect to display them."

"I'll make sure she makes a special one just for you."

"Thank you for your kindness. I'm not one to ask for anything because although I live alone I have many friends, but I do love her doilies."

Mrs. Barnett moved forward to approach her daughter, but Mother Shea's words stopped her. "I notice you have Janet in blue."

"Yes." She shrugged. "One can only hope."

"I noticed her eyeing the Original."

"She's just curious like the rest of us."

"He is very good looking."

"I hadn't noticed."

"She did."

"It's nothing," Mrs. Barnett said, pressing down a flicker of fear. She toyed with the collar of her dress.

"I'm sure it is, but it would be nice to see her safely married." Mother Shea leaned in closer. "It is my understanding that Jeffrey likes a special type of blue. Turquoise. Just like this." She held up a cloth necklace with a small turquoise stone in the middle.

"Really? But Sister Daniels did say—"

Mother Shea moved her hand in a quick dismissive gesture. "You notice that her niece is wearing this precise color blue herself."

Mrs. Barnett saw the young woman then pursed her lips. "I should have known."

"But that can be easily remedied. I don't need this anymore."

Mrs. Barnett turned to her stunned. "You mean to give it to me?"

"Yes."

She reached for it then stopped. "But it's a necklace. My husband is against any large adornments."

Mother Shea lowered her gaze and stroked the pendant. "I've heard that Janet's schooling may be putting funny ideas into her head, like leaving your house and living on her own." She glanced up. "Do you want to see Janet married or not?"

Mrs. Barnett stiffened in fear. How had Mother Shea found out about Janet wanting to move out? Probably Mrs. Lind told someone, who told someone else, she didn't dare think of who else knew. She stared at the necklace, longing evident in her gaze.

"Times are changing Sister. If we want our girls to compete against those with their crafty worldly allurements they must have their own special charms. Don't you agree?"

Mrs. Barnett grasped the necklace. "Yes."

Mother Shea smiled. "Put it on her as soon as you can."

"I will do it right now."

"You know I have a very large sitting room. Only two doilies will get lost in it. I've always wanted a lovely table runner too."

"You will not be disappointed."

"Thank you," Mother Shea said. "You're so generous because I am too modest to ever ask."

JANET WATCHED the festivities with an artistic eye noting the elaborate way the ballroom had been decorated. Colorful ribbons, streamers, and large helium balloons draped the windows. Bright red damask tablecloths covered round tables, dressed up with fine white chinaware, and small round glass bowls, filled with live flowers floating in red-colored water, provided artful centerpieces. It was a boisterous affair with lots of people and although few people danced (though no one from their church because they didn't believe in dancing) the musical ensemble played an exciting mixture of upbeat classical music, intertwined with several recognizable Caribbean tunes.

Her gaze turned to the lavish feast, a buffet bursting with an assortment of familiar dishes such as jerk chicken, fried fish, cassava cup cakes, some unfamiliar dishes, and a wide assortment of desserts, including sliced banana sweets. Waiters, wearing tuxedos and white gloves, stood ready to assist. Off to the side a group of young children were playing to their own tune, singing a favorite childhood song "Brown Girl in the Ring", and laughing hilariously at the various dance movements each girl introduced.

Her quiet thoughts were violently interrupted when something wrapped around her neck threatening to strangle her.

"Don't gasp like that," Mrs. Barnett said. "It's very unattractive."

Janet coughed trying to get her breath back then finally wheezed, "You nearly choked me."

Mrs. Barnett clasped the necklace then stood in front of her. She patted the stone in place satisfied. "There. Much better."

Janet touched the necklace confused. "But Daddy—"

"Won't mind. Mother Shea gave it to me. She'd never give you something improper to wear."

"No, but—"

"Don't you trust your mother?"

Janet sighed knowing that was the end of the argument. Yes, she trusted her mother, but Mother Shea was another issue. However, she knew to keep her suspicions quiet.

"I happen to know that Jeffrey likes this particular color blue," Mrs. Barnett said leaving no room for discussion.

"It's too tight." Janet reached up to stretch it.

Mrs. Barnett slapped her hand away. "You're just not used to it. Stop fiddling."

Francine approached them. "I saw one like that at the museum. It's called a choker."

"It's aptly named," Janet said.

Mrs. Barnett glanced around looking for her two legged prey. "A gathering of women always makes a man nervous. Francine, go entertain someone else with your trivia. And fix your face. You're not pretty enough to pout so don't try." Once Francine was gone Mrs. Barnett said, "Why are you standing here alone?"

Janet adjusted the choker with a sigh. "I didn't do it on purpose."

"There aren't enough men," Mrs. Barnett said in disgust as she surveyed the room. "I see Jeffrey. Why is he talking to Valerie instead of you?"

"Maybe because he likes her."

"He'll like you too if you give him a chance."

"I've already tried to speak to him, remember?"

"Try again."

"I'll wait for my chance."

"Chance is merely a well orchestrated opportunity. You never wait for it. And I can see he's ready to leave her. Good. Now it's your turn. Oh no, that Anita Maxwell has gotten to him first. Wait... oh he's going to Beverly to give his congratulations." They both watched Jeffrey approach Beverly and Janet saw how her sister's face lit up. She glanced at her mother who visibly looked concerned, then her gaze fell on Brother Jerome, but he was too self satisfied to notice. The knot in her stomach began to ease until she saw Mother Shea's keen, observant gaze and knew that Beverly had to be very careful.

CHAPTER 10

Jeffrey flashed a warm grin as he took her hand. "I want to offer you my congratulations."

"Thank you," Brother Jerome said before Beverly could reply.

Undeterred Jeffrey continued clasping Beverly's hand. "It's been a long time."

Again Brother Jerome spoke for her. "Yes, it is amazing how time passes. Time is such a fluid thing and runs through our lives like water. I once read somewhere that *'The time which we have at our disposal every day is flexible...'*

"Elastic," Jeffrey corrected recognizing the quote from Proust.

Brother Jerome didn't hear him. *"And the passion we feel makes it bigger..."*

"Expands it."

"Correct. Expands it. That's my favorite quote."

"You know so many quotes," Beverly said, looking directly at Brother Jerome. "You are very clever."

Brother Jerome patted her on the shoulder as he would a beloved pet. He beamed from her praise, always taking special

86

pride when someone noticed his intellect. His father never did. "I have many years behind me and have learned that knowledge is the victor over ignorance. In time you too will develop a fine mind."

Before Jeffrey could speak, Beverly looked at her intended and said, "You must remember to drink something before your speech. It is very important that you do not sound hoarse."

Brother Jerome grasped his throat as though it were about to shrivel up from lack of moisture. "Yes, of course. Excuse me." He rushed away.

Jeffrey sat beside her. "You handled that well."

"I don't know what you mean," she said looking innocent until a smile touched her lips. A smile that made his heart ache and introduced feelings of regret he hadn't known were still there.

"May I ask a favor?" she asked.

"Yes."

"May I have my hand back?"

"I'm sorry." Jeffrey quickly released it surprised that he'd held it for so long without noticing. It had felt so natural and right in his. He lowered his gaze. "It has been a long time."

"Yes."

"There's another quote about time that I remember." He lifted his gaze and stared deep into her eyes. "*Time is too slow for those who wait.*"

Beverly grinned remembering the Van Dyke quote from school. "*Too swift for those who fear.*"

"*Too long for those who grieve.*"

"*Too short for those who rejoice.*"

His gaze held hers. "*But for those who love, time is eternity.*"

Beverly turned away, her hands trembling in her lap.

He resisted the urge to cover them with his own. "I'm sorry I never wrote."

"You were too busy with your adventures." She looked at him

and smiled. "Besides we were childhood friends. We are adults now."

"Yes." There was so much he wanted to say but time was short and he could see Brother Jerome making his way back to them. "I was surprised to hear about your engagement."

"My engagement surprised all of us."

"I think—"

"Now I feel refreshed," Brother Jerome announced again placing his hand on Beverly's shoulder.

Jeffrey looked at Brother Jerome's empty hands annoyed that the older man had neglected to get Beverly anything to drink. He turned to her. "Would you like me to get you something?"

"No," Brother Jerome said quickly, recognizing his blunder. "I will get it for you. After all I might as well get used to my duties as your husband." He walked away.

"You didn't need to send him off again," Beverly said. "I'm perfectly fine."

"But he should have brought you something to drink. I know I would have. You'd never be forgotten if—" Jeffrey bit his lip. "You two don't seem to have much in common."

"We have enough in common."

"Like what?"

"We love our families, our church and our ways."

"It's a new time Beverly some ways have changed."

"Not in Old Hamsford."

"I've seen the world. A world where fathers and churches don't determine your destiny."

"I see."

"Old Hamsford can't stay this way forever. It has to change. And it will."

"Well, it's not going to change right now."

"And if Brother Jerome were to take you away from Hamsford, what will you have in common?"

"We will find other things. Probably children."

Jeffrey's gaze pierced hers as though he could see into her soul. "Would you still marry him if there was someone else?"

A look of fear crossed her face. "Don't ask me a question like that."

"Why not?"

"Because it's too late."

"Is it?"

Brother Jerome thrust a glass in her hand; a few drops fell to the floor. "There you are, my darling. You look a little pale. This will put color in your cheeks."

She absently took the glass and said, "Thank you, my dear."

Beverly's quiet but clear term of endearment hit Jeffrey like an anvil. He swallowed. "I wish you both lots of happiness," he said in a curt tone before walking away.

JANET WEAVED through the crowd trying to stay out of her mother's sight and found Valerie at the banquet table. She made a small plate, although she wasn't hungry, and winked at her friend across the table. "I saw you talking to Jeffrey."

"Yes, but he spoke to Beverly longer."

Janet frowned. "You noticed that too?"

"Everybody noticed."

"Except Brother Jerome."

"Yes, except him. Thank goodness."

"I doubt he'd notice an angel sitting on his head unless it introduced itself and said it knew God personally." Janet lifted a Jamaican meat patty and took a bite.

"You're not being fair."

"I'm not trying to be," Janet said then she made a face.

Valerie laughed then moved from the other side of the table. "It's probably better that he doesn't notice too much."

Janet shrugged, trying to make light of a matter that was serious. "They used to be old friends. They're just becoming reacquainted."

Valerie sent her a significant look. "Don't try to deceive me. I saw exactly what you saw. They like each other very much."

Janet let her gaze fall and kicked a wayward crumb. "Yes, well he is a very likeable person."

"Too likable," Valerie said concerned.

Janet looked at her surprised. "What do you mean?"

She dragged Janet to a corner where they could not be overheard. "Beverly should marry Brother Jerome as quickly as possible and not think about it. She should focus on how fortunate she is and think of nothing else."

"How fortunate she is?" Janet scoffed. "But he's—"

"Rich, Jamaican and in the Church. He will give her status and security. That's all that matters."

"So you think they're well matched?"

"They are equals. His money affords her youth and beauty and vice versa."

"But his mind—"

"He has his Master's degree. It doesn't matter in what," she added before Janet could argue. "It shows that he's not as feeble minded as you pretend to think."

"Pretend?"

"He's a little pretentious, but he's not cruel. He has a good heart. Think of all the charities he's involved in at church."

"The ones he doesn't add his name to?"

"At least he contributes," Valerie said with patience. "Beverly will make him happy and by marrying him she will make your parents happy too."

"And what about her happiness?"

"If she focuses on the right things she will be happy too. Happiness is a matter of choice." When her friend continued to frown, Valerie took her hand. "Janet, stop thinking like an artist and be sensible. It's easier to form a partnership with someone who knows what he wants. Everyone knows Brother Jerome wants a wife, we all only suspect Jeffrey does. So we have to resort to the art of persuasion."

Janet glanced at Valerie's dress. "That's why you wore blue."

"As did you."

"Against my will," Janet said looking down at her raspberry tart.

"I bet if Jeffrey Farmer asked you to marry him you'd say yes."

Janet looked at him. He was attractive and she knew he'd be easy to live with. His sisters would be a pain, but she'd learn to tolerate them. He passed the JCE test with flying colors and wouldn't be as demanding as most of the men she knew. He was one ticket to freedom. "Maybe," she admitted, then let her gaze travel to his friend. She'd never seen a man so beautifully made. His dark suit only emphasized his wide shoulders, small waist and impressive build. *Men were created for a lot more than sketching,* she remembered Ramani say. A slight grin touched her lips. Watching him, Janet could imagine the various different uses. "I could say yes to him." She shook her head, embarrassed by her thoughts. That was impossible. She turned to her friend.

Valerie stared at her open mouthed.

"I said that out loud, didn't I?"

Valerie nodded.

Janet burst into laughter. "Relax. I was joking."

Valerie blinked several times. "You shouldn't joke about things like that. Your parents would have a fit if they heard you."

Janet dismissed the thought with a wave of her hand. "It's never going to happen so don't worry." She sighed. "Now back to Jeffrey. It still seems unfair."

"Unfair or not, he's a definite prospect. However, there's one minor problem."

"What?"

"Although he may be in the church he's not a part of *our* church. That makes things uncertain." Valerie looked at something in the distance. "What is your mother doing?"

Janet looked at her mother who was making gestures towards Jeffrey. "She doesn't like me standing alone."

"You're with me."

"You're a woman, you don't count. Excuse me while I try my best to disappear." Janet dashed into the coat closet, certain she'd found the perfect hiding spot. She sat with her plate precariously balanced on her lap, thrilled that she wouldn't have to deal with any distractions when she heard Jeffrey's voice.

"Frederick, what are you doing out here all by yourself? Come on and have some fun. I'm your friend. I can't leave you out here all alone. You look pathetic."

"I'm fine," a cultured African-British voice replied. "But you have to join in. People will think you don't like them."

"So what?" he said with a note of scorn. "I don't care what people think. Especially these people. I can see why you left here the first moment you could."

"It's not really so bad," Jeffrey said. "The people may seem a bit provincial, but they're not so bad. Not all of Hamsford is like the church set."

"Provincial? A person from a small town of less than twelve thousand I call provincial. A group of eight thousand people who all come from the same Jamaican parish and the same ten families, borders on in-breeding."

Jeffrey laughed. "That's not fair. There are nearly 20,000 residents here and not all of them have Jamaican heritage, although most do. I know it seems strange to you, but that's how it is here. And we're not all related. We have distinct family groups."

"You can tell the difference? Half the girls—I use the term loosely—are wearing the same dress."

"I don't notice dresses, I notice faces and there are plenty of pretty ones. Fashion isn't a big deal here."

"Neither is education. There's no one I'd want to talk to. They all seem to have read only one large book and even that, not very well."

"No," Jeffrey admitted. "But not everyone can be a theologian, Frederick; however, they are strong in their beliefs. If you'd give them a chance they'd open up."

"And why do they keep calling me Durand? I've told them my name is Frederick."

"It's a sign of respect. Those in the church are called Brother or Sister. Those who've left but are still part of the community like myself, are referred to by their first name. But outsiders like you, are called by your surname. Close friends of similar age can be referred to by their first names. It helps people to know the structure of things."

"Sounds old fashioned."

"It is, but the younger ones are easier to talk to and there are plenty of young women here."

Frederick glanced at Beverly. She stood out not only because she was the most beautiful woman in the room but her green dress was a nice reprieve from the river of blue. "The only interesting woman is engaged."

"Yes, Beverly is wonderful." Jeffrey sighed, a hint of regret in his voice. "Perhaps I should have come back sooner."

Frederick sent him a sharp glance. "For what?"

"Nothing." He snapped his fingers as an idea came to him. "I know who you could talk to. Her sister."

Janet stiffened.

"Which one?" he said without interest. "She has lots of them."

"Just four. Janet is second to Beverly in age and looks. She is someone I know you would find very interesting. I'd wanted to introduce you earlier. She's studying at the university and she's very talented." Jeffrey surveyed the room trying to spot her. "That's funny, she was here earlier. She was wearing a—"

"Blue dress," Frederick said bored. "Just like all the others. I've already met her."

Janet leaned closer intrigued.

Jeffrey stared at him surprised. "You have?"

"Not formally, but I saw her."

"Where? When?"

"About a week ago at the University. I was meeting someone and then these papers blew into my path. I saw a girl struggling to get them so I decided to help. I saw what they were by accident and felt like a pervert when I handed them over. I gave her some half-baked compliment and she denied the pictures were hers and pointed out Janet. So your little Hamsford girl may have talent, but it's coupled with a dirty mind."

"What?"

"She'd drawn nudes in positions that would make the *Kama Sutra* turn red."

"That can't be right," Jeffrey stammered certain his friend was talking about someone else. "Janet is entirely pure. She's an artist. There must be an explanation for her drawings."

"Her body may be untouched, but her mind certainly isn't. I know what I saw and I know what she's like. When she isn't throwing herself in your path or piling her plate with food, she is gossiping with that woman over there." He pointed to Valerie who was talking with her mother. "No other man has spoken to her and I don't intend to be the first."

Jeffrey shook his head. "You're wrong about her. First off, she's majoring in Art History and plans to work for a museum or art institution after she graduates. She's—"

"Do I look drunk?"

"No. You never get drunk."

"Exactly and I never lower my standards."

"I think your standards are too high."

"Only because you don't have any. You enjoy everything and everyone."

"I guess it's my nature," Jeffrey said without offense. "I like people."

"Then go and enjoy them and don't worry about me."

Jeffrey left his friend and Janet left her hiding place eager to find Valerie.

Valerie stared at her in disbelief when Janet finished her story. "Did he really say that?"

"I was paraphrasing. What he actually said was worse. I can't believe that for a moment I was actually attract... I was wrong. I should have known better. Originals always think they're so superior. He is clueless about my work, it's mostly abstract. Yes, some of the sketches were from my live figure drawing classes, but they were hardly obscene. He's the one with the filthy mind. Besides, who is he to be so high and mighty? You'd think he'd come from a continent where women never went topless."

"It was a simple misunderstanding."

"That I hope he keeps to himself. Could you imagine if anyone overheard him talking about my portfolio? I'd kill him if he ever let my father hear him."

"Don't worry, he hasn't spoken to anyone except the Farmers so you're safe."

"I'm glad he doesn't pass the JCE test. Now I have a perfectly good reason to hate him."

Valerie shook her head. "No you won't. Hate is a cruel and dangerous emotion."

"True," Janet said suddenly feeling ashamed. "I'll just strongly dislike him. Who could possibly like a man who can't tell the difference between art and pornography? You'd think a man who appears to be cultured would be able to make the distinction. I can't believe he said *I* had a dirty mind."

"He didn't mean for you to overhear him."

"But I did! And I'm glad – I have never in my life met anyone so arrogant and haughty. But you know what? Pride comes before a fall. And from where he's standing I hope he falls far and hard."

Fortunately, Janet's anger didn't last long. She was a young woman with a sense of humor and after talking to Valerie, she spent the rest of the evening entertaining others with her tale of the snotty Original and his dismissal of her—leaving out the particular reason why—and soon everyone agreed that the Original was a very unpleasant individual and best ignored.

"Ladies and Gentlemen, can I please have your attention," Brother Jerome said, standing at the podium holding a microphone.

Valerie approached Janet. "He prepared a speech?"

"Of course he prepared a speech. He has an audience doesn't he? How come men aren't encouraged to keep their mouths shut like women are?"

"Because someone has to listen."

And listen they did as Brother Jerome droned on about his blessings and the fact that God had selected the most beautiful woman in Hamsford to be his wife. And then he went on to tell everyone about Mother Shea's dream, not wanting anyone to think it wasn't an ordained union. And just in case some residents had not heard, he spent another ten minutes going into detail about his considerable financial blessing and the property he had acquired following the death of a relative.

"Don't frown, Janet," Valerie said in a low voice. "He's going to be your brother in law."

"I know. The thought makes me wish this choker were tighter."

Everyone applauded when he was finished. Mr. Barnett

came up to Janet. "He's not a fine speaker, but he'll have to do." He paused then ripped her necklace off. "What's that rubbish round your neck?" He demanded holding it out to her.

Janet could feel a trickle of blood slide down her back but she didn't move. "Mother Shea told Dee-dee I should wear it."

"And no one asked me?" He spun on his heel. "We'll talk when we get home."

CHAPTER 11

"So what's your report, Frederick?" Karen asked him the moment they reached home. She was eager to hear whatever cutting remark he had to say about the party. "I know you have one."

They sat in the living room of their family home. Jeffrey's new home was still unfurnished and he had repairs he wanted completed before moving in. He felt comfortable staying in his old room and his sisters were thrilled to have him. He was also happy to be there and stood by the large bay window in the living room, remembering that his beloved father was gone.

Although his sisters still lived there, they rarely ventured into Hamsford (especially Old Hamsford) or associated with the evangelical church scene. They attended a different, more contemporary church and frequently traveled. They felt no ties, but Jeffrey loved Hamsford because his father had and he was glad to be back and reacquaint himself with everyone.

Things had started to change with many of the elderly moving into senior living centers and several families leaving for other opportunities. Hamsford had begun to get some undesirable inhabitants due to a high vacancy rate downtown. So his father had helped create a cultural district that included converting an old train station into the Michael T. Brown Cultural Arts Center and Museum. In addition, through the City Council, his father had worked to offer small businesses "friendly" loans and tax incentives to revitalize the downtown and attract new homebuyers. So far the improvements had worked and Jeffrey was determined to keep his father's vision alive.

"Karen, don't tease him," Tanya said. "The evening was bad enough."

"I enjoyed myself," Jeffrey said, staring out at the lights along their driveway.

"You always enjoy yourself."

He turned. "It's easy to do with great food and good company."

Frederick frowned from his position by the fireplace. "Define the word *good.*"

Jeffrey returned his gaze to the window.

Karen jumped into the conversation. "The food was adequate," she said, as though she was being generous with her praise.

Tanya nodded. "I believe Brother Jerome selected the Red Mango Company."

"Second rate West Indian cuisine."

"It was what he could afford."

Karen lifted a brow. "And that speech—"

Jeffrey spun around. "I think he made an okay speech."

"I'm surprised you were able to stay awake for it," Tanya said, suppressing a yawn.

Karen crossed her legs and swung her foot. "Did you notice that every eligible woman wore your favorite color? That alone should have spoiled the evening."

Jeffrey shook his head. "No, it's nice to be admired." He

shoved his hands in his pockets. "Besides, it's understandable. They want to get married. There's nothing wrong with marriage."

"No," Frederick said. "But marriage is serious. It has to be approached with caution."

"I know."

"You have to consider her background, her temperament."

Karen flashed a malicious smile. "And her family."

Frederick nodded. "Yes, they will be a part of your life. You also have to ask yourself if you would want to travel with her or introduce her to your friends."

"Yes," Karen said eager to agree. "You should marry into the best of one's culture not the worst of it. Or the best of someone else's," she said sending Frederick a significant look. She'd hated the engagement party. It brought back too many memories. She liked Beverly, but the Barnetts represented everything she disliked—ignorance, old rules and tradition. They were a reminder of her immigrant roots and she loved all things American—capitalism, individuality, prosperity. "She's so backwards. So Trinny-trinny," she said using the Hamsford slang term for new immigrants.

"No, she's not," Tanya said. "She's grown up here like we have. All the Barnett girls have."

"They're nothing like us. We're American. Our family has been in this country for generations. We're Americans first and Jamaicans second."

"We're Jamaican-Americans. I don't see why we have to choose."

"We're American," Karen said fiercely. "That hyphen is an insult and makes us foreigners in our own country." She looked at Frederick, her heart skipping at the sight of his handsome face. She admired him and all he represented—a proud, distinct culture of constant privilege. He could trace his heritage back centuries and would never sully that distinction by marrying the wrong woman. "But that doesn't matter. What matters is *who* you marry."

"I didn't say I was ready to settle yet," Jeffrey said with an impatient move of his shoulders.

Frederick's gaze didn't leave him. "Good."

~

"YOU RESORT to this behind my back!"

"Winston, keep your voice down."

"I'll talk at the top of my lungs if I want to. When I see danger I'll shout 'Fire!'" He waved the necklace under his wife's nose. "Fire!"

Mrs. Barnett keep her gaze downcast used to her husband's railing. She sat in a chair off to the side of their bed and waited for his anger to pass. She knew it was best to keep her voice low and appear as obedient as possible. It was her role to follow the dictates of her husband. He was the head of the house and deserved that respect. But inwardly she didn't regret her minor rebellion. Mother Shea knew more about getting husbands for her daughter than any man could. "Mother Shea thought—"

"I don't care. My girls don't wear jewelry and I mean none. God made them as they are. You are supposed to follow my lead."

"I'm sorry."

"Why did you do it?"

Because I thought it was best. But Mrs. Barnett didn't say that. Instead she searched for a reason that would appease him. "I so didn't want to," she said in a soft whine. "It's just that I wanted Janet to stand out. She'd had her feelings hurt."

He paused. "Really?"

"You didn't hear the gossip?"

"You know I don't listen to it."

"Well, that Original said some terrible things about her."

Mr. Barnett rested his fists on his hips. "He insulted our daughter? Why?"

"I don't know exactly, but it doesn't matter." She sighed as though it took every effort to do so. "I just wanted Janet to feel better so when Mother Shea suggested I let her wear it," she motioned absently to the object in his hand. "I didn't think it was wrong. I know I shouldn't have."

"I understand your intentions were good." He dropped the necklace into her lap. "Now get it out of my house."

THAT SUNDAY, like every Sunday, Janet woke up to the smell of coffee, Jack—a bread similar to flatbread—fried in butter, ackee and saltfish. But she didn't get a chance to enjoy it because her mother rushed them through breakfast eager to get to church where Pastor Wainwright would formerly announce and bless Beverly's engagement.

Neither Janet nor her sisters minded as they tied scarves over their hair or pinned on their hats, knowing there was no other place to be. On Sunday, Hamsford turned into a ghost town. One of Hamsford's main roads, High Street, was called Church Row because over a distance of three miles sat an assortment of churches—two evangelical, three Baptist, two Seventh Day Adventist, two non-denominational (one of which was the church the Farmers attended), one Jehovah's Witness and a Catholic Church, the largest and most grand building on the strip. A new ordinance restricted holding church services in private homes, resulting in several store front churches.

Throughout the morning service, following the hymnal, bible reading and offering, Mrs. Barnett beamed with pride, and she nearly danced when Pastor Wainwright and the congregation blessed her daughter's engagement and celebrated their joy. Unfortunately, she wasn't as happy two days later.

"The Williams are having a party next week," Mrs. Barnett announced at dinner.

"You don't sound pleased," Beverly said.

"How can I be pleased when I know that the only reason they are holding one so soon after your engagement is so that they can invite Jeffrey Farmer? You know that Sister Williams plans to have her daughter marry him."

"Valerie is too old for him," Maxine said.

"And plain," Mrs. Barnett added. "Although she is a very decent young woman and I would never talk about her lack of looks publicly. God created both the peacock and the sparrow. I'm glad that I don't have the problem of a plain daughter who I have to throw parties for in order to attract eligible men." She looked around the table, her gaze conveniently skipping over Francine.

"Perhaps the Williams just want to celebrate spring," Janet said. "How do you know Sister Williams has a hidden agenda?"

"Because I'd do the same if I had the money." Mrs. Barnett glanced at her husband, who sat quietly at the table pretending not to hear the conversation. She returned her gaze to Janet. "You'll have to be more aggressive this time. You can't let Valerie or anyone else take up all his time."

Janet glanced at Beverly, who kept her gaze focused on her plate. "But I don't—"

"I know," Mrs. Barnett interrupted. "Take your large sketch pad. You can do quick portraits. That's always fun."

"I wish you wouldn't look at me every time Dee-dee mentions

Jeffrey's name," Beverly said as she sat on her bed looking at Janet, who stood in the doorway.

"I saw the way you looked at him at the engagement party."

"I was thrilled to see him again. That's all. I don't mind that Daddy and Dee-dee want me to get married."

"I heard that Brother Jerome plans to move to Pennsylvania."

"So what? I'll go where he goes." She gripped her hands. "I am fine."

But Janet didn't believe her sister and believed her even less when she saw Beverly and Jeffrey talking at the Williams' party. Unlike the engagement party, it was a more subdued affair, but no less impressive. Mrs. Williams, a short, thick woman, with shoulder length wavy hair, was a woman used to entertaining and knew how to dress up her house for any occasion. All the colors were coordinated, the table covering matched the chairs and napkins; fresh spring flowers from their garden were placed throughout the house, including each of the bathrooms. White lace curtains graced the windows and a wonderful woodsy aroma swept throughout the home from the logs burning in the fireplace.

For dinner, Mrs. Williams' cook presented a large pot roast, baked potatoes, red beans and rice, and a fresh salad. Dessert consisted of cinnamon rice pudding. And a variety of music from gospel to jazz played throughout the evening.

"Your sister needs to watch herself," Valerie said in an anxious whisper. "She's an engaged woman. She shouldn't act as though she's single."

"One doesn't stay out of the garden because they have a bouquet inside the house," Janet said. "Just look at Brother Jerome and Sister Daniels."

"Yes, I see them but they don't look like a couple. Perception matters more than truth. No one should doubt her faithfulness."

"Beverly would never be unfaithful."

"That's not the point. It doesn't matter what she would or wouldn't do. She can't afford a hint of suspicion. She's giving Jeffrey too much encouragement and if *I* notice it, others will too."

Janet sighed. "Maybe she loves him."

"Then I feel sorry for her."

"You pity love?"

"I pity anything with no room to grow. We don't know if he wants to marry her."

"I'm sure he would ask her if she were free."

"But you don't know for certain. If she's not careful she could put herself in a very dangerous position and lose two opportunities."

Janet frowned. "What do you mean?"

"What if her behavior raises doubt in Brother Jerome's mind and he decides not the marry her?"

"That's fine."

"And Jeffrey never offers to marry her?"

Janet hesitated. "Then she could live with me."

Valerie rested a hand on Janet's arm. "I want you to think this through. She might give up stability, station and her family's honor because of a feeling for a man she hasn't seen in years. Love is one of the flimsiest things to base a marriage on. A strong marriage's greatest foundation is a love of God, a commitment to each other and common goals. That is all."

Janet stared at Valerie perplexed. "You can't really believe that."

"How many love matches have lasted for not just years but decades? How many times have you seen love turn to disdain? Feelings change. Rationality is constant."

"Yes, maybe," Janet said with some hesitancy. "but you don't go about marriage as though it were some business transaction."

"I'm only suggesting that one use one's head in these matters instead of one's heart. Think of the words from Jeremiah: *The heart is deceitful above all things and beyond cure. Who can understand it?* Emotions have betrayed human beings for centuries, which is why we turn to God and if Mother Shea is to be believed, this union has His blessing." She lowered her voice. "Be careful Janet on how you persuade your sister. There's a lot more at stake than you realize."

"Yes, I can see that." Janet suddenly groaned. "Oh no Dee-dee is looking at me again. She's probably wondering why I'm not talking to Jeffrey."

"My mother has already resigned herself to be disappointed, but she wants me to play the piano later." Valerie glanced away then said, "Your mother isn't the only person watching you. Durand has been staring at you since you arrived."

Janet bristled. "I don't know why. He probably finds something immodest about my dress. Perhaps he expects me to strip down and assault him."

"Janet!" Valerie said scandalized.

"He's so intimidating. I bet he wants to belittle me by making his disgust clear."

Valerie glanced at Frederick, suddenly thoughtful. "Actually, I think he likes you."

Janet gently patted her friend's cheek. "Poor Valerie, you've just lost your mind." She took her hand. "Quick, let's go to the piano before my mother separates us. I'll play and you can sing something. And we'll walk past Durand and ignore him."

Janet would have accomplished her goal had Valerie's father, Brother Williams, not stopped her just as she was to pass Durand. "Where are you both dashing off to?"

Janet anxiously pointed to the piano. "We're just—"

"I noticed you brought your sketch pad. That must mean you're going to do some portraits."

"Yes," Janet said trying to inch away. "Later."

"She's very talented Durand," Brother Williams said addressing the quiet young man. "You should be one of the first in line."

Frederick didn't smile, but his face softened. "I just might."

"I'd hate for you to waste your time. I'm sure you have better things to do," Janet said, then looked at Brother Williams. "He's likely traveled the world and has seen many fine artists. I doubt he'll find my little sketches interesting."

"You're wrong. I'd like a portrait," he said.

Janet sent him a cool look. "I couldn't do your face justice. Excuse me." She nodded then walked over to the piano.

"Janet," Valerie scolded as she led her away. "At least be gracious if not tactful. He's Jeffrey's friend."

"I don't know why."

"It's not for you to judge."

Janet sat at the piano and lifted the lid. "I would rather break all my pencils than ever sketch a line of his face. I'll never draw it. Ever." She flexed her fingers over the piano keys. "Now what should I start with?"

They made a selection from the song book that was available, then began. Valerie had a beautiful, melodious voice. The room hushed to hear her. Although Janet's playing was far from spectacular, it complimented her friend's singing.

Frederick watched her, intrigued. He'd had no intention of enjoying himself when he'd first arrived. He'd planned to come and endure as he had the last time, but this time was different. This time his gaze kept falling on Janet Barnett. He didn't intend to but he couldn't seem to help himself. She wasn't in blue this time, but a cream yellow that complimented the red undertone of her lovely brown skin. And although her dress was conservative, her figure—slender, with enough curves to keep a man interested —made it seem a little less so. Her laughter was the first thing to catch his attention. It was surprisingly free and genuine. From the moment he heard it, he found himself studying her and questioning his first assessment. After further thought her drawings weren't that obscene—he'd seen most of them upside down—and though bold they weren't indecent.

He'd met many women in his life and in his travels and here in some backwards community was a woman who was like no other woman he'd ever met before. Her smile was quick and without pretense; she was innocent yet her gaze was sharp—nothing escaped the scrutiny of those bright brown eyes. He'd been disappointed that he hadn't been able to engage her in conversation, but not bothered. Watching from a distance was much more entertaining.

Frederick wasn't easily offended. He'd come from a line of conquerors. A powerful family descended from royal patronage, who'd only gained dominance under the threat of slavery and colonialism. By the use of cunning and mastery, they'd increased their prestige and wealth. He knew nothing of oppression. His family had assimilated to the ways of the West without fracturing their pride in their culture.

Hamsford and its culture fascinated him. This time he watched the church members and didn't find them strange but amusing in the fierce ways they held onto their beliefs, while the world around them changed. And one woman made all the difference. She held him in a strange rapture. His guarded heart responded to her light and slipped past his defenses. He didn't know what it was, but he knew he'd never be the same.

CHAPTER 12

The audience applauded when Janet and Valerie completed their duet. Before anyone could make another request, Francine raced over to them and announced, "I have a poem that I've set to music."

"Why doesn't she just call it a song?" Valerie whispered to Janet as Francine settled at the piano.

"Because Francine won't use one word when she can use many."

The moment Francine hit her first note it pierced the air like a chicken being strangled. Janet folded her arms, although she wanted to cover her ears. She looked around the room embarrassed by the look of pain on people's faces. She caught Tanya's wince and Karen's smug grin then glanced away. Thankfully, she was soon dragged away to do people's portraits and Valerie was asked to organize a game of charades. Within minutes Francine's audience had disappeared except for three young children who knew her from Sunday school and applauded loudly when she finished. Their enthusiastic applause however, was enough to encourage her to share another poem set to music, but before she could, Mr. Barnett whispered something in her ear forcing her to leave.

~

"I WISH Francine Barnett didn't think she could sing," Karen said in the backseat of her brother's car.

"I know," Tanya said beside her. "My ears are still ringing."

Karen leaned forward and touched Frederick's shoulder. "And what do you have to say about this evening?"

"I enjoyed myself," he said.

Stunned silence followed his statement then Jeffrey slapped the steering wheel and laughed. "I knew you would once you gave everyone a chance! What did you like the most?"

"I liked Janet's duet with her friend."

Tanya lowered her window a crack, letting the cool night air seep into the car. "Yes, that was nice."

"It was okay," Karen said.

Jeffrey glanced at her in the rearview mirror. "I also enjoyed it. Valerie is one of the best singers around."

Karen sighed. "But Janet isn't one of the best pianists."

"No," Frederick agreed. "But she makes up for it with passion and vigor. A true music lover."

"Artists always seem to be full of some strange passion," Karen said annoyed by the topic of conversation.

"Not all artists," Frederick said with subtle warning.

Karen quickly said, "I didn't mean her... I just... well it just takes getting used to being around them again. I've attended many grand events and have heard truly gifted concert pianists. Since Dad's death you know we haven't attended any of these small events."

"I think it was fun," Jeffrey said.

Tanya rolled her eyes. "*Quelle surprise.*"

"We only attended because of you," Karen said. "By the way, why did you buy that property east of town? Everyone's whispering about it."

"I know," he said.

When he didn't say more, Tanya said, "Janet did my sketch. It's very good. She said I had the perfect nose." Tanya traced the slope with her finger. "I put the drawing in the trunk because I didn't want it to get wrinkled."

Frederick tapped his knee. "She's very talented."

Karen raised her brows in soft mockery. "High praise again. My, my, has someone developed a crush?"

He met her gaze in the rearview mirror, the night lights highlighting his dark eyes.

His cold look sent chills through her. Karen folded her arms then turned to her sister. "Put up the window. I'm freezing."

The temperature in the car hadn't changed much, but Tanya was used to Karen's moods and did as requested. "They've changed don't you think?" she said.

"Who?" Jeffrey asked when no one else did.

"The Barnetts. It's been a while since I've seen them."

"I don't think they've changed much," Karen said. "Beverly is still beautiful."

"Yes, I like her. She was always so sweet and kind."

"I'd like to invite them for dinner," Jeffrey said.

His sisters glanced at each other as though he'd lost his mind then Karen said, "The entire family?"

"We used to be friends."

"Yes, but why have them *all* over?"

"As a special congratulations for Beverly's engagement."

Frederick tugged on the cuff of his jacket. "I think you've offered her plenty of congratulations."

Jeffrey frowned. "What does that mean?"

"You spent most of the evening 'congratulating' her."

Jeffrey gripped the steering wheel. "We were talking about old times."

Frederick sent him a cool look. "You must have a long history."

"We do," Jeffrey said in a terse voice.

Karen tapped her chin. "I remember when we were young and Beverly used to come with us to the lake house."

"Wouldn't that be nice?" Tanya said.

Jeffrey furrowed his brows. "What?"

"Inviting Beverly to come with us to the lake house."

"Yes," Karen agreed. "We're going next weekend let's invite her. She's always been good company."

"I think it's a perfect idea," Tanya said before he could reply.

Karen nodded. "We've made up our minds and it's settled. I'll call her tomorrow."

"Janet used to come with us too," Jeffrey said.

His sisters shared a look then Tanya said, "Yes, she can be pleasant too."

"Sometimes," Karen added.

Jeffrey drove up the driveway and parked the car. "Invite them both. It'll be fun." He got out of the car and looked at Frederick over the hood. "Don't you think?"

He nodded. "I think it will be interesting."

"Great." Jeffrey closed the car door then pointed at Karen. "Call them." He turned before he could see his sister's scowl.

Beverly hung up the phone then stared at it as if it threatened to turn into a live creature.

"Well?" her mother demanded.

She turned to her mother and four sisters who all sat in the living room staring at her. Private phone calls didn't exist and people rarely called to speak to Beverly. "The Farmers have invited Janet and me to spend the weekend at their lake house. They're going to plan a picnic as well."

Mrs. Barnett jumped up as though the Holy Spirit had seized her. She bounced around for a bit then patted Janet on the cheek. "I knew you'd made an impression on him. Didn't I say that necklace would work? And you performing with Valerie to get noticed was an excellent idea."

Janet stared at her mother horrified. "I didn't play so that Jeffrey—"

"The reason doesn't really matter. He's interested."

Janet shook her head. "No, I don't—"

"Why else would he invite you? He invited Beverly to come too so that he wouldn't look over eager." Mrs. Barnett clasped her hands together thrilled. "You'll wear your pink two-piece outfit and the necklace, I mean the chocker—"

"Choker," Francine corrected.

"Yes, that. The one I gave you the other night."

"But Daddy—"

Mrs. Barnett pressed her finger against Janet's mouth. "Won't be there to see you. Once you're married it won't matter what your father says." She turned to her eldest daughter. "Beverly you'll wear the drop-waist purple dress I bought you and those nice heels your Aunt Bernice sent you."

"Heels?" Janet said. "This is a picnic not a dance. Those shoes won't be sensible."

"She's a fine lady now and she must dress the part. The Farmer girls almost always wear heels."

"But that's them," Janet protested. "Beverly isn't accustomed to walking all over the place in heels."

"She'll grow accustomed."

"I'll wear them," Beverly said before Janet could argue further.

"Good." Mrs. Barnett gazed at her daughters with tears brimming in her eyes. "At this moment I'm the happiest woman alive." She kissed them both on the cheek. "Praise be to God."

Later that evening, Janet sat on her bed hugging her knees to her chest. She stared at her sister who rested against the bed post. "They don't really need me to come, you know. I'm just a spare."

"That's not true," Beverly said. "They wouldn't have invited both of us if they didn't want you. Dee-dee thinks you made an impression on Jeffrey."

Janet raised a sly brow. "*Someone* in this room made an impression, but it wasn't me."

Beverly blushed.

"You like him."

"I've always liked him." She lowered her gaze. "But let's not have this conversation."

Janet rested her chin on her knees and groaned. "Too bad his sisters will be there."

"They are very nice."

"You think everyone is nice."

"At the core every human being has something decent about them."

"Perhaps," Janet said unconvinced. She straightened her legs and stared at her feet. "I suppose the problem with me is that I don't like people as much as I should."

Beverly grabbed her sister's hands and said in an urgent voice. "To truly love God you must love man. Just understand that everyone is a child of God and made in His image."

Janet grinned to ease her sister's worry. "Yes, but some more than others."

JANET DIDN'T EXPECT to enjoy the journey to the lake house and she certainly didn't expect the seventh traveler who joined them.

Beverly and Janet stared at him not sure what to make of it. However, he smiled back at them unconcerned as he sat content in his cage.

"His name is Milton," Jeffrey said loading their suitcases into the trunk of his SUV. "He belongs to Frederick."

Beverly leaned forward and the dog's smile seemed to widen as he pressed a paw against the cage. "What is he?"

"A border collie."

"He seems very friendly."

"He is." Jeffrey closed the trunk. "Once he's out of his cage he'll be all over you. He's one of the friendliest dogs I know."

"Perhaps he could teach his owner a lesson or two," Janet mumbled.

Beverly pinched Janet hard then got in the car.

After a two hour drive they reached the lake house. It was a beautiful brick structure situated on a pristine landscaped property only a few feet away from a natural lake surrounded by evergreens and lush foliage. Boats zipped across its surface and in the distance a couple fished.

The front door flew open and Les and Abigail Horowitz, the caretakers, rushed down the steps to greet them.

"It's been ages," Abigail said crushing Janet to her large frame. She smelled like cinnamon muffins and had her dark braids twisted in a bun on her head. She stood back and looked at her. "You haven't changed one bit."

"They've both gotten prettier," Les said with a wink, stroking the white streak in his beard.

"Later you must tell us what you've been up to."

"Beverly's getting married," Karen said pushing past them to walk up the stairs.

Abigail widened her hazel eyes surprised and pleased. "Really? Who's the lucky man?"

Beverly hesitated. "You don't know him."

"But he's a good man and you love him very much, right?"

Beverly avoided her gaze. "Yes, he's a good man."

Abigail opened her mouth, but Janet interrupted her. "Could you show us our rooms?"

Abigail closed her mouth and did.

CHAPTER 13

The evidence of the Horowitz's attention to detail showed throughout the house. From the gleaming hardwood floors, glistening double paned windows and fresh bed linens. Once everyone was settled in their rooms, Abigail stayed behind to help Janet unpack. "What's going on?" she asked.

Janet opened a drawer. "I don't know what you mean."

"Your sister didn't seem too keen to talk about her upcoming wedding. Usually young women can't stop talking about their special day."

Janet picked up a blouse. "You know how it is with us."

"Yes." Abigail sat on the bed then let out a heavy sigh. "Your parent's are involved?"

"When aren't they?"

"You know that my family had to break from the Orthodox traditions of my grandfather and it was very painful. Until the day he died my father felt guilty. I know how important it is to want to honor your parents but sometimes you cannot please them. My choice did not make my father happy at first, but he grew to understand."

"I wish it were that simple."

"But if Beverly doesn't feel right about it, she may have to go against your father."

"No," Janet said adamant. "We could never go against him. Ever." She remembered the rage and anguish she'd seen on the face of Ramani's father and couldn't imagine doing that to her own. No, it was an impossible choice.

"Maybe, but you never know what you can do until you're forced to."

Janet shrugged resigned. "It's settled."

Abigail nodded. "If you or your sister ever need someone to talk to I'm here."

Janet hugged her, tears burning her eyes that she refused to let fall. "Thank you."

Abigail stood. "I'd better get downstairs before I'm summoned. The food is all ready for your picnic."

Janet forced a smile. "I'm looking forward to it."

JANET WAS the last person to reach the picnic site. She stared in amazement. A white canopy stood with a table underneath covered with a rose colored lace tablecloth and white china. She took a seat and inhaled the aromatic scent of the feast that awaited them. Pitchers of lemonade, ice tea, and sorrel were placed off to the side, atop a large cooler filled with ice. There were cucumber sandwiches cut into quarters with the rind cut off, deviled eggs, a black-bean salad, ginger-spiced chicken legs, baked breadfruit and fried sweet potatoes and Mrs. Horowitz's delicious homemade banana-nut-raisin bread for dessert.

"There you are," Tanya said. "We were about to start without you." She pointed to Jeffrey. "Now you can begin."

He said a quick prayer then they piled their dishes. Beverly looked down at Milton who sat at Frederick's side. "He's so well-behaved. Most dogs start to beg when they smell food."

"He's trained," Frederick said, not looking up from his food.

Jeffrey picked up a deviled egg. "He's a world champion, you know."

"Really?" Beverly said.

"Yes, he's extremely athletic. For a time Frederick volunteered with animals. He adopted dogs from the pound and turned them into service dogs."

Beverly looked at Frederick impressed. "That's wonderful," she said then sent Janet a private glance.

Frederick shrugged then gestured to Milton with his elbow. "Unfortunately, this one failed so I couldn't give him to anyone. I had to find another talent."

Jeffrey laughed. "Don't believe him. The moment Frederick saw him, he wanted to keep him. Milton was skin and bone, but he didn't care. He nursed him back to health and now they're inseparable."

Frederick stroked Milton under the chin. "He's a good dog."

"Who makes me feel like I'm your *second* best friend," Jeffrey said without offense. "I wouldn't be surprised if you prefer animals to people."

Frederick kept his gaze focused on Milton, his voice neutral. "Animals are trustworthy. They'd never betray you."

"And they're easier to control," Janet said.

He looked at her, but didn't reply.

Jeffrey clasped his hands behind his head and stared at the dog with admiration. "He has more trophies and ribbons than most people. Always first place."

Janet flashed a smug grin. "Of course. His master wouldn't accept less."

Frederick lifted his glass, his gaze meeting hers over the rim. "No, I wouldn't."

Jeffrey let his arms fall. "He's got this guy who wants to buy him, but Frederick refuses to sell."

Frederick took a sip of his drink then set it down. "He's priceless."

Janet tilted her head to the side. "And you don't need the money."

Again his dark eyes met hers, but he didn't reply. Undeterred Janet boldly met his gaze until Tanya admitted that she was helpless with animals but loved plants and changed the subject. After lunch Jeffrey and Frederick played a game of badminton on the lawn while Karen and Tanya encouraged Beverly to talk about her wedding plans. Janet went inside, grabbed her sketchbook and sat over to the side to draw.

She watched her sister with a feeling of both love and envy, seeing the ease with which she spoke to Karen and Tanya. She saw Beverly's glances at Jeffrey as he made athletic leaps to catch Frederick's serves, but only she could interpret the depth of her sister's gaze. To an untrained eye Beverly looked like a happy bride-to-be. Janet wanted to believe it, despite her sister's awkward response to Abigail, but knew she couldn't. She sketched the three lounging women—Karen's sleeveless sundress, showing off her smooth skin and her white leather sandals and bare legs and took care drawing Tanya's colorful spaghetti strap top and Capri trousers. In contrast, Beverly looked nice, but conservative in a long sleeved peasant top and skirt that reached her ankles. Soon wedding talk drifted towards Janet. She stopped sketching the women, turning her attention to the men.

Milton started to bark excitedly as he watched them, so Frederick and Jeffrey adjusted their game and involved him in their fun. Frederick gave a signal and the dog jumped up, pushing off his chest, and did a back flip. He then did the same with Jeffrey. Janet sketched Jeffrey's features in detail but left Frederick's in silhouette. She'd promised herself never to sketch his face.

However, she couldn't resist sketching his physique. The guy was a jerk, but he had a great body. He moved with the quick, graceful movements of a trained athlete and his command over Milton impressed her. Janet smiled at their antics and nearly jumped from her seat wanting to join them to see what other tricks Milton could perform. She turned towards the women, wanting to comment on the dog's tricks, but saw them deeply engrossed in conversation. Janet returned to her sketch knowing that they wouldn't be interested in what she had to say.

For the three young women, weddings and marriage appeared to be much more important than enjoying the spring day. Janet wished she could feel the same, but in a few months her sister would be like a canary owned by a cat.

Jeffrey and Frederick stopped their play with Milton and returned to the table to get drinks.

Tanya motioned to Janet, who still sat apart from the group. "Come and join us."

Janet smudged a line with her thumb, giving Milton's coat more character. "I'm fine here."

"All you like to do is draw," Karen said. "But most artists are anti-social."

"Only some. Some are also suicidal, drug addicts and promiscuous, but so are some non-artists." She sent Karen a pointed stare. "I just enjoy the view from where I sit."

"Janet likes to study people," Beverly said.

"And what do you uncover?" Jeffrey asked stretching his legs out.

Janet kept her gaze lowered and smoothed out a line defining Milton's front paw. "Nothing. I just watch."

"Impossible," Frederick said, folding his arms on the table. "No one is an impartial observer. Observation is always tainted by one's own bias and prejudice."

Janet lifted her gaze. "I do my best to keep my prejudices from tainting my viewpoint."

"So you study people like a child? No preconceived notions? That's amazing."

"When I study people I let their flaws reveal themselves."

Frederick poured more lemonade into his glass. "And from a distance you think you can assess the true nature of anyone?"

"Yes."

Frederick took a sip then set his glass down. "Then you think you know me."

Janet paused, recognizing the challenge. "Not intimately, but close, yes."

He stared at the ice swirling in his lemonade. "I see. Are my flaws that evident after such a short time?"

Janet set her sketchbook down. "I'm surprised you admit to having any."

He looked at her. "Then you don't know me well."

"I know you well enough."

"And my flaws too?"

"Yes."

Karen lightly touched his arm. "No, you can't. Frederick is perfect."

He shook his head amused by her statement. "No, I'm not. I have flaws like any other man."

Janet leaned forward and rested her chin in her hand. "Like what?"

The corner of his mouth kicked up in a quick grin. "I thought you already knew."

"I want to be sure."

Frederick hesitated. "I have a short temper, can be impatient and resentful. Once I've crossed you off my list, it's final."

"You're right. Those are flaws that I couldn't have observed from a distance."

"Correct. It takes time to completely know someone."

Janet picked up her charcoal and rolled it between her forefinger and thumb but her gaze never left his face. "If one has the patience."

His gaze didn't waver. "Or the inclination not to judge and dismiss."

Their eyes clashed in combat, but neither said another word. Karen felt the charged atmosphere and sought a way to change it. She turned to her brother who was fixing another plate. "Don't be a pig, Jeffrey."

Jeffrey placed two large spoonfuls of the black-bean salad on his plate. "I'm never a pig." He smiled then winked at Beverly.

"You just pretend not to be."

"I admit I like a good meal, but I always leave enough to share."

"We don't have to worry about Beverly," Tanya said. "She eats like a tiny bird."

"So, Janet," Frederick asked. "How would you describe your appetite?"

Janet didn't respond at first, surprised that he'd asked her. "It depends on the meal. If I enjoy it, I can be shameless."

"It's always good to know what you like."

Karen piped up eager to get his attention. "I know that I love raspberry cheesecake." She turned to Frederick who was also going for seconds. "Oh, before I forget, how is your sister?"

"Fine."

Karen sent Janet a haughty look. "She's an accomplished visual artist. She started displaying her work at ten."

"I'm surprised," Janet said.

"Why?"

"I had the impression that Durand didn't like artists very much."

"Why would you think that?"

"Oh, just something I overheard," she said in a casual tone sending Frederick a sharp look.

Karen frowned. "You shouldn't listen to gossip."

"Perhaps."

"I admire artists," Jeffrey said. "I like how you can translate what you see before you, or in your mind, and put it on paper. It's incredible. Artists are so talented."

"Not all artists," Karen sniffed. "Some just claim the title and persuade people to agree."

Janet set her charcoal pencil down and wiped her fingers with a damp napkin. "I'm not an elitist. Whatever work of art someone creates I consider the creator an artist."

Karen applied a new coat of tinted lip gloss. "A true artist should be able to master any medium, have an encyclopedic knowledge of all the great masters, be bi- if not multi-lingual and develop a prodigious amount of work. Plus he or she should possess a certain air of class or style not burdened or enhanced by any outside stimulants."

Janet laughed. "I've never met an artist like that. You've just described an imaginary figure."

Karen recapped her lip gloss then dropped it in her handbag. "No, I just described Frederick's sister."

Tanya nodded. "She's a prodigy. Barely eighteen and she's done gallery showings around the world and there've been several documentaries done about her on Canadian T.V. I think the last one was done when she was exhibiting in Vienna."

Janet blinked. "I see."

"Yes, she's an extraordinary young woman," Tanya said.

"But she's a perfectionist," Frederick was quick to add. "She doesn't sketch as adeptly as you."

Janet snapped her notebook shut. "Yes, but any hack or board-walk artist can sketch quickly. True artists take their time."

Before Frederick could reply, Karen jumped to her feet and

said, "Let's go pick honeysuckle and grapes. They grow wild along Roden Way."

Jeffrey also stood. "Good idea. It will be a nice walk."

They grabbed several empty baskets, and Janet grabbed her sketchpad then started out.

The group strolled along a nice path through the woods and across a railroad track that curved around an empty train station, where the track split. Years earlier the desolate area flourished with the influx of visitors, but the growth of nearby towns made the stop unnecessary. Now only the occasional freight train would lumber through the country side leaving Brickstone Station empty.

Janet was across the tracks when she heard Milton barking then Beverly cry out her name. She turned and saw Beverly trying to pull her foot free. The heel of her shoe had gotten caught in a wooden section of the track where the line diverged.

Janet dropped everything and dashed back.

"My shoe's caught," Beverly said, stating the obvious. The heel of her shoe sat wedge tight in the crevice.

"I'll get you out," Janet said, although her racing heart threatened to beat out of her chest. "Don't worry."

That's when they heard the loud rumble of a train.

CHAPTER 14

"Help!" Janet said.

Jeffrey, who was several feet away from them, spun around first. She could tell how fast the train was approaching by the look of horror on his face. It mirrored that of his sisters and friend. He raced towards them and she could feel the movement of the rails beneath her knees, the gravel biting into her legs. Soon Jeffrey was at her side and on his knees trying to remove the shoe. Janet tried to unlatch the strap wound around her sister's foot at the ankle. The buckle on the side was caught in the tracks preventing Beverly from pulling her foot out. Nothing budged. The roaring drew closer.

"God help me," Janet begged.

"Leave me here," Beverly said. "Or we'll all be killed."

"I'll never leave you," Jeffrey said through clenched teeth, the veins in his arms raised as he tried frantically to remove the shoe.

Beverly tried to push Janet away. "Please, go! If this is my fate I accept it."

"But I won't." Janet struggled with the strap, tears blurring her vision. "This can't happen. I won't let it."

"But it is happening. Accept it. Go!"

The train whistle drowned out Tanya and Karen's screams, the tracks trembling increased as the train barreled down on them like an unstoppable monster puffing black smoke. In moments it would be all over. Suddenly, someone brushed Janet aside.

"Get ready to lift," Frederick said to Jeffrey. He pulled out a knife then slit the ankle strap in one swift motion. Jeffrey grabbed Beverly; Frederick grabbed Janet and they jumped off the track. Seconds later the train roared past chilling the sweat on their skin.

They lay on their side and Jeffrey gathered Beverly close and whispered, "Thank God."

"Yes," Beverly said, calmer than she truly felt.

Janet watched them, her heart breaking. Who could tear them apart? God? Was that the deity she served? What omnipotent being would cruelly separate two people who loved each other and belonged together?

She absently accepted Frederick's help to her feet. He lifted her with such nonchalant strength that for one moment she dangled in the air before he set her down again. There were no tender moments from him, not that she would have expected any. He gave her a cursory look. "You're fine," he said. It was a statement rather than a question so Janet felt no need to respond beyond a curt nod. He turned away. She looked down at her torn skirt, now covered in dirt and bent down to brush off the remains of gravel on her legs.

Beverly stood then let out a cry and would have fallen forward had Jeffrey not caught her.

"What's wrong?" he asked.

She cringed. "It's my ankle."

Frederick came over to them. "Sit down."

Tanya and Karen huddled around her and Tanya said, "Is it broken? I hope it's not broken."

"I doubt it is."

"How can you be sure?" Karen asked.

Frederick ignored her. He knelt in front of Beverly and prodded her ankle. She let out another soft cry. "I'm sorry," he said in a low voice that was more polite than sincere. He touched another section and she winced.

Janet took a step forward ready to stop him. "You're hurting her."

He continued his examination. "I know."

"Then stop doing that."

"I have to." He rested his hands on his lap. "Fortunately, it's not broken. However, I can see that it's very tender. You've sprained it." Tanya and Karen sighed in relief. "We'll have to clean that cut," he said, noticing a small gash on the side of her ankle.

Jeffrey bent down and lifted Beverly up in his arms. "I've got you."

"I hope the Horowitzs have antibiotics," Karen said as she and Tanya followed.

Janet stared at Jeffrey and Beverly in the distance. Soon her sister would marry Brother Jerome and become an obedient sacrifice. She spun away unable to look at the image anymore. Her gaze fell on the shoe still caught in the crevice. She suddenly hated it and all it represented—a life stuck ready to be run over and crushed into conformity. If only they could all be cut free.

She fell on her knees and yanked at the shoe, determined to release it. She yanked with all her strength and it finally came loose causing her to fall backwards. She stared at it. So simple, so ordinary yet it had changed her life—changed her view of things. Janet watched Jeffrey and Beverly become smaller and smaller before they completely disappeared into the woods. She wanted to shout, scream, wail against the injustice of it all.

Tears burned her eyes. Oh how she disliked Brother Jerome

and her mother's stupid, stupid plan. She gripped the shoe in her fist then pounded it against the track with such force that the heel snapped off, hitting the metal trashcan sitting on the station platform. The loud thud echoed down the now silent track. She sat back exhausted.

"Are you okay?"

Janet stiffened at the sound of his voice, but didn't look up, mortified that he would find her this way. She quickly wiped away the tears. "I'm fine."

Frederick stood beside her. "It's only a sprain. She'll recover."

"Yes. I know. Thank you."

He shoved her sketch pad and pencils in front of her. "You wouldn't want to forget these."

For a moment Janet wanted to forget everything. If only she could draw a picture of herself in a new life. Or be as brilliant as Frederick's sister. Was she really talented or was she revered because she was rich? His sister lived a vastly different life compared to hers. Janet knew that even if she became a renowned artist her father still wouldn't let her go. She would still belong to him.

Janet took a deep breath and gathered her scattered emotions then retrieved the items he offered her. She calmly stood and dusted off her skirt. She stiffly walked back towards the house then stopped and turned to see Frederick staring at her, an unreadable look on his face. She remembered her manners and returned. She held out her hand. "Thank you, Durand."

"You can call me Frederick."

"No, I can't." She continued to hold out her hand.

He glanced down at the hand confused then shook it. "I don't need thanks."

"I know," Janet said in a curt voice amazed by how his hand swallowed hers. Was there nothing about this man that wasn't oversized? "But I give it all the same."

"You're welcome."

She pulled her hand free and walked away, still feeling the strength of his gaze and the heat from his grasp.

By the time Janet reached the lake house, Beverly was settled on the couch in the living room, with pillows and blankets. Janet set her things down and went over to her sister. "Are you all right?"

"Yes."

Moments later, Frederick entered and stared at them. "What the hell is this?"

"What do you mean?" Janet asked offended more by his tone than his language.

He removed the pillows from behind Beverly's head and placed them under her ankle.

"What are you doing?" Janet demanded.

"Jeffrey knows," Frederick said, sending his friend a cutting look. "She's suffered a sprain not a fainting spell. Did you clean the cut?"

"Yes," Jeffrey said affronted.

Frederick rested his hands on his hips, his voice aggressive. "With what?"

"I'm sure he's taken excellent care of my sister," Janet said annoyed with Frederick's tone. "You shouldn't talk to your friend this way."

He lifted a sardonic brow. "Really?"

"Yes, now leave her alone to rest."

He nodded then turned on his heel. "Fine."

"Durand," Beverly called to him.

He took a deep breath before turning. "Yes?"

"I don't know how to thank you."

"You don't have to," he said as though he'd done nothing at all then left.

Janet shook her head as she watched him go.

"Don't worry about him, Janet," Jeffrey said. "I'm used to his ways."

"He shouldn't talk to you like he's your father."

"He talks to everyone that way."

Janet looked at Beverly. "Are you okay?"

"Yes, I'm fine. Please don't be rude to Durand."

"I was only mirroring his behavior. Did he hurt you?" she asked looking at Beverly's wrapped ankle.

"Of course not."

"Everything is all right now," Karen said.

But all was not right when Janet woke up that night to her sister's moans. She'd decided to spend the night with Beverly to look after her. Janet turned on the lights and looked at her sister. A clear sheen covered her face and sweat soaked her pillows. Janet touched her forehead. It burned with fever.

Janet shook her awake. "Beverly."

Beverly slowly opened her eyes, her gaze unfocused. Janet grabbed her robe, dashed to Jeffrey's room and knocked. Frederick answered.

Janet stumbled back shocked.

He rested a hand on the doorframe and stared down at her equally surprised. "What's wrong?" he demanded.

"I was looking for Jeffrey."

He tapped impatiently on the doorframe. "What's wrong?"

Janet stiffened at his tone, but answered him. "It's Beverly she's burning with fever."

"Get her dressed."

"Why?"

"We're taking her to the hospital." He turned.

"For a fever? I think—"

Frederick turned back to her his voice unyielding. "Don't argue with me."

Jeffrey came out of his room and stared at them. "What's going on?"

Frederick answered before Janet could. "Get dressed. We're taking Beverly to the hospital."

Jeffrey started down the hall towards Beverly's room. "What's wrong with her?"

Frederick blocked his path and quietly said, "Get dressed or I'll go without you." He pinned his gaze on Janet. "You have two minutes or I'll take her as she is." He went back into his bedroom and shut the door. Jeffrey and Janet shared a look then quickly did as told.

"That man," Janet muttered gently changing her sister although she wanted to kick something. Beverly was too weak to respond so Janet dropped the subject and finished dressing her before changing into her own clothes. They were both ready by the time Frederick and Jeffrey arrived. Frederick walked over to the bed where Beverly still lay. He lifted her leg and unraveled the bandage to look at her ankle.

"Is it infected?" Jeffrey asked.

"Yes." He gently set her leg down.

"But I did everything. I—"

Frederick walked to the door. "This is not the time for blame. Let's go."

Jeffrey looked at Janet with anguish as he gathered Beverly in his arms. "I'm really sorry about this. I—"

"Let's go!" Frederick said not caring if he woke up the entire household.

They obeyed.

CHAPTER 15

"I was sure I cleaned that wound," Jeffrey said as he, Frederick and Janet sat in the waiting room of the local hospital. Fortunately, it was a slow evening and Beverly had been seen immediately when they entered the emergency room.

Frederick casually flipped through a magazine. When it became apparent that he was not going to reply, Janet responded, "It will be okay." She was determined to offer Jeffrey the comfort that Frederick would not.

"I took my time with her and was very careful."

"I know."

"I thought I was thorough." He buried his face in his hands. "I guess I wasn't."

"Everything will be okay." She glanced at Frederick, vexed by his nonchalant manner. "I know how much you care."

Frederick closed his magazine, tossed it on the table then selected another one.

"I can't believe this," Jeffrey moaned. "I thought I was helping."

Janet felt some of her patience thinning, but still kept her voice gentle. "I know."

Frederick turned a page and addressed his friend without looking up. "Stop feeling sorry for yourself."

Jeffrey lifted his head. "What?"

"You heard me."

Janet pursed her lips. "You shouldn't talk to him that way, he's upset."

Frederick looked at her. "More than you?"

Janet hesitated taken aback by the question. "No, but—"

"Then he should be comforting you. You're the one who woke up to your sister burning with fever. You're the one whose sister is in a hospital."

Janet opened her mouth but didn't know what to say.

"He's right," Jeffrey said ashamed.

"No, he's not right," Janet said appalled by Frederick's callous comment and the picture he painted of Jeffrey. "He's your friend. He should stand up for you not bad talk you in front of others."

Jeffrey grinned. "Frederick takes some getting used to."

Frederick set his magazine aside. "Jeffrey knows I will always be there for him, even if he has a bad habit of over dramatizing things and indulging in excessive guilt."

Janet scowled. "And you're intolerant of both."

"I know he's better than that."

Jeffrey stood then stretched unaware of the tension in front of him. "I'm thirsty. I'm going to the vending machines, would you like anything?"

Janet and Frederick shook their heads and he left. Without Jeffrey to distract her, Janet didn't know what to do with herself. She wasn't interested in the magazines, the TV was reporting another sad story about a war torn country and she certainly didn't have anything to say to Frederick. She crossed her legs and swung her foot, staring at the strange pattern in the carpet.

Unfortunately, the silence made her wonder what was happening to Beverly. What was wrong with her? Had the infection spread? Had they been able to reduce her fever? When would the doctor talk to them?

"Your sister will be okay," Frederick said.

Janet didn't look up at him, she especially didn't like the cool, casual way he said the words, but they made her feel better all the same.

Minutes later Jeffrey returned with three cans of soda and three bags of chips. He handed the drinks and chips to the others as though giving them a peace offering for his past behavior. Frederick said nothing. Janet smiled. She had nearly finished her drink when the doctor came out.

She was a tall Hispanic woman with short hair and a wide smile. "Your friend will be fine. She suffered a really nasty sprain. While examining Miss Barnett, we discovered some minor nerve damage that will probably heal on its own. However, when we looked at a CAT scan of the injury, there appears to be a shadowy area, which our radiologist believes is where some of the gravel and dirt from the tracks went deep into the open wound. That is probably the cause of her fever.

"I spoke to Miss Barnett and explained that in order for us to do a deep cleaning of the area, which would be extremely painful, we will need to give her some local anesthesia. The procedure can be done here in the emergency room. However, I would like to keep her in the hospital for a day or two, at least until her fever and some of the swelling goes down."

Janet thanked the doctor then turned to Jeffrey. "What do we do now?"

"Go home," Frederick said. "Get some sleep so you can be with your sister tomorrow."

~

MRS. BARNETT HUNG up the phone with a satisfied click. She looked at her husband as he played chess against Francine who was failing miserably. "Three extra days!" she announced.

"What are you going on about?" Mr. Barnett said, studying the chessboard.

"Beverly twisted her ankle wearing those new high heels and had to be rushed to the hospital because of an infection. She's all right now. She's taking antibiotics, but the doctor wants her to stay in the hospital for a day or two."

Francine clicked her tongue and adjusted her frames. "Such is the price of vanity. Janet knew those shoes were ridiculous."

"They are not ridiculous. She got her heel caught in a train track."

Mr. Barnett kissed his teeth in disgust. "And could have been squashed like a beetle or carried away to heaven by a fever because you forced her to wear them."

Mrs. Barnett rested her hands on her hips. "I didn't force her. Besides no real harm came to her and now Janet gets to stay longer and charm Jeffrey even more. Before summer I hope to have two daughters engaged." She clasped her hands together and stared up at the ceiling. "God works in mysterious ways."

Mr. Barnett shook his head, stared at the chessboard then up at Francine. "I taught you how to play, how come you're so bad?"

Francine tentatively moved a piece. "I do try."

He took one of her knights and knocked it off the board. "I can never beat Janet this easily."

"That's only because she lets you win," she muttered resentfully.

"What was that?"

"Nothing."

"Tell me what you just said."

Francine pushed back her chair and stood. "I'm tired. I'd like to go to bed."

"It's early yet."

"I have a lot of homework."

"You always finish your homework first thing." He gestured to the board. "Come finish the game."

Francine looked to her mother for help.

"Leave her alone, Winston," Mrs. Barnett said. "We all know you've beaten her. That should make you happy."

"But she has a few choice moves that she could take and—"

Mrs. Barnett nodded at Francine. "You can go to your room."

Francine smiled grateful then left.

Mr. Barnett sat back disappointed. "You spoil them."

Trudy sniffed from her position on the couch where she'd fled after her father had demolished her at the game earlier. "I hate losing."

Mr. Barnett set the table up again. "Then you should learn how to win."

"That's why I never play against, Daddy," Maxine said curled up in a chair watching a game show on T.V. "I never play games I know I can't win."

"I'm glad you're finally getting better," Janet said to her sister as she changed for bed. Beverly had been released from the hospital early that morning. "Two evenings by myself with them was a little too much. This is not how I planned to spend my spring break."

"I don't like this anymore than you do," Beverly said from her position on the bed. "Hopefully we can go home in a day or two. I'm missing time off work and we could use the money. And I hate spoiling everyone's fun."

"You haven't spoiled anything. Everyone decided to extend their stay and make the best of it. Karen and Tanya don't work and Jeffrey and Durand are on track with their project so a few days delay won't matter. I just want to go home."

"I'm sorry."

Janet pulled on her nightgown then looked at her sister with regret. "Don't be. I'm just feeling a little sorry for myself. I'm not blaming you."

"I know and I'm doing my best to get stronger. I'm sure I won't be so tired tomorrow and can join you downstairs."

"That will be a relief. When I'm with them nothing I say is right. Especially about art."

"But you love art."

Janet climbed into bed and drew up the blankets. "Not the right kind to suit Karen and Tanya. I say I like Mondrian and they say they prefer Cezanne. I like the illustrator Tom Feelings, they like Jacob Lawrence. It's impossible to agree on anything."

"Never mind. Tomorrow will be better."

Janet liked her sister's optimism, but didn't agree. She turned off the lights then lay on her side. She waited until she was confident her sister had fallen asleep, then she snuck out of bed. She changed back into her street clothes then left the room.

She loved roaming the house at night. The quiet hush of evening invigorated her. Unlike her own house, the lake house had many rooms in which to explore and no one would wake up and ask her what she was doing. She could truly be alone.

At this sacred hour there was no one to answer to. She could eat what she wanted or look through the extensive library without anyone commenting on her selection. There was no one to impress or explain to. Sweet freedom. Janet went out onto the porch. She stared at the lake as the moonlight touched the dark surface that reflected its image like a mirror. Then her gaze fell on a dark, still figure. She knew immediately who it was. His large silhouette was enough to identify him. Beside him sat the shadowy figure of a dog. Her pulse quickened. Durand seemed to enjoy the night as much as she did.

Janet frowned. He was an intruder. She knew the thought was irrational, but the feeling didn't leave her. The night was hers and she didn't like his claim on it. He embodied the dominance and control she wished to escape. And there he was again dominating the very scene she'd come to admire.

Since leaving the hospital with Beverly he rarely spoke to her and when he did it was always brusque. Yet she knew he watched her, his piercing ebony gaze assessing and intense. What did he see when he looked at her? She didn't like him, but everyone else did. She wasn't surprised by the Farmers, and Beverly liked everyone, but even Abigail and Les seemed to enjoy his company. How could they all be so blind?

Janet folded her arms. *What kind of man are you, Durand?* He turned as if she'd spoken aloud. Janet gasped and stepped back from the railing trying to hide in the shadows. He soon turned away and Janet disappeared inside.

The next day Beverly was strong enough to join them, although she needed to use crutches. They ate brunch on the porch then each found ways to entertain themselves. As Abigail cleared the table she watched the group of young people. Jeffrey stayed by Beverly's side eager to attend to her every need. He'd given her a blanket, which she wrapped around her shoulders. She smiled at him. Janet sat on the railing with her sketch pad pretending to draw the lake, but always sending curious looks towards the pair. Frederick sat on the stairs stroking his dog and watching Janet. Karen sat at the table while Tanya painted her nails and she watched Frederick. Abigail lifted the stack of dishes and shook her head at the drama unfolding in front of her, before returning inside.

"I can't believe Janet said she likes Feelings over Lawrence,"

Karen said, glancing at Janet. The porch was large enough that she knew Janet couldn't overhear, but that Frederick could.

When Tanya didn't say anything, Karen kicked her. Tanya jerked her hand spreading nail polish on Karen's finger. "Look what you made me do."

Karen narrowed her gaze and hissed in a low voice. "Say something."

"About what?" Tanya said applying nail polish remover. "You've ruined a nearly perfect manicure."

"Who cares? Reply to what I just said."

"About what?"

"About Janet's artistic taste." She raised her voice. "Don't you agree that Janet wasn't being honest last night about Tom Feelings?"

"No, I mean yes," Tanya hastily corrected when Karen growled. "I don't believe her."

"Janet likes to be contrary because it gives her a reason to voice an opinion. Don't you agree Frederick?"

He absently turned to her. "What?"

"Never mind." Her gaze fell on Jeffrey. "I'm glad Beverly is feeling better."

"Yes," Frederick said.

"Watching her with Jeffrey is so amusing."

He sent her a sharp look. "You think so?"

"Don't worry," she said amused by the look of concern on his face. "It's nothing serious. You should know him by now. He falls in love so easily." She looked at Tanya. "Remember that woman in Morocco?"

Tanya nodded. "And Italy?"

Karen smiled. "It's harmless."

Frederick didn't return her smile. He studied the pair for a long moment then abruptly stood. "Jeffrey, help me give Milton some exercise."

He walked down the steps towards the lake before Jeffrey could protest. Jeffrey said something to Beverly then followed. Janet filled the seat Jeffrey had vacated and watched the two men. "It looks like Durand has two pets instead of one."

"Don't say that," Beverly said. "Jeffrey really enjoys Durand's company. They're good friends."

Janet took off her shoes and tucked her feet underneath her. "Their friendship is a mystery."

"Not to me. Jeffrey told me they met when they were both volunteers with the American Red Cross and stationed in an East African village helping dig wells. They also gave vaccinations against childhood diseases and illnesses that were responsible for the high infant mortality rate in the region. Twice they had to deal with rebel invaders and Jeffrey swears that Durand saved his life, although he won't go into detail."

"Sounds commendable," Janet said surprised.

Beverly made her voice firm. "It *is* commendable."

"But it's no surprise. The Originals pride themselves on being warriors, right?"

Beverly frowned. "You should give Durand more credit."

Janet shrugged. "He gives himself plenty."

"I don't think so. He has sad eyes."

"No, he doesn't." Janet's voice cracked with astonishment. "His eyes are as hard as steel."

Beverly shook her head then stared out at the lake.

FREDERICK WORKED on his laptop but couldn't focus. After dinner, everyone decided to watch TV, but he was too restless to join in. So he sat to the side staring at the screen, but seeing nothing.

"You're supposed to be on vacation," Jeffrey said when Frederick refused to join them.

"I have a few people I have to respond to."

He needed the work to occupy his mind, but it wasn't working. His thoughts still entertained hopes and desires he wanted to repress. He liked Janet more than he wanted to. He was infatuated. The cadence of her voice had become the sweetest sound; her eyes like sunlight. When she looked at him, he felt tongue-tied. He was a fool. She was all wrong for him, but his thoughts didn't care, so he kept his distance.

Unfortunately, he couldn't stop watching her. He watched her when she played with Milton when she thought no one was looking; as she helped chop vegetables or made potato pancakes with Abigail, or pulled weeds with Les in the garden. He remembered catching her looking at his Blackberry. She'd thought she was alone in the room and had rushed over to the table where he'd left it, her slender fingers sliding across the tiny keys.

When he entered the room, she'd turned around and stared at him looking guilty. "I was just looking," she said in a rush. "I didn't turn it on or anything."

"That's okay." He picked it up and held it out to her. "Would you like me to show you how it works?"

"No." She backed away from him. "That's all right I've satisfied my curiosity." She dashed out of the room.

He impatiently drummed his fingers on the wrist rest remembering his disappointment. There were a lot of things he wanted to show her. He wondered how much of her sheltered existence had prepared her for the world. But that didn't matter. It couldn't. Their lives were too different. He was just bored. He needed to work.

He wanted to return to Hamsford.

Janet wanted to return too. On the day of their departure she hugged Abigail and Les then took her seat next to the window, eager to go home. Tanya was equally ready to go because she'd run out of her favorite moisturizer. Karen sat beside her eager to return home so that she could have all of Frederick's attention again. Only Jeffrey and Beverly seemed reluctant to leave. Abigail watched the SUV drive away wondering if she'd ever see them all together again.

~

"WELL WHAT HAPPENED?" Mrs. Barnett asked upon her daughters' return. They all sat around the dinner table and everyone looked at Janet and Beverly eager for answers. Janet began to share their activities but her mother waved that away. "I meant what progress have you made?"

"I don't think I've made any progress."

"You must have. You had nearly a week."

"Dee-dee, I—"

"Never mind. The next few weeks will likely seal the deal."

Brother Jerome came to visit the next day with a bouquet of flowers for Beverly. He stayed for dinner and spent the entire evening declaring how happy he was that she had healed completely.

That evening Janet lay in bed strangely thrilled to be back home among the noise of her sisters and her mother's questions. Although the lake house had been a brief escape the company had been wearisome and she was glad to be away from them. She was about to turn off her bedside lamp when she heard muttering next door. She knew that Beverly didn't sleep with the radio on. Curious, Janet grabbed her robe and walked barefoot to her sister's room. She gasped when a sharp, metal object bit into the bottom of her foot. She hopped around on one leg and removed it. It was an earring. Mrs. Lind must have lost it while cleaning. Janet gingerly put her foot down then dropped the earring in her robe pocket. She looked up and saw a faint light seeping from her sister's bedroom.

Janet stood in the doorway and saw it came from the glow of a candle. Beverly kneeled before it, with her head lowered and covered by a scarf. She held her hands together in prayer, words rushing from her lips.

"Beverly?"

She didn't turn and the flood of words continued to flow.

Janet came closer. "What's wrong?"

Beverly turned to her, her eyes bright with fear. "Do you ever think about burning in hell?"

CHAPTER 16

Janet shut the door, making sure not to close it completely, so that their voices wouldn't carry. She flipped on the light switch and they squinted against the sudden glare. "What are you talking about?"

"I've been thinking about hell."

"Why?"

"I don't want to marry Brother Jerome."

Janet sank into the bed with relief. "I don't think you'll go to hell for that."

Beverly pushed the scarf from her head in a swift angry motion. "Don't make fun of me."

Janet blinked, taken aback. "I'm not."

She softened her tone. "I know. I'm sorry." She wrung her hands together. "It's awful."

"I know," Janet agreed with vehemence. "The thought of you and that man—"

Beverly shook her head. "No, that's not what I meant. My feelings are awful. It's all been arranged. This marriage will help us so much. Our parents are depending on me. Dee-dee has always wanted us to marry well."

"Jeffrey's rich."

Beverly stood, placing her fingers to her lips. "Quiet. You mustn't say his name."

"Why not?"

Beverly sat beside Janet. "Because you shouldn't speak with such certainty about things that you're unsure of."

"I'm certain about your feelings for him and his feelings for you."

Beverly looked hopeful. "Has he told you anything?"

"No." When she saw her sister's face crumbled, she quickly added. "But I've seen the way he looks at you."

"A gentle look is not a confession of love or a proposal."

"But—"

"I know he likes me as he always has, but that doesn't mean he wants to marry me."

"A man can be encouraged. I don't know how, but I'm sure there's a way. You should have seen his face when that train was coming towards you. He would have given his life for you."

"Durand was there too."

Janet scowled. "Durand doesn't count."

"He had the knife that cut me free."

"Most savages have knives. I won't give him credit for that."

"You're being spiteful."

"Yes, if he can accuse me of having a dirty mind I can accuse him of being a savage."

"Despite his money and education?"

"He is clever and resourceful, but he is still arrogant and condescending."

"And he saved my life."

"Yes," Janet said in a terse voice, not wishing to reflect on it. "but we're not discussing him. You love Jeffrey."

"I can't admit it."

"You don't have to."

Beverly knelt in front of the candle again and replaced her scarf. She gripped her hands in prayer. "God forgive me. I am a selfish, miserable creature. God please change my heart or take my life."

Janet blew the candle out and lifted Beverly to her feet. "Don't say that. It's going to be okay."

Beverly yanked her arm away. "How can it be okay?" Her voice shook. "I am the eldest. I am supposed to bring my family honor. Be a source of pride. Mother Shea said she saw it in a vision."

"I know."

"And father said it's God's will."

"I know."

"And Dee-dee said it's the answer to all her prayers."

"I know that too, but I'm sure they all want you to be happy."

"By shaming them? By spitting in the eye of God? You don't really believe that."

Janet hesitated then sighed. "No."

Beverly grabbed the front collar of her nightgown, her knuckles pale. "I have no choice. This is my fate. I must accept it." She turned to the window her voice flat and as weak as a decayed oak tree. "Yes, I will bear it."

"You do have a choice."

"Perhaps I did something horrible in my past and this is God's punishment."

Janet stepped in front of her. "No."

"Yes, you're right." She squared her shoulders. "I shouldn't indulge in self-pity. God is wise. Brother Jerome will provide us with all that we need," she said as tears gathered in her eyes.

Beverly's misery threatened to crush Janet's heart like a steel weight, shattering it to pieces. But when she saw her sister put the candle away resigned, anger began to build then morphed into defiance. "You will not marry Brother Jerome," she said with such ferocity it surprised them both.

Beverly looked at Janet unsure. "But—"

"I will fix things for you."

"How?"

Janet didn't know and part of her regretted making such a bold promise, but the glint of hope on her sister's face gave her courage. "I'm not sure, but I'll think of something."

"Janet, you can't afford to get into anymore trouble. I can't let you risk it. If you fail—"

"I won't fail."

"We've seen what disobedience can do to a family."

"Everything will be fine. Now sleep."

Beverly hesitated then climbed into bed. Janet turned off the light and left the room. Once she reached the hallway she sank against the wall and whispered. "God help me."

God didn't hear her. Janet woke up the next morning with no ideas. However, she gave her sister a smile of reassurance at breakfast and again told her that everything would work out as Beverly headed for work. Her sister gave her a fierce hug then left in high spirits. Janet's spirits plummeted. She barely paid attention in class and nearly missed a lecture she'd signed up for. Back at home she met Mrs. Lind in the kitchen. "Oh, I found your earring," she said placing the object on the table. "I had it in my pocket this morning but forgot to give it to you."

Mrs. Lind glanced at the earring then shook her head. "Dat isn't mine."

"But it has to be, none of us have pierced ears."

"That may be true, but it still isn't mine."

Janet lifted the earring and studied it. "But it was upstairs, if it's not yours then..." She gripped it in her hand a feeling of dread twisting her insides. "But it can't be." She glanced at Mrs. Lind but the other woman's face remained expressionless. Janet left the kitchen and paced the living room until she heard the front door slam. She ran to the foyer and saw Francine hanging up her coat.

"Where're Maxine and Trudy?"

"At the market, Dee-dee told them to pick up some things. Why?"

"No reason." Janet forced a smile so that Francine wouldn't suspect anything. "Did you have a good day at school?" She folded her arms trying to appear casual, although the tiny earring in her pocket felt like a large boulder.

"Oh yes," Francine said eager to share the events of her day. She led Janet into the family room and told her about every subject and even included what she'd eaten at lunch. Janet listened trying to appear interested. Twenty minutes later she heard the front door slam and two female voices.

"He was not!"

"Yes, he was!"

Janet met Maxine and Trudy in the foyer. "What is going on?"

Maxine spoke up. "At the market there was this man."

Janet frowned. "You're not supposed to be talking to strange men."

"We had to," Maxine said as though her sister was slow witted. "He's just opened his craft stand and he carries the most beautiful scarves and I wanted to buy one. So I asked him which would look perfect on me."

"And I also asked him which one would look good on me," Trudy interjected.

Janet rested a hand on her hip. "So what are you fighting about?"

"Which one of us he liked better. I know he liked me better

because look what he suggested I buy." Maxine pulled her scarf out of her backpack.

Trudy also took out her scarf. "And me. I think mine's a lot prettier."

Janet didn't like either, but looking at them suddenly gave her an idea. "Francine, I'm sorry I kept you. I'm sure you'd like to complete your homework before dinner."

"Oh yes." She left.

Janet turned her attentions to the scarves. "I think you'll both look wonderful. On campus I saw this very stylish woman wearing one just like this. Do you want me to show you how she wore it?"

"Oh yes," they said.

She took them upstairs to their bedroom then ordered Maxine to sit. "She wore it in her hair," Janet explained. She then folded the scarf and used it to pull Maxine's hair into a ponytail. Janet stumbled back the moment she saw what she'd feared. Maxine had pierced her ears.

"Well, how do I look?" Maxine asked then frowned when she saw the look on her sister's face. "What?"

Janet leaned forward and tugged on Maxine's ear. "When did you do this?"

Maxine quickly covered her ears then glanced at Trudy. Janet turned to her and pulled back Trudy's hair. She also wore two studded earrings.

"Maxine did it first," she said in a small voice.

"And if Maxine does something you have to do it too," Janet said in a low grim tone. She pointed to the place next to Maxine. "Sit down."

Trudy scurried over to the bed.

Janet stared at them stunned. "What were you thinking?"

Maxine shrugged and removed the scarf so her hair would cover her ears. "We just wanted to try it. There was this girl at school who said there was a really cheap place you could get your ears pierced."

"You're not *supposed* to get your ears pierced."

"Mrs. Lind has pierced ears."

"Mrs. Lind isn't in the church."

"Neta has her ears pierced," she said referring to a young woman in their church.

"Sister Gordon lets Neta wear jewelry. We can't."

"But Neta—"

"Doesn't live in *this* house. This is Daddy's house."

"It's no big deal," Maxine grumbled.

"Is that so?" Janet turned to the door. "Then let me go get Daddy right now."

Both girls jumped up and grabbed her arms. "No!"

"We're sorry," Maxine said.

"Very sorry," Trudy said.

"We thought it would be fun."

Janet sent them a look and they sank back onto the bed. She folded her arms not knowing what to say. She understood the temptation, especially when other young girls in the church had fathers who were more lenient. Fathers who allowed pierced ears and some makeup. She too had imagined piercing her ears the moment she left the house. Years ago she'd tried colored lip gloss, but had removed it before coming home.

"I know it's difficult, but while you live under this roof you must respect Daddy's rules."

"He'll never find out," Trudy said. "We only wear them to school and not to church. You can't tell anyone."

Janet held out her hand. "Give me your earrings."

Both girls pulled them out and handed them to her.

"Is that all?"

"No," Trudy said.

"Yes," Maxine said.

Janet frowned and kept her hand held out. Maxine sent Trudy a look then sighed and reluctantly retrieved her other earrings, which she'd kept hidden in a drawer.

Janet clenched her teeth when Maxine gave her four more pairs. She closed her hand. "I won't say a word." She held up her fist. "This time."

The two girls kissed her on the cheek. "Thank you, thank you."

"You're welcome."

Maxine draped the scarf on her head and tied a knot under her chin. "I think I'll wear it like this. Now all I need are sunglasses to look like a movie star."

Trudy imitated her. "Me too."

Janet watched them. "That's fine, just promise to behave yourselves."

The two girls turned to her with their heads covered and smiled looking as pious and innocent as postulants. "We will."

Janet left their bedroom wishing she believed them.

CHAPTER 17

"So you enjoyed yourself at the lake house?" Mr. Barnett asked, looking through Janet's sketches as they sat in his study. He would never admit how much he'd missed her and how glad he was to have her home again.

"Yes."

"It is a grand place," he said studying the details she'd been able to capture. One day he wanted to own a big house on a lake and be able to take his family there on holidays. He glanced at Janet who wore a sweater that was over eight years old with the knitting unraveling at the hem. One day he would like to afford her, his wife and his other daughters, fine clothes. Newly purchased and not from the thrift shop.

"How is Brother Jeremiah?" Janet asked.

"Doing very well. I told him about seeking counsel and he did. He's set up a monthly payment with the customer until the balance is paid. In the meantime, Pastor Wainwright advanced him a portion of what he was owed from the church's emergency funds. So Bessie will be pleased. He will repay the church once he is paid."

"Good." She hesitated. "I don't think Maxine and Trudy should go to the market without Francine."

"Why not? You went there at their age."

"I know, but there are certain market men there."

"They won't bother my daughters. Everyone knows that the Barnett girls are to be left alone." He closed the sketchbook and leaned forward. "But something is troubling you. You've been quiet since your return. What's wrong?"

Janet wrung her hands together. "I don't know if I can tell you—"

He fell back and threw out his hands. "Of course you can tell me. If you can't tell your father, who can you tell?"

She cleared her throat. "I have a friend who's unhappy."

"Is it Valerie?"

"No, it's someone else."

He sat up alarmed. "Who could it be? What other friends do you have? I should know who your friends are."

She sighed. "Maybe *friend* is the wrong word. She's an acquaintance and she told me a problem but I don't know how to help her. A problem so bad it keeps her awake at night."

"She can't sleep? Is she having nightmares?"

Janet suddenly looked thoughtful. "Yes, terrible nightmares. That's the problem."

"If she's having trouble with her dreams she should go to Mother Shea. She can help interpret them for her."

"Of course. Mother Shea," Janet said slowly. "I had never thought of that." She leaped to her feet. "Thank you, Daddy."

"Yes, yes," he said feeling both embarrassed and pleased by her enthusiasm. "Come to me with your troubles any time."

~

"IT WILL NEVER WORK," Valerie said as they walked back from

an event at the church. They had attended a special service to welcome home a missionary and his family who had just returned from Rwanda. The evening had consisted of watching a slide show of an orphanage their church had funded following the genocide. The early evening sun had yet to disappear and a weeping willow swayed as though dancing to the sound of cicadas. "She'll see right through you."

"Not if I come up with a good enough dream."

"It will have to be very good."

Janet spotted Brother Jerome walking to his car. She smoothed down her hair, adjusted her blouse and moistened her lips. Brother Jerome appreciated a woman looking her best. She patted the side of her cheeks for added color then called out to him. "You look very distinguished today."

He turned to them and stood straighter, basking in her attention. "Thank you."

Janet walked towards him. "Such a distinguished, cultured man deserves the same in his wife."

"Yes, Beverly is perfect for me." Brother Jerome said, opening his car door.

"Oh, yes she's very beautiful and will look perfect on your arm. Too bad she's not as cultured as you."

Valerie nudged her and whispered out of the corner of her mouth. "What are you doing?"

"You know what I'm doing," Janet whispered back.

Brother Jerome rested his arm on the car door and frowned at her. "What do you mean?"

"Beverly hates most gatherings or public events, she finds them boring."

"She didn't appear that way to me."

"She hides it well. But I guess that as long as she presents herself one way in public it doesn't matter how she behaves at home."

He furrowed his brows. "She's different at home?"

"Well, I don't think it's appropriate—"

His gaze grew intense. "No, I'm curious."

"She snores terribly."

He chuckled. "That can be corrected."

Janet glanced at a passing car. "Then there are the crying bouts."

"Crying?"

"Yes, she has these hysterical crying fits. She just bursts into tears for no reason." This was partially true, Beverly was known to cry at the slightest bad news she heard and would sob if she watched a heartbreaking movie.

"Hmm."

"And Beverly tends to leave her dirty clothes on the floor. But that shouldn't be a problem for you, I'm sure you're rich enough to hire a maid."

"Hmm."

"Just forget what I said. Come on Valerie, we need to pick up some books, Beverly needs to learn how to cook!" She turned.

"Sister Janet?"

She looked back at him.

"Thank you," he said staring at her in a new way.

Janet only smiled and left.

Valerie tugged on Janet's arm. "You lied," she whispered.

"Partially. Beverly does snore, when she has a cold, she cries at sentimental commercials and soppy movies. And she does forget to put her clothes away. As for being able to cook, she can but she's not very good."

"I hope you're prepared to live with the consequences if he decides not to marry her."

"Consequences? That's my goal. I have to convince Brother Jerome and Mother Shea to stop the wedding. I've never seen my sister so miserable. I have to do something."

Valerie sighed. "Well, if that is the case then perhaps, just perhaps, I can help. I know something about dreams."

"Good."

"But it's a gamble."

"It's a gamble I'm willing to take."

JANET SAT in her Art History class silently rehearsing her plan for Mother Shea, when her professor handed her the grade for her last project: a D.

She gripped the paper and stared. "This has to be a mistake."

"It's not," Marisa said. "Professor Blakemore always grades harsh after a midterm."

"Especially the female students," another young woman said behind them. She had a deep voice that seemed incongruous with her tiny frame.

"But that's not right," Janet said. "I can't get a D. It will ruin my grade point average."

Marisa shrugged. "That's the way it is."

"Yep," the girl with the deep voice said. She unbuttoned the top of her blouse to let her cleavage show. "And I'm getting an A." She gathered her things and walked to the front of the class.

Janet watched her as she leaned over the professor's desk. "What is she talking about?"

"Don't be naïve. You know what she's going to do." When Janet continued to look blank, Marisa said, "She'll get an A when her legs spell a V."

Janet fell forward. "She'll do *that* for a grade?"

"Lots of girls do, but you don't have to go that far. I'm not." Marisa shoved her books into her book bag.

"What are you going to do?"

"What most of the female students do." She glanced around

then lowered her voice. "Professor Blakemore has these 'tutoring' sessions after class at his place. It's simple—you play the rules, stroke his ego and you'll get your A."

Janet glanced at her Professor unable to imagine going to his house let alone doing anything else. "But I can't do that. I *won't* do that."

"Come on. Don't be so uptight. We're artists, remember? Free-thinkers. All you have to do is drink a little, flirt a little and it's over. That's the way things are."

"Not for me."

Marisa shrugged. "Fine then you'd better hope he'll let you pass with a C. There are only a few more weeks before summer break. You don't have much of a choice." She walked off.

Janet drummed her fingers on her desk. She did have a choice. She wasn't going to sleep with her professor or entertain him at his home. She would get her A on her terms.

"JUST ACCEPT your D and forget about it."

Janet stared at her counselor as though she'd just spouted gibberish. "I don't understand."

"I can see that," the woman said taking off her glasses and letting them hang down her chest. They got tangled in her equally long silver necklace, but she didn't notice. Janet resisted the urge to stamp her feet. Mrs. Upton didn't have time to notice much, which explained why she had two pencils sticking out of her bun and a pen behind her ear. Folders and papers covered nearly every surface of her office and a line of students waited outside. Mrs. Upton turned to her computer, made a few unintelligible comments then said, "You're an excellent student this shouldn't affect you."

"It is affecting me. He gave my project a D."

"So you'll get a C in the course. It's not critical."

"But he—"

Mrs. Upton slowly turned from the computer and sat back with her arms folded. "Let me tell it to you straight. Professor Blakemore is a powerful man. Not only does he have tenure, he has connections. Do you know who his father is? Do you know who his wife is? No you don't, but that's okay because the only thing you need to know is that his family donates a lot of money to this school." She waved her hand. "No, honey, don't open your mouth. I'm telling you something important. Money means some-thing. He spends a lot. He can't be touched." Mrs. Upton leaned forward and rested her arms on the table. Her elbow knocked over a tray of paper clips. She didn't notice. "You only have a few weeks left. You're going to pass the course. Be grateful for that." She glanced at the computer. "Besides you're an Art major. Nobody's going to be looking at your grades that closely. You'll be lucky if you can get a job without also getting an MA." She returned her gaze to Janet. "I suggest you take your grade and leave me to deal with students who have real problems."

Janet stormed out of the building and blindly walked across the campus silently calling Professor Blakemore every horrible name she could think of then adding Mrs. Upton to the mix. There was no one she could talk to. Not her father, not Pastor Wainwright (he was a good man, but would just encourage her to accept the grade or leave school), Beverly would worry, and Valerie would say that's what she should expect when dealing with 'worldly' people.

"Hey!" someone called out to her. Janet turned and saw Marisa. "I saw you come out of Mrs. Upton's office. She isn't any help, is she?"

"As helpful as a twig in the ocean."

Marisa grinned. "I know." She pulled out a piece of paper from her tight black jeans and handed it to Janet. "Here's the place and time. This is your only chance to get an A. It's up to you." She walked away.

Janet stared down at the address then crumbled the paper in her fist. It was hard enough to live by her father's rules; she would not live by another man's. She didn't care how much money and power he had. But she wasn't sure how to fight him.

She headed to the street and nearly got run over by a corvette when someone violently pulled her back.

"Hey slow down," Jeffrey said as Frederick released her.

Janet turned and saw them looking at her concerned. She groaned. Just what she needed—more rich, powerful men. They were the last people she wanted to see right now. "I will, thanks."

"What's wrong?"

She hadn't planned on telling them, but something about Frederick's direct, hard gaze forced the words from her and the story poured out before she could stop it. "But I don't know what to do," she finished feeling helpless.

The two men stared at her speechless then Jeffrey said, "Did you say Professor Blakemore?"

"Yes."

"Sam Blakemore?"

"I don't know his first name, but that might be it."

Jeffrey raised his brows and turned to Frederick. "Do you think—?"

He nodded then flashed a ruthless smile that made Jeffrey laugh. Before Janet could ask him what was so funny, Jeffrey patted his friend on the shoulder then winked at her. "Don't worry Janet I think we can help."

"You'll stretch the fabric!"

"Are you saying I'm too fat?"

"Certainly not," Mother Shea said keeping her grip on the skirt she wanted. "I would never say that. But your hips say it for you. The cut will not flatter your shape."

The other woman, middle aged with dusty ebony skin, loosened her hold on the skirt, curious.

Mother Shea smoothed back a stray hair that had come undone during the struggle. She held the skirt against the woman's waist. "See? And this color does nothing for you. Few colors flatter me the way they would you." Mother Shea tucked the skirt into her shopping bag. "It's so difficult for me to find the right color. I know you don't have that trouble."

The woman glared at her then stormed away.

Valerie watched Mother Shea then turned to Janet. "When are you going to do it?"

Janet didn't look up as she helped her sort clothes for the church's weekend charity event. "I better hide some pieces. Mother Shea always grabs the best one for herself before we can put them on sale."

"Did you hear me?"

Janet glanced up and saw her sister Maxine pouting as she helped a church sister with decorations. Usually her three younger sisters were kept busy on weekends helping in the church pantry. Every other Saturday the homeless and needy families would come to get free food baskets. Maxine had missed two Saturdays and had been forced to help today. Janet knew her mother had a hard time getting Maxine and Trudy to stay longer than an hour or two while Francine stayed all day doing what she called 'the Lord's work'.

Janet turned her attention from Maxine to Mother Shea. "Yes I heard you."

"You better talk to her soon."

"I've had other things on my mind."

"Like what?"

"School," Janet said not wanting to elaborate. She held up a purple and green polka dot dress with lace trimming the sleeves, hem and collar. "How hideous. We can't give this away."

"When you're desperate you're not picky."

"I don't care how poor you are, no one should be forced to wear this." Janet looked around then dropped the dress on the floor and kicked it under the table.

"You know it's not too late to back out."

"I'm not going to back out. I'm going to visit Mother Shea just as planned. But before I do, I have to teach someone a lesson."

CHAPTER 18

Samuel Blakemore loved his job. He'd been at the University for fifteen years and every year the students got more desperate and his semester became more interesting. He grew older but the students remained the same. He wasn't an attractive man. He wore a goatee to hide the fact that he barely had a chin, and his eyes were a little too far apart, but he had the height and thick sandy hair that made him look younger than he was. But most important, his course was required for all art majors, before they could graduate, and he had the power of tenure behind him.

He sat grading papers, looking at the names and grading them based on the students he wanted to know on an intimate level. He was ready to give one coed a low mark when someone knocked on his door.

"Come in."

A young, black woman with a long braid, wearing jeans and a decorative purple tunic entered. She was a striking woman although she didn't wear make-up or jewelry. He tried to place her then suddenly remembered. Yes, Janet Barnett. She fascinated him. She was an outstanding artist but didn't act like the other students. He'd taken a risk giving her project a low grade, but he'd been curious to see what she'd do about it.

Her presence in his office gave him the satisfaction that he'd been right. The sight of her pleased him more than he thought it would. Perhaps there was more to her than he thought. But that wasn't a surprise. Usually the quiet, conservative ones were the most adventurous. He stood and walked up to her. "Janet, a pleasure to see you. Please take a seat." He gestured to a chair and watched her sit then quietly locked the door behind him. "Now, how can I help you?"

"I want to discuss the grade you gave my project."

He returned to his desk feigning regret. "I was disappointed to have to do that, but your project wasn't up to standard."

"I disagree, but that's not why I'm here. What do I need to do to get an A?"

Blakemore felt his mouth go dry. He flexed his fingers to keep from rubbing his hands together. His eyes scanned the length of her. She had a gorgeous figure that the loose tunic and jeans couldn't hide and a mouth that begged to be kissed. He took a deep, steadying breath already feeling himself grow hard as he imagined caressing her bare skin. "I'm glad you asked because there is a way." He walked around the desk and stood in front of her letting her see the full evidence of his desire. "A very easy way."

He suppressed a smiled when he saw her gaze fall to the front of his trousers then drop to the floor. God he loved when they were shy. It made the conquest that much sweeter. He wondered if he'd have to chase her around the room for a few minutes, or play some other coy game. "Do I make you uncomfortable?"

Her gaze remained on the floor. "No."

"Good. I think it's best to approach this like two adults."

"Yes. I agree. So let me get one thing clear." She lifted her gaze—her brown eyes meeting his green ones with an expression of such fury blood drained from his face. "You will give me an A because I earned it."

He laughed and folded his arms, getting back his courage. What could she do to him? She was nothing—a nobody. "I'm tenured baby and there's nothing you can do. You could complain from here to the dean and nothing will change. I haven't raped anybody and I haven't killed anybody so I'm not going anywhere and this course is my little kingdom. You have to follow my rules."

Janet crossed her legs, her gaze unwavering.

Blakemore moved his shoulders feeling antsy. "So do you want that A or not?"

"I'm going to get an A and this is what I'll do. I will complete another project and hand it in to you. You will grade it with the correct mark and that will be the end of it."

He shook his head. "Now that doesn't seem fair to me because I don't get anything out of it." He moved forward to touch her arm.

She pulled out an X-ACTO knife from her backpack and pointed it at him. "Any part of you that touches me will be sliced off."

He yanked his hand back. "What is wrong with you?"

"Do we have an agreement?"

He marched to the door and unlocked it. "No. You don't play the game you don't get the grade." He opened the door. "Now get the hell out of my office."

"Is that the way you speak to your students?" a familiar voice said.

Blakemore turned and saw two catlike eyes in the face of a beautiful woman. She stood in the doorway. "Charlotte!" He gripped the door handle and nearly swallowed his tongue. "What are you doing here? You're supposed to be out of town."

"I know, but I got a call."

He spun around and glared at Janet. "You called *my wife*? I'll—"

"Now, now," Charlotte said in a soothing voice. "Don't say anything that you'll regret." She strolled into the room with the panther like grace she'd acquired as a dancer. She tossed her purse on the desk then faced him. "I've been taking this crap for years, but this machine isn't accepting your quarters anymore. Your game is over. We're playing by my rules now." She began to tick items off on her fingers. "First you're going to give this student an A. Second you're going to permanently cancel that little tutoring session you have scheduled and give all those other students the grades they deserve. Third, you'd better get used to thinking of this place as your castle because by the time my lawyers are finished with you this is all you'll have left."

"Charlotte." His voice trembled.

She picked up her purse. "Come Janet. Professor Blakemore has a lot of work to do."

Blakemore watched them go then sunk into his chair and cried.

Outside his office Janet stared at Charlotte amazed. "I can't thank you enough for your help."

"It was time. I knew what was going on but no one was bold enough to confront me about it. I liked your gumption."

"Thank you."

"I also like your work. I got a chance to see some when Samuel brought his work home."

Janet narrowed her eyes. "But I didn't do many drawings for his class."

"Yes, I know, most of the papers are narratives describing different artists and their work. But I remember the report you submitted comparing the skillful use of light and dark between impressionist and modern day techniques in portraits. Samuel was blown-away by your submission. It was one of the best he had ever seen.

"I agreed with your argument and your samples."

Janet nodded remembering the project. She'd created several small portraits, some mimicking the style of the old masters, and others incorporating the controversial styles of several modern day artists.

"It was a brilliant," Charlotte continued. "I don't usually use undergrads, but I've heard good things about your work and could use someone like you. What are you doing this summer?"

"I don't have anything planned," Janet replied, cautious.

"How would you like an internship? I have an interior design business and could use an assistant. I also have an artist who could show you how to do faux painting and a lot more if that's something you'd be interested in."

A job to paint and make money? "I'd love it."

"Here's my card. Call me after you've completed your last class and we'll get together."

Janet stared at the card as if it were gold. "Thank you so much."

"No, thank *you*. I've been fixing up other people's homes for so long I'd forgotten to get rid of my own trash." Charlotte put on her sunglasses then strutted down the hall, drawing the attention of everyone she passed.

Janet pumped the air with her fist then put the card away. She'd defeated Professor Blakemore now it was time for Mother Shea.

other Shea hated nightfall. It wasn't the silence, it wasn't the loneliness, it was the emptiness. In her house there was no one to admire her, to seek her advice or listen to her dreams and no one to care that sometimes she feared growing old. Hamsford and the church people meant everything to her and she wondered if she served them well. They were all that she had and they made her feel important. She'd grown up poor and unremarkable until the day she had that one dream that changed her life.

At times she feared that she'd have another dream that would do the same thing. And Mother Shea feared change more than anything. She sat in her living room with a cup of tea ready to settle into the night and soak her swollen feet when someone knocked on her door.

Mother Shea glanced at the clock, her heart beginning to pound. Nobody could be coming to her house at this hour with good news. She put on her slippers and tied the sash of her robe then went to the door. "Who is it?" she asked trying to see through the peephole.

"Janet Barnett."

She swung the door open surprised. "It's late for you to be here."

"I know but I desperately need your help."

Mother Shea opened the door wider. "Come in."

Janet entered trying her best not to stare. Few people were allowed into Mother Shea's home. She had a special back entrance that lead to a social room where she talked to visitors. Janet didn't want anyone seeing her there, so she had chosen nighttime to sneak out, and had decided to go to the front door. She'd stood outside praying for God's forgiveness and blessing, knowing what she was about to do was deceptive but hoping He'd understand. The moment she saw the interior of Mother Shea's house she saw that being a Seer paid considerably better than she'd imagined.

While Mother Shea didn't possess many furnishings, the few she had were finely crafted pieces. A number of framed quotes, professing God's love, lined the walls. She led Janet into her small sitting room, where on a large marble center table, lay an enormous family bible.

"Take a seat," Mother Shea said. "And tell me what's troubling you. I must say, I'm surprised your parents let you stay out so late."

Janet sat on a plush couch determined not to be distracted from her mission. "No. They don't know I snuck out tonight. But I *had* to see you. I had this terrible dream last night that disturbed me."

Mother Shea leaned forward. "Yes?"

"I need you to interpret it for me."

"Of course. You came to the right place. But why not wait until morning?"

"Because I have been having this dream every night for the past five days. The same dream and I am afraid to go to sleep tonight. The dream really scares me and I can't sleep until I understand it."

Mother Shea sat back ready to listen. "Very well tell me about it."

Janet wiped her sweaty palms on her jeans and did, remembering every detail of the dream she and Valerie had rehearsed. Mother Shea's expression didn't change. When Janet was finished she swallowed and said, "That's it."

"You've had a dream that your dead Grandma Lucy ripped a wedding veil off of Beverly's head?"

"Yes."

"And you've had this dream five times?"

"Yes."

Mother Shea folded her arms. "Why did you come here to lie to me?"

Sheer fear swept through her. "What?"

Mother Shea's crafty eyes studied her. "That dream was pure fabrication. Do you want to know how I know?" She didn't wait for a reply. "Because you're not the type of woman who dreams at night. You dream in the day. You dream of leaving your parents' home and being on your own. You dream dangerous dreams."

Janet licked her lips.

"I'm not going to ask why you don't want your sister to marry Brother Jerome because I don't care. But I will tell you this." She leaned forward and Janet looked into the face of a woman who wasn't only cunning, but clever. "Start to dream at night and let those other dreams die or you are headed down an ungodly path. You will bring more shame to your family than you ever knew possible." She sat back. "Now let me tell you about a dream I've had. If your family deviates from the wishes of the Lord your family will suffer. I see your house in mourning and shame. Your sister *must* marry Brother Jerome. Do you understand me?"

"Yes, Mother Shea."

She held out her hand. "So this conversation never happened."

Janet opened her wallet and handed her ten dollars.

Her hand didn't move. "How your mother would weep if she knew you'd been here."

Janet gave her another ten.

"And your father too."

Janet sighed and gave her last ten. "That's all I have."

Mother Shea stood and folded the bills. She opened the door and Janet walked past. "Drive safe." Her mouth spread into a thin lipped smile. "And sleep well."

SHE'D FAILED. Janet sat in her car and rested her head on the steering wheel. Her sister would marry Brother Jerome and there was nothing she could do. She steeled herself from tears and drove home. She didn't park her car all the way up the drive. Although her family could sleep through a tornado, she didn't want to risk waking them. She crept to the front door then halted when she heard movement close by. It sounded like a large animal. Janet picked up a rock and threw it into the bushes.

"Ow!"

Janet jumped back. "Who's there?"

"It's only me," Francine said, emerging from her hiding place.

"What are you doing?"

"Conducting an experiment."

"An experiment?"

Francine pulled out a leaf caught in the zipper of her jacket. "Yes. I wanted to see how easy it was to sneak out of a house and get back in. I was able to sneak out, but getting back in has proved difficult." She pointed to her bedroom window. "The vines aren't strong enough to hold me and we don't have a nearby tree or something else to climb."

"But why would you want to?"

"A girl at my school was bragging about how she sneaks out to meet her boyfriend and in three books I've read the heroine has done the same. I wanted to prove that it was possible." She sighed. "Unfortunately, I've come to the conclusion that the house must have a certain structure to allow for those types of nighttime activities." She narrowed her eyes. "Then again, you're trying to sneak back inside without detection. How do you plan to do that?"

Janet held up her keys. "Through the front door."

Francine pushed up her glasses and nodded. "Oh yes... I'd never thought of that."

Janet shook her head. "Come on."

"What are you doing out this late anyway?" Francine asked as Janet opened the front door.

"I had an errand." She turned the knob then turned to Francine with a finger to her lips. Francine nodded in understanding.

They crept inside then Janet gently shut the door behind her and bolted it. Francine took off her shoes, accidentally letting one drop and hit the floor with a thud. They stiffened waiting to hear movement from upstairs, but the house remained silent. Janet removed her shoes then waited a few moments to let her eyes adjust to the darkness before heading to the stairs.

Francine followed close behind her and whispered, "This is a lot more sensible than climbing the side of the house."

"Shh."

They'd reached halfway up the stairs when the hall lights came on. They stopped like startled night creatures caught on a roadway.

"Come here," Mr. Barnett said from the bottom of the stairs. He disappeared into the living room.

Francine turned and plodded down the stairs. "A serious miscalculation."

Moments later they sat in front of their father patiently waiting for his anger, but his tone was surprisingly calm.

"What were you two doing out at this time of night?"

Francine spoke up before Janet could. "It's all because of my experiment. Janet was helping me." She explained her theory in long detail until her father's eyes began to glaze over then finished with, "And I've discovered that it doesn't work unless the house is structurally conducive to that manner of escape and re-entry."

"I heard a car."

"Again my fault. I wanted to try different strategies and we drove around the neighborhood looking at different house structures."

Mr. Barnett turned to Janet. "Is this true?"

She hesitated and Francine continued. "I'll let you read my report once it's done."

Janet looked at her sister astonished that she was willing to cover for her. Her plain features gave nothing away. Although she'd seen that face all her life she felt as though she was staring at a stranger. How well did she know her? Who was she really?

Mr. Barnett stood. "No, I don't need to read your report, but next time use your imagination. I expect better sense from you Janet."

Janet nodded. "Yes, Daddy."

"Now get to bed." He turned and left.

Janet looked at her sister and mouthed "Thank you."

Francine squeezed her hand and for a moment their eyes met with a depth of understanding neither could voice. For an instant Janet wanted to share all her troubles, but knew that Francine couldn't help her. She watched her sister enter her bedroom and sighed feeling alone.

~

BROTHER PETER JEROME knew he had God's favor. He'd been blessed with a good family, good friends, good fortune and now he was set to marry a good woman. He'd come far from his father's scorn. In the church he'd learned that he was important. Therefore he did his best to hold on to God's favor by doing all that was right. But his thoughts were wrong. He kept thinking about Janet's words and started having doubts about Beverly. She was right. He did need someone educated and who would complement him. He needed advice because his doubts weren't the only thing wrong with his thoughts.

"I need to speak to you," he said to Mother Shea after bible study the following Tuesday night.

"I'm busy. Perhaps another day we—"

"No, I must talk to you now. I have troubles."

This piqued Mother Shea's interest. Brother Jerome rarely admitted to having trouble. "What is it?"

He pulled her to the side and looked around to make sure no one could overhear them. "I can't marry Sister Beverly."

"Of course you can. It's all settled." Mother Shea patted his arm. "You're just nervous, you'll get over it."

"It's not that. I've searched my soul and prayed but I think it would be wrong."

"What are you on about?" Mother Shea adjusted the pin in her hat and pursed her lips.

"I'm having carnal thoughts of another woman."

Mother Shea quickly looked around the church as if lighting were about to strike him dead then dragged him outside. "Say that again?"

"You heard me. I'm having carnal thoughts about a woman who *isn't* my intended."

"At work?"

"No, here in the church."

Mother Shea hesitated. "How carnal are your thoughts?"

"Very carnal," he said in an anxious whisper. "I think about doing things to her lips and her body in a way that no decent man should."

Mother Shea widened her eyes. "Good Lord!"

"These thoughts assault me the most at night... when I'm in bed."

"Oh Jesus!"

"And when I see her all reason leaves me and I want to be with her and—"

"Enough!" Mother Shea said waving his confession away. "Dear God, you can't be sinning in your heart this way and still marry."

"I know," he said miserable. "But I think the woman returns my uh... affection."

Mother Shea stumbled over to a bench near the church entrance. "You think she's... enticed you on purpose?"

"She's not a jezebel. She's a good woman. Sister Beverly deserves better and I think I can make things right with the Barnetts."

"Then what do you want me to do?"

"Pray for me."

"I will." Mother Shea went home and that night she dreamed.

Errol set the phone down with a thud. "Sigonya, come quick!"

"What?"

"Come here."

His sister appeared in the living room where Errol stood motionless. "What you wan? Lawd man. Mi can never get mi work done when you call mi all di time."

He put down the phone. "The wedding done. Him not getting married."

"Who?"

"Peter Jerome."

She fell into a chair. "No wedding?"

Errol shook his head.

Sigonya threw up her hands in disgust. "What am I supposed to do wid the outfit and matching shoes mi buy?"

"And the non-refundable tickets?"

She glanced over at the older woman who sat staring out the window as she did most days. "And Auntie was looking forward to this trip." She folded her arms. "I knew he was an odd bwoy. Didn't I tell you? No woman will hav him."

The hot breath of summer made an early appearance in spring then wiped its memory away with sweltering heat and long days. The Barnetts experienced a similar change, Francine graduated from high school, Maxine and Trudy's pierced ears began to close, Janet got her A and Beverly didn't marry Brother Jerome. Everything seemed to settle back to normal at the Barnett house.

But things were anything but normal in Hamsford. Gossip about Brother Jerome's change of heart and Mother's Shea's vision that God wanted Beverly for someone else continued to spread with unrelenting speed. However, Mother Shea was worried. She knew something wasn't right. Brother Jerome was an honorable man. She was glad he had told her of his problem, but she wanted to know who had tempted him away from Beverly. In her latest dream she had seen Beverly with another man, but she still felt her first vision was the right one.

Mother Shea sat in church and watched the second eldest Barnett daughter with special interest. She was sly. She looked pious, but Mother Shea knew the truth. She barely listened to the tearful admission of backsliding and slipping into worldly habits, by a young woman who told the congregation she'd twice submitted to the temptation of fornication and drunkenness.

She felt that something wasn't quite right. Her gaze fell on the two younger sisters as they stared at something in their laps instead of Pastor Wainwright. She frowned. Brother Barnett would be wise to watch those two. A solid marriage would have been a perfect solution and she'd had hope for the family, but now she sensed something bad was going to happen in the future. Something big would change. Yes, the hand of change loomed large around them and she didn't know how to stop it.

"I wish you'd tell me exactly how you did it," Beverly said as she, Janet and Valerie planted flowers in the garden. They knelt beside each other preparing the ground for the new plants Mrs. Barnett had purchased. "I still can't believe I'm no longer engaged."

Janet scooped up some dirt with a hand shovel. "I didn't do anything. I tried but it didn't work. It's a miracle. Now you can marry Jeffrey."

"Who says I'll marry him?"

"It would be a perfect choice. I wouldn't mind staying in that grand house of his."

Valerie shook her head. "Be careful, Janet. You're talking about things that haven't come true yet."

"But they will. You'll see." She winked at her sister. "Mrs. Beverly Farmer."

Beverly glanced around nervous. "Shh, someone might hear you."

Janet removed a plant from its pot. "It's a pity his name is

Farmer. I would have wanted a more distinguished name for you."

Valerie shook her head. "Remember the words of Solomon, *Do not boast about tomorrow for you do not know what a day may bring forth.*"

Janet placed the plant in the ground and covered its roots. "Yes, that's true, but all the signs are there that this is going to be a wonderful summer. Next month I start my internship with Mrs. Blakemore." Janet grabbed another pot. "Beverly's been invited over to the Farmers house four times already."

"As Tanya's guest," Beverly quickly added.

"Doesn't matter."

"And Brother Jerome has no hard feelings," Beverly said. "Actually he almost seems relieved and he's invited the family over for dinner twice. He has a lovely home."

Janet lifted her shovel. "It's too cluttered." She pointed to another pot.

Valerie picked it up then stopped before handing it to her. "You should listen to your sister's caution. The sky may look bright, but clouds can still gather on the sunniest of days."

"I'm not worried." Janet took the pot and set it down beside her. "But there is one thing I find strange."

"What?"

"Our parents don't seem upset. I thought it would take Dee-dee at least two months to get over her disappointment, but she didn't respond."

"Because Brother Jerome spoke to Daddy and Mother Shea said that it wasn't meant to be," Beverly said.

"Yes." Janet chewed her lip. "but I wonder what they told them that made them react so calmly?"

Mrs. Barnett stepped outside. "Get cleaned up I've just invited Brother Jerome to stay for dinner."

Janet suppressed a groan. "Can Valerie stay?"

"Yes, that's fine," Mrs. Barnett said absently. "Just remember to look your best." She went back inside.

Janet stood puzzled. "It's the strangest thing. We see him more now than when you were engaged."

"Perhaps he feels guilty," Beverly said. "And wants to show the community that everything is okay between our family and him."

"Perhaps, but I think he's over doing it. Everywhere I look he seems to be there. He sat beside me on church movie night; he waves at me every Sunday and seeks us out after church. Ugh. It's creepy."

"He wants to ease the gossip."

"I just hope it ends soon." Janet took Valerie's hand. "At his house I was left alone with him for twenty minutes while he showed me his art collection. I never want that to happen again. Please stay with me."

Unfortunately, Valerie didn't get a chance to. Brother Jerome placed himself beside Janet the moment he entered the house and never left it. Francine offered to say the blessing and started before anyone could protest. After several minutes her mother interrupted. "And Lord bless this food and keep it warm." Everyone said "Amen" except Francine who felt annoyed that her blessing had been cut short in front of a guest she'd wanted to impress.

Janet cringed each time Brother Jerome's knee accidentally touched hers, and avoided his gaze. He talked about the property he had inherited in Pennsylvania and the enormous five-bedroom, three-bath colonial there. He then went on to share, in detail, his connections there with several rich and influential people.

Janet wondered if he'd ever come across the scripture *Be not boastful in your manner*. Or had he just glossed over that one.

"You'll love it there, Janet," he said. "They have a fantastic museum I can show you."

Janet forced a smile. "You're very kind."

He returned her smile and looked at Mrs. Barnett whose face beamed. At the end of the meal, Mrs. Barnett jumped up and said, "Maxine and Trudy, help Mrs. Lind with the items for the church yard sale. Francine and Valerie I need the two of you to sort a few things for donation. And Beverly, please help me with something in the kitchen."

Janet looked at her mother with panic. "Isn't there anything you'd like me to do?"

"No. Just finish your meal."

In seconds they were all gone. Janet sat paralyzed left alone with her father, who continued to eat, and Brother Jerome. Suddenly Brother Jerome picked up his napkin and daintily wiped the corner of his mouth. He slowly rested the napkin down. "Let's go for a walk," he announced as though he was about to take her on a grand voyage. He pushed his chair back and stood. "Do you mind Brother Barnett?"

"Not at all. Enjoy yourself."

Janet sent her father a pleading look, but he'd lowered his gaze to his meal.

"Come Janet," Brother Jerome said. "It's a beautiful evening."

Janet looked at her father again and this time caught his eye, but his stern expression made no allowance for disobedience. She reluctantly rose to her feet and followed Brother Jerome into the garden.

"Everything's all set," Brother Jerome said with pride as they walked the small garden path with its broken red bricks and aromatic mint growing along side. He tucked her hand through the crook of his arm. "You have nothing to worry about now."

"What are you talking about?" Janet asked shocked by his brazen behavior.

"Don't be coy anymore, Janet. You know what I mean."

Janet eased her hand away. "I'm afraid I don't know what you're talking about."

"Fine," Brother Jerome said with an indulgent shrug. "If you need me to say it, I will. We are now engaged."

Janet halted and stared at him open-mouthed. "What?"

"I spoke to your father this evening and he gave me permission to take you as my wife. Your mother, of course, is overjoyed because this lifts a heavy burden from her. She'll have a daughter married. I thank God I can be of service this way."

Janet collapsed onto a wooden bench behind her, stunned. "But this can't be true." She placed a trembling hand against her forehead. "This is unbelievable."

"No, my dear. It's very true. We're engaged and will be married before the end of summer."

Janet squeezed her eyes shut. "I'm not hearing this. It's not happening."

Brother Jerome sat beside her and took her hand in his. "I know you were probably upset because I selected your older sister first; however, I want you to know that once we are married, you will always be number one in my heart."

Janet sat speechless. How could her father have agreed to this? He of all people? How could he have put her in this awkward position? She snapped back to attention when she heard his plans for them.

"You're moving?"

"*We're* moving, yes. That's why we will need to get married right away. You'll enjoy Pennsylvania. And the house will suit us."

Janet pulled her hand away and stood. She took a deep breath to steady her voice. "I'm honored and flattered that you would choose me, but I cannot marry you."

"Of course you will. You have to." He stretched his legs out and rested his hands at his sides. "What other prospects are out there for you?"

"I don't know about my prospects, but I do know that I'll make a terrible wife."

"Don't worry my dear. I decided that if Mother Shea's vision hadn't altered, I would have married your sister, and I was willing to accept her many faults. I came to realize that God was testing me to see how humble I am. You're from a Christian family, and no matter what your failings, I am willing to accept them."

Her temper snapped. "Brother Jerome you must listen-"

His face lit up. "Your passionate nature is what I love most. It's invigorating. Don't concern yourself. I know the prospect of being my wife might seem intimidating, but you'll grow into the role. We'll have a quick wedding then you'll be mine." He leaned forward to kiss her.

Janet stepped back with her hands held out. She swallowed then chose her words carefully. "I think I framed my response wrong. I didn't mean I can't marry you. I mean I won't. I am sorry." She turned and ran into the house.

Brother Jerome watched her departure with amusement. His little wildcat. Poor Janet was just overwhelmed by the prospect of leaving her family and having her dream of marrying him come true. He should have been gentler in explaining the move. But he would next time, with Brother Barnett's help. He went inside and saw Mrs. Barnett first. "Where is your husband?"

"In his study. How did things go?"

"She said she wouldn't marry me, but I know that's only because of the shock of moving." He walked past her to Mr. Barnett's study. "Don't worry, I know how to handle women," he said seeing Mrs. Barnett's angry expression. He knocked on the study door then went inside.

Mrs. Barnett stared at the closed door then spun around desperate to find Janet. "Where is your sister?" She demanded when she saw Francine heading to the family room.

"Which one? I could tell you where Maxine and—"

"Janet. Where is Janet?"

Francine pushed up her glasses. "I think she's in her room."

"Then get her."

Francine tapped her chin. "However, she didn't look happy when I told her Valerie had gone home so she may not still be there."

"Then find her," Mrs. Barnett said in a tight voice.

"And tell her to come to me." She stormed into the family room.

Moments later Janet entered. Mrs. Barnett stared at her for a long while then quietly said, "You *will not* ruin this opportunity."

"What opportunity?"

"Brother Jerome. This is the best opportunity for all of us."

Janet began to shake her head. Mrs. Barnett leaped from her chair and pointed at her. "You must marry Brother Jerome. Do you know how much your father and I have sacrificed for you children over the years? Him working two jobs in New York and me having to scrub floors, until my knuckles were raw and my hands calloused. This is God smiling on us. Don't throw it away."

"I don't want to marry him."

"I don't care what you want. You will. This is the way it will be."

Janet's voice cracked with anguish. "My soul belongs to God, my house belongs to my father. Shouldn't my life belong to me?"

They heard heavy footsteps head towards the front door, Mrs. Barnett followed them. "Brother Jerome, you're leaving?"

"Just for the night," he said flashing a bright smile. "We've talked and everything is settled." He left.

"I will not marry him," Janet said in a low voice.

Mrs. Barnett spun around. "Yes, you will. Do you know why I married your father?" She continued before Janet could reply. "Because of my pastor. I knew your father by reputation and nothing else. I knew that he'd returned to the church and he seemed a good man, but I hardly knew him. But he went to our pastor and told him that I'd won his heart and that he wanted to marry me. Soon my father was telling me I was getting married because the pastor said so. I did not go against my father or my pastor. I did as I was told and that was it. And we've had a good marriage and you will too." She seized her daughter's shoulder. "You must do this for us. Remember the scripture *Honor thy father and thy mother.* This is your chance to do so. Besides he is rich."

"I'll make money this summer. I have a chance to work with a very rich woman."

Mrs. Barnett folded her arms in disdain. "With her or for her?" she sniffed. "I've worked for rich people most of my life and trust me, it's nothing special. I've scrubbed their floors, washed their clothes and watched their children. That's not the life I want for you. Your father works, Beverly works, I take in work, but still it's not enough." She opened a desk draw and waved a stack of papers at Janet. "These are requests from back home: Emails and letters that never stop coming." She tossed them one by one in Janet's direction. "People asking for clothes and food and tuition money. People who expect us to help them. Can you lift that burden from our shoulders with this new job?"

Janet picked up the papers strewn on the ground. "I will try." She handed them back to her mother.

Mrs. Barnett snatched them, shoved them back in the draw then slammed it shut. "Trying isn't enough. Your father has been *trying* for over twenty years! Trying to make it big in this country. I thank God for how far we've come, but we haven't come far enough. Your father is a strong man, but it has not made the struggle any easier. I've seen so many of my dreams die away as the years have past." She held out her hands in a plea for understanding. "I've always wanted my daughters to marry well. Make my dream come true."

Janet stared at the ground. "I hope to one day, but I can't marry him, Dee-dee." She raised her gaze. "I will work hard and I will help you."

Mrs. Barnett's hands fell and hung limp by her sides. "So you still refuse to marry him?"

"Yes."

Mrs. Barnett pursed her lips. "Come. Let's see what your father has to say."

CHAPTER 21

Mrs. Barnett dragged Janet towards Mr. Barnett's study. She pounded on the door then opened it and shoved Janet inside.

"What is this?" Mr. Barnett said in surprise.

Mrs. Barnett rested her hands on her hips. "Winston, talk some sense into this *dawta* of yours."

His brows shot up perplexed by the anger in his wife's voice. He had to tread carefully when she was in one of her moods. "Daughter of mine? You no longer hold claim to her?"

"Only if she starts acting as a daughter should." She gestured to Janet as though she were some stranger she'd picked up off the street. "This girl tells me that she won't marry Brother Jerome. She won't have him." Mrs. Barnett pressed her hands together as tears filled her eyes. "No matter what I tell her she won't listen." She pounded her chest. "This girl stomps on my heart every time she opens her mouth."

"My dear, calm yourself," Mr. Barnett said, saddened by his wife's tears.

She stomped her foot. "Tell her to marry him!" He held up his hand and Mrs. Barnett took a deep breath. "Tell her," she said in a softer tone.

Mr. Barnett moved his gaze from his wife's tormented expression to stare at his daughter's cool one. "Is what your mother saying true? You refuse to marry Brother Jerome?"

Janet nodded. That simple gesture made something inside Mrs. Barnett burst, forcing her to raise her hands upward. "My heart is breaking. Dear God in heaven help me." She pointed at Janet as if her hand were a weapon. "Tell her that she must marry him, or I'll never speak to her again."

"Be careful wife, you don't want to give her another reason to say no."

Janet hid a smile, while Mrs. Barnett narrowed her eyes finding no humor in his comment. "Talk to her." She approached his desk and rested her hands on it. "Or I promise you that you will not rest tonight."

Mr. Barnett lowered his voice and said in a gentle voice, "I will. Trust me. Now go. I will talk to her alone."

Mrs. Barnett saw a small glint in her husband's eyes that reassured her and she wiped her tears and nodded. "Good." She turned to Janet. "Listen to your father," she said then left.

"Sit down, Janet," Mr. Barnett said once the door was closed.

Janet sat then waited.

He clasped his hands together and looked at her pensive then sighed. "I know what this is all about. You're afraid."

"I'm not afraid," she said in a clear voice.

He ignored her. "You are afraid that marriage will interfere with your schooling, but I can assure you it will not. Brother Jerome says there are excellent schools in Pennsylvania and you can finish your last year there."

"I can't marry him"

"But you will."

"Daddy—"

He pounded his hand on the desk. "This is not a discussion. You will marry Brother Jerome. Do you hear me?" Janet nodded but he saw the defiance in her eyes. The look propelled him to his feet. "I don't understand you. Only months ago you wanted to leave my house and now that I have arranged that for you, you look at me as if I have betrayed you." He tapped the desk with his forefinger. "I was made to believe that you had grown to like him. He can pay for the rest of your schooling. You'll live in a grand house. A house of your own."

"The house of my husband," Janet said bitterly.

"He will be good to you. I will make sure of that."

"You do not need to make sure of anything because I won't marry him."

Mr. Barnett stared at her his eyes turning to onyx, his tone flat and hard like steel. "Yes. You. Will." He sat back at his desk and resumed what he'd been doing before being interrupted.

Janet felt like all the air had been sucked out of the room and the walls were closing in on her. Her fate was sealed and he would not retract. She had two choices: She would either honor him or dishonor him. He would either claim her as his daughter or... There was no option. Without her family she had nothing. Although she dreamed of freedom, she didn't want it at the risk of being forced into exile. She didn't want to be shut out from the only life she knew. She would cease to exist like her friend Ramani.

But she couldn't obey him without the seeds of her resentment coming to full bloom. *Please don't force me to hate you*, she wanted to scream. She loved him, but at times felt that that love was tearing her apart. Janet stood and stared at him, searching her mind for something to say.

She had to make her father understand. She rushed to his side and fell on her knees, tears filling her eyes. "Daddy, please listen," she said, desperation making her voice shrill. "I'd rather die in this house than live with that man. He is rich, but he is not bright." Mr. Barnett continued to write as though she was not there. "Who will I play chess with? Who will listen to my advice?" She gripped her hands together. "He will trample my soul with his condescension and vanity. Is that the man you want me to give my life to? Please father, my provider, my counselor, please don't force me to do this."

Mr. Barnett set down his pen and turned to her. "I. Gave. My. Word."

"I will leave school immediately and get a job. Name your price and I will pay that debt with every breath in my body."

Mr. Barnett shook his head. "Don't talk like that." He placed a hand on her shoulder and gazed down at her with pain. "If only I could rid you of your unholy passion. Why can't you be like the others? Why can't you do as you're told and listen to our guidance? What has happened to obedience?"

"I wish to be obedient but—"

Mr. Barnett threw up his hand and stared at the ceiling, anger making his accent more prominent. "My God! Why did You choose to saddle me wid a stubborn dawta like this? Am I not a good man? Am I not trying to serve You in all the right ways?"

"Daddy—"

He surged to his feet, knocking over his chair. "We shook hands! I gave him my word. My *word*. You know I am not a rich man, my only golden possession is my word and I do not give it out freely. But you." He pointed at her. "You want mi fi throw it away."

Janet shook her head. "No, I—"

Mr. Barnett took a deep breath, trying to reign in his temper. "You wish to rip the joy from your mother's face. Your mother is so happy. It's done. The future of your sisters remains unstable. Who would want to marry daughters from a man who cannot control his own children?"

"But Beverly can help us."

"What does she have to do with anything?"

"She's been at the Farmers' house a lot lately, and I believe Jeffrey Framer is interested in her."

"He hasn't come to me yet."

"I know, but—"

"That means nothing." He tapped the desk. "This is settled. You will marry Brother Jerome and that is final. It was not to be Beverly, but it will be you!"

Janet lowered her head in defeat. "Very well." She loosened the long braid that hung down her back. "I will not shame or dishonor you." She grabbed a pair of scissors lying on a stack of papers nearby, then lifted her hair. "The end of my life starts right now."

Mr. Barnett grabbed the scissors and threw them across the room. He violently shook her. "Why won't you see reason? Why can't you see dat I've thought of nothing but you? I'm not a monster, and yet you turn away from mi as though I am some kinda beast. Is it wrong for a father to lead his child in the right direction? I have prayed all my life asking God to help mi make all my children happy, but wid you I always seem to fail."

Janet fell to her knees again and clung to his trouser leg, weeping. "Please, I don't want to dishonor you, but I can't marry him. Please, Daddy. Please."

Mr. Barnett shut his eyes feeling his resolve drowning under the flood of her tears. Finally the weight of resignation descended and he touched the top of her head and gently said, "Okay, okay, don't cry. I won't force you to marry him."

Janet leaped to her feet and hugged her father kissing him on both cheeks. "Thank you." She kissed his hands. "Thank you."

Mr. Barnett patted her on the back, pleased to see her joy. "Yes, yes. I'll take care of everything."

Janet kissed her father one last time and then dashed out of the room.

Mr. Barnett picked up the scissors and replaced them on the desk and sat. He looked at the pile of bills waiting to be paid then pushed them aside. Dear Janet. She wouldn't try to leave home now.

He'd been surprised when Brother Jerome had stated that Janet was interested in him, but his wife had said she thought the same when he described her behavior. Because it made her happy, he went along with their assumptions. But they'd been wrong about Janet. Mr. Barnett smiled. He and his daughter were very much alike. How he loved her and now she would remain with him: Safe.

Mr. Barnett opened his drawer and pulled out a picture of Elvis Presley as a young man, thinking of how his life had been tragically cut short. He didn't keep the picture because he liked when Elvis sang the gospels, but because he felt close to him. He used the image as a reminder of what can happen when godly people are tempted by the wrong things. He knew it was only God's grace that he hadn't fathered any illegitimate children or gotten addicted to drugs. Like Elvis, he had grown up in the church and left. But unlike Elvis he'd gone back before succumbing to the demons that could destroy a man's soul.

"I saved her Elvis." He sighed. "If only someone had saved you, but you save me every day and I thank you." He gently put the photo away and rested back satisfied. Then a cold chill swept through him. Now he had to tell his wife.

He didn't have to wait long. Mrs. Barnett burst through the door. "Well?" she demanded.

He held up his hands as though giving God an offering and began to pray. "Lord I thank You for the wisdom and insight you gave me to handle this situation. I thank You for letting my daughter be frank with me so that I knew which way to direct her."

Mrs. Barnett glared at her husband. "Winston."

He put a finger to his lips then continued. "I thank You for giving my wife an understanding heart that will help us move forward in this time. How I thank You." He closed his hands and his eyes then began to mutter the rest of his prayer in silence. He peeked through one eye to see what his wife was doing and saw her pacing. He continued to pray until she finally sat. "Amen," he said then smiled at her as though she'd been patiently waiting for him instead of looking at him with an expression of cold fury. "Yes, my dear?"

"Don't try your tricks with me. What happened?"

"I talked to her."

"And?"

"And she agreed to marry him."

Mrs. Barnett widened her eyes then rose from her seat and jumped up and down, clapping her hands. "Praise God." She stopped. "I knew you would handle her." She turned to the door. "I'll start preparing for—"

"Not yet."

She looked at him curious. "What?"

"I haven't finished."

"What else needs to be said?"

"Plenty. Sit."

"But Winston—"

"Sit, woman. You might faint and I'm in no mood to catch you."

"I've never done such a thing," she grumbled returning to her seat. "What do you have to say?"

"There won't be a wedding."

Mrs. Barnett gaped at him unable to breathe. "Didn't you just say that she'd agree to marry him?"

"Yes, but I decided that I didn't want her to."

"But you gave your word."

"I changed my mind."

Her voice hardened. "Change it back. Everything is settled. Don't do this to me, Winston. We need this marriage."

"No, we don't. Business is picking up and Janet will be working for a rich woman this summer."

"It's not the same. Winston, please—"

"I've made up my mind."

"But—"

"My decision is final," he said in a voice that allowed no argument. "Other men will come along that will suit her better. Trust me."

Mrs. Barnett gaped at him, but knew she couldn't argue with him. His word was law. She burst into tears.

Mr. Barnett came from around his desk and rested his hand on his wife's shoulder. "Quiet, my dear. It will be okay, I promise. God has better things in store for us. In time you will agree. Besides you may have a wedding yet."

She sniffed and looked at him suspicious. "What do you mean?"

"It seems our Beverly has captured Jeffrey's favor." He shrugged. "Who knows, with a little more prompting you may get your wish."

She wiped her eyes suddenly thoughtful. "Yes, they do make a handsome pair."

He nodded.

Mrs. Barnett slowly rose to her feet, her eyes brightening with promise. "And he has more money than Brother Jerome."

"Yes," he said leading her to the door.

"And a young man like that would give us wonderful grandchildren."

He opened the door and gently pushed her out. "Yes." She still continued talking to herself as he closed the door behind her.

"THANK YOU FOR MEETING ME," Mr. Barnett said as he entered Brother Jerome's office. As a bank manager, Brother Jeromes' space was well furnished and impressive in size. Mr. Barnett sat in a chair that looked comfortable. He soon discovered it was overstuffed and stiff.

"Always a pleasure."

"Yes." He cleared his throat and shifted in his seat. "My daughter has disappointed me."

"How so?"

"Although, Janet was—I mean is—willing to marry you, her behavior let me know that she is still young and has a wild streak that needs to be tamed."

Brother Jerome leaned forward eager. "Yes, I had noticed it when she ran away, but I am more than willing to tame it."

"And she still talks back."

"Talks back?"

He nodded. "Yes. All the time. To her mother. To me. No man wants a wife who talks back."

Brother Jerome rubbed his chin. "That is a problem."

"I could not in good conscience give you a daughter like that. A woman who is too hot can burn a man's reputation."

"Hmm."

"You deserve someone more ripe and seasoned."

Brother Jerome grinned. "But Janet is spicy."

"Too much spice can make a man ill."

Brother Jerome leaned back deep in thought. Brother Barnett was right. He needed to think sensibly. He'd wanted Janet to fulfill some—many, if he was honest—lustful urges, but a man in his position couldn't be led by such wanton emotion. And, besides, who would know a daughter better than her father? "Yes. Thank you, Brother Barnett. Thank you for looking out for me. Let's consider the engagement dissolved."

Mr. Barnett stood and held out his hand suppressing a smile.

And with that everyone was happy. Brother Jerome was grateful he'd avoided a bad marriage, Mrs. Barnett was hopeful to hear news for Beverly and Mr. Barnett had his house back in order.

~

IN THE SUMMER, "LITTLE CARNIVAL", an annual event for children and teens was held in Hamsford to show off the rich culture of the Jamaican residents. It consisted of a clamorous and colorful parade downtown where participants wore elaborate costumes, steel bands played reggae and competed for prizes, and an array of seafood dishes were in abundance. Given the region's location along the Chesapeake steam blue crabs, crab cakes, and lobster were the items of the day. And, of course, there was the obligatory beer drinking contest. Janet and her sisters never missed this event, although they had never been allowed to participate.

June turned into July and Janet flourished with her work at The House of Design, learning faux painting and *trompe l'oeil* under the patient tutelage of one of Mrs. Blakemore's partners. To her joy, Beverly spent many weekends at the Farmer house, which made Mrs. Barnett very happy.

However Valerie was less enthused when Janet told her. "I still don't think you should make too much out of it," she said as she and Janet walked the marketplace.

"It's wonderful. I know we'll hear good news soon." Janet saw Darika who shook her head at Janet's silent question. Janet looked away then halted and stared at something in the distance. "Oh no."

"What?"

"There's Brother Jerome." Janet was about to turn when he saw them.

"There's no need to look so horrified. He's not going to attack you," Valerie said. Janet had told her about the engagement and because it was quickly dissolved she was the only one, beside the Barnett family, who knew.

Brother Jerome stopped in front of them and offered Janet a wide smile determined to be cordial. He knew that young women's hearts took time to heal and didn't want to be insensitive. He asked about their families and was about to leave when Valerie offered him a bright smile and asked about his property.

He was surprised at first then pleased, eager to tell her about it. He talked at length before Janet interrupted him saying they had an errand to run and said goodbye. He watched them leave thinking that Sister Valerie wasn't as plain as he'd previously thought.

"Dear God," Janet groaned dragging her friend away. "I thought he'd never stop talking. Is he still watching us?"

Valerie glanced back. "Yes."

"Then we'll have to go to the far side of the market until he leaves. Thank you for diverting what could have been an awkward situation."

"Hmm."

Janet looked back to see that Brother Jerome was out of view. "I couldn't have handled him better myself."

Valerie smiled, but didn't respond. She had no intention of telling her friend that she hadn't started the conversation with Brother Jerome to smooth over the situation. It was an attempt to turn his attention in her direction. All that Janet disliked about him, Valerie knew she could tolerate.

She had the extra years to know the loneliness of being unmarried and hoped to change that very soon. She anticipated that it would take time, effort and strategy. At church she made sure to compliment Brother Jerome every time he spoke. She invited him for dinner, and started attending both Monday and Wednesday night bible study, which were lead by Brother Jerome. She took note of his schedule, making sure to "accidentally" meet him in the market and in Anita Maxwell's bakery, where he loved to buy pastries and cakes. Yes, she was a shrewd woman with a mission and had anticipated everything in order to accomplish her goal.

What she didn't anticipate was a rival.

anet watched in amazement as she stood in the back of the church. "I must have been adopted," she said, watching her sister Francine talking to Brother Jerome and gushing about his latest speech. "You should see how she prepares herself for church. Three weeks in a row she's asked me to help her with her hair. Goodness look how he eats it up. He loves it. Ugh... I think he likes her."

"She looks very nice," Valerie said in a neutral voice.

"But she's still plain, poor thing."

"We can't all be beauties, Janet."

Janet turned to her friend ashamed. "No, I didn't mean it like that."

"I know," Valerie said quickly. "I'm just tired. Excuse me." She hurried out of the church desperate to be alone and walked home. If she were a woman easily led to tears she would have wept. But she didn't, although she felt her hopes dissipating; her weeks of effort coming to nothing—again. Thirteen years of hope dashed. She'd noticed Francine's attention to Brother Jerome before anyone else had. Every time Valerie sang or played,

Francine would make sure she was on the program and recite a poem. Every time Valerie complimented Brother Jerome, Francine complimented him more. In their bible study class, Francine would ask him questions, wisely appealing to his ego.

No one really knew Francine. Her family only saw her as plain, but Valerie saw much more. She saw a young woman filled with the same hopes and desires she had: To be looked at, to be cherished. She was somewhat silly, but she was still young and that was what hurt the most.

Valerie knew she could never be young again. Everyone knew Brother Jerome favored the Barnett girls. He admired Brother Barnett and the conservative upbringing of his daughters. She knew that he'd probably convinced himself that Francine would make him a proper wife and he would enter into a family he respected.

Valerie turned when she heard quick, pounding footsteps then someone call out her name. She turned and saw Janet running towards her. She stopped in front of her and said in a breathless rush, "Valerie, I've upset you and I'm sorry."

"It's okay."

"But I've hurt you."

Valerie began to walk again. "It's not you," she said with a bitter smile. "It's life."

"What's wrong?"

"I just need time alone."

Janet took her arm concerned. "But Valerie—"

She yanked her arm away. "Janet, please. I just want to be left alone."

Janet backed away startled. "Okay."

"Thank you," she said in a calmer tone then walked away. When Valerie reached her house, she did not go inside. Instead she went around to the back garden and sat in the gazebo among the lush aroma of lilacs, roses, peonies and the buzz of honeybees.

The Williams' garden was one of the grandest in Hamsford because they could afford the landscaping and weekly lawn care. But at that moment, sitting amongst its vast beauty, Valerie felt like a weed. Despite the fine clothes, parties, high profile social events, and her job at her father's company she still carried the stain of being unmarried. And she had lost another opportunity to remove it.

Valerie sat, feeling defeated. No she wasn't a beauty, but some of the happiest women she knew were not. Surely there were men who would look beyond her face and age and take time to get to know her. She had dreamed of getting married since she was a little girl. She wanted to be a wife, to cook for and care for a man. She wanted to be a mother and have three or four children. She wanted to have her own house to decorate and clean. She knew she would make any man the perfect help mate. But no one had given her the chance.

Tears swelled up in her eyes, but she rigidly held them in check. She was too sensible to deceive herself. Brother Jerome had given her no hint or sign of his interest and he'd certainly never looked at her as he had Francine. She took a deep breath and blinked until all her tears were gone.

She hadn't come to the garden just to be alone and feel sorry for herself. She also came for her cigarettes. She found them under a hollow rock where she'd hidden her carton then lit one and took a long drag. She exhaled, feeling all her anxieties slipping away. She knew it was a bad habit, but it made her feel good. She stretched out her legs and decided to allow herself to enjoy being out in the sun. She would not wallow in self-pity, always hopeful that new opportunities would present themselves. She inhaled letting the smoke fill her lungs and shut her eyes then exhaled. *Good, plain, old Sister Valerie smoking in the garden.* What an odd sight she must be and how they would gossip if they knew. Valerie opened her eyes and blew two smoke rings and watched them fade into the sky. If God ordained that she was not to marry, then she would remain single and dedicate her life to the church. She glanced up and saw a hanging vine and stood to twist it around a post. When she did that, she saw Brother Jerome coming up the drive.

Her heart stopped as she watched him head to her front door. Valerie opened her mouth to call out to him then realized she still held her cigarette. She quickly stubbed it out, hid the evidence of her habit then sprayed the area with an aerosol can she hid nearby. She then popped a peppermint in her mouth and called out his name. He turned to her.

"What an unexpected pleasure to see you here," she said as he approached.

"Yes," he said, a little uneasy.

"Would you like something to drink?"

"No, no. I want to talk to you."

Valerie sat down and watched him, worried. He seemed agitated and her hopes dimmed. Perhaps he came to talk about his feelings for Francine because she was a close friend of the Barnetts. She steeled herself and gestured to the seat beside her. He sat, but didn't say anything.

Soon the silence lengthened into awkwardness and Valerie felt forced to speak. "I always enjoy talking to you. What's on your mind?"

"You left the church early before I could talk to you."

"I didn't know you wanted to speak to me."

"No, you wouldn't." He fell silent again.

"I saw you speaking with Sister Francine," she said determined to introduce the topic, although it pained her.

"Yes." He smiled. "She's an interesting young woman."

"Yes," Valerie agreed in a dull voice certain that she'd have two cigarettes once he left. She stood. "Are you sure you wouldn't like something to drink?"

Brother Jerome held his hand out to her then let it fall. "Please, sit down. I don't mean to take up your time, but I don't know how to begin."

Valerie sat beside him and clasped her hands together, wanting the moment to end, but she smiled instead. "Just start, Brother Jerome."

"This isn't how it's usually done, but after the fiasco with the —" He stopped and rubbed his chin unsure. "But then again I could be reproached, so I won't speak of it."

Valerie touched his arm, eager to end the suspense. "Brother Jerome. I know how you feel, but as your friend I suggest you do it. I won't fault you and I doubt anyone else will either."

"You think so? You understand?"

"Yes."

"And you won't think badly of me?"

"No. Please, Brother Jerome. I am your friend and I will support you in this."

He grabbed her hand and kissed it. "I knew I was right to come to you."

"Yes," she said startled by his exuberance.

"I sensed that you wouldn't take offense to this informal way." He kissed her hand again.

Valerie stared at him. "I don't—Brother Jerome, what are you talking about?"

"Our engagement. I want you to marry me."

Valerie's mouth fell open; he took it for joy and said, "I know I should be asking your father first, but oh, my dear Valerie. I wanted to make sure how you felt." He kissed her on the cheek then hugged her. "You've made me very happy. I will speak to your father at once." He raced to her front door. A few minutes later her mother ran out and hugged her with such force Valerie couldn't breathe. Next her father congratulated her and her sister and brother realized, with joy, that their dear sister would not die an old maid.

Valerie's mother hugged her again then lifted her collar and sniffed. "Do I smell cigarette smoke?" she said appalled.

"That's my fault," Brother Jerome said. "I was briefly at the market in town."

"Of course," Sister Williams said accepting his explanation then turned and went back inside.

Brother Jerome briefly shared a significant look with Valerie, then followed her. Naturally he stayed for dinner and Valerie sat beside him with smug satisfaction. She had accomplished her goal. She was not a romantic and did not expect men or matrimony to give her any real happiness. She was too observant to know some did not. But she was ambitious and her goal was to be a wife and mother, and now she would soon achieve that. She knew it would raise her above the pitying looks and the upper-middle class status of her family.

Valerie looked at her intended with an uncritical eye and saw him for what he was and his flaws didn't matter. She did not need to love him or like him very much. She just needed to marry him and no longer be a burden to her father, and a worry to her mother. Now she wouldn't have to care about her plain features or advancing years.

But there was one thing that did make her uneasy—Janet's reaction. Although she had learned to guard herself against the thoughts or feeling of others, Janet's opinions mattered.

She shared her uneasiness with Brother Jerome as they sat in the dining room finishing their dessert together. Her family had left them alone.

Brother Jerome rested his spoon down. "Don't worry. I will handle it. I would hate for any jealousy to break up such a solid friendship. She can't fault you for accepting me and in time her feelings for me will dim, although they may never fully disappear."

"Yes," she said, feeling no need to correct him. "But it's still a delicate issue. I need to tell her first."

❧

JANET SAT on her bed and stared at Valerie horrified. "Of course you're joking. You just told me this incredible story because you want to have a good laugh."

"It is not a joke," Valerie said in a grave voice.

Janet jumped to her feet. "But it has to be." She shook her head stupefied. "I'd seen him eyeing you in "that way" and I knew he was giving you special notice, and I'd thought to warn you. But I'd never thought it would lead to this!" She gripped the bedpost. "You're engaged to Brother Jerome? You're going to *marry* him?"

"Yes," Valerie said in a quiet, but firm voice. She did not have Janet's fiery spirit and could always calm it with a rational soothing tone. "Why are you so surprised? Do you think that all men you dislike, other women are bound to dislike as well? Do you think because you believe a man is unmarriageable that everyone should agree? Come on Janet, is that naïveté or arrogance?"

Hit with that cool reprimand, Janet sunk back down on the bed and hung her head. "You're right. I shouldn't be so disrespectful. It's your decision. I'm sorry." She took a deep breath, tracing a pattern on her skirt. "I am happy that Brother Jerome has impressed you so much that you want to spend your life with him. I wish both of you many years of happiness."

Valerie lifted her friend's chin, forcing Janet to look at her then smiled with affection. "You little liar. You don't mean a word of it." Janet looked at her in surprise and Valerie's smile grew. "I know you, Janet. I listened to your words but read the expression on your face. I know how you feel. Yes, it is a strange incidence, especially when he asked you to marry him only a few weeks ago."

Janet frowned. "And my sister before that."

"Yes, but if you take the time to reflect you will understand and applaud what I've accomplished. I want security and position; Brother Jerome will give me that, along with his family ties, his property and his connections. I want you to be happy for me, because I am happy."

Janet sighed. "Because you're getting what you want I can truthfully say I am glad."

Valerie hugged her, "Thank you Janet. That means everything to me."

Janet hugged her back, feeling numb. *I make a poor substitute for Ramani, don't I?* Valerie had once said. Sometimes she felt that was true, but she loved Valerie and her friend hadn't caused her as much trouble. After Valerie left, Janet paced her room trying to understand, but she couldn't. Valerie and *Brother Jerome?*

The thought made her want to laugh, but mostly it made her want to cry. Janet tried her best to shut it from her mind.

However, when Mrs. Barnett found out about the upcoming wedding, Janet had no choice but to face it.

"That Williams woman is going to have a daughter married," she announced to Beverly and Janet as she put on her shawl in the foyer. She glanced at her image in the mirror then looked at her two eldest daughters. "I should have been preparing for a wedding. But I'm not. She is. She only has two daughters and I have five," she said holding out five fingers with such venom it looked like an obscene gesture.

Janet shook her head. "But Brother Jerome is —"

"Still a man. You may not like everything about him, but he has one special power: he can turn a woman into a wife. And you both had your chance. Although I can't blame you, my dear Beverly."

"What about me?"

Mrs. Barnett sent Janet a cool look. "Somehow you bewitched your father."

"Don't give up hope. Beverly is close friends with the Farmers especially, Jeffrey."

Mrs. Barnett stroked Beverly's cheek. "I know and you'll have exciting news for me soon?"

"I hope so," Beverly said.

Mrs. Barnett nodded, pleased. "Good. You will catch Jeffrey Farmer for a husband and rectify this." She swung open the door. "But now I have to go and hear all of Sister Williams' news." She left.

Beverly turned to Janet. "I wish you wouldn't keep mentioning Jeffrey Farmer. We're just friends and nothing more."

"I'm sure he's just gathering up the courage. I've no doubt that you'll be getting a proposal very soon."

Beverly smiled, but there was worry in her eyes.

Errol nearly fell out of his chair when he saw the invitation. He ran into the kitchen where the scent of jerk chicken filled the air. "Sigonya!"

"What is it now!"

He waved the invitation. "Dat Peter fellow get himself another woman."

"To marry?"

"Yes. Here's the invitation."

Sigonya sent a worried glance to her Aunt who was shelling green peas.

Errol followed her gaze. "She might like to go."

"She wouldn't know the difference. We're not going. We'll just send dem a gift."

THE NEWS of Valerie's impending wedding didn't matter much to Maxine and Trudy although they did look forward to the celebration. Francine was disappointed but quickly rebounded when she convinced herself that he was too old anyway.

The Barnetts invited the Williams over for dinner with Brother Jerome. Janet watched her friend as she sat next to him feeling a keen sense of loss. Brother Jerome would be taking Valerie away. Janet had hoped to release her friend to a worthier man. She tried to be happy for her, but knew her friendship with Valerie would never be the same. As she worked on a portrait for them, Janet tried to reconcile how much everything would soon change.

VALERIE'S WEDDING was one of the biggest events to occur in Hamsford that year. The church had been transformed into a beautiful sanctuary. Pale blue, silk sheer curtains draped the stained glass windows; cream colored silk cushions camouflaged the church's drab wooden benches. A trellis arch stood in the entry way of the chapel, and another at the altar where the couple said their vows. Billowing white satin ribbons and yellow and white miniature roses were attached at the end of each bench, forming an elegant pathway for the wedding party to descend.

Three girls and three boys, between the ages of three and five, preceded the wedding party. Each carried small baskets filled with white petals, which they threw on the red carpet down the center of the church. And every few seconds the bright flash of a camera would pierce the air.

At the reception, which was held immediately afterwards in the hotel ballroom, Janet sat in a chair watching everyone: unsupervised children chased each other, Sisters of the church commented on the decorations, Brothers commented on the food, and the rest of the townspeople talked about whatever came to mind. Janet turned her attention to the trio ensemble playing music and while there was no dancing the guests didn't complain because the enormous banquet was enough.

Following lengthy toasts, given by what seemed like everyone who attended; it was time to cut the cake. The wedding cake was a five-tired, rum cake expertly decorated, with icing resembling finely woven Italian lace and trimmed with edible gold leaf motifs. Alcohol flowed, but not too freely, drunkenness was strictly forbidden. However, a few guests did appear inebriated but no one said anything because they were not church members. Suddenly, loud sucking noises, coming from a table nearby, assaulted Janet's ears. She didn't need to turn around to know that it was the Gordon family. They were among the poorer residents of Hamsford and when eating meat of any kind, loved to suck out the bone marrow then chew the bone. "You children don't know how to eat," Mrs. Gordon once chastised her when Janet had stared at her amazed. "People in many countries could survive on what you throw away." Janet knew the Gordons would likely leave the reception with their bags full of food, but it was expected and no one cared.

"You're worried?"

Janet looked up and saw an extra wide straw hat with large blue and black flowers and a hand beaded trim. Her gaze fell to Mother Shea's face. "Why would I be?"

"Because that should have been your sister."

Janet tilted her head. "You envisioned she'd be with someone else."

Mother Shea narrowed her gaze. "Only because he'd been led astray by some woman, but he never told me her name."

"Perhaps she's the one he's marrying."

"No, I don't think that's her. Sister Valerie doesn't stir up such lascivious thoughts in a man." She stared at Janet, who boldly stared back with a slight smile.

Beverly rushed up to her. "Come on Janet. Valerie is about to throw the bouquet."

Mother Shea walked away.

Janet watched her leave. "You can catch it for me."

Beverly glanced at the gathering crowd of women then sat beside Janet. "You haven't been yourself all day. Is it because of Durand? I'm surprised he's here I know, but has he said something to upset you? I know how much you dislike him."

"No, I've hardly noticed him actually." That was only partially true, everyone noticed his entrance, as people always seemed to, but Janet was too preoccupied to care. "It's just this wedding." She took a sip of her sparkling cider then set it down. "The idea is so appalling. No matter what angle I try to see it from, it is all so wrong."

"Wrong?" Beverly said surprised. "Have you seen Valerie's face? Look at how proud her parents are. It's a glorious day! They will be perfect for each other and will create their own happiness. You may not like him, but he's not an awful man and he passes the JCE test."

Janet took another sip of her drink. "And that's all that matters," she mumbled.

"She's free Janet. At least be happy about that."

"From the house of her father into the house of her husband."

"Yes. We cannot choose our fathers but we can choose our husbands and she's made her choice. It's *her* choice Janet. Accept that."

Janet sighed finally facing what she didn't want to see. Valerie's dreams were different from hers, and it was okay. "I thought I knew her, but you're right. I will be happy for her. She'll be free of this place and her father's rules." Janet squeezed her sister's hand. "At least I know I will fully approve of your husband. I know he'll make you happy." She glanced at Jeffrey. He sat at one of the tables with his sisters and Frederick. They made a handsome group. Tanya and Karen wore elegant designer outfits, Jeffrey a dark blue suit, while Frederick sported a fitted Italian double-breasted suit, accented with a bold striped tie.

People were still uneasy around him, but the Williams felt they had to invite him because he'd attended their last party. He was still considered aloof, but people had grown accustomed to his mannerisms and thought of him as they did the three stray cats that roamed the neighborhood—he belonged there but no one would claim him.

At the beginning of the reception, Janet and Beverly had exchanged customary 'hellos' with them, but each had been so busy that they hadn't gotten an opportunity to say anything more.

Beverly sighed. "Janet, are you listening to me? Jeffrey makes me happy now, but I'm not going to look into the future because he does not seem to be inclined to want to marry."

"Just give him time, he will."

Valerie interrupted Beverly's reply by rushing over to Janet and pulling her out of her chair. "Come with me." She dragged Janet to the stage then grabbed the microphone. "May I please have your attention?" The room quieted and everyone turned to her then she handed the microphone to Brother Jerome. "Husband," she said as though she'd been calling him that for years.

Brother Jerome turned to crowd. "We know it is not customary to open gifts at the reception but this was one gift we wanted to share with all of you. As you know we will be leaving Hamsford and starting a new life in Pennsylvania. Thanks to Sister Janet, my wife and I will always have you close."

"What is he talking about?" Janet whispered, wanting to leap off the stage.

Valerie sent her an enigmatic smile. "You'll see."

Brother Jerome continued. "I will always have a memory to hold onto of this special day. Of the love of a dear friend. Of the kindness of a close neighbor—"

As Brother Jerome droned on, Valerie instructed her father to bring out the gift.

Brother Williams set the covered canvas on an easel then left the stage. Valerie looked at her husband and whispered, "Now."

He completed his speech then lifted the cover off, revealing an oil painting Janet had done. It was of Valerie in her wedding dress surrounded by images of her life in Hamsford. The portrait stunned everyone and applause soon broke through the silence.

Valerie turned to Janet and hugged her then drew away. "I know I wasn't supposed to look at it yet, but I couldn't help myself. When Daddy saw it, it was the first time he called me beautiful."

Janet's throat tightened. "You've always been beautiful to me."

Valerie blinked back her tears. "Oh, my dear, dear friend, I'm going to miss you." She looked at Janet and held her hands. "We will be back for the dedication of the expanded library in the fall and you must come and visit."

"I will."

Brother Jerome took Janet's arm and handed her the microphone. "Please say a few words."

"What?"

"Say something," he urged. "I know you're not as skilled at these things as I am, but don't let that intimidate you. You're among friends. Go ahead."

What could she say? Janet awkwardly took the microphone and glanced at the crowd then looked back at the new couple. Valerie beamed and Brother Jerome looked proud and she let her prior feelings fade away. Today, at this moment, she would be joyful. "I truly don't deserve the applause. If there is to be congratulations, let it be for this couple. Brother Jerome I know that you will cherish my dear friend and take care of her. And my beloved Valerie I know you will be a wonderful wife. To the both of you, God bless."

Everyone applauded again and Janet looked at Beverly for reassurance. Her sister nodded and mouthed, "Well done" and beside her Jeffrey winked. Frederick's expression was enigmatic, but Mother Shea's was not. Her penetrating glare shot across the room. Janet lifted her head higher in defiance. She would not wilt. The festivities continued into the early morning, with the married couple leaving in a limousine, shortly after two in the morning. They were scheduled to fly to Italy that day for their honeymoon. After some coaxing, the wedding planner was finally able to get the last guest to leave at five o'clock.

A week after the wedding Janet returned to the university to complete her final year expecting another uneventful semester. Then she met him.

CHAPTER 24

"Are you going?" Marisa asked Janet as she stood in the hallway reading a flyer about lecturing artist, Russell Wilcox. This semester her green streaks were purple and red.

"I'm not sure."

"The man is fantastic. Have you seen his work?"

"Yes, he is impressive, but not all artists are great speakers. Remember Manfred Walters?"

"Oh yes, that was awful. I considered giving him a brownie just to see what would happen."

Janet looked at her confused. "What would a brownie do?"

Marisa began to smile. "You know I'm not talking about a regular brownie, right?"

She frowned. "No."

"Your parents are from Jamaica and you don't know about brownies?" When Janet continued to look blank Marisa said, "Laced with marijuana."

"We don't believe in that."

"I'm not surprised. It's amazing all the things you don't know about. It's like you're from another world."

Janet turned back to the flyer, used to comments like that. "He's not bad looking."

"Better in person. I saw a glimpse of him yesterday. I think you should go. It's free and only thirty minutes." She shook her head. "I can't believe he's the artist in residence this semester."

"Hmm." Janet pulled out a sticky candy and offered it to Pamela.

She hesitated. "What is that?"

"A coconut drop," a male voice said behind them. They spun around and looked up at Russell Wilcox. "I haven't seen these in years. May I?"

Speechless, Janet held it out to him.

He popped the candy in his mouth. "Delicious."

Janet continued to stare. The man was beautiful. He had fine symmetrical features that begged to be captured on film or paper. He looked down at both of them through liquid brown eyes that reminded her of melting chocolate, and then he smiled—his strong, white teeth complimenting his brown skin. He held out his hand. "Who should I thank?"

"I'm Janet Barnett and this is Marisa Espinoza."

"A pleasure to meet you both. Are you Jamaican?" he asked looking directly at Janet.

"I was born there but my parents lived there much longer than I did."

"Which part are they from?"

She told him and he nodded. "I know that place well. Where did you get these?"

"There's a wonderful marketplace close to where I live. I could give you directions."

"I'm new around here. Perhaps you could show me."

Janet didn't speak until Marisa nudged her. "Yes," she said in a rush. "I'd love to."

"Good, I look forward to it. I'm free tomorrow. Will that work?"

"Yes."

"I'll see you then." He took another sweet then walked off.

Marisa grinned. "I bet you're going to the lecture now."

Janet kept her gaze on Russell as he walked down the hall. "Nothing could stop me."

FEMALE STUDENTS CROWDED the lecture hall, leaving little room for their male counterparts. They sat in theatre-styled seats, listening to his every word. When the presentation was over, they rushed up and surrounded him, flooding him with questions. Janet knew it was impossible to try to talk to him so she headed for the door.

"Janet," he called out to her.

She turned and saw the envious eyes of the other female students. "Yes?"

"Don't forget."

She felt her cheeks grow warm, flattered that he would seek her out like that. "I won't."

Janet barely remembered how she got home or what she ate for dinner. She sat in the family room without hearing her sisters fussing or what was on TV. Later that night she slowly changed for bed unable to recall any events of that day except for one.

When someone knocked on her door she absently said, "Come in."

Beverly entered and stared at her worried. "What's wrong with you?"

"What do you mean?"

"Did something happen at school today? You don't seem like yourself."

"I'm not." Janet grabbed her pillow and hugged it. "I'm not sure who I am." She sat on her bed. "Today I met the most amazing man." She hugged the pillow tighter. "Smart, attractive, talented. His name is Russell Wilcox and he's an artist in residence at the university. I heard his lecture and he is wonderful. He's so easy to talk to and doesn't have airs even though he's famous. And he's Jamaican by birth."

"Someone you can fall in love with?" Beverly asked.

Janet tossed the pillow on the bed then rested her head on it. "I'm in danger but I'm not there yet. Tomorrow he wants me to show him the market."

"By yourself?"

Janet sat up. "It's nothing improper. He's just not familiar with the area and I offered to show him around."

"I think I should go with you. I could get off of work early and meet you."

"Fine, you'll get to see how wonderful he is too."

Beverly certainly agreed when she met him and so did every woman who saw him in the marketplace. Even Darika mouthed 'Who is that?' when she spotted him and Janet just winked. The men liked him as well. Although he was an artist he didn't have the flamboyant mannerisms that would put them off and they accepted him quickly.

The following week Janet invited Russell for dinner, where he impressed the entire Barnett clan. Mr. Barnett liked his deference to him, Mrs. Barnett liked the fact that he was Jamaican and single and although he was an artist, at least he was established, which meant he was employed. She slyly asked about his religious affiliation and was pleased with his stories about his mother and his church upbringing. So Mrs. Barnett ascertained he passed the JCE test.

The two younger Barnetts didn't care about the test; they

liked his good looks. Francine didn't find him intellectual enough to interest her, although she also liked him.

To everyone's surprise, Russell attended church that Sunday and immediately became a prize all the single women in the church wanted to win. He soon became a fixture by visiting Mother Shea and other church members, and influential people in the community on a regular basis.

Within three weeks their church claimed him as one of their own and respectfully referred to him as Brother Wilcox. Although the women in the community tried to catch his attention it soon became clear that the Barnetts held precedence. He ate Sunday dinners at their house, and twice took Janet to Movie Night at the church.

Janet loved all the attention and made sure to be in his company every chance she got. When she heard that he was interested in architecture she offered to show him the construction for the new library addition and persuaded Beverly to come along. That day Janet dressed with special care and wore one of her stylish Sunday hats that people at church told her framed her face.

"You look wonderful," Beverly said when she saw her.

Janet laughed. "Good that's exactly what I want to hear."

"It's impressive," Russell said staring at the massive structure. Autumn leaves scurried past pushed by a gusty wind that rattled the branches of surrounding trees.

"Yes," Janet said, holding on to her hat.

"Jeffrey is very pleased to finish his father's work," Beverly added.

"He has the eye," Russell said. He ran up to the side wall and rested his hand there. "And do you know what this would be perfect for?"

"A mural," Janet said.

His gaze met hers. "You can read my mind. That might be dangerous."

Her heart began to race and there was tingling in the pit of her stomach. "Do you have any other dangerous thoughts?"

"Only when it comes to pretty women."

Before Janet could reply, a gust of wind blew off her hat and sent it tumbling behind the building. She and Russell raced after it. Russell reached it first and bent to pick it up when the wind playfully blew it out of reach and sent him running again. Janet laughed as she watched him. Finally he captured it and jogged back to her.

He gave a low bow. "For my lady."

She held out her hand. "Thank you, sir."

He gently placed the hat on her head and said in a low voice, "The pleasure is all mine."

Their eyes met and for a moment nothing else mattered.

"Janet," Beverly said pulling her sleeve. "Look who's here."

Janet reluctantly turned her gaze away and saw Jeffrey.

"This is a happy surprise," he said.

Beverly gestured to the building. "I see it's coming along."

"Yes, we're right on schedule. Frederick and I were just looking over details. I don't know where he disappeared to." He looked around then shrugged. "You'll be coming to the opening, right?"

"Yes, we'll be there," Janet said. Before she could introduce Russell, Jeffrey spotted something behind them and said, "Good. There he is."

Janet turned and saw Frederick with Milton. When Milton saw them, he looked up for permission then burst into a run to greet them. Janet knelt down and petted him and turned her cheek to let him lick her face. Frederick approached them at a more sedate pace but looked pleased to see them. "Hello," he said with a warmth that surprised Janet.

"Hello," they replied then Janet noticed that Russell hadn't turned and felt embarrassed that she hadn't introduced him. "I'm sorry. Let me introduce you to our friend, Russell Wilcox."

"Nice to meet you," Russell said to Jeffrey then slowly turned. "Durand."

Frederick's face became a hard mask. He snapped his fingers and said, "Milton. Come." Once the dog came to his side he nodded to Beverly and Janet, muttered, "Excuse me," then walked on.

Jeffrey glanced at his friend confused, then looked at them and offered a sheepish grin. "Umm, it was nice to meet you. I hope I see you all at the dedication."

"We won't miss it," Janet said.

His gaze lingered a moment on Beverly as if he wanted to say more then he said, "I'm glad," before running after Frederick.

Janet turned to Russell to ask his opinion of Frederick's rude behavior, but before she could, Russell apologized that he had to take care of an important errand and left. She didn't get to speak to him again until a few days later when he unexpectedly appeared at their church game night. She was further pleased when he sat besides her at the refreshment table and brought up the subject she couldn't.

"I see that you are good friends with Jeffrey Farmer," he said, breaking a chocolate chip cookie in half.

"Yes. We've known him since we were children."

He took a bite. "Do you know much about his friend?"

"No. Only that he's helping Jeffrey with the building."

He nodded then sipped his drink. "How long have you known Frederick Durand? Has he been in the area long?"

"Long enough. A few months. He knows a lot about architecture apparently and that's why Jeffrey's using him and it's my understanding he has a lot of property and money."

"Yes, I know about his background." Russell rested his arms on the table and sighed wistful. "Probably more than most."

"Really?" she said intrigued.

"Yes. But my opinion probably won't agree with the way most people see him." He finished eating his cookie.

"Almost everyone in Hamsford can't stand him. He is arrogant and cold."

Russell wiped cookie crumbs from his fingers. "Do you know how long he plans to stay here?"

Janet shook her head. "Hopefully he'll leave right after the dedication. At least that's *my* hope."

Russell sat back and studied her, curious. "You surprise me. Most people can't see beyond the name and the money."

"We are spiritual people. We respect money, but we certainly don't worship it or a person who has a lot of it."

"Hmmm," he said unconvinced.

Janet stiffened concerned. "I hope he won't stop you from enjoying being here in Hamsford."

"Durand won't keep me from doing anything I want to. He never has, although he's tried," Russell said in a grim tone.

"He's probably tried to tame that wonderful wild spirit in you. A man like him wouldn't understand it."

"Exactly. His family has a large property in Jamaica and my mother worked there. We used to play together when he'd come home on holidays from his schooling abroad. His father took a liking to me and had me do odd jobs. He paid for my schooling, which allowed me to attend private boarding schools and the finest art institute on the island. He had high hopes for me and put me in his will. But when he died, Durand did not honor it."

"What do you mean?"

"If I had my choice I would not be an artist in residence. I would hide myself away and paint, and only come out for gallery openings and interviews. But that is, unfortunately, not my lot in life. I have to make a living. It wasn't supposed to be this way; Mr. Durand had specified that I would always be financially secure as long as I continued doing my art. But Frederick and I had a disagreement." He pulled up his sleeve and showed her a large scar on his forearm. "You probably don't know this but he always carries a knife with him."

"Yes, I did notice that," Janet said remembering the incident at the train track.

"Well, one day we argued and he gave me this scar and gave away my inheritance."

Janet listened in disbelief. "But how could he do that if it was written in a legal document?"

"He could and he did. I was trying to teach his sister a painting technique; he took it to mean something else and attacked me."

"So brutally?"

"Yes, he has a mind that can twist the most innocent of situations into something more... sinister."

"I can believe that, but—"

"Have you ever seen his sister's drawings?"

"No."

"They are safe little things. I'm more aggressive and bold in my taste and they didn't suit him and he didn't want me to show her how to paint in that style."

"No," Janet said with disgust, remembering his comments about her work. "He wouldn't understand."

"Also, I speak my mind and told him what I truly thought, which he disliked. That's why he hates me, but he's a clever man and I underestimated him. That's always a dangerous thing to do. He found a legal loophole and I cannot fight him. So I paint and teach."

Janet tapped the table. "You should expose him."

"Eventually someone will, but it won't be me. I respect his family too much to put them through that shame."

"You are a good man," Janet said her admiration growing. "But besides disliking your work, what would have made him behave so cruelly?"

"Jealousy. His father cared for me more than he did for him."

Janet shook her head in amazement. "I knew I didn't like him, but I didn't know he was capable of this; such malicious disregard for his father's wishes. That he's capable of stealing away the livelihood of a childhood friend because of jealousy. He has the heart of Cain."

Russell held up his hands in surrender. "I won't speak against him."

"I remember his haughty behavior at the lake house, his temper and his arrogance. He's a horrible person. I can honestly say he is one of the worst men I've ever known. To mistreat a man like *you* is unforgivable. You're so kind, easy going and generous, it's unimaginable. No wonder his father liked you better. He couldn't help it. Durand is Essau and you are Jacob, the one loved best. But pride cometh before a fall. Just you wait and see."

Russell glanced at a group playing charades then turned back to her. "He's never seen pride as a fault. He has a lot to be proud of: His family, his property, his generosity—he's made large donations to important charities and foundations, and his sister. He's the most proud of what he has accomplished with her in terms of his guardianship. Frederick's father traveled a lot and his mother was one of those overindulged rich wives who didn't have time for children."

"What is his sister like?"

"You can read all about her online."

"And the reports will all be glowing," she scoffed. "But what do *you* think?"

"Her success is more a result of her name and her money. I don't think she has any extraordinary talent, although her work is decent. Unfortunately, she is too much like her brother, proud. We were once good friends and I doted on her, but things have changed. She's become a snob and she moves in different circles. She must be eighteen by now, a very attractive young woman, but extremely cold."

"I can't believe that Jeffrey can be so blind to Durand's true character."

"Most people are. He can be charming when he wants to be. But when he doesn't think you're worth his time, he lets you know."

"BUT THAT CAN'T BE TRUE," Beverly said when Janet told her what Russell had shared. She sat at her desk and shook her head. "There must have been a great misunderstanding."

"There is no misunderstanding. You have to face the truth when all the facts are there. I saw Wilcox's scar and we've both seen Durand's knife."

"But some facts must be missing because Jeffrey wouldn't be friends with such a cruel person."

"Unless he's been deceived."

"I can't see Durand as deceitful."

Janet folded her arms. "So you think Wilcox is a liar?"

"No, but—"

"You can't have it both ways. One is a devil and one is a saint. And the saint is Wilcox. Sincerity flowed from his every word."

Beverly looked distressed. "I still don't know what to think."

Janet let her hands fall to her hips. "That's okay because I do."

CHAPTER 25

Janet could hardly conceal her excitement the day of the dedication ceremony. Not only would she get to see Valerie again, but she looked forward to seeing Russell and having an opportunity to sketch him. Jeffrey had planned a bazaar-like atmosphere inside the library. There were several food vendors selling Jamaican beef patties, hotdogs, hamburgers and ginger beer, and a live steel band playing an assortment of popular music, causing some of the spectators to stop and sway. Janet had been assigned a booth where she offered to do quick portraits and she'd brought her favorite box of charcoals along.

Janet set up her materials, arranged the area, and waited to see Russell. After a half hour she searched the crowd and still didn't see him. When an hour passed, she asked Brother Jeremiah, who'd become a friend of his.

"He's not coming," he said.

Janet's heart fell. "Really?"

"He had an appointment in D.C. But we can both guess that there is a certain person here he'd rather not see." He glanced in

Frederick's direction as Frederick pointed something out to a council member.

Janet frowned. "There's a certain person we'd all rather not see."

"Can I get a portrait, Miss?" a familiar voice said.

Janet turned and saw Valerie. She flew into her arms with joy. "You're here!"

"I told you I'd be back."

Valerie looked like a stylish married woman. "You look fantastic."

"I'd say the same, but you don't look happy."

"I'd hope to meet Russell."

"Janet," Valerie said scandalized by how she'd addressed him. "Have you forgotten yourself? You can't be so informal and call him by his given name. You don't know him."

"I know enough about him. I feel as though I've known him my whole life."

Valerie frowned. "So you've said in your emails, but that doesn't change anything."

"But the church—"

"Calls him Brother Wilcox, not Russell." Valerie shook her head. "And I don't care if all the students on your campus call him that. You can't. You shouldn't. You've known him only a few months and you don't have any particular tie. Don't be so casual. Guard yourself at least until a year has passed."

Janet nodded. "Yes, you're right, but if you met him you'd know how tempting it is to call him by his given name." She looked down at her clothes. "And I dressed up today, just for him and he's not coming."

"I'm sure you'll get to impress him on another occasion."

"My dear," Brother Jerome said, waving his hand to Valerie. "I have people I want you to meet."

Valerie touched Janet's arm. "I'll talk to you later," she said then left.

Although Janet was disappointed by Russell's absence she was determined to enjoy herself and soon did so by completing several quick sketches of the children and adults who stopped by. But there was one person she was not happy to see.

"May I have a sketch?" Frederick said, taking the small seat in front of her easel.

She stared at him, searching her mind for a reason to refuse him, but couldn't find one. She made up an excuse that she was thirsty and would be with him in five minutes then left the booth to get a drink. Janet finished the lemonade in one long swallow then crumbled the cup up in her hand.

Beverly came up to her and whispered, "You look like thunder."

"I have to draw Durand, when I promised myself I never would." She threw the cup into the wastebasket.

"You should be flattered."

"Should I be pleased that the devil smiles in my direction?"

"Janet, don't be so harsh. I've spoken to Jeffrey and he is certain that Wilcox is not all that he claims."

"He's Durand's best friend. Of course he would say that." Then Janet glanced at her watch annoyed. "My five minutes are up."

Beverly pinched her. "Behave. And smile."

Janet used her hands to widen her mouth. "Will that do?"

Beverly shook her head. "Please be serious, Janet. This day means a lot to Jeffrey."

"I'll do my best." Janet briefly shut her eyes as though doomed for a root canal then returned to the booth, where Frederick waited. She didn't offer him any greeting or direct him on how to sit. Instead she began her sketch in silence. But after a few moments, the silence began to bother her. "The new wing is quite impressive," she said.

"Yes."

When he didn't say more, she said, "Now it's your turn to say something. Perhaps about the walls or the landscaping?"

"I didn't know you wanted to talk."

"As long as people don't move too much, talking helps me to get to know them more."

"I don't believe idle chit chat reveals much about a person."

"Or perhaps like me you only talk when you want to make a point."

"You think you know me well." He paused then said, "Do you like architecture?"

"Yes I do. When you saw us the other day I was showing a good friend of mine this building." She studied him and got the reaction she wanted. His eyes darkened and he clenched his jaw.

"Russell is very lucky. He makes friends easily. Whether he can keep them is something else."

"Unfortunately, he lost your friendship, but I remember you once said that when you cross someone off your list it's final."

"Yes."

"And you don't make mistakes? Because I know your choice caused Wilcox a lot of pain."

Frederick sniffed. "He makes due."

"He keeps his suffering silent."

"Really?"

"Yes."

"Then how come you know so much about it?"

Janet opened her mouth to reply, but Brother Williams interrupted when he glanced over her shoulder to study her sketch. "Oh Janet, how clever of you to capture Durand's likeness so quickly." He patted Frederick on the shoulder. "Durand you will be pleased."

"I'm sure I will," he said.

"She painted a beautiful portrait of my Valerie in her wedding dress."

"Yes, I remember," Frederick replied, looking at Janet with respect.

"And I'm certain we'll soon see another happy bride." Brother Williams glanced at Beverly and Jeffrey. "What an exquisite bride she will be. But let me not stop you. I'm sure you two want to finish."

Frederick hardly paid attention to Brother William's departure, his gaze focused on his friend. He and Beverly were talking with such animation they seemed to block out the rest of the world. He soon remembered himself and returned his attention to Janet. "I forgot what we were talking about."

"Nothing," she said. "I don't believe we have anything to say to each other."

"How about music?"

"I sincerely doubt we have the same taste in music."

"You don't have to have the same taste in something to talk about it. We can express our different opinions."

"But sometimes different opinions can lead to arguments, and I would hate to argue with you."

He drummed his fingers on his knee. "One doesn't necessarily follow the other."

"True. I also remember you telling me that once you turn against someone you never change. I hope you're not too quick to form opinions."

"No, I am not."

"And you don't look down on others?"

"No." He furrowed his brows. "Why are you asking me these questions?"

"I'm just trying to figure you out. I want to know what kind of man you are."

"And have you figured me out?"

"Not yet. I have found too many varying accounts to create a complete picture."

"Take your time. Rash judgments can lead to mistakes."

"But I may never have another opportunity." Janet set her charcoal down. "Done." She handed the drawing to him. Frederick stared at it for a long moment then quietly said, "Thank you." He stood.

"Don't you want me to package it?"

"I'm sorry?"

She impatiently held out her hand and he gave Janet the drawing. She deftly rolled it up then placed a ribbon around it and handed it back to him. "There."

"Thanks again."

She nodded.

He tapped the picture against his palm and looked at her, as though he wanted to say more; Janet busied herself by arranging her pencils. Finally he left without saying goodbye.

Frederick wasn't aware of his abrupt departure. His only focus was creating a needed distance from her. She was like a splash of color in a black and white photograph. His eyes always sought her. As she'd sketched him, he'd studied how dark her eyebrows were, how she bit her lip as she concentrated. She had pretty lips—lush, full and wonderful just like her. Frederick glanced down at the drawing in his hand and smiled as though he'd received a sacred souvenir.

Janet watched him go, glad the ordeal was over, then pushed him from her thoughts.

Hours later, Janet closed her booth, hoping she could spend some time with Valerie before she left. As she flipped over the sign, Karen approached her. "I know that you've been blindsided by Wilcox, but I must tell you that although I don't know everything that happened between Wilcox and Frederick, Frederick is above reproach and he can't stand hearing that man's name. It is so awful to have one's house staff turn against you and try to air dirty laundry, especially when it's false."

"You're right," Janet said. "You don't know everything that happened. I believe you don't know anything at all." She brushed past her.

Minutes later Janet stood at the buffet table next to Valerie. "This is a terrible habit of ours," Valerie said.

"What?"

"Finding refuge at the buffet table."

Janet laughed. "At least I'm not hiding from anyone this time."

Valerie looked at Beverly. "Your mother is still determined to have Jeffrey Farmer as a son-in-law."

"She may get her wish."

"Only if your sister moves fast otherwise she'll lose him."

"Beverly is shy."

"How many months has it been? A man cannot be left dangling on a hook that long. She needs to reel him in."

"How?"

"By letting him know, without any doubt, how she feels. He cannot read her mind. She likes him, true, but is she willing to spend her life with him? She must let him know that."

Janet blinked. "But that would be brazen."

Valerie spotted a place to sit and walked towards it. "How can he know how she feels about him, if she doesn't show it?" She sat.

Janet sat beside her. "I'm certain he knows."

"Men need to always be certain of a woman's feelings. A woman should always show more than she really feels."

"You sound certain about this theory," Janet said taken aback by her friend's advice.

"I'm married, aren't I?"

Janet folded her arms.

Valerie looked at the crowd. "I'm glad to see that your family is doing well. They seem to be enjoying themselves."

Janet agreed. Her family was enjoying itself, perhaps too much. She'd overheard her mother talking to two of the Sisters in the church, about Beverly's impending marriage with Jeffrey and how it would help them financially; Maxine and Trudy openly flirted with the catering staff, the workers, and any other male guests attending the affair. And then, as if there could be no further embarrassment, Francine surprised everyone by announcing that she had written a special poem for the dedication in honor of Jeffrey's father. From the look on Jeffrey's face, Janet surmised he had given her permission, not wanting to say no. She then proceeded to read. Thankfully a piano was not nearby. When it was over their father clapped the loudest.

Janet felt herself become smaller and smaller as she recalled her family's behavior. Fortunately, Beverly kept Jeffrey from noticing. Unfortunately, everyone else did. She could see Frederick's cold assessing gaze and Tanya and Karen's amused looks.

Mother Shea also watched, but for an entirely different reason. The outside world's influences were becoming stronger and lasting longer. The Barnetts were a little too liberal with their two younger daughters and that should not be tolerated. Their church community was as liberal as it needed to be.

She had heard about other churches in their faith collapsing as daughters left home to live by themselves, or went off to find jobs away from home, and sons no longer asked permission to marry but instead, told their parents who they would marry.

Their traditional ways and strict beliefs would be wiped out if they were not careful. Mother Shea glanced at Frederick and frowned. The Other—she no longer thought of him as just the Original—had to leave soon. It worried her how some of the Hamsford residents had accepted him. They weren't church members but it still concerned her. She did not like the influence he seemed to have over his friend. Jeffrey openly showed Beverly undue interest and yet had made no offer of marriage.

She looked at the crowd and saw many faces she didn't recognize. Jeffrey had invited many outsiders who she knew would leave after the dedication, which suited her. She then turned her gaze to Brother Jerome and his new wife. She still felt that something was very wrong with it. She would not let herself admit that their union had been a personal blow. Why hadn't he come to her? Last night she'd had a bad dream that had frightened her. If the people in her congregation did not continue listening to her, they would all pay.

"Where is it?" Maxine asked checking through the papers on her desk. Outside their bedroom window they could see the glow from jack-o lanterns and scarecrows in the distance as the October wind howled.

"I don't know," Trudy said searching through her own desk.

Maxine lay on her stomach and crawled under her bed. "You have to know!"

Trudy lifted her mattress. "But I don't."

Maxine's muffled voice came from under the bed. "This is awful."

Janet stood in the doorway watching Trudy flip through her books then throw them on her bed. "What's going on here?"

Trudy froze. Maxine peeked her head out and smiled. "Nothing."

Janet rested her hip against the door unconvinced. "You're both obviously looking for something."

Maxine scrambled out and stood. "It's nothing important really."

"You're sure you don't want me to help you?"

Trudy handed her a book. "Well, if you could—"

Maxine snatched it away from her. "We can find it on our own."

Janet shrugged then left, missing Maxine hitting Trudy with her pillow before disappearing under the bed again.

What they didn't know was that three days earlier, Mrs. Lind had found what they were looking for.

CHAPTER 26

Mrs. Lind had spent the majority of her forty-three years working for others. She didn't mind working. Her mother had worked hard and so had her grandmother that was the lot in life for the women in her family. They suffered bad marriages to worthless men and lived hard. Although the women before her had given up hope of good things ever happening to them, Mrs. Lind never did. No matter what, nothing stopped her from desiring one thing. And one day her desire was answered in a very unusual way.

She was dusting the few books Maxine and Trudy kept in their bedroom when several sheets of paper fell to the ground. She began to replace them until she saw what was on them. When she did, she fell on the bed with her hand to her mouth. "Dear God," she whispered. She rarely called his name because she wasn't a religious woman and she didn't believe He was listening anyway. But in this instance the words escaped her lips as she stared at the drawings.

She thought of all the trouble it would cause if anyone were to find out. Her hands trembled as she looked at each one. The disgrace. It would ruin the Barnetts. No one could ever know about them. She stood ready to tell Mr. Barnett then stopped at the door as an idea began to form in her mind.

As the idea grew a smile spread on her face. The Barnetts would not want anyone to discover the truth and that could be very useful to her. But who to tell? She could tell Mr. Barnett but he would just rant and rave and she couldn't bargain with him. Mrs. Barnett was too soft. She would weep. Beverly? Definitely not... but Janet. Yes, Janet would do anything to make sure these drawings were never discovered and she would be able to negotiate her silence.

Mrs. Lind folded up the drawings, carefully put them in her large apron pocket then continued dusting, this time softly humming to herself.

"MI NEED FI TALK WID YOU," Mrs. Lind said to Janet three days later as Janet worked at her desk.

Janet spun around in her chair and faced her. She did not like Mrs. Lind. She found her ways too even tempered, too obliging. She found her looks sly and her eyes even more so, but she could not deny that she was a fine worker and an excellent cook. She gestured towards her bed. "Yes?"

Mrs. Lind entered the room, but did not sit. "Your sisters have been frantically looking fi someting."

Janet rolled her eyes. "Yes, I know."

"Well mi find it."

"Good," Janet said confused why Mrs. Lind would tell her about it. "They'll be happy to hear that." Janet turned back to what she was doing.

"Mi need fi should show you first." She held out a folded paper.

Janet took the paper and unfolded it. She leapt to her feet when she saw it: A pencil sketch of Maxine lying on a bench wearing nothing but a see-through piece of fabric. "What is— How can—I don't understand." She shook her head and stared at Mrs. Lind. "What is this?"

"You know what it is," Mrs. Lind said softly. "You see who sketch it?"

Janet's gaze fell to the signature: Russell Wilcox. She felt ill. "I can't believe this."

"There's more."

Janet held out her hand desperate. "Please give them to me before anyone else sees them."

Mrs. Lind sat on the bed and clasped her hands together in her lap. "I will give dem all to you and never speak 'bout dem again, but first we need fi come to an agreement."

"What? What kind of agreement?"

"I need a more permanent way to stay here."

"Permanent way?"

"My residency status."

"What do the drawings have to do with your residency status?"

"I want to stay here for good. I hate only having a six-month visa, an' having to go back an' forth. I don't want fi leave again."

Janet slowly sat down as she realized what Mrs. Lind wanted. "But I can't help you with that."

Mrs. Lind shrugged nonchalant. "Then I guess you don't need these drawings as badly as you say." She stood.

Janet jumped up and closed the door before Mrs. Lind could leave. "Wait. I just need to think."

"You better tink fast. Mi visa expires soon."

Janet tossed the drawing on her desk. "Oh Maxine. You stupid, stupid girl."

"Your fadda should watch her more."

"I know."

Someone pounded on the door. "What is going on in there?" Mr. Barnett demanded. "Why is this door closed? Janet, open the door."

Her father barged into the room. He glanced at Mrs. Lind then Janet. "I've told you, I will not have closed doors in my house. What is going on here?"

"Nothing," Mrs. Lind said. "The door closed by accident."

He walked over to the window. Janet inched towards her desk and hastily covered the drawing with a book. Mr. Barnett turned and Janet folded her arms. "You know I don't like secrets," he said.

"There are no secrets," Mrs. Lind said smoothly. "It is just as I said. I was helping Janet shift someting an' the door done close itself."

"Very well. I'll get you a proper doorstop." He sent them a look then left. They waited for his footsteps to disappear. When they did, Mrs. Lind checked the hallway then closed the door a fraction before she continued. "So you understand me."

"You want a U.S. husband?"

"Yes. You will not get the rest of the drawings until mi have a ring pon mi finger."

Janet rubbed her forehead as though she were developing a headache. "How am I supposed to find you a husband?"

"I've been watching you. I saw how you helped Valerie get Brother Jerome."

"I didn't have anything to do with that."

But Mrs. Lind ignored her and continued, "And I've also seen how you keep pushing your sister towards dat Jeffrey fellow. You make a proper matchmaker when you want to. You're a clever girl and mi trust you. You have four months or your parents are going to learn what their daughter has been doing in her spare time."

She pointed to the drawing on Janet's desk. "Oh, and I should let you know, dat's the tamest one."

Once Mrs. Lind left, Janet stormed into Maxine and Trudy's room. They lay on the bed together looking at a magazine. When they heard her footsteps they tossed it under the bed.

Janet rested a hand on her hip and pointed at Maxine. "I found what you were looking for."

Maxine sat up in relief. "Oh good. I was worried."

"What were you thinking?'

She frowned. "What do you mean?"

"How could you have posed for those sketches?"

"You act like I did a bad thing. You sketch nudes at school, right? Wilcox said I made an excellent model."

"You're too young."

"He told me that models start at sixteen and older."

"Not doing these types of poses."

"Yes, they do," Trudy said. She pulled out the magazine and showed Janet the cover of a teenaged girl posing in a sheet. "She's a singer."

Janet rolled the magazine up. "It's still not appropriate and you're not supposed to be looking at these."

Maxine swung her feet. "Nothing happened. I wasn't naked or anything. I kept my underwear on and I was covered with a cloth."

"But the drawings—"

"He just sketched me, that's all. Are you jealous that he didn't choose you?"

"Don't be ridiculous, but you know you shouldn't have done them or you wouldn't have worried about Daddy finding them."

"You've never told Daddy about some of your classes," Maxine shot back. "Does that make it wrong or is it just that he wouldn't understand? I think you and I know the answer to that."

She was right. Janet had never shared the fact that she had

taken several live nude figure drawing classes. And she had kept all her sketches carefully hidden behind a panel in her closet. How could she condemn Wilcox's sketches if she did the same? The models in her class were someone's sister too. But somehow she felt the sketches of Maxine were wrong.

Janet tossed the magazine down and Trudy quickly hid it, but Janet didn't care. Her focus remained on Maxine. "Your body is God's temple. It belongs to Him, then you then your husband."

"No. My body only belongs to me and Wilcox didn't touch me so there's nothing wrong with it. Anyway, it's not the first time."

Janet stared at her sister as fury crawled up her spine. She clenched her hands into fists. "Shit!"

The word left her mouth before she could stop it. Someone spun her around and knocked her to the ground with the back of his hand. She held her hand against her burning cheek and stared up at her father, his face a mask of rage.

"Stand up," he said in a quiet tone as lethal as a rattlesnake.

Janet sat paralyzed.

He raised his hand. "Do I need to hit you again?"

Janet scrambled to her feet. He grabbed her chin and held it until she felt her lower jaw would break. "Is this the language they teach you at school? They teach you to swear at your sister? To say this filth?"

Trudy tentatively stepped forward, tears shinning in her eyes. "Daddy, please—"

He pointed at her. "Quiet."

She lowered her head and stepped back.

He turned his attention back to Janet. "For the next three days you will stay in this house and cleanse yourself."

Janet widened her eyes. She could take the cleansing, which meant praying and fasting, but staying home for three days would be torture. "What about school—"

"Do you want me to make it a week?"

Janet swallowed and lowered her gaze. "No."

Mr. Barnett shoved her towards her bedroom as though she disgusted him. "Start your prayers now."

"Daddy, I'm sorry."

He squeezed his eyes shut. "I don't want to hear your voice. Leave your words for God."

Janet glanced back at her sisters—Trudy in tears and Maxine looking bored—then left.

"I STRUCK her hard across the face with all the strength I could manage," Mr. Barnett admitted as he sat in Pastor Wainwright's office. The familiar seat where they usually discussed church affairs today offered him no comfort. It felt worn and stiff. "There is something in that child I don't understand."

Pastor Wainwright stroked his mustache with his long delicate fingers then said after a moment, "Or perhaps you do and that's what frightens you." When Mr. Barnett didn't reply he said, "Has she repented? Shown regret?"

"Yes, the moment she said the word she regretted it."

"Then if God can forgive her you can too. Janet is a nice young woman. Even the most righteous have their faults." He clasped Mr. Barnett's hand. "I will pray for you now and for your family on Sunday then I want you to let it go. Will you do that for me?"

Mr. Barnett swallowed hard. "Yes, Pastor. Thank you."

That Sunday, Pastor Wainwright stood at the pulpit after his sermon and stared out at his congregation. He briefly met Mr. Barnett's eye then raised his hand and said, "Today one of us needs special prayer. Sister Janet, please come down to the altar."

Janet gripped the pew, but didn't move until her father

nudged her. She took a deep breath then rose and slowly walked down the aisle amid the curious and accusatory eyes of the congregation who stared at the purple bruise on her face. She stopped in front of the pulpit and stared up at the pastor.

"Turn to the congregation."

"No," she said in a soft voice.

The Pastor stared at her as if she'd suddenly grown horns. He blinked then covered his microphone. "Janet, do not shame your family. Now turn. You know this has to be done."

"No," she said in the same quiet voice. "I am truly sorry for what I have done and I have cleansed myself. I have prayed to God and asked for His forgiveness. I know I am a sinner and I know my sins and I am ashamed. However, I will not stand here for man to judge me when I know that others in this congregation have done far worse," she said thinking of Russell who sat in a few rows behind her family. "I accept your prayers, but I *will not turn.* Please send me back to my seat. I do not want to disobey you or dishonor my family unless you force me to."

Pastor Wainwright took out his handkerchief and wiped the sweat gathered on his forehead then stuffed it back in his pocket and addressed the congregation. "Brothers and Sisters it seems there was a misunderstanding. Sister Janet and her parents only need our prayers that she does well in her studies. Sister Janet, please return to your seat."

She did and everyone remained quiet until the end of the service. On the walk home Mr. Barnett said, "What you say to the Pastor?"

"I told him I had repented."

"But—"

"Daddy, there are worse things happening right before your eyes."

"What worse things?"

Janet glanced at her younger sisters who looked at her with fear. She let her shoulders fall. "Just things."

"If you can't be specific then don't speak at all." He frowned annoyed. "We'll watch *The Harder They Come* tonight," he said then marched past her and joined Mrs. Barnett. In the distance Janet saw Russell surrounded by a group of church sisters. Behind him she saw a hawk glide through the sky.

CHAPTER 27

Janet slammed the sketch down on Russell's desk. "How dare you come to our church and sit there all righteous when you know what you've done."

Russell held out his hands confused. "What have I done?"

She shoved the sketch across the table. "Does that help?"

Russell glanced at it. "Oh, that."

"Yes, that and there are others." Janet tapped the image. "She's sixteen."

"I know." He looked at Janet's face then surged to his feet. "Wait. Are you accusing me of something more? My honor and reputation means a lot to me Janet, be careful how you handle it." He came from around the desk. "Don't make this anything more than it is. I admired her body and sketched it. I thought you, of all people, would understand that the artistic eye worships anything of beauty. Don't let your father's teaching pollute your mind. Don't make something beautiful dirty by judging it." He sniffed. "Or perhaps you're more like Frederick than you think."

Janet blinked, stung by the comparison and surprised by his

vehemence. "That's not fair. I'm nothing like him, but she's a child."

He sat on the corner of the desk. "And innocent. I know. She's still innocent. As untouched as the day she was born. It was my imagination, Janet. Your sister was clothed."

"Barely. She was in her underwear!"

"And covered in fabric."

"Which was transparent. And why does she look naked in the sketches?"

"Janet, you're an artist, you know about artistic license. I added the extra elements. Your sister was thrilled with the result. But you've disappointed me." His brown eyes bore into hers with chilling intensity. "What kind of man do you think I am? I'd expected you to think better of me. Do you honestly think I would enter your father's house and disrespect him like that? That I would enter a church with no fear of God? Is that how you see me? As depraved, deceitful and a hypocrite?"

Janet opened her mouth then closed it, embarrassment and regret making her mute. She stepped back from his desk and fell into a chair. "I'm sorry. I didn't—"

"No," he said his tone more gentle than before. "It's good." He pulled up a chair and sat beside her. "I think we should have this conversation. Your sister is a free spirit. A girl like that cannot be caged for long."

"She still needs guidance."

"With a firm hand or a lenient one? What do you think when you see those nude models you sketch in class? Have you ever thought of living without inhibition?"

She thought of Ramani. "No, some rules are needed for our survival."

"Is that the church talking or you? Do you know the difference?"

"I am not blindly following rituals and beliefs," Janet said defensive.

"But you find them constraining at times. I know. I can tell. I grew up with them and I respect them. But why is it that the *Song of Solomon* is rarely spoken about?" He lowered his voice to a husky tone. "*... the joint of thy thighs are like jewels, the work of the hands of a cunning workman. Thy navel is like a round goblet, which wanteth not liquor: thy belly is like a heap of wheat set about with lilies. Thy two breasts are like two young roes that are twins, which feed among the lilies.*' Sex, love, beauty are just as important as honor and obedience.

"We are all tempted and it is important to understand those temptations so that we do not fall prey to them." He took her hand in his, his liquid gaze smoldering with fire. "The scripture tells us to 'yield not' to temptation He didn't promise us there wouldn't be any." He leaned closer.

Janet didn't move. She couldn't. She'd never had a man hold her hand like this and she knew she should pull away, but didn't. He held her mesmerized because he understood temptation and didn't judge her. Her skin tingled at his touch and Ramani's words came to her again, *Men were created for a lot more than sketching.* She wondered how it would feel to succumb to the delicious pleasures of the flesh, of how it would feel to kiss a man and have him hold her in his arms. How it would feel to be one with him.

"You know I would never take advantage of your sister," Russell said. "That's why I gave all the sketches to her. I didn't think that she was going to keep them. You know you can trust me. Haven't I always been honest with you?"

Janet didn't speak. She trusted him and knew there was nothing to fear. Everything about him was trustworthy, the way he honored her father, he attended church every Sunday, and socialized with people in the church and in the community. He was a very popular instructor and in spite of his full schedule, he had made time to tutor her with her watercolors.

Unlike other artists she had met, there were no visible vices and everyone who knew him liked him. Janet liked him too—a lot. She admired his freedoms: His freedom of thought, his freedom of speech. Nothing about him was guarded. He was like no other man she'd met. Yes, he'd always been honest with her. Would another man have been so open to share his misfortune and Frederick's terrible treatment?

Frederick. Her judgment of Russell's sketches reminded her of his coarse judgment of hers. The sketches were innocent. She was the one who'd seen more into it. She looked down at their clasped hands then met his eyes. "Yes, I do trust you."

He smiled.

UNFORTUNATELY, Russell's explanation still didn't solve her problem. Mrs. Lind had the rest of the sketches and threatened to show them to her parents. Janet knew that couldn't happen. Her mother would drop dead and her father would send all five of them to a cloistered monastery, somewhere in the hills of Jamaica, where none of them would be allowed to leave until they reached eighty.

Janet paced her bedroom. She had no one to confide in. Valerie was gone and happily married. Beverly would not be able to understand and certainly not her sisters. She had to find a man before Mrs. Lind acted on her threat. She stared up at her picture and shook her fists. *Why me?*

Janet fell face down on her bed and buried her face in her pillow. What was she going to do? Then she stared at the pillow and pounded it. She wasn't going to find a man in her bedroom. She had to search.

Janet grabbed her coat and jumped into her car. She drove aimlessly for a while trying to sort her thoughts then drove to the market.

The cold chill of the coming winter didn't bother her as she made her way from the parking lot to the building. She needed a man and she might find one there. Janet strolled along the different stands checking her options. There was Mr. Crawford, a man with a short stature who sold music and movies but liked to smoke and favored something much stronger than tobacco.

And there was Mr. Shelton Morris. Depending on the day, he could be considered handsome, but he liked the bottle too much and had gone through three wives already. Janet sized up each man feeling her hopes dimming. Finding a suitable man outside the church might prove just as difficult as those inside. She was about to give up hope when she heard Mr. Beecham say, "I can't do that kind of thing."

"But it's not normal for a man your age to live alone," his companion said.

"I prefer to be just the way I am."

"But you haffa big house, an' no woman to clean it. Don't you want a woman to cook fi you and be there fi you?"

"I don't need dat."

"How about to keep your bed warm?"

Mr. Beecham made a tsking sound. "I'm not good wid women. After mi wife die, I met a few at the community center, but I don't know what fi say to dem. The last time I tried to ask a woman out, Mrs. Maynard, the woman who sells fish here in di market, she just look pon mi and laugh."

"You can do better than dat. You don't want a woman like her anyway."

"Why not?"

"You ever see how large her backside is?"

Both men fell out laughing.

Janet knew this was her opportunity. Mr. Beecham was a widower with a grown son, but most importantly he was a US citizen. She approached the two men, startling them and smiled. "Good afternoon Mr. Beecham."

"My, it's nice to see you here, Janet. It's always a pleasure. So what you need today?"

"Well, Mrs. Lind is going to be making a delicious pumpkin pie and I am looking for the best pumpkins in town. I know you carry the best." Mr. Beecham bid goodbye to his friend, and led Janet over to a private collection of pumpkins he had kept behind his stand. "These are my best."

"Mrs. Lind loves your fruits and vegetables. She is always asking me where I get them. I also think she likes you."

"Mrs. Lind? Dat woman's never looked at mi."

"She's shy."

"She wasn't shy the last time she was at the market. I heard her telling off Clifton Bishop. She didn't tink his cheese was wrapped properly; she didn't look shy to mi."

"You know how we women are. She's shy with men she likes." Janet's insides clenched, she didn't want to tell an outright lie. "Would you mind bringing over a fresh basket of vegetables to our house, around six pm on Sunday?" Janet hurriedly selected various items, and paid Mr. Beecham.

Janet knew that Sunday at six would be perfect because Mrs. Lind was in the habit of baking several pies, and prided herself in cooking the best Sunday dinner in Hamsford.

"No problem. But don't you want to take a few with you now?"

"Thank you, but no I can't. I'm on my way to school. I'll see you Sunday. I promise you'll get a great tip." Janet dashed away before he could change his mind.

She did not go to the university. Instead, she went to the local Salvation Army and picked out a few items, for Mrs. Lind. She gasped when she saw the polka dot lace dress she'd gotten rid of at their charity function. She glanced around then bundled it up and threw it away determined that no one would be forced to wear it. After feeling she'd done her duty, she continued searching for clothes for Mrs. Lind. If she was going to be successful at finding a husband for her, she needed to spruce up the package. That would be a challenge.

CHAPTER 28

"Why?" Beverly said staring at her sister surprised.

"Because you're the one who knows how to do this," Janet replied.

Beverly looked at the clothing items spread out on Janet's bed. "You want me to help... um... pretty up Mrs. Lind? Will she allow me?"

"Yes, she will."

"Okay," Beverly said then headed for Mrs. Lind's room.

"Even if I have to force her," Janet muttered following behind. Beverly gently tapped on the door. When they didn't hear a response, Janet pounded on it.

The door swung open and Mrs. Lind appeared. "No need for all dat noise. What you want?"

Janet pushed past her and walked into the room. "I've found you a husband, but he can't see you like this."

"You found her a husband?" Beverly said.

"Yes." Janet shook her head and held up her hand. "Please don't ask."

Mrs. Lind folded her arms. "What's wrong wid me?"

Beverly and Janet shared a look, but wisely said nothing. Janet placed the clothing on the bed. "We have no time to discuss the issue. He's coming on Sunday at six o' clock. You're going to meet him at the back door and you're going to be wearing this." She held up a wool top and tweed skirt. "But that's just the beginning."

Beverly and Janet worked on fixing up Mrs. Lind, after she agreed to their scheme, but it wasn't easy because she firmly told them, "I don't want to look like a painted woman."

Janet didn't think that was possible as she looked at Mrs. Lind's makeup selection. She barely had one. Although she had no religious restrictions regarding makeup or jewelry, she rarely wore any. Janet looked at Mrs. Lind's face the way she would a blank canvas then at her supplies. Mrs. Lind had two tubes of lipstick, a bright red rouge, black eyebrow pencil and translucent face powder. Janet sighed then went to work.

"You're putting on too much," Mrs. Lind said.

Janet kissed her teeth annoyed. "I've hardly started."

"You sure you know what you're doing?"

"You'll have to trust us."

She was able to convince Mrs. Lind to let her use the eyebrow pencil to fill-in her eyebrows, which were almost non-existent. Next, she used the same pencil to outline her eyelids, top and bottom, giving them a sparkle. Pleased with the outcome, Janet used the pencil to outline and fill in her lips. She then added the more subdued dark raisin lipstick color as a topcoat.

The clever mixture created just the right shade for Mrs. Lind's dark skin. Janet then used the other lipstick as an eye shadow. She finished Mrs. Lind's face by applying a thin layer of the translucent powder then fixed the look with a spray of cold water.

Once the makeup was completed, they made Mrs. Lind try on the outfit and selected a pair of shoes from her limited selection. Then Beverly worked on Mrs. Lind's hair. It was thick and course, but she didn't want to press or relax it so she gave Mrs. Lind a hot-oil treatment and pulled her hair back into a bun.

"What do you think?" Janet asked Beverly as they stared at the finished result.

"She looks wonderful."

Janet opened the closet door where Mrs. Lind kept a full length mirror. "What do you think?" she asked her.

Mrs. Lind looked at herself. "It'll do," she said but they could tell she was very pleased.

THAT SUNDAY, Mr. Beecham walked up to the back of the house and knocked on the kitchen door. The smell of fried plantain and curry chicken was overwhelming, bringing back memories of his own dear wife, Matilda, and the lovely Sunday dinners she used to cook.

Mrs. Lind opened the door and looked down at what he was carrying. "Oh, dem vegetables look good," she said.

She looked wonderful. He'd never seen her like this before; he could hardly believe it was Mrs. Lind. Her hair was pulled back off her face and held in place with a gold headband. She wore a pair of small pearl earrings, a stylish, short sleeved wool top, and a pencil thin tweed skirt. He entered the kitchen and placed the basket on the table, unable to take his eyes off her. He cleared his throat feeling awkward. "Let me help you put them away."

Mrs. Lind pointed towards the food pantry. "Put dem in there. Do you like oxtail and butter beans?"

"Mi love it but haven't had it in years."

"Would you like some now?" She motioned to a seat.

He hesitated. "Are you sure? I don't want fi take someone else's share."

"I made it yesterday. I always make plenty. Please sit."

Mr. Beecham flung his coat behind the chair, washed his hands in the sink then sat. He knew he was staring, but lacked the energy or desire to stop. He watched as she ladled the food on his plate, appreciating her figure. *Clifton was right. It would be nice to have somebody fi go home to. Fi go to bed wid.*

Throughout the meal (she also convinced him to have some fresh papaya juice and rum cake) he practiced in his mind what he wanted to say, but let her do most of the talking. By the time he'd finished his dessert he had the words down, but they wouldn't come out.

Annoyed by his cowardice, he got up and put on his coat. He thanked her for the dinner, wished her a nice evening then left.

Mrs. Lind sat at the table staring at the dirty dishes feeling defeated. She slowly stacked them and placed them in the sink.

Janet came into the kitchen. "So what happened?"

Mrs. Lind turned on the faucet. "Him naym di food an' left."

"That's it?"

Mrs. Lind pulled on her plastic yellow gloves. "Dat was it. Him gone."

"But he can't be gone." Janet glanced at the object on the floor. "His basket is still here."

"But di man isn't."

"Never mind," Janet said, her tone sounding more hopeful than she felt. "This was only the first try. I'll think of something." She left the kitchen.

Mrs. Lind continued washing the dishes and then stacked them to dry. She was about to leave when she heard a soft tap on the door. She opened it and saw Mr. Beecham.

He shifted awkwardly. "I—"

"Yes, I know. You figet your basket." She turned and retrieved it then handed it to him. He looked at it then pulled her towards him and kissed her. When he drew away she only stared at him.

"Do you want to slap mi?" he asked.

"No."

"Laugh at mi?"

"No."

"Go out wid mi?"

"Yes."

"Marry mi?"

"Yes."

He lifted the basket that had fallen from her hand. "Good. I'll call you tomorrow." He turned.

"You not goin' fi say goodbye?"

Mr. Beecham looked confused then smiled. He kissed her again, this time covering her mouth with his and she kissed him back. Janet returned to the kitchen ready to share Plan B, but halted when she saw them. She quietly backed out of the room and pumped her fist in triumph.

"What are you doing?" Mrs. Barnett said, coming down the hallway.

"Nothing. Where are you going?"

Mrs. Barnett glanced down at the dishes she held. "Where do you think? Into the kitchen."

Janet reached for them. "Let me take those for you."

She moved them out of reach. "I can carry them myself."

"But I want to help you."

"Then move. Why are you blocking my path? I want to go into the kitchen."

"You can't."

"Why not?"

"Mrs. Lind is busy."

"Don't be stupid." Mrs. Barnett pushed past Janet and went inside. Janet shut her eyes waiting for her mother's outcry, but she didn't hear anything. She turned and peeked inside the kitchen through the slit created by the door jam and saw Mrs. Lind standing at the sink calmly washing the pots, as though nothing had happened.

BUT SOMETHING definitely had and Mrs. Lind told the elder Barnetts about it.

Mr. Barnett stared at Mrs. Lind as though she'd turned purple. "You're going to get married to Mr. Beecham?"

Mrs. Lind sat in the living room calmly staring at both of them. She had expected this reaction, which was why she'd waited a week to tell them. "Yes."

"What do we know of this man?"

"It's not about you. It's about mi, and I know enough."

"Why do you want to go off and get married?"

"I want to live mi own life."

"You can have your own life here. You married before, wasn't that enough?"

"No. But you know what, I didn't come here fi argue wid you. I'm leaving Winston. You've been good to mi but it's time fi mi to be gone."

Mr. Barnett shifted in his seat, vexed. "You should have come to me first."

"I'm a grown woman, mi nah need your approval. Besides, I'm not your dawta. You should be keeping a close eye on dem, and not mi."

"What you mean?"

"Exactly what I said."

Mrs. Barnett spoke up before the two could argue. "I hope you'll be happy," she said, extending her hand to congratulate her.

"Tank you. I will. One day I hope fi pay you back fi all your kindness to me."

"Oh you don't need to worry. You've done plenty. We'll miss you."

Mrs. Lind hesitated then said, "Perhaps... perhaps you can come and visit." She knew it was a bold request. Mrs. Lind wasn't of their class and they'd likely have no reason to associate with her, especially with Mr. Barnett objecting to the marriage. But Mrs. Barnett took her hands and looked at her as equals and said, "Just tell us the day and we'll be there."

Tears sprung to her eyes. "Tank you."

Mr. Barnett, who hadn't moved from his position, threw up his hands. "But this is—"

Mrs. Barnett cut him a glance. "That's enough Winston." She smiled at Mrs. Lind. "It's settled."

Soon after, Mrs. Lind's engagement was announced in *The Hamsford Daily*. Two weeks later Mrs. Lind got married at the courthouse and moved in with her husband. Janet burned the sketches. Maxine and Trudy stayed out of trouble, and Francine continued doing well at the Junior College she was attending as did Janet with her studies. Everything seemed to have settled into a nice routine until one day that changed.

Janet returned home from the university in high spirits and Francine greeted her at the door with bad news. "Dee-dee's singing."

Janet felt her spirits fall. "Where is she?"

Her mother's voice told her soon enough as her mournful song slipped out the door of the family room. "Oh Lord how I suffer for thee..."

Janet squeezed her eyes shut. "Oh no, not that one." She knew her mother only sang when she was unhappy and sang *that* song when she was especially disappointed and didn't want to discuss it.

Francine cleaned her lens with the corner of her shirt. "It's better than *On My Way to Hell* or *Dying for You*."

"Not much better," Janet said as she hung up her coat in the closet.

Francine put her glasses on. "You know she makes them up. I've never found any of her songs in a hymnal and I've looked."

"I know she makes them up, but she remembers every word." Janet sighed. "I'll talk to her." She set her backpack down then entered the family room where her mother sat staring out the window.

Mrs. Barnett glanced up at Janet, but continued her song. "Oh trouble comes to me..." she sang reaching a high note.

"Dee-dee what's wrong?"

"Such troubles I've seen..." She lowered her head. "She lost him."

At first Janet thought it was part of the song, but soon realized it wasn't. "What are you talking about?"

"He's gone."

"Who's gone?"

"Jeffrey Farmer. He's gone off with the Original. He's gone to Detroit. Something about a new opportunity or some such nonsense. I thought something would happen, but he left without making any promises."

Janet left her mother and sprinted upstairs. She found Beverly reading a book. "I can see that Dee-dee told you," she said before Janet spoke. She put her book down. "Don't look at me like that."

"Like what?"

"With pity."

"I don't understand."

"There's nothing to understand. It's very clear. He's gone. He returned to Hamsford to accomplish what he meant to, and now he's moved on to better things."

Janet sat. "What's better than you?"

Beverly smiled. "You're sweet."

"No, I'm annoyed."

"Karen told me that his moving to Detroit was what he really wanted, and I have no right to claim him." Beverly went over to her desk and pulled out a sheet of paper. "It wasn't like he gave me a ring, or even asked me to wait for him. And he didn't leave without saying goodbye." She held the paper out to Janet. "He sent me an email."

Janet scowled. "An email. How gallant," she said meaning the opposite.

"Read it."

Janet scanned the contents but didn't find anything to improve her mood. Jeffrey said how much he'd enjoyed being back in Hamsford and seeing her again and wished her the best of luck. She tossed the email on the bed. "No, this isn't him."

"Janet—"

"I refuse to accept this. He gave you all his attention. He bought that house. He showed all the signs of settling down here. How dare he waltz back into your life, sweep you off your feet then leave like this."

Beverly's eyes filled with tears. "Forget about it, Janet. I'm going to."

"No. You were meant to be together. Something doesn't fit and I'm going to find out what."

~

"THANK YOU FOR MEETING ME," Janet said to Karen as they sat in the university Student Lounge.

Karen looked around in distaste. She would have preferred more elegant surroundings, but planned to make this meeting short. The lounge was warm, but she refused to remove her cash-mere coat. "I'm glad to clear up things."

"What is the truth about Jeffrey?"

"I told your sister."

"I'm asking you to tell me."

Karen flicked a crumb off the table annoyed by Janet's tone. "He's bought property there that he wants to develop. Jeffrey's a city boy at heart and Detroit suits him."

"So he left without saying goodbye?"

A bead of sweat slid down Karen's back. "No. He sent her an email wishing her the best."

"Pretty shabby treatment after months of courtship."

"Courtship?" Karen laughed. "I wouldn't call it that. When Beverly came to visit she spent most of her time with Tanya and me. Jeffrey occasionally joined us, but you know him. He was just being his over friendly self. I think your sister read more into his attention." Karen tugged on the collar of her coat feeling as if she were in a sauna but determined not to show it. "The truth is he didn't want to encourage her anymore. I didn't want to hurt your sister's feelings any further, so I didn't tell her everything."

"What?"

"He's currently seeing a female executive who he's known for several years. It's possible they'll get married. I know you had high hopes for your sister, but she's just not the one." Karen abruptly stood, afraid that if she didn't leave soon she'd faint.

FREDERICK SAT on the edge of the whirlpool and stared at Jeffrey worried. His friend was withdrawn. Even the vibrant energy of their favorite sports club couldn't alter it. Usually after a game of basketball, where they'd rib each other and pretend to be sports stars, Jeffrey would be rejuvenated, but not today. Today his heart wasn't in it. Frederick frowned. Jeffrey had fallen harder for Beverly than he'd guessed, but the distance would do him good. It would give his friend perspective.

"Cecilia is here," Frederick said.

Jeffrey glanced at him, but didn't respond.

Frederick tried another tactic. "Your father would be proud that you're doing this," he said, referring to Jeffrey's new property. "This opportunity is a good bet."

"Yeah."

"Sorry I couldn't make it to the funeral."

Frederick finally got the reaction he wanted. Jeffrey's gaze sharpened. "You had other problems. Don't worry about it. I know I can depend on you."

"So you trust my judgment?"

"Of course. Always." He smiled, but the smile was fleeting.

"Now I understand," Beverly said when Janet told her about the conversation that evening. She watched Janet pace her room. "It's okay."

"How can you understand when I don't? Did he mention this woman to you? Did he mention wanting to live in the city?"

"No, but we didn't talk about personal things."

"You just talked about everything else."

"Yes. We were only friends like I am with Karen and Tanya."

"They are not your friends," Janet muttered.

"What?"

"Never mind."

"Accept the fact that he's never coming back. I have."

But Janet couldn't accept it and told Russell so as they sat alone in his classroom the next day.

"Don't be too surprised," he said putting his things away in a box. "Frederick rubs off on people. Your sister didn't measure up."

I never lower my standards, she remembered Frederick saying. "But I expected better from Jeffrey. I'm still determined that they belong together."

"Good." He pointed a thin paintbrush at her. "Don't let anyone take that fierce determination from you." He resumed his packing.

Janet watched him with regret. "I'm sorry to see you go."

"It's the end of the semester and my time to move on. I do have some good news. I have accepted a great position with The Detroit Art Institute. I promise to keep in touch. You have my email and phone number, don't you?"

"Yes, and you have mine."

Russell touched her cheek with a gentle caress. "I know."

JANET USUALLY LOOKED FORWARD to winter break but she missed Russell's company and was worried about her sister. Beverly barely spoke at dinner. Each day she went to work, came home and after dinner went straight to her bedroom. She was hurting, but would never burden anyone with her pain.

"What's wrong with her?" Mr. Barnett asked one evening when Beverly excused herself early from the table.

"Jeffrey's gone," Janet said.

"For good," Mrs. Barnett added.

"Oh," Mr. Barnett said with little interest. "Well, never mind a broken heart always mends."

However, Janet couldn't wait for her sister's broken heart to heal. One evening she lay in her bed, listening to her mother's mournful songs which mingled with the soothing voice of Elvis seeping from her father's study. Janet knew she had to do something. She searched her mind then came up with a plan. Two weeks later she burst into Beverly's room and shrieked, "Aunty Thelma said she'd love to have us come visit."

"What?"

"We're going to spend a week at her place. She lives in a suburb just outside Detroit, remember?"

"Janet—"

"I'll be on winter break and I know you have plenty of vacation time." She smiled. "Who knows what will happen?"

CHAPTER 29

Their father's sister, Thelma Nelson, was thrilled to see Beverly and Janet. She had a small house, lived alone and always welcomed visitors. She had been married but readily told people he'd gone on. Only a few people knew that Amos Nelson hadn't had the decency to die, but had left her for another woman. However, Mrs. Nelson wore black as though she were a widow; not because she missed him or wanted to deceive anyone, but because she thought that the color made her look slimmer and more elegant.

They spent the first two days sight-seeing and catching up on family stories. By the middle of the week, Janet asked permission to visit Russell.

"That's fine," her aunt said. "You've told me so much about him in your emails I feel as though I know him."

"Shouldn't we come too?" Beverly asked.

"You'll be bored," Janet said. "We'll probably just talk about art. I won't be completely alone with him. He has a studio at the Institute. I'll meet him there."

"I think that sounds like fun," her aunt said. "We'll find something else to do. Beverly, you could visit your friends here."

Janet looked at Beverly curious. "What friends?"

"I sent Tanya an email that you and I were coming and she told me to call when I arrived."

"Why don't you and Bev visit the Farmers." Janet clapped her hands excited. "We'll all have a wonderful day."

JANET LOOKED at the address then the studio door. She hadn't called first, eager to surprise Russell, but now she wondered. She took a deep breath then knocked.

He opened the door looking annoyed then surprised. *"Janet."*

"Hi."

"What—I didn't expect to see you."

"I wanted to surprise you."

He pulled on his lip. "You certainly did."

"Are you busy?" she asked seeing a teenage girl in the background.

He glanced at her. "I'm just finishing up. Stephanie, glad you could come for your lessons," he shouted over his shoulder.

The girl laughed. "Okay."

"I uh... offer tutoring." He lowered his voice "It's not glamorous, but pays the bills."

Stephanie walked past them with her backpack. "When should I—"

"I'll see you next week. I'll call you beforehand." He forced her out the door and took Janet's arm. "Come in."

Janet stepped in and saw a large painting in process. "I didn't know you had time in your schedule to give private lessons to young people."

He shrugged. "As I said, it pays the bills. I'm part of a

nonprofit organization that's trying to encourage young people in the arts."

"That's very commendable," Janet said awed by his spacious studio.

"I always make do with what I have." He sat. "I'm happy to see you. What are you doing in Detroit?"

His easy manner made her relax. At first she'd thought coming had been a mistake, but now she knew it wasn't. Janet sat in front of him. "We're visiting our aunt. She lives just outside Detroit. She invited Beverly and me to visit. Since I was so close, I decided that I wanted to see you."

But something had shifted. Her heart no longer raced and her stomach didn't tingle. Janet enjoyed being with him, but realized that her girlish infatuation had changed into deep affection and nothing more. She still admired him and reveled in the time he took to offer her a tour of the Institute and they discussed his upcoming exhibit. Janet shared with him how her classes were going and that she had sold one sketch and a portrait, not for much, but it was a start.

"How does it feel to be out of Hamsford?" he asked as they sat in the Institute's café.

"It's a breath of fresh air."

"And Beverly needed a change of scene," he said with a knowing look.

"Yes." Janet lifted her hot chocolate. "But I didn't come to talk about her. I don't want to burden you with my family's problems."

"I don't mind. I respect your family. They're like my own. Beverly will soon see that she can do better than Jeffrey Framer. Hopefully you will too."

"What do you have against him?"

He stretched his arm along the booth. "Nothing personally, but his behavior shows Frederick's influence and anyone like that rates low on my list."

"You're right," Janet said remembering Russell's story about Frederick.

"Do you have some time?"

"Sure. Why?"

"I'd like to go back to my studio." He paused. "I'd like you to sketch me. I've heard about your talent and want a chance to have a memento of your visit."

Janet blushed, pleased by his praise and interest. "I'd love to."

Moments later, Janet stood in Russell's studio smoothing down the large drawing pad propped on an easel and then organized the assortment of charcoal almost giddy with excitement. At last she'd get to sketch that beautiful face of his. He'd disappeared into the bathroom to shave. He said he hadn't had a chance that morning. She hadn't noticed a difference, but didn't want to tell him so. "I'm ready when you are," she called out to him.

"Good. I'll be right with you."

Janet closed her eyes, clasped her hands together hoping she would do a good job then took a deep breath.

"Where do you want me?"

Janet opened her eyes and gasped. Russell stood naked.

He casually walked over to the couch and sat. "I think I'll sit here." He rested his arms on the back of the couch. A slight smile touched his lips at her startled expression. "Just think of me as one of your models. Whatever thoughts are in your mind have nothing to do with me or this situation and everything to do with you. I believe it was Shakespeare who said, 'There is nothing good or bad, but thinking makes it so.'" He rubbed his chin. "So what do you think, Janet? Is this bad?"

Janet looked away and picked up a piece of charcoal. It snapped in her fingers. She set it down and picked up another one. "No, I've spent the last several years drawing naked men."

"And this is the way we were meant to be before sin entered the world." He adjusted his position.

Janet didn't respond and began sketching, determined to remain composed, although her throat was dry, her thoughts raced and her heart pounded as though she'd run a thousand miles. He was beautifully made and she had to force herself to be objective and not stare. Fortunately, she was skilled and completed the sketch in a matter of minutes. "I'm done." She placed the charcoal down and stepped back.

Russell rose to his feet, wrapped a small towel around his waist, then stood beside her, staring at the image. "Excellent. You are definitely talented." He leaned forward. "But you haven't signed it."

"Oh, um... yes." Janet hastily scribbled her name.

He smiled. "Much better."

Janet didn't move afraid that she might touch him, his nakedness seeming to grow larger and larger in her mind. She fought to ignore the tantalizing scent of his cologne. "Thank you."

"Do I make you nervous?"

"My models don't usually critique my work after I've sketched them," she said wiping the charcoal residue off her fingers.

"I see."

To her relief Russell disappeared into the bathroom again and came out clothed. He went into the kitchen and offered her a drink, which she refused. He poured himself a glass then leaned against the counter and watched her as she put on her jacket. "Janet, you have a chance to go far with your art. After you've graduated I'd be more than happy to mentor you and connect you with key people."

"I'd love that, thank you, but I've got a job waiting."

He paused surprised then asked, "Doing what? Not teaching I hope."

"No, I interned with an interior designer and she..." Janet stopped when Russell shook his head.

"You're meant for better things than prettying up some rich person's house."

"But I like—"

"Don't limit yourself Janet. When you graduate call me. Promise."

JANET LEFT Russell without promising him anything, feeling both conflicted and wonderful. He'd opened her mind to so many things. Sketching him wasn't bad. It was art. It was innocent. It was freedom. But she rode back in the taxi feeling confused. Would working for Mrs. Blakemore be limiting? She loved the work, but what if she could become a gallery artist? Was that better? She returned to her aunt's house ready to share her wonderful afternoon only to find Beverly in tears. She looked up at her aunt. "What happened?"

Mrs. Nelson looked bewildered. "We visited the Farmers, although Jeffrey wasn't there, and had a lovely time until Karen handed Beverly a copy of a newspaper from Hamsford. She said we should read it when we get home in case Beverly was feeling a little homesick. I thought that was very kind of her."

Janet folded her arms. "Hmm."

"So when we got home, Beverly read it and then burst into tears."

"Let me see it." When her aunt handed her the paper, Janet flipped through it then saw the headline: *Jeffrey Farmer engaged!*

Beverly sniffed. "I'm sure she didn't know how to tell me so she did it this way. There were hints but I didn't listen."

"Perhaps I should have read it first," Mrs. Nelson said near tears.

Janet shook her head. "Aunty you didn't do anything wrong." She turned to her sister. "I don't believe Jeffrey would have done this to you."

"Then why would the announcement be in the paper?"

"Anybody can put anything in the paper. And I bet you it wasn't him."

"I shouldn't have come here."

"But—"

Beverly squeezed her eyes shut and held her fists to her chest. "I'm not strong like you, Janet. I'm sorry." She opened her eyes. "I want to go home."

JANET SAT in her bedroom and stared out at the light snow falling. She'd hoped that being home would have helped Beverly, but each day her sister became more and more despondent. She barely ate dinner and only went to work and her bedroom where she would stay all weekend. Janet was concerned but didn't know what to do.

Suddenly, Francine burst into her room. "Come quick," she said grabbing Janet's arm and dragging her out of her bedroom and down the stairs. She led Janet into the kitchen then pointed at Beverly who was on her knees scrubbing the floor. "She's been at it for *hours*. That's not like her."

"No," Janet said quietly. "It's not."

"Daddy and Dee-dee aren't here. Should I call them?"

Janet shook her head. "No, I'll talk to her. Go. Leave her to me."

Francine looked unsure then left.

Janet cautiously approached Beverly and knelt down in front of her. "What are you doing?"

"I'm cleaning."

"But we don't need to do that."

Beverly wiped her forehead with the back of her hand. "With Mrs. Lind gone, Dee-dee needs help around the house."

"But you know that Sister Alma comes and helps her once a week."

Her scrubbing increased. "It's not enough."

Janet placed her hand on the brush to stop her. "Yes, it is."

Beverly sat back on her heels, her eyes filled with anguish. "Don't you understand? I should have married Brother Jerome. I shouldn't have encouraged you to change his mind because I thought that Jeffrey might..." She shook her head. "I put all my hopes on a stupid dream and it didn't come true. I could have made my parents so proud instead I've disappointed them. I can't clean enough or make enough money to make up for the mistake I've made."

"You haven't made a mistake," Janet said troubled by her sister's words.

"Yes, I did and now God is punishing me. It was God's will. Instead I was lead by my own vanity."

"But Mother Shea had another dream."

"Only because of my wickedness. I disobeyed Him. I should have brought honor to my family instead of shame. Everyone looks at me with pity. I'm a disgrace. I—"

Janet grabbed her sister firmly by the shoulders. "Beverly, listen."

But Beverly was beyond listening she continued to ramble, her words growing wilder and more hysterical. Soon they became gibberish. Then her eyes fell to the back of her head and she started to shake, her arms and legs flailing about.

"Francine!"

Francine immediately appeared and shrieked when she saw Beverly.

"Call 911," Janet told her. Minutes later the EMTs arrived

and stabilized Beverly then whisked her into the ambulance. Janet jumped in her car and followed them, instructing Francine before she left, to let their parents know exactly what happened when they returned home from prayer meeting.

Janet waited alone in the emergency room for about an hour before her family joined her. She calmed her mother and told her father about the seizure then they all fell silent. Nearly an hour later a doctor came and spoke to the family. He explained that Beverly had suffered a stress induced seizure. He also explained that she was dehydrated.

The doctor ordered that Beverly be kept in the hospital for several days then released her, but not before recommending that she make a follow up appointment with one of their psychiatrists.

Mr. Barnett tore up the referral. "You think my daughter is crazy?" he asked the young doctor.

"No, but we believe she had a nervous breakdown."

"A nervous what?"

"Breakdown," the doctor said patiently. "Her mind—"

"Her mind is fine. Perfectly sound. And any demon of the mind can be prayed out." Mr. Barnett wagged his finger at him. "The Evil One has not taken hold of her. Her body just needs rest and we'll take care of that."

And they did. When she returned home, no one spoke about Beverly's hospital stay. They all tried to help her recover and pretended as if nothing had happened. Beverly's boss put her on extended sick leave, for as long as she needed, and promised to hold her job. No one mentioned Jeffrey Farmer. But Beverly didn't recover and finally Mrs. Barnett decided the winter weather was bad for her and sent her to Jamaica to stay with her sister.

～

In April Janet accepted Valerie's invitation to visit and spend spring break in Pennsylvania. However, she regretted telling her mother so early when she went into the kitchen. Even though the window was open, heat baked the room and the scent of oil, cinnamon, ginger and vinegar permeated the air. Janet saw bowls of crescent shaped meat pies, jerk chicken, bulla cake and peas and rice fighting for space on the table.

Janet rested a hand against her chest. "What are you doing?"

Mrs. Barnett wrapped the meat pies in foil. "You can't go empty handed."

"Dee-dee, I can't take all this food with me."

"You can and you will."

"But Dee-dee—"

"They'll need it. Who knows what kind of shops they have up there. They need nourishment from home." She pointed to the stove. "Mind my fish."

Janet went to the stove and saw fried fish simmering in coconut milk and spices. "This is too much."

"What was that?"

"Nothing."

Mrs. Barnett nodded and tapped Janet on the shoulder. "Just do as I say. You'll thank me."

Mrs. Barnett was right. Valerie and Brother Jerome were overjoyed by the food Janet brought them and that evening they ate and talked about Hamsford and their new life in Pennsylvania. The next day Janet stood in the main living room, looking at the Jeromes' expansive property. "It's so good to be here."

"It's good to have you here," Valerie said excited to see her.

Janet turned to her friend and smiled. Valerie had certainly done well for herself. "It's a beautiful home."

"It's a mausoleum. Don't look surprised Janet. Remember I can read you. Peter can't help himself. Whenever Mrs. Amsted recommends or mentions something she thinks he should have, he goes out and buys it right away."

"Mrs. Amsted?"

"She's an associate who he does some investing with." Valerie pointed out the window. "Her house is over there."

Janet peered through the window and saw the large structure in the distance. "It's enormous."

"Peter hasn't seemed to notice that. She's always throwing out and replacing things. Unfortunately, objects that fit her house only crowd ours, but he loves getting them. He respects her opinion above anyone because she's so cultured."

Janet rolled her eyes. "Of course."

"I don't mind. He has a large barn that he renovated where he keeps the rest of his collectables. It makes him happy."

"And what keeps you happy?"

"I'll show you." Valerie led Janet to the attic where she had created a restful sewing and reading room. Janet looked at the uncluttered space and smiled. Yes, this would make her friend very happy. "It's wonderful."

"Thank you." She sat. "He does his thing and I do mine and we are very satisfied."

"Valerie!" Brother Jerome cried from below. "Come, I have something to show you and Janet."

Moments later they entered the living room and saw Brother Jerome holding up a large ornate lamp. "Isn't it exquisite?"

When Janet didn't reply, Valerie did. "Yes, where did you get it?"

"Mrs. Amsted was going to donate it, but she was kind enough to give it to me." He rested it on the table. "I'll have to find the perfect place to put it."

Janet looked around the crowded room and mumbled, "That should keep you busy."

He snapped his fingers. "I also have fantastic news. Mrs.

Amsted has invited us for dinner this evening." He looked at Janet. 'She wants to meet you. How lucky you are. She's very choosy about the people she entertains. You'll be fine."

However, Brother Jerome changed his mind when he saw what Janet wore that evening. "Don't you have anything else?" he asked.

"Peter," Valerie scolded.

"I'm sorry, my dear. You're right." He stroked his chin and looked critically at Janet's outfit. "Valerie is now acquainted with dressing formally, but whatever you have will have to do. Mrs. Amsted is very gracious. And-"

Valerie tapped her watch. "The time Peter."

He glanced at the clock then ran to the door. "Yes, yes we can't be late." He held out their coats. "Come on." He quickly shuffled them into the car and drove to the Amsted house. Janet stared amazed by the expanse of property while Brother Jerome provided a narration on the history of the land—who owned it before the Amsted's and any other trivia that came to mind.

Fortunately, it was a short drive. Brother Jerome continued his narration as they walked towards the large ornate door and only stopped when the butler answered. The butler led them into the main hall where their host sat with her daughter. Mrs. Amsted was a commanding figure who held her years well— although most people didn't know exactly what they were. She had pale skin, green eyes and a silver streak that cut through her soft brown hair, which was pulled up into an upsweep.

Her daughter, Daphne was a lively young woman of twenty-five with shoulder length ash blond hair and rosebud lips. She patted the seat next to her when she saw Janet.

"We're going to have another guest arriving soon," Mrs. Amsted said. "He's staying with me for a few days." Before anyone could ask who, she continued, "He is one of the many young people I have sponsored over the years to attend our universities. I've had students from India, Saudi Arabia, and other countries around the world. But I have to admit that Frederick was one of my favorites and still keeps in touch. Ah, there he is. Your ears must have been burning. We were just talking about you."

Frederick strolled into the room with his hands in his pockets. "Good things I hope." He halted when he saw Janet and she stared at him, equally startled. "Hello."

"Hi."

Mrs. Amsted's gaze darted between them. "You know each other?"

"Yes," Brother Jerome said. "Durand spent time in Hamsford. That's the town I told you about. I, we lived there before coming here. Janet and her family still live there."

"I see. So this is a mini-reunion. How exciting."

Frederick overcame his paralysis and walked over to Janet. "How is your family?"

"They're doing fine." She wanted to mention Jeffrey's abrupt departure and sudden engagement but didn't.

"I'm glad to hear that."

Mrs. Amsted stood. "You can become reacquainted another time, right now I want everyone to join me in the theater room." She turned and left. Daphne groaned and Frederick looked less than enthused.

CHAPTER 30

"Ohat's in the theater room?" Janet asked following Daphne down the hall.

"Mom's vacation photos. We're going to be in for a *long* night."

Brother Jerome, ingratiated himself by commenting on each image and saying how fascinating the scenery was, while Janet and Valerie could not help noticing that Mrs. Amsted was prominent in each picture, leaving the scenery as a spot in the background. Daphne was conspicuously absent. Frederick's expression did not reveal his thoughts and he remained quiet throughout. Fortunately, the butler announced dinner saving them from a showing of her trip to the Andes.

Janet marveled at the sight that greeted them as they entered the dining room. The table was exquisitely decorated with so many settings it looked ready for a large party. A massive bouquet of live flowers sat in the center of an enormous rosewood dining table. The place setting consisted of white bone china trimmed with silver, Italian crystal glasses and linen napkins with the family seal. Janet wasn't intimidated by the assortment of utensils. Her Aunt Bernice had made it her task to teach all her nieces proper etiquette, including which fork or spoon to use, how to use a napkin, and other very helpful tips.

Janet's eyes widened when the appetizer arrived—a steaming bowl of clams flavored with ham, charred tomatoes and parsley oil. This was followed by the main course: olive-oil poached salmon served with steamed asparagus, and risotto made with three kinds of onions. The desert was a roasted pineapple split with macadamia brittle, served in delicate Austrian crystal bowls. Throughout, two butlers stood at attention, anticipating each guest's request.

Frederick sat across from Janet and twice tried to engage her in conversation, but she stopped his attempts by talking to Daphne, who sat next to her.

"You're not at all what I expected," Daphne said. "The people that Brother Jerome usually knows are, are...." She searched for the words.

Janet smiled. "I'm glad to say that we are not all the same. Besides I've known Valerie much longer."

Daphne nodded. "That explains it. Do you like bicycle riding?"

"Yes very much."

"We have a wonderful bike path that leads to the parkland at the back of our house."

"What are you two talking about?" Mrs. Amsted asked from her position at the head of the table. "Private conversation amongst guests is rude. I hate feeling left out, especially in my home. Tell me about yourself, Janet."

"There's not much to say. I'm finishing my last year at the university."

"What is your major?"

"Art History."

"Art History? What a useless degree."

"She's an artist," Frederick said.

"I hope your family is wealthy enough to sustain you," Mrs. Amsted said unimpressed. "It's not likely you will be able to make a living from it."

Frederick lifted his glass. "She's very good."

"As good as your sister?"

"Better."

Mrs. Amsted raised her brows amazed. "That's high praise indeed, Janet. I hope I will be able to see your work one day."

Frederick cut his asparagus. "She's excellent at doing portraits."

"Good, how long will you be here?"

"I have five more days," Janet said uncertain.

"Perfect, that's plenty of time. I would like you to do a portrait of me."

"But I didn't bring any of my art materials, and—"

"That's not a problem. Whatever you need I will have them here for you by tomorrow. Just give Frederick a list. He knows more about supplies and such than I do." She placed her napkin on the table. "I'm finished. Let's go into the sitting room." Mrs. Amsted left and Daphne, Frederick and Brother Jerome followed. Janet seized Valerie's arm. "This is awful."

"You didn't like the food?"

"No, the portrait. I can't do it. That's not why I came to visit. I had planned to spend as much time as I could with you."

Valerie patted Janet's hand in reassurance. "You'll have time with me in the evenings. Just think of the honor. If she likes what you do, and I'm sure she will, you could get a lot of commissioned work. Mrs. Amsted is well known in high society. She knows judges, senators, and top executives with multi-billion dollar companies."

"But—"

"Plus, Peter will never forgive you, or me, if you say no."

Janet slumped her shoulders, resigned. "Why did Durand have to mention my art?"

"I think he admires your art... and you."

"I think he's just trying to frighten me by comparing me to his sister."

"I think you're wrong."

But Valerie wasn't able to expand further because Mrs. Amsted called them to join her. They all gathered in the sitting room where Mrs. Amsted and Brother Jerome busied themselves looking at an antique catalog while Valerie looked on and smiled. Daphne convinced Frederick and Janet to help her complete a 3D puzzle of a castle.

"Where's Milton?" Daphne asked.

Frederick studied a piece then put it in place. "Upstairs sleeping. How come every time I visit you're working on one of these?" he asked her.

"Because I know you can help me finish them. I have three more upstairs." Daphne turned to Janet. "He's very handy that way." She picked up a puzzle piece and tried to put it in place but it refused to fit. "What were you doing in Hamsford?" she asked him.

"Helping a friend with a building."

She pounded the piece in place. "Figures."

"That doesn't fit."

Daphne sighed and removed it. "I know." She frowned at the bent end.

"The key is to find pieces that fit together and build one side of the structure." He quickly assembled five pieces.

"I told you he was good. Oh look, Janet, your piece matches his."

Janet stared down at the small window piece she held then placed it next to his.

Daphne grinned. "A perfect fit."

Janet folded her arms. "I'm not really good at puzzles."

"Oh, please don't stop. With your help we can finish this thing in no time."

Janet picked up another piece that matched Frederick's. "Well done," he said when she fit it in place.

Janet nodded. "Thank you." Then they shared a look that fueled their competitive nature and soon they each raced to see who could build faster. They grabbed pieces, fitting them together. At times Janet's hands brushed his but she didn't notice, determined to beat him. Daphne sat back knowing she couldn't compete with their quick eye and dexterity so she just watched them. An hour later the castle stood completed.

"That was amazing," Daphne said. "Did you two get on this well in Hamsford? You make a great team."

Janet gasped astonished. "Work together?" She shook her head, not knowing whether to laugh or scream in horror. "Oh no. We hardly spoke to each other."

"Why not?" Daphne wagged her finger at Frederick. "Did you work too much as always?"

Janet flashed a sly smile. "The first time I met Durand was at a party and he refused to talk to anyone."

Daphne looked at him in disbelief. "Frederick, she's lying, right?"

He cleared his throat. "I was feeling awkward at the time."

"Awkward?" Janet said surprised. "Even though half the people were in awe of you and the other half impressed by you? You're a wealthy, attractive man who has traveled the world. How can that be?"

He leaned forward, resting his elbows on his knees. "I don't find it easy mingling with strangers."

Janet tilted her head, doubtful. "You're shy?"

Daphne laughed; Frederick sent her a look that made her stop. "No, it's more complicated."

"I see." Janet also leaned forward and held his gaze. "Well, you will notice that I never offer to sing, because I do it badly. I make sure to avoid situations that put me in a bad light."

Frederick lowered his gaze. "Point taken."

"She's just teasing you Frederick, right Janet?" Daphne asked unsure. "He's the most sociable person I know."

Janet shrugged. "I suppose it all depends on the type of people."

He met her gaze. "No, it depends on whether I feel accepted, or not."

Janet felt her cheeks grow warm, remembering how quickly everyone had called him The Original. "True, but one can gain acceptance with minimal effort. You didn't try."

Daphne jumped to her feet, tiring of the conversation and not understanding it. "How about I get another puzzle?"

"No," her mother said. "It's time for the Jeromes and their guest to leave. It was a pleasure to meet you Janet. Did you give Frederick your list?"

"Uh—"

"I know what she needs," Frederick said.

Janet blinked, stunned by his assumption.

He cleared his throat and softened his tone. "I mean I can guess."

Daphne glanced at Frederick then Janet and began to smile. "I'm sure you can."

He shot her a glance; her smile grew.

Mrs. Amsted beamed. "Then it's all set." She patted Janet on the back as she led her to the door. "I expect to see you very soon."

"Yes."

"Tomorrow at two."

Janet inwardly groaned knowing she had no choice. "I'll see you then."

~

JANET ARRIVED at two on the dot, Brother Jerome made sure of it. The butler, Stephens, led her into the solarium where Mrs. Amsted sat in a chaise lounge talking to Frederick while Milton slept at his feet. The solarium looked like a designer showroom one would see in an upscale magazine. And Mrs. Amsted looked like the perfect model.

She stretched her hand out to Janet. "Ah, there you are," she said in a booming voice that jolted Milton awake. He yawned and stretched then, seeing Janet, ran over to greet her. "This is how I want you to paint me, sitting on this lounge chair."

Janet stroked Milton. "That's fine, but I don't see any supplies."

"I think I should have an animal in it too. Can you paint dogs? Of course you can that was a silly question. Frederick, I'm going to borrow Milton. Do you think he'll be able to keep still?" Before Frederick could respond she called Milton to her and placed him on her lap. "Yes, that's better. How do I look?"

"Wonderful," Janet said. "but I need supplies."

"Yes, and I've taken care of everything."

At that moment, Stephens and another young man entered carrying an easel, paper, canvas pad, a selection of brand new watercolors, pastels and charcoal, pens, and an assortment of the finest brushes. Janet stared amazed by the quality. Throughout her years at college she had only dreamed of being able to afford the kind of collection she was looking at.

"If you don't like it, you can blame Frederick. He made the selection."

Daphne came into the room and noticed Janet's face. "I think she likes them. I think she likes them a lot. Don't you Janet?"

"They're wonderful," she said unable to look away.

"Frederick would have bought half the store for you."

Janet glanced at him. "Maybe he thinks I need the help."

He shook his head. "No I—"

Daphne interrupted him. "Are you kidding? He thinks—"

Frederick spun to her. "Don't you have something better to do?"

She fluttered her lashes. "Not really."

"Find something," Mrs. Amsted said. "You're distracting us."

She made a face at Frederick then left.

Mrs. Amsted gestured to Janet, eager to start. "What do you plan to do?"

"I'm thinking."

"Think faster. I can't be here all day."

Janet agreed and decided to do a quick study in watercolor. Oils would take too long to dry, and she didn't like working with acrylics, although they dried quickly. Watercolor was her favorite medium, next to charcoal, and she wanted to complete this task as soon as possible.

Janet picked up a pencil. "Now we can get started."

She expected Frederick to leave, but he didn't. Although she tried to become engrossed with her drawing Janet couldn't ignore his presence. When Janet left to go home, she found Daphne reading and asked her questions about Frederick, hoping she could find out news about Jeffrey, but Daphne didn't give her the information she wanted so she gave up.

Frederick sat in on the session the next day as well, again saying nothing, but she could feel him watching her. Janet completed the watercolor by the end of the second sitting.

Mrs. Amsted examined it. "Nice. Very nice. If you keep on practicing, one day you may be able to make money as a professional. Of course you'll be competing with computers that do just as well."

Janet opened her mouth to respond, but Frederick interrupted her. "Actually, this portrait is one of the best I've seen.

Observe how elegant you look and the way she captured your hand on Milton's fur. Computer graphics can't do that."

Janet stared at him speechless, surprised by his praise.

Mrs. Amsted tilted her head to the side considering his words. "Yes, you're right. I do look wonderful. I'll have it framed right away and hang it above the mantle. Well done, Janet."

JANET LEFT RELIEVED to have completed the assignment. Now she had a chance to spend more time with Valerie and avoid Frederick. But he surprised her by showing up at their house the next morning while Valerie and Brother Jerome were out.

She motioned towards a chair and he placed a package on the coffee table, then sat. "Mrs. Amsted wanted to thank you for the portrait by giving you the supplies you used."

Janet stared at the package. "But they are expensive."

"They'd go to waste in her house."

"I see."

Silence fell. They sat facing each other, but Frederick made no move to leave.

"Thank you."

He nodded then tapped his knee. "Your friend seems to be happy here. I see that they displayed your picture." He looked at the painting Janet had given the couple as a wedding gift.

"Yes, it reminds Valerie of Hamsford."

"Does she miss it?"

"No."

"Would you miss it if you had to leave? I know it's hard to leave family and friends, but some people are more tied to a place than others."

Janet frowned unsure of what he was trying to say. "I don't understand."

"Never mind." Frederick stood. "I better go." He pointed to the package. "Enjoy the paints," he said then left.

Janet watched him walk away and softly said, "I will."

~

"It's obvious that he's in love with you," Valerie said when Janet told her of Frederick's strange visit and his behavior at Mrs. Amsted's.

"That's ridiculous."

Valerie sighed. "Think about it."

"I have thought about it. I think he's bored. Fortunately, I'm going bicycle riding with Daphne tomorrow so he won't catch me home alone again."

~

"You're tormenting yourself." Mrs. Amsted said when she found Frederick on her tennis court hitting a ball against the wall. Milton watched him.

"I'm working on my backhand." He hit the ball again.

"You've been working on it for nearly three hours. Take a break."

Frederick hit the ball once more then stopped. "I was just thinking." He walked to the bench where he'd left his things and picked up a towel.

"About Janet?"

He wiped his face then draped the towel around his neck, chagrined. "Am I that obvious?"

"Only to Daphne and me. We know you too well." She handed him a bottled sports drink. He thanked her and twisted off the top. "You're like a brother to Daphne and a son to me," Mrs. Amsted said resting her hand on the chain fence. "Any woman would be lucky to have you."

Frederick took a long swallow then replaced the top.

"I've seen the way she looks at you. She's asked Daphne lots of questions about you."

He turned sharply to her.

Mrs. Amsted grinned at his interest. "Yes, that's right."

"I'm not sure how she feels about me."

"She likes you. It's clear. We women know these things."

Frederick thought for a moment then put his towel in his bag and zipped it up. "I have to consider my family. Her family. How different our lives are."

Mrs. Amsted tugged on his arm and forced him to face her. "You're right. But I've seen how the Jeromes live, it's not so very different from us and you can make compromises. I wouldn't have chosen someone like her for you, but sometimes the heart knows what we need. Follow your heart. Do you love her?"

Frederick took a deep breath then nodded.

Mrs. Amsted cupped his face in her hands. He was so young and so far life hadn't been fair. She was the mother he no longer had and she wanted to see the lingering sorrow in his eyes disappear. "Then go after her. You've suffered so much. It's time you reach for the joy you deserve."

He took Mrs. Amsted's hand and kissed the back of it then flashed one of his rare smiles. "I will."

JANET LOVED LONG BIKE RIDES. She and Daphne rode the bike path along the lake in the park then rested under a tree. Dragonflies skittered over the lake while the grass looked brilliantly green against the sandy dirt path.

Daphne leaned her head against the trunk. "It's been great

having you visit. Usually Frederick is the only ally against my mothers' dreadful dinner parties."

"So you and he are good friends?" Janet asked curious, hoping she'd have better luck getting the information she wanted.

"The best. Frederick is a wonderful person to have as a friend. Loyal, generous and he takes good care of those he cares about. He recently told me about his friend Jeffrey."

"What did he say?" Janet asked in a halting tone.

"I can't go into detail, he's a very private man, but he told me he saved him from marrying some deacon's daughter."

Janet swallowed hard and yanked a blade of grass from the ground. "And did he give a reason why his friend needed to be saved?"

"Sort of. Jeffrey wanted to marry this woman but Frederick didn't approve."

"I see." But she didn't see. She couldn't understand how Frederick thought he had the right to ruin her sister's chance at happiness.

"Janet, are you all right?"

Janet abruptly stood. "I'm getting a headache." She strapped on her helmet then picked up her bike. "Do you mind if we go back?" Janet climbed on her bike and sped away.

WHEN JANET STORMED into the house, Valerie met her at the front door. "You won't believe who's here."

"I can honestly say I don't care."

"You will when I tell you. It's Durand. He's been waiting for the last thirty minutes just to talk to you."

Janet headed for the stairs. "I don't want to see him."

"But what am I supposed to say?" Valerie said anxious. "You

have to see him, he knows you're here. I can't send him home and I can't lie to him."

Janet gripped the railing but didn't turn.

"Please? For me? I have to live here and he's a guest in my home."

Janet took a deep breath, harnessed her anger then calmly walked into the living room.

Frederick got up when she entered, but Janet walked past him, as though he were a piece of furniture and sat in the armchair facing him. "You wanted to see me?"

He sat. "Yes."

She crossed her legs and swung her foot impatient. "About what?"

"I would like to discuss something very important with you."

Janet stood unable to look at him any longer. "Well, we'll have to do it outside. I promised Valerie I would trim some of her bushes." Janet left the room before he could object and marched into the garden. She pulled on a pair of Valerie's gardening gloves then grabbed a large pair of pruning shears and headed for the rose bushes.

"Valerie keeps a beautiful garden," Frederick said.

Janet viciously snipped off a branch. "Yes." She attacked the bush with such vengeance that it seemed to tremble under her assault.

Frederick frowned. "Are you sure you should prune that much?"

"You wanted to talk to me about something?" She chopped off the head of one of the roses. It fell to the ground as though it had been decapitated.

Frederick stood on the opposite side of the bush hoping to get her attention. "I came here initially to tell you about an art exhibit I thought you might like, but it doesn't seem important anymore."

Janet let the shears fall to her side and looked up at him. "And what *is* important?" When she saw him pull a small black box from his coat pocket she nearly laughed at the absurdity of her thoughts. "Let me guess. You came here to ask me to marry you because despite how different our worlds are you've fallen in love with me."

He stared at her amazed. "How did you know?"

"What?"

"I knew we were of the same mind but this borders on telepathic. I've been carrying this ring in my pocket for days and you knew it all along."

Janet sent him a wary look. "Knew what?"

Frederick held his hands out in helpless surrender. "The fact that I love you." He placed a hand on his chest. "I am hopelessly and deeply in love with you." He shook his head amazed by his own declaration. "Saying these words to you is completely out of character for me, but I can't help myself. I know that our lives are as different as the sun is from the moon, your family is not the sort I typically associate with and you're not even the type of woman I'd usually consider. But that doesn't matter.

"My family probably won't approve of you because of your background and upbringing. But I don't care. In spite of an ocean of contrast between us, I hope my love for you will bridge that gap. Janet, I want you to marry me."

Janet slapped the shears against her palm and stared down at them. A rose petal stuck to one of the blades. She slowly raised her eyes and looked at him. "I'm sorry. I—"

He shook his head. "There's no need to apologize. I know it's amazing. I listed all the reasons why I shouldn't marry you and it was a long list. I could've filled pages. I thought about all the people I would be disappointing and struggled with my feelings but nothing helped. Nothing could override my love for you. So, I accepted my fate and here I am."

"Yes," she said in a flat tone. "Here you are." Janet brushed the petal off the blade. She looked up at him. "But you must let me apologize. I am sorry that your thoughts about me have caused you pain. I had no idea. And I hope that you will quickly forget everything you just said. I am also sorry that you wasted your money on a ring. But most of all I'm sorry that you asked me to marry you thinking that I'd say yes."

Frederick stared at her as if she'd just spit in his face. "That's it?"

"What more do you want me to say? I think I've made myself clear." Janet tossed down her shears and walked towards the back of the garden.

He followed her. "Not clear enough. A man doesn't bare his heart to a woman so she can stomp on it. I need to know why."

Janet stopped and stared at him. She yanked off her gloves and slapped them hard against her thigh. "*I* also have an extensive list of why *I* would never marry you. One being the fact that I just learned that you're the reason Jeffrey Farmer dumped my sister."

He blinked.

"Do you deny it?"

"No I don't. Why would I? I didn't see that relationship going anywhere. I could see that your sister liked him, but she also liked Brother Jerome and I assume, any other man who pays attention to her."

Janet trembled with outrage. "What?"

"She seems to be a very sweet girl, but I never saw her do

anything to show that she liked Jeffrey more than anyone else. Besides, their personalities are too different. Their aspirations are worlds apart." He threw up his hand. "It seems I was more correct in my analysis of his situation than I was of mine."

"She was hospitalized for an entire week because of your self-righteous meddling."

Frederick's jaw twitched. "I'm sorry to hear that, but I had no choice. I was only thinking of my friend's happiness."

Janet spun away from him, marched up to a small tree and pulled off a dead leaf. "At the expense of hers!" She took a deep breath then faced him and hit the gloves against her palm as though she were applauding him. "Congratulations, you saved your friend from a terrible fate. But I'm sure you don't need any congratulations. You're already very proud of how you take care of your friends. But aside from ruining my sister's happiness, there's another reason why I hate you." She saw a flicker of pain in his eyes, but didn't care. She reveled in the power of saying the word. "Yes, hate." She rested her hands on her hips. "Your treatment of Russell Wilcox was and is despicable and validates what I think of you."

Frederick lifted a branch. "I see you're eager to believe anything that man says."

"I believe the facts he told me."

He lowered the branch and shook his head in disgust. "What facts?"

"He told me of his suffering and how you stole his inheritance from him. How you attacked him." She held out her arm. "He showed me his scar. The one you gave him."

'Yes," Frederick said his voice low with venom. "I gave him that scar and if he hadn't moved his arm I would have gotten his heart."

"And probably eaten it like a cannibal."

Frederick turned away.

His silence angered her more. "He's done nothing but kind things for my family. I have yet to come across a more selfless, more caring man. While you —you have broken my sister's heart and treated my family with nothing but contempt and disdain."

He shot her a glance. "No, I haven't."

"You just told me that my family is 'not the sort you typically associate with' as if they were beneath you. You then tell me that I am not the type of woman you usually like and that you're disappointing your family with your choice. What do you expect me to say?"

"Did you want me to lie? I thought you were above the simple art of flattery."

"You didn't even try."

"I was being honest. I thought you'd appreciate how I felt and all I had to think about. That's just how I am."

"Yes, and I can't stand you. I think you're arrogant, resentful, proud and barbaric. You may consider yourself above others, but I think you're lower than dirt." Janet stepped towards him and dropped her voice. "The first moment I saw you, it took me only five minutes to decide that you were the last man on God's green earth I would ever marry."

Frederick held up his hand. "Okay. You've made yourself perfectly clear." He took a step back eager to leave. "Don't worry. I'll never bother you again." He turned and left.

Janet watched him go then stumbled over to a stone bench and sank down in shock. She wished she could laugh at the absurdity of it all, but she couldn't. *He'd wanted to marry her?* How could that be? It was too ridiculous to be true.

Valerie raced up to her. "I just saw Durand leave. What did he want to talk to you about?"

Janet stared at the mutilated rosebush. "It was a misunderstanding," she said in a soft voice. "Nothing important."

~

FREDERICK BURST into the Amsted house and headed for the stairs, but stopped when Mrs. Amsted said his name.

"Frederick is that you?" she called again from the solarium.

He briefly shut his eyes, gripping his hands into fists, and composed himself before he faced her.

"I've been working with Stephens on where to put my portrait." She turned to him. "So how did it go?"

His expression gave nothing away, his voice remained neutral. "I was right. She doesn't like me."

"I knew she might be backwards but I didn't believe she was imbecilic. What do you mean she doesn't like you?"

"She said no."

"Did she say why?"

He took a step back and jerked his head to the stairs. "I need to take Milton on his walk."

Mrs. Amsted took a step towards him, her voice rising. "How could she refuse you? Perhaps she didn't understand the question."

"She understood it."

Mrs. Amsted spun around to Stephens and gestured to the portrait in anger. "Get rid of it at once."

"No," Frederick said. "How she feels about me doesn't... She still..." He stopped then tried again. "It's an excellent portrayal of you."

"But Frederick—"

"I don't want to talk about her again." He took another step back. "Now I'll take Milton on his walk."

Mrs. Amsted watched him leave feeling as if her heart were breaking. Daphne came in looking worried. "What's wrong with Frederick? He walked right past me as if I wasn't there."

She looked at her daughter. She didn't want to share his pain. His proposal would remain a secret. "It's business."

"What should I do with the painting?" Stephens asked.

Mrs. Amsted glared at the image. She'd encouraged Frederick to take a risk and the girl had made a fool of her. She'd never forgive Janet for replacing the sorrow in his eyes with anguish. "Put that thing in a place where I'll never see it."

FREDERICK WALKED to the local park, which was over two miles away, but he didn't notice. He couldn't erase Janet's words from his mind. They echoed as though she'd shouted them in a cave and pierced him as if she'd laced each word with poison.

She'd refused him. Not with embarrassment or apology, but with vehemence. She thought he was "lower than dirt." "Barbaric." Him. Frederick Durand—A man who had parents lining up their daughters to marry him. She didn't just dislike him, she *hated* him. She didn't just hate his actions, she hated *him*.

Fine. Let her believe what she wanted to about him. Why should he have to explain himself? He'd never had to before. He was used to doing what he wanted without argument. He'd been the youngest prefect in his boarding school and had commanded respect and loyalty. If he wanted someone to do something, they did it. They never asked why.

Frederick stopped and looked at the lake and the ripples that Milton created as he lapped up water. He hung his head and clasped his hand behind his neck. No. He had to defend himself. He had to challenge her accusations and rectify his reputation. She may never love him or like him, but he wanted her to understand him.

"Mrs. Amsted wants to see you," Valerie said in an excited whispered when she entered Janet's room.

Janet lay on her bed and pulled the pillow over her head. "Tell her I have a headache."

"That won't be necessary," Mrs. Amsted said. "This won't take long."

Janet lifted her head. "You wanted to see me?"

Mrs. Amsted looked at Valerie. "Do you have a place that's more private?"

"Yes. The attic."

She waited. Valerie got the hint then led the way. Janet reluctantly followed. Once they'd reached the attic Valerie left them alone and shut the door. Janet took a seat. Mrs. Amsted did not.

"Frederick told me about his visit here today. No, you don't have to speak. I don't care about anything you have to say."

Janet crossed her legs and swung her foot.

Mrs. Amsted lifted her nose as if she smelled a foul odor. "I don't know who you think you are, but it's obvious you don't know the man you've just rejected. He's one of the finest young men I've ever known. I'm glad this news will get no further than us. I wouldn't want anyone to know that he stooped so low as to ask a high minded nobody to marry him. He wouldn't have asked you if I hadn't encouraged him and I resent that immensely."

"You don't know—"

"I know that you deserve to stay in your little town, with your little friends and have your talks about your little thoughts and not venture out into the real world, which you know nothing about. You are talented but not wise. You can't discern quality from charm. And you deserve any heartbreak you get." She walked to the door. "I wish you no success and I hope never to see you again." She opened the door and left.

"The feeling is mutual," Janet muttered. She went to the

window and watched Mrs. Amsted get into her car. Her words stung, but Janet brushed them aside because she knew Mrs. Amsted didn't know who Frederick really was. Just like Karen and Tanya and Jeffrey, she was blind to the beast underneath the money and prestige. But Janet knew the real man and felt proud of her decision.

"What was that all about?" Valerie asked behind her.

"She wanted to talk about art."

A FIERCE SPRING rain pounded against the windows as Janet waited for her ride to the station.

"I wish we could take you," Valerie said.

Janet looked at the sky darkened by clouds. "It's not your fault I'm leaving a day early. You had other plans. At least Daphne can take me."

"Yes, cheaper than a taxi." She paused. "So you still haven't changed your mind?"

Janet shook her head then peered through the rain. "I think I see her car." She turned to her friend and hugged her. "It was great to see you."

"The same."

Janet picked up her luggage and opened the door.

Frederick stood there.

Her mouth fell open. "Where's Daphne?"

Valerie pushed Janet aside and opened the door wider. "You're getting soaked, Durand. Come inside."

He stepped in and pushed back the hood of his mackintosh. "Daphne had an emergency. I'll take you." He noticed her luggage in the hallway and picked them up. "The car's open." He pushed his hood up and dashed back outside.

Janet didn't move.

Valerie nudged her. "I know you don't like him, but don't keep him waiting."

Janet reluctantly opened her umbrella and stepped outside. Sheets of rain fell around her, deafening any other sound. She stopped then turned to her friend. "Pray for me," she mouthed.

"Always."

Janet steeled herself then got into the car with the man she'd never wanted to see again.

~

THE CAR FELT LIKE A TOMB—DARK and cramped. Janet fiddled with the air vent and seatbelt, wishing she could roll down the window. The rain sounded like golf balls as it bounced off the roof.

"I need to talk to you," Frederick said as he merged onto the highway. He held up his hand to wave off any protest. "Don't worry. I won't bring up the subject I mentioned before. I told you I would never bring it up again. I want to forget about it as much as you do. But I can't let you leave without knowing the truth about me. You said you had many reasons for hating me and listed two: my role in persuading Jeffrey not to marry your sister and my dealings with Russell Wilcox. I want to defend myself against both accusations."

Janet watched the windshield wipers move back and forth.

"First, I want to tell you about my involvement with Jeffrey and Beverly. The decision wasn't done callously. I saw how your sister captured Jeffrey's heart. But I was not surprised. I've seen him in love before. However, it was at the dedication and later at Valerie's wedding that my apprehension of Beverly's true feelings emerged. I watched and saw that she was friendly, but she was no friendlier to him than she was to his sisters or anyone else she was with.

"Obviously, you know your sister better than I do, and I am sorry that I misjudged her feelings, but I made my assessment based on what I saw. I didn't want to see it, but to me it was clear. She is a very beautiful young woman used to men's attention. I didn't think Jeffrey had a chance of happiness with someone who could as easily marry him or any other man. I also know that your ways in Hamsford are different than I'm used to and that was another concern I had.

"Jeffrey returned to Hamsford after seeing a lot of the world and I was afraid that your sister wouldn't fit easily into his new life. I apologize, in advance, if I offend you, but I have to speak honestly." He altered the wipers to go faster. "I also objected to your mother's loud announcement of her daughter's conquest to marry a Farmer, your middle sister's habit of demanding attention, your two younger sisters' propensity to flirt with anyone of the male gender and, I hate to say this, your father's lack of observation of what was going on around him."

Janet sat rigid, pressing her foot against the floor in hopes that the car would move faster.

"I can't say anything about you or Beverly, but I couldn't ignore the rest of your family and the impact they would have on my friend. As the months passed I knew that it would be in Jeffrey's best interest to leave Hamsford and sever his connection with Beverly.

"Karen felt the same way I did so we met with Jeffrey and told him about a wonderful opportunity for property development. Although the idea intrigued him, he had no interest in staying in Detroit to see it through because he wanted to marry your sister. I persuaded him not to. I showed him all the reasons why it would be a terrible decision. To my surprise he didn't listen to any of them. However, there was one area where he wasn't certain—Beverly's true feelings for him. I made it clear that she probably only saw him as a friend and because he had his own doubts and trusted my observations I was able to convince him that I was correct."

Janet glared at him. "Is that when he got engaged?"

"What are you talking about?"

Janet turned away. Of course he'd never have read *The Hamsford Daily*. It was beneath him. "Forget it. Go on."

Frederick adjusted the rearview mirror. "I did what I thought was right at the time and have no regrets except that," he faltered. "I wish I had let Tanya tell Jeffrey that Beverly had come to visit him in Detroit when she asked me what to do. I'm not proud of that. I'm sorry that what happened hurt your sister. I didn't do it on purpose and I have nothing more to say."

Janet folded her arms and watched the ominous storm clouds grow darker.

"Now about what you consider my reprehensible treatment of Russell Wilcox," Frederick said with a note of sarcasm. "Because I don't know the particular accusation against me I can only refute his story by sharing my own.

"Let's start with his name. He was born Bernard Rupert Strickner. His father was an admirable man who worked on my family's property in Jamaica where my parents lived for many years. My father's strong feelings and high regard for Mr. Strickner naturally spilled over to his immediate family. He gave Mrs. Strickner a position in his office and treated Bernard as one of his own. He paid for his schooling and encouraged his ambitions. My father liked Bernard as a son and put him in his will and gave him an allowance.

"Unfortunately, Bernard began spending time with a Jamaican gang and spent his allowance on women and parties. One day members of that gang broke into our home to rob us. They thought no one would be there, but that wasn't the case. My mother had returned with my little sister and the housekeeper. The robbers brutally attacked the housekeeper with a machete and..." He bit his lip. "one of them raped my mother. We found Elani hiding in a cupboard under the stairs. She still has nightmares of that night.

"Three men were apprehended and convicted. One piece of evidence against them was a detailed map showing the layout of our house. None of the thieves would name Bernard but we knew he was involved." Frederick gripped the steering wheel. "One day I forced him to admit it. I could have killed him that night, I admit that too, but I didn't. He confessed and was sent to a home for juvenile delinquents. My father changed his will and disowned him. He died six months later. After his release, Bernard left Jamaica and changed his name to what it is now.

"I don't know how he lived and didn't care. I thought he was out of my life until about two years ago." Frederick took a deep, steadying breath. "The memory of this incident and the one I'm about to tell you still—" He stopped. "I hate to talk about it, but I can't leave my story incomplete. I'm asking you not to share it with anyone." He glanced at her. Janet nodded. "My sister is considerably younger than me and presently living with an aunt in Vermont. Our mother never fully recovered from her attack and had to be institutionalized. She died a few years ago. I'm glad her misery is over. My sister too is very sensitive about certain things and I've looked after her. For most of her life she's been home schooled and traveled with her tutor Mrs. Ambrose. Little did I know that Mrs. Ambrose was close to Russell's mother and Russell himself. Nearly two years ago he reentered my sister's life and told her that if she didn't do as he said he would repeat what had happened all those years ago and worse. Elani was only sixteen and terrified so she agreed to elope with him. But his plans were spoiled when I came to visit unexpectedly and she told me what he was up to.

"You can imagine how I reacted. I'll just say that when Russell came to get her, I didn't say a word to him, but he felt my anger. That's when I used my knife. And we have never spoken since. I fired Mrs. Ambrose, because I found out she also played a role by being conspicuously absent each time Russell came to visit my sister. That was the last I saw of him until the day I saw him with you.

"I know his main objective was to marry my sister for her money and an act of vengeance against me. He failed."

The rain had lightened to a drizzle and Frederick reduced the speed of the wipers.

"I know it's a lot to take in and I probably should have told you this the other day, but I couldn't think clearly then.

"Mrs. Amsted and Daphne know everything because they helped me in dealing with Russell and my sister, so if you don't want to believe me you can ask them." Frederick pulled onto a side road then parked in front of the train station. "And that's it. I wish you a safe journey back home." Frederick got out of the car and retrieved her bags. He set them on a cart. "Do you need help inside?"

Janet took the cart from him. "No, I'm fine."

He returned to his car. "Goodbye," he said and she knew he meant forever.

CHAPTER 32

Janet scarcely remembered her train ride home.

She repeated every word he'd spoken. She completely rejected his observation of her sister, because she knew he'd been wrong about that. However, she couldn't dismiss his observations of her family. Her mother had been a bit too presumptuous in her speech with the Sisters in the church, and she certainly shouldn't have made her assumptions so obvious that strangers could hear, especially since no formal announcement was ever made.

And yes, she couldn't deny her three younger sisters' behavior. She had no excuses for them. But they were her family and she loved them and accepted them for who they were.

She didn't like his vague apology for interfering because she felt that it was insincere. He still felt justified that he'd done the right thing. But he'd no right to part Jeffrey and Beverly and she couldn't forgive him for not regretting that. It was obvious that his pride wouldn't allow him to admit that he was wrong about their relationship and that he'd hurt her sister. Just as she thought, he was arrogant and domineering.

But his story about Russell had astonished her. As he spoke she didn't know what to think and still didn't. At first she refused to believe it and told herself that it was false. She clung to that belief because she couldn't release her admiration for Russell. Frederick's story had to be false. How could his character be so odious? How could she have misjudged him? It couldn't be true.

However, her mind wouldn't let her rest and she compared Russell's story to Frederick's. Both mentioned a family connection and a will, but the similarities stopped there. She recounted Frederick's talk about Russell's bad behavior and searched her memory for evidence of it, but couldn't find any. He'd attended Sunday dinners with her family and treated everyone in the community with respect. She hadn't seen a hint of wild spending or partying.

But Frederick wouldn't have told her to confirm his story with Mrs. Amsted and Daphne if it was false. Her heart slowly cracked as she faced the realization that Russell was not the man she thought he was.

No, she didn't know where he'd come from before meeting him at the university. She'd assumed his reputation was solid because she had heard about him and his accomplishments. To her horror, Janet realized that she'd assumed a lot about him. His Jamaican background had provided an instant affinity.

Because of his easy smile and charm she didn't question why he'd probed her about her feelings towards Frederick, before sharing his story. Now with a clearer mind, Janet knew he shouldn't have been so familiar with a stranger. He'd been overeager to tell her his sad tale after he learned Frederick wouldn't be around for long. And although he'd boasted that Frederick couldn't tell him what to do or how to behave, he avoided seeing him by not going to the dedication.

And she couldn't ignore Russell's behavior with Frederick's sister. To use a young girl with such calculating motives made her stomach turn. She briefly thought of the inappropriate drawings he'd done of Maxine; the teenage girl she'd seen in his studio; even how he'd manipulated her into drawing him in the nude, using her attraction to him and her desperate need to appear sophisticated and cosmopolitan as a weapon to seduce her. A sinister image of Russell began to form in her mind. She was glad he was gone. Her family was safe.

Janet tapped her finger against the armrest annoyed. Why had Russell showered attention on her? Did he think her family had more money and connections than they had? Or maybe *she* had flattered and *encouraged* him. As her opinion for Russell darkened her opinion of Frederick grew.

She couldn't blame Jeffrey for his behavior. Nothing about him was cold hearted and Beverly had never said anything about him to make her doubt his character. Poor guy, he'd truly felt that Beverly was not interested in him and believed Frederick a trustworthy friend.

Everyone who knew Frederick spoke of him with praise and Janet remembered the warmth with which he spoke about his sister. Even Russell had to admit he treated his sister very well. Janet remembered his actions at the railroad tracks, and how he was at the hospital. At first she'd used his brusque manners as evidence of him bullying Jeffrey and had used Russell's assessment to complete her picture of him. But she'd been wrong.

She'd been unfair to Jeffrey by assuming that he was easily deceived and naïve, and definitely unkind to Frederick, by believing a stranger and not relying on her own observation.

Janet banged her head against the window. *What an idiot!* She banged it again two more times then sat back and muttered, "I'm so stupid."

The tattooed young man sitting beside her sent her a strange look, but she ignored him.

How different everything looked now! How blind she'd been!

What horrible words she'd used. She'd called him barbaric based on the story of a liar. Janet's heart fell. She'd been just as narrowed minded as those residents in Hamsford who still called him 'The Original' as though he were a creature from another world and not a man. Janet squeezed her eyes shut in disgust. She'd always thought she was a good judge of character, but she'd been wrong. Wrong in so many ways.

She'd been enamored with Russell because he was the opposite of her father. And although she hated to admit it, Frederick was right about her sister. Hadn't Valerie told her that Beverly needed to show more feeling? That a man needed encouragement? And as much as she hated his comments about her family; thankfully he'd left Beverly and herself from his criticism.

Janet slowly exited the train in low spirits and waited for her father to arrive. So much had happened to her. So much she couldn't share. Yet there was one thing she knew she could not conceal.

BEVERLY STARED at Janet as they stood between the bookshelves at the campus library. Although she looked a lot healthier after her trip to Jamaica, Janet's words made her go pale. "He asked you to marry him and you said 'no' so bluntly?"

Janet glanced around to make sure no one could overhear. "I told you why."

"Yes, I know. And you're right. He wasn't romantic, but Originals aren't known for that."

"Please don't call him that," Janet said.

Beverly fell silent and Janet picked a book off the shelf.

Beverly pressed her hands together and tapped them against her mouth then let her hands fall. "I know it was arrogant of him to expect a 'yes', but your refusal must have been devastating. I can't even imagine his disappointment. Poor Durand. To have loved you all this time. So much that he actually asked you to marry him."

Janet opened the book and flipped through its pages. "Are you trying to console me or make me feel worse?"

"I'm on your side, but oh, poor Durand."

Janet snapped the book shut. "Stop saying that. I already feel bad about how I spoke to him, but he'll get over it once he thinks everything through."

Beverly shook her head. "Perhaps. He didn't even care what his family thought. Oh poor—"

"Beverly!"

"I'm sorry."

Janet shoved the book back on the shelf and grabbed another one. "You understand why I said no, right?"

"Yes."

"Good." Janet flipped the book over. "It doesn't matter because I still feel awful."

"About what? You did what you had to."

"I feel awful about how much I liked Wilcox. I praised him to the skies and he didn't deserve a word."

"What do you mean?"

Janet saw someone and pulled Beverly to another empty aisle then told her what Frederick had shared with her in the car (but not every sordid detail). Beverly listened wide eyed, then rested a hand on her chest when Janet had finished. For a moment she was too stunned to speak and when she did, her voice trembled. "Wilcox can't be that evil. I don't want to believe it, but I guess I have to. Durand wouldn't share such an intimate story about his sister if it wasn't true. Oh the poor man, he must have suffered having to listen to you tell him how much you hated him. Hate is such an ugly word. The poor man."

A bitter smile touched Janet's lips. "Well, the fact that my behavior was completely foolish and ridiculous should ease any suffering he's endured. I've never felt more like an idiot."

"We had him in our home," Beverly said still in shock. "Trusted him. Wilcox ate at our table and attended our church."

Janet groaned, remembering the times she'd met with him alone. "I know."

"He seemed to be such a nice man. I remember you calling him a saint."

"I called him a lot of things, I was wrong. If I were a jeweler, I would have discovered that my diamond was actually glass, and my rock a precious stone." She ran her finger along the spine of the book. "My question is should I tell everyone about Wilcox's true character?"

Beverly hesitated then said, "Wilcox is gone so it doesn't matter. I think we should keep this to ourselves. Besides I don't see any reason to discredit him. He's not a threat to anyone here and let's pray that one day he'll redeem himself."

"I doubt it, but you're right. Durand didn't tell me the story so that I could tell others. I just want to forget this horrible ordeal."

Beverly lowered her gaze and her voice. "Did he mention anything about Jeffrey?"

Janet glanced at a moth splayed on the window behind Beverly. "No."

Beverly smiled rueful. "Of course not, his mind was filled with you. Oh po—uh... dear Durand."

Janet set her book down. "Beverly, you're going on as though I killed him."

"I'm sorry, I just know how it feels to be disappointed in love."

Janet didn't move. "Hmm."

"But I'm glad you're home. Maxine and Trudy have been unbearable."

"Why?"

"They want to go on the end of the year summer trip for

Juniors and Seniors. They have been hassling Daddy and he's finally relented."

Janet rested her arm along a bookshelf. "You mean the special overnight camp affiliated with the school?"

"Yes."

"The one that lasts for three weeks?"

"Yes."

"That will be a disaster."

"Daddy doesn't think so."

Janet headed for the exit. "Then Daddy needs to think again."

"You're questioning my decision?" Mr. Barnett tapped his chest and stared at his daughter. "Am I not a deacon in the church?" He tapped his desk. "Am I not the head of this household?"

Janet leaned forward in her chair. "I just believe you should think this through."

"I have thought it through. Do you think my mind is so soft that I let things flitter in and out of it without consideration?"

"No."

"Then it's settled."

"Daddy, you can't let them go."

"Tell me why not, Miss Janet Barnett." He waved his hand at her. "You are always telling me how strict I am with you girls. Now I am trying to be lenient and you disagree. What is wrong with me saying yes this time?"

"Maxine and Trudy tend to act silly, especially in co-ed groups." Janet struggled to find the right words to tell her father without letting him know what her sisters had been doing. "You can't trust them —at least not yet."

"Yes, I know they can be silly, but that is nothing new."

"If you only knew how people see them. Maxine already has a reputation as a flirt."

"Yes, but what has she done?" Mr. Barnett grinned. "Taken away a possible male interest of yours? Janet, don't worry, any man interested in Maxine more than you isn't worth your time."

Janet opened her mouth, ready to share about the pierced ears and the drawings but knew better. Their ears had closed and the drawings were gone. If she told him now, he would blame her and be angry with her for not telling him sooner. It would be the Ramani incident all over again.

"It's not that," she said. "I'm not talking specifics, but in general Maxine's behavior is of concern. Please use a firm hand with her before she is completely out of reach."

"Maxine's young, I agree, but you don't have to worry, she will be with her sister."

Janet glanced at the ceiling exasperated.

"And they will be looked after. There are going to be a total of ten adult chaperones and besides Sister Gordon's daughter, Neta, will be going on the trip as well."

"I'd sooner trust a dog to watch my food than that woman's daughter to watch anything."

"I think you're jealous."

"I'm not—"

"Yes you are, because I didn't let you and Beverly go on school outings when you were younger. I want to mend my ways. I don't want to be rigid and inflexible. I love my daughters, I don't want them to hate or despise me." It was a mounting fear. He already felt his children slipping out of his grasp and he didn't know how to control them. They were good girls and he was very proud of them, but he was used to the way girls behaved back home. He wasn't used to some of their demands wanting to date and stay out with their friends, but he was also afraid of being too strict. Then he could lose them forever.

"They won't despise you Daddy, please listen to me."

"You've been traveling all over, haven't you? I've not said a word. One moment you're in Michigan the next you're in Pennsylvania, your sister goes off to Jamaica and mi say nothing."

"We're fully grown. It's not the same."

"I've already said yes. And my word is my word."

"But—"

Mr. Barnett cupped his ear. "Do you hear that?" He paused. "It's called peace. I like peace. And I did not have any until I said yes. Even your mother saw no harm in their going so why should you?"

"I've told you why. I think you should endure a week, or even a month of their bad temper and sulking, instead of allowing them such a big taste of freedom. Maxine is vain, arrogant, and without restraint and you know that she influences Trudy. Whatever Maxine does Trudy will follow. All we have is our good name. One stain can ruin it. Please Daddy, I'm begging you, don't allow them to go."

Mr. Barnett slowly stood then came from around the desk. He took Janet's hand. "We survived the scandal with the Maliks and the incident with Brother Jerome. I know how to protect my name. I can assure you that neither you nor Beverly will be judged by your sisters' behavior. Everyone knows them to be silly, and perhaps a taste of the world, under the trained eye of a church sister will sober them up. It will keep them busy this summer. I've heard you, but I have decided. They are going. The discussion is finished."

Janet left her father's study, knowing that there was nothing more to say. She headed for her bedroom, but her mother stopped her in the hallway. "Talk to me," she said then walked into the family room.

Janet glanced up at the ceiling and inwardly groaned then followed.

"How are the Jeromes doing?" Mrs. Barnett asked easing into the couch.

Janet fell into a chair. "Very well."

"Do they have a large house?"

"Medium sized and very comfortable."

"Naturally, Brother Jerome has the money to furnish it sufficiently. I'm sure they have no financial worries."

"We didn't talk about money."

"No, wealthy people never have to. Oh, if only Beverly had been able to get Jeffrey. I can't blame her, she tried, but what a blessing that would have been. I'd hoped she might have come back from Jamaica with some news, you know about meeting someone there, but nothing." Her mother kissed her teeth in disgust.

Janet blinked appalled. "Dee-dee she was recovering from her illness."

"I know, but a mother can still hope. At least Trudy and Maxine are in high spirits. Isn't it wonderful that your father is letting them go on the trip?"

Janet made a noncommittal sound.

"You disagree? Is that what you were talking to your father about?"

"I just think—"

Mrs. Barnett held up her hand. "There are two parents in this house not three. We know how to raise our children."

Janet slumped further into her chair as she watched her mother leave. She released a weary sigh, feeling the weight of being under her father's roof.

Over the next several weeks Janet busied herself with her studies and by May finished her last class. As everyone else raced out of the room, Janet sat at a desk knowing she would never have to enter another classroom again. She'd accomplished her goal and earned her degree. Janet knew there would be no ceremony, no congratulations, but she was proud of herself. The only certificate she knew her parents would be proud of was one that began with the letter "M".

Before going home, she treated herself to an ice cream cone then walked the campus grounds.

"Hey Janet!"

She turned and waited for Marisa to catch up with her.

"What happened?" Janet asked amazed by Marisa's transformation. Her nails were clear, her hair an ordinary brown and her nose ring gone.

"My grandfather's visiting from Spain. I didn't want to give him a heart attack."

"You look great both ways."

"Thanks. So are you finished?"

"Yes. You?"

"One more course this evening then I'm through. So what are you going to do to celebrate?"

Janet gestured to her cone. "I *am* celebrating."

Marisa looked at her as if she'd suddenly started to fly. "What? No party. No big trip. Nothing?"

"My family isn't into degrees. But I'm going to visit my aunt and uncle in Montreal this summer."

"Well, my family is celebrating and they're sending me to Paris for six months."

"That sounds fabulous."

Marisa looked embarrassed. "Yes, well they're okay." She pulled out a piece of paper and slid it across the table. "When I get back, if you're ever interested in hooking up sometime we can get in touch."

"I will."

Marisa smiled then left.

Janet tucked the paper away and finished her ice cream. She

still didn't feel like going home yet so she lay back on the grass, letting the sun warm her face.

"Mind if I join you?" a male voice said from above.

Janet's eyes flew open and at first the sun cast the speaker's face in shadow. She sat up and shielded her eyes to see who it was. When she did, she nearly ran.

CHAPTER 33

"Wilcox!"

He grinned. "See? You're not the only one who can deliver surprises."

Before she would have been flattered by him seeking her out and charmed by his smile, but now his attention seemed self-serving and his easy smile made her skin crawl. "What are you doing here?"

He sat on the grass beside her. "I had some business in the area. I'm surprised that I hadn't heard from you before you'd completed your courses. I offered to help you, remember?"

"I'm going to be working at The House of Design."

"But interior design is—"

"Is what I've chosen to do," Janet said in a tone that surprised him. "I don't need to be a gallery artist."

"Well, if you ever change your mind, call me."

Janet glanced at a passing bicyclist.

He cleared his throat, unsure of her strange mood. "I stopped by your house and said hello to your family."

Janet turned to him and gasped as if he'd undressed himself.

"You stopped by my house?"

He frowned. "You sound surprised. I've visited there many times before."

Her tone turned grim. "Yes, I'm aware of that. Who did you speak to?"

"Everyone. Your mother and father seem to be in good health and his business is going well. Francine told me that she's doing well at junior college and Maxine and Trudy went on and on about their upcoming school trip. They're very excited."

"Yes. You know I've had a chance to travel myself. I visited my friend Valerie in Pennsylvania. I saw Durand there. He was staying with an acquaintance, Mrs. Amsted and her daughter Daphne. Do you know them?"

A series of emotions crossed his features—shock, wariness, alarm—but his smile soon returned. "A little." He searched her face. "How long did you stay?"

"A while," she said purposefully vague.

"And did you have the misfortune of seeing Durand often?"

Janet lowered her gaze and ran her hand along the grass, her tone nonchalant although her words were not. "I saw him nearly every day."

"I'm sorry. That must have ruined your holiday."

"Not at all." She drew up her knees, looking Russell squarely in the face. "He improves the more I get to know him."

Russell's brows shot up. "Really?" He laughed. "Perhaps you're confusing him with Milton. That animal is a charmer and perhaps his presence puts Durand in a different light."

"No," Janet said in a quiet tone. She boldly met his gaze. "I can tell the difference between a dog and a man."

"Right. Perhaps that joke was in poor taste." Russell ran a hand over his head amazed. "It's no big deal. He knows how to behave with people he wants to impress. And he always puts on a good appearance when he is around his sponsor. I'm glad that he's kind to others in public, although in private we know how his behavior truly is. Every day I'm reminded of his cruel treatment of me. I know his father would weep at the man he's become." Russell leaned back, his expression smug.

"Yes, he probably would weep for both of you, but for very different reasons."

Russell frowned, not sure how to interpret her statement. "My father would be sad to know how my life has turned out."

Janet only smiled. She would not allow him to reopen the subject. She'd never be an audience for his stories again.

"I—" His mobile phone rang cutting him off. He looked at the number and scowled then stood. "I have to go." He waved then left.

Janet watched him and muttered, "Yes, please go and never come back."

As EXPECTED, there was no big to-do about Janet completing her degree or starting her new job at The House of Design. Weeks later the Barnetts bustled with excitement as they stood outside the high school beside the luxury tour bus hired for the trip. Mrs. Barnett fussed over her daughters, telling them all the ills of the world that they had to be careful of. Mr. Barnett only nodded in agreement. Then they watched them get on the bus and stared as it drove away.

"The house will be so quiet without them," Mrs. Barnett said.

Mr. Barnett grinned at Janet. "Thank God for that."

But Mr. Barnett wasn't smiling the next week when Janet told him about her job. "What do you have to go to Delaware for?"

She looked at the books lining her father's bookshelves. "It's a job."

"What kind of job takes you out of state for a week?"

"Many jobs do."

"But you're an interior designer."

"Sort of."

"What do you mean, sort of?"

"My specialty is faux painting and *trompe l'oeil*. For the job I've been assigned, I'm painting a mural for one of Charlotte's important clients."

"Charlotte?" he repeated shocked that she'd used the woman's first name.

"Mrs. Blakemore. I worked for her last summer and have known her nearly a year. She's my employer and doesn't mind the way I address her. She prefers it. Don't worry, I am always respectful."

He nodded his consent. "At least she's a woman and not a man."

"She wants me on this project because the artist they hired fell ill and she thinks I'm the perfect one to finish it."

He sighed resigned. "Very well."

Janet reveled in her freedom as they sped down the highway in Charlotte's yellow Corvette. Even though she was still living at home and was still under her father's rule, for a week she would be a working woman in the modern age and wouldn't have to answer to anyone. No friends or family to impress. She could be completely herself.

"I'm so glad you're doing this Janet," Charlotte said, turning the radio station to classic rock. "I was determined to get you on this project, even if Sara hadn't fallen ill. You're going to love it. Frederick Durand is always a pleasure to work with."

Janet stiffened. "Durand?"

"Yes, your friend."

"*My* friend?" she stammered. "I hardly know him."

"Oh, I'm sorry. I thought you were close since he recommended you for this position."

Janet felt as if her throat was closing. "He did?"

"Oh damn, I guess he didn't want me to mention it." She shrugged. "Oh well at least I kept it to myself this long."

"He didn't want you to tell me?"

"No, he hates to be thanked. You'd think he'd like it since he's always helping people." She checked her lipstick in the rearview mirror. "He is one of the most generous clients I know, an absolute doll. I love working with him on his homes." She glanced at Janet and laughed. "Don't look so worried. He's not going to be there looking over your shoulder. He's traveling abroad."

Janet began to breathe again. "Oh."

"But he has wonderful taste. Some single men are nightmares, but Frederick is sweet, gorgeous and rich. I can't believe he's still single." She ran a hand through her hair and let the wind blow it. "My divorce is almost final and I know he's considerably younger, but..." A teasing smile spread on her face. "he'd be a great distraction, don't you think? He always makes me laugh."

Were they talking about the same man? "Durand is funny?"

"Hilarious when he wants to be." Charlotte flashed a knowing smile. "You should *really* see some of the tricks he's taught that dog of his. He's not as straight-laced as you'd think. He's full of surprises."

Frederick's house was definitely one. It was a designer showpiece, a stately stone and brick estate situated on a sprawling wooded lot. Charlotte had a copy of the key and let them in. Unlike many grand homes inside wasn't cold and didn't feel like a museum. Janet saw pictures of his friends and those she supposed to be his family, everywhere. Charlotte gave her a brief tour of part of the house. Janet marveled at the grand foyer, formal living and dining room, library, master bedroom which had its own private deck; four full baths, two fireplaces, wraparound porch, and fully finished basement with a wet bar and media center. There was an in-law apartment, but it was locked.

When they entered the conservatory Janet saw a grand piano. *He plays the piano?* She turned to a window and saw an obstacle training course where he probably trained Milton.

In the main hallway Janet looked up and saw a large oil painting of a lake scene. She looked at the signature, *Elani Durand*—his sister. But it was the drawing next to it that shocked her. He'd framed the sketch she'd done of him. She wanted to turn away but remained transfixed.

How strange it was to hear him described by Charlotte. Generous, funny, warm? He'd recommended her for this job? How far did his connections reach? How powerful was he in organizing or arranging people's lives? Who was he really? But she knew the answer. He was a great client, a kind brother, a loyal friend and he'd once loved her.

The thought brought heat to her face. She dismissed it and focused on her sketch. It had been adequate, but not accurate. If she had a chance to draw him again she would soften the lines of his mouth and make the look in his eyes more tender. She had seen that expression once and it haunted her at the oddest moments.

Janet turned from the drawing and continued down the hall amazed by its vastness. She didn't have more time to look around before Charlotte called her to show her the partially completed mural. The finished product would be an image of a stained glass window. Working from the artist's sketches, Janet got to work.

That night she lay in one of Fredericks' guest bedrooms, running her hand over the sensuous feel of the fine linen sheets. If she'd said 'yes', she'd be home right now. The thought sobered her. That was impossible. He was a wealthy man and their cultures and lives were too different. But she couldn't help wondering if he wandered the halls at night as he had at the lake house.

The next couple of days Janet worked hard. She wanted the final picture to be so magnificent anyone looking at it would think they could open the window and see the sun. Each day, she went to work early and left late. She barely saw Charlotte, who busied herself working on renovating one of the bedrooms. On the fourth day, although her shoulders ached, Janet finished the final detail of the sun cascading through the glass.

She was so engrossed in her task that at first she didn't hear the soft paws padding on the wooden floor. When she did, she turned and saw Milton. Before she could react, Frederick came around the corner.

He halted as if he'd hit a wall.

Janet stood frozen. She knew him, but felt like she didn't know him at all. In his dark suit, he looked much like what he was —wealthy, attractive, privileged—but now she knew there was much more to him. That his hands had saved her sister's life; that his arms had carried her to safety; that his mouth had spoken words she'd never thought she'd hear and that his heart had once been hers.

They stared at each other then both spoke at once, apologized, then Janet said in an awkward tone, "You're here."

"I came back early. I'm sorry I didn't let Charlotte know."

"Why would you? It's your house."

"Yes." He flexed his fingers and cleared his throat. "How's your family. Are they all okay?"

"Yes, thank you." Her mind briefly went blank then she said, "You have a beautiful house."

He nodded, rubbed the back of his neck then glanced at her work. "I thought someone else was doing this."

"They got sick so I'm finishing it."

He took a hasty step back. "I didn't mean to disturb you. I'll leave you to finish what you were doing. Come Milton." In seconds he was gone.

Janet sank to the ground and covered her eyes. She shouldn't have come. The last time she'd seen him was when he'd dropped her off at the train station, after showing her how foolish she'd been. What did he think of her now? She didn't want his opinion to matter but it did. He obviously didn't love her anymore, but she didn't want him to feel the opposite.

Janet opened her eyes and looked down at her stained clothes. She looked a mess. How apt. He was Lord of the manor and she merely a servant.

Charlotte raced up to her. "Did you see him?"

Janet slowly rose to her feet. "I think I should go."

"Why? You're nearly finished."

Janet tripped over her bag, but caught herself before she fell. "I'll finish the rest tomorrow. I need to take a break. Get some air."

"You do look a bit ill. Okay, let's go for a drive. I'll get my things."

Janet quickly cleared up her supplies then waited by Charlotte's car. Soon the front door open and Charlotte came out followed by Frederick.

"Where are you two off to?" he asked looking more causal in jeans and a T-shirt.

He reminded her of how he'd looked at the lake house when he was playing badminton with Jeffrey and her fingers itched to sketch him. All of him.

"Taking a break," Charlotte said.

"Will you be back for dinner?"

Janet blinked. "Dinner?"

"Yes. I can whip up something. I've learned to feed myself when I let my chef take holidays."

"You can cook?"

Charlotte grabbed Janet's arm. "Honey, you're in for a treat."

CHAPTER 34

Charlotte and Janet watched Frederick cook and before long the familiar scent of fried plantain and steamed vegetables filled the house. Janet mentioned the similarity between some of his food and Jamaican ones. He showed her other foods like pounded yam and okra, although he called them by different names. They reminded Janet of the African influence in the Jamaican culture and why those from the continent were called The Originals.

Janet continued to watch, amazed by how comfortable Frederick was in the kitchen. He had prepared a savory hot pepper stew filled with onions, tomatoes, goat meat, kale, and other ingredients she wasn't familiar with. Along with fried plantain, he also prepared a delicious dish called acara made from ground black eyed peas, which he scooped up in a large spoon and dropped in hot oil. They reminded her of fritters—fried mini cakes made with flour and shredded saltfish.

When they entered the kitchen nook to eat, Janet gasped at the picture she saw. "You have *The Scream?*"

Frederick shoved his hands in his pocket. "At times I feel like I know how the chap feels."

"Me too. I have the poster on my ceiling."

"Your ceiling?" Charlotte asked.

"Yes. My father won't let me hang any images on the wall."

Frederick glanced up. "That's interesting. I thought people only hung mirrors on the ceiling."

Janet furrowed her brows. "Why would they do that?"

Charlotte burst into laughter.

Frederick's lips twitched, but he lifted his brows in innocence. "I have no idea."

DINNER WAS DELICIOUS. Charlotte flirted and Frederick made her laugh, but Janet remained silent unable to think of anything to say. Her eyes couldn't leave his face. Why hadn't she noticed how long his eyelashes were or that he had sparks of gold in his brown eyes? That his skin was smooth and rich like cinnamon.

"I've got other posters. Would you like to see them?"

Janet stared before she realized he was talking to her. "Uh... sure."

Frederick showed her his collection of posters in his study, then others displayed in the in-law apartment.

"Mondrian!" Janet said rushing over to the picture. "And Feelings!" She dashed across the room. "And O'Keefe."

Charlotte chuckled at Janet's enthusiasm. "They aren't the originals, honey. Just reproductions, he has originals in another—"

Janet didn't care. She ran her hand along the frame in awe. "I know, but you don't understand. It's perfect. I've dreamed of living in a place like this." Her gaze met Frederick's and her cheeks burned as she remembered his rejected proposal. An awkward silence fell. Janet snatched her hand away from the frame and folded her arms.

Charlotte stretched her arms. "I'm going to go have a nice soak," she said then left the room.

Janet shifted from one foot to the other trying to come up with an excuse to leave.

Frederick straightened a picture. "Want to help me exercise Milton?"

Janet felt her anxiety falling away. "I'd love to."

Because he had an audience, Milton decided to show off. He raced through his obstacle course in record time and performed his tricks to perfection. When he was through training, Frederick let Janet give Milton a treat.

Janet watched Milton eat then knelt down and stroked him. "He's a smart dog."

"He's a good listener too and has been with me through some trying times."

"I can see why you'd never part with him."

Frederick handed Milton an extra treat. "Yes. He's priceless."

JANET WOKE up early the next morning, eager to finish the mural. She went down the hall and turned the corner, but stopped when she saw Frederick standing with another man looking at her work. She quickly backtracked and hid.

"He's still not for sale."

"He could fetch a lot of money as a breeder. A pure bred like that shouldn't go to waste."

"He's not going to waste. He's happy here. Now what do you think of it?"

There was a brief pause then the man said, "It's amazing. What did you say her name was again?"

"Janet Barnett."

"Does she do anything else?"

"Yes, portraits, paintings, sketches."

"Commissioned work?"

"She's available for that, but she has to approve the project. She won't work on anything that doesn't interest her."

"What does she charge?"

"Her fee begins at fifty-thousand."

Janet gasped. Fortunately the man's laughter covered the sound. "Come on Frederick, she's a recent graduate I bet she'd jump up and down for ten thousand maybe even five."

"If you can't afford it—"

"You know I can."

"Then there's no need to discuss it. You don't have to pay her fee, but others will."

"The work is amazing," the man said pensive. "Give me her contact information."

"When you're interested you can contact me."

"She doesn't have an agent, does she?"

"She will," Frederick said then Janet heard their footsteps fade away. Fifty thousand dollars! She'd never thought to charge that much. Did he really think she was that good? Good enough to get an agent?

For the rest of the day, Janet concentrated on finishing the mural. She spent several hours finishing off minor details, before applying a thin layer of an acrylic-based product as the final coat. She didn't stop for lunch with Charlotte, but instead drank a protein shake. Throughout the day Janet hoped Frederick would come and see her progress, but he never did.

It was late in the evening before Janet added the last touch and finally decided it was done. She stood back and surveyed her work trying to see if there were any areas that needed to be touched up.

"It looks perfect to me," Frederick said, coming towards her.

Janet shook her head, ignoring the thrill of delight at seeing him again. "Nothing is perfect."

"It comes pretty close." Before Janet could disagree he said, "So are you interning with Charlotte over the summer?"

"No, it's my permanent job. Thanks to you."

"Thanks to me?"

Janet couldn't stop a smile. "She told me that you recommended me for the job."

Frederick looked away embarrassed and shoved his hands in his pockets. "Well, she had an opening and I thought it would work out for you."

"It did."

He nodded. "So you're going to work and go to school?"

"No, I've finished."

"Congratulations." He held out his hand and she shook it, again amazed by its size but this time finding nothing wrong with it. It was warm and strong. "Did your family celebrate?"

"No, they're not impressed by degrees, but my Aunty Bernice and Uncle Godfrey are very proud and have invited me to stay with them for two weeks in Montreal at the end of the month."

"Montreal?"

"Yes."

"Amazing. I'm meeting Karen, Tanya and Jeffrey there around the same time. We'll be attending my sister's gallery opening."

"Oh," Janet said not knowing what else to say. But hearing Jeffrey's name and the mention of his sister brought back the memory of their last conversation. Frederick rubbed the back of his neck clearly remembering the incident too.

"I'm sure they'd like to see you again," he finally said.

"Perhaps one day."

"I know my sister would like to meet you." He glanced at the mural, then the ground then her face. "Would you be interest-ed...?" He folded his arms. "I mean if you'd like..." He sighed and tried again. "Could you find the time to attend her opening? I could get tickets for you and your aunt and uncle."

Janet stared at him unsure that she'd heard him correctly. He wanted her to meet his sister? Why would his sister want to meet her? "Of course, I'd love to meet her."

A smile tugged the corner of his mouth. "Great. Give me their address and I'll send them the invitation. Um, just wait a minute." He left the room then came back scribbling something down on a pad of paper. "Here's my mobile number, the phone number of the place where I'll be staying, the gallery's number, and my email address in case for some reason the phones don't work—"

Janet reached for the paper. "I think that's enough."

He turned to block her. "And here's my sister's address—"

Janet moved around him and tried to snatch the paper, but he moved it out of reach. "Durand!" she said exasperated.

"My name is Frederick," he said softly, his gaze focused on the notepad.

"I know."

He captured her eyes with his. "But you can't call me that."

"No," Janet said with a note of regret. Her father wouldn't approve.

He ripped the paper from the notepad then handed it to her. "Okay." Their fingers touched when she reached for it, sending a delicious shiver through her.

"I'll see you then," he said taking a step back. "Now I'd better go give Milton his exercise before he gets grumpy." He turned and left.

Janet closed her eyes and held the note against her chest not sure what she felt. Giddy? Excited? Confused? She opened her eyes and stared down at the note. "Montreal, here I come."

CHAPTER 35

ernice Perry loved her niece as though she were her own daughter. As Mrs. Barnett's older sister she felt that Janet favored her more than the others and she loved the chance to spoil her. They were not part of the evangelical faith the Barnett's belonged to and valued education, the arts and fine living. They lived in a luxurious three level townhouse with a family room that boasted a cathedral ceiling and a brick fireplace flanked by nine-foot high windows.

The day Janet arrived, her aunt and uncle surprised her with an ice cream cake and a leather bound portfolio as her graduation gift.

Mrs. Perry had started her career as a nurse and had had the good fortune of finding a suitable surgeon, Dr. Godfrey Perry II, to fall in love with. Together they had built a wonderful life together and now enjoyed their retirement. But even though Mrs. Perry loved her niece and was delighted to have her visit, she loved the invitation that arrived in the mail even more.

"I know you told me it was coming," Mrs. Perry said holding it in her hand.

331

Dr. Perry stood next to her. "But it's still a shock to actually see it."

She waved it in front of Janet unable to let it go. "Just look at it. Isn't it beautiful?"

Janet nodded trying to get a glimpse of it. "Yes, very elegant."

"We have wanted to go to this gallery for a long time," Dr. Perry said.

"But have never been able to get tickets," Mrs. Perry said.

"Much less attend—"

"An Invitation Only event."

They both shook their heads as though a puppeteer were orchestrating their movements.

Mrs. Perry put a hand to her mouth. "What should I wear?"

"The blue one," Dr. Perry replied, and winked at his wife.

"And you'll wear your new suit." She turned to Janet and giggled like a young school girl. "We'll have so much fun. Too bad it's from that horrible Original you emailed us about, but we'll have fun anyway."

"No," Janet said, regretting her correspondence with them. "He's not as bad as I described. I've gotten to know him better and I think I was wrong."

"I doubt it," her aunt said. "you're a clever judge of character and my sister told me all about his behavior at Beverly's engagement party. He acted as though he was better than everyone else."

"The Originals are always like that," Dr. Perry said. "They all like to claim that they come from chiefs and such."

"Please don't call him that," Janet said clenching her hand. "His name is Frederick Durand and he has a very impressive heritage and he's considerate and generous. Plus he's also been kind enough to invite us to this function. For that reason alone we shouldn't make fun of him."

"I'm sorry," her aunt said surprised by Janet's fierce defense of him. "I didn't know your feelings about him had changed so much."

Janet stared back amazed. "Neither did I."

IT WAS a chilly evening the night of the gallery opening, which was located in downtown Montreal. A large flood light, situated at the entrance, illuminated a red carpet that led to large glass doors. The evening sky sparkled with the lights coming from towering office complexes. The gallery's ultra chic architectural design of translucent glass blocks and its minimalist interior reflected the gallery owner's love of space and depth. A large sign, "Elani Durand Exhibit," directed visitors to a small salon on the second floor.

"Stop fidgeting Janet," Mrs. Perry scolded as Janet frantically searched the gallery. "You'd think you had bees in your panties."

"Aunty!" Janet said shocked.

"It's true. Keep still." She adjusted Janet's shawl. "You *never* search for a man; you let him search for you. Isn't that right Godfrey?"

"Definitely."

Janet briefly stood on her tip toes. "I just want to make sure that he knows I'm here. I'd hate to miss him and his sister. There are so many people here."

"Isn't it fabulous?" Mrs. Perry said grabbing a wine glass from a passing waiter. "Oh look Godfrey, there's the president of Montreal's Cultural Arts Commission."

"Yes, I see. That lovely lady must be his wife. She looks rather young."

"When a man reaches that age, the women usually are."

Janet didn't hear them as she scanned the crowd. She was about to give up when he came into view so clearly she wondered how she'd missed him. Again, he was the tallest man in the room, but before she could reach him, he disappeared again. In this elegant setting, Frederick didn't look out of place. She was the one who felt as if she didn't belong.

"Janet!" Jeffrey shouted when he saw her. He rushed over to her, gave her a big hug then shook her aunt and uncle's hands, introducing himself, before turning back to her. "Frederick told me you were coming, but I wasn't sure. You look great." He tugged on her sleeve. "Blue suits you."

"Only sometimes," she said remembering the hideous dress she'd worn to Beverly's engagement party. "Is everything going well in Michigan?"

"Yes, it's fine," he said without much interest. "How are things at home? Is your family doing well? Is *everyone* still at home?"

Janet suppressed a smile knowing his real question. Her heart leapt. Perhaps he still had feelings for Beverly. "Yes, *everyone* is very well and still at home."

"I'm glad," he said. "That everyone is well," he quickly added.

"But we're all wondering what you're going to do with the Westland property since you don't plan to live there."

Jeffrey made a vague motion with his hand. "I plan to find a use for it."

"Hopefully sooner rather than later. If you won't occupy it, perhaps you'll find a family who will."

His two sisters came up from behind him before he could reply. "Janet, it's nice to see you again," Karen said extending her hand. Tanya stood beside her. Janet shook Karen's hand and forced a smile. The sisters forced even wider ones.

"You two look well," Janet said. Then she looked at Jeffrey. "I was surprised that I hadn't seen you around Hamsford preparing for the wedding."

Jeffrey frowned. "Wedding?"

"I'll tell you later, Jeffrey," Karen said, nudging him.

"Why not now? Is it a secret? Who's getting married?"

"You are," Janet said. "Or perhaps you already have. It was presumptuous of us to think that you would return to Hamsford to get married."

Karen tapped his arm. "Jeffrey, I think—"

Jeffrey impatiently brushed her hand away. "What are you talking about?"

Janet ignored Karen's fierce stare. "Your engagement was announced in the paper."

He looked incredulous. "What are you talking about?"

"Was your engagement supposed to be a secret?"

"There is no secret because I'm not engaged." Jeffrey spun to his sister. "Karen?"

She shrugged helpless. "It was just a terrible mix-up. I'd sent in one story and they printed another."

Janet toyed with the end of her shawl, keeping her voice nonchalant. "Yes, a terrible mix-up. *The Hamsford Daily* had a picture of you and your fiancée and story of how you'd met and your plans. My family was shocked when we saw the article. We thought you would have told us, but you'd left so suddenly so..." She let her words fall away.

Jeffrey's eyes flashed with anger. "You mean she—uh—your family and the people of Hamsford think I'm engaged?" He looked at his sister in disbelief and anger. "What is going on?"

Karen flashed a sickly smile. "You were engaged."

"I broke it off."

"Exactly," she said in a small voice.

"Years ago," Jeffrey said in a tight voice. He turned to Janet eager to explain himself. "I'd been engaged when I first returned to Hamsford for my father's funeral and I bought the house intending to settle there with my new wife. The engagement had been announced in several newspapers and society magazines, but I broke it off before going to—uh—seeing everyone again. My decision made some people unhappy, but that's how I felt. I couldn't marry her. I don't know if it matters, but please let Bev—the people of Hamsford know that I'm definitely not engaged."

"I will," Janet said gently. "I can already tell you that the people of Hamsford will be very glad to hear it."

"Really?" he said searching her face for the answer to another question.

"Definitely."

Karen took her brother's arm, uneasy with the direction of the conversation. "Oh well. Misunderstandings happen."

Jeffrey pulled his arm away and glared at her. "And after we leave here, you're going to tell me all about it." He marched off.

Karen sent Janet an ugly look then turned away, dragging Tanya behind her. "That was interesting," Janet said then realized that she was alone. Her aunt and uncle had disappeared. For a moment she felt lost, but the look Jeffrey had given her had bolstered her spirits. He still felt something for Beverly. Perhaps he would come back to Hamsford and clear up everything himself. She could see the joy on her sister's face and envisioned her mother dancing in the living room.

Janet grabbed a glass of wine. She rarely drank, but felt like celebrating. She studied the art collection amazed by the scope. One piece in particular grabbed her attention. It was a beautifully rendered illustration of Milton done in colored pencil, a technique she'd never tried. "Janet?" a deep voice said from behind her.

A voice she'd been waiting to hear.

CHAPTER 36

Janet spun around so quickly that her drink splashed to the ground and onto his shoes. "I'm so sorry."

Frederick stopped her before she bent down to clean it up. "It's okay."

"But—"

He motioned to a waiter who immediately came towards them with a cloth. "Never mind, they'll clean it up."

"So much for trying to look sophisticated," Janet said rueful. "Please take this," she said once the waiter had cleaned up the mess. "I haven't even taken a sip and I'm already clumsy." She smiled at Frederick. He looked like African royalty in a dark blue brocade two-piece traditional outfit, and a small hand woven, embroidered cap. She then noticed the young woman standing beside him.

She was nearly as tall as Frederick and for a moment made Janet feel as if she'd entered the land of giants. The young woman wore an elegant floor length, layered outfit, made out of exquisite white lace, and an elaborate gold damask headdress. Janet knew who she was before Frederick introduced her.

"This is my sister Elani."

She wasn't as physically stunning as her brother but she had nice eyes and pretty features, but her mouth turned down at the corners as if she were bored. She didn't appear like the successful, talented artist she was.

Janet didn't know what to say to her so she decided to make light of their awkward meeting. "So have I disappointed you or convinced you of everything your brother has told you about me? Never mind," she said when Elani looked confused. "It's a pleasure to meet you." Janet extended her hand.

"No, the pleasure is all mine," Elani said giving her a firm handshake.

Frederick said, "I'll leave you two to get to know each other," then left.

Janet resisted the urge to call him back. She didn't know what she would say to this pretty, quiet person. But she didn't need to worry. Once Frederick had gone, Elani looped her arm through Janet's, as though they were best friends and said, "I've been waiting for this day for months. My brother has told me so much about you."

"So you know all my faults."

"Oh no," Elani said horrified. "He's always telling me how accomplished you are. How talented you are and kind."

"He was exaggerating."

"Impossible. Frederick never exaggerates. When he says something about someone he means it." She continued before Janet could protest. "I'm so glad you're here. I rarely get to talk to other artists. Or people who will be honest with me, but I want to know your opinion. What do you really think of this?" She pointed to a large, wood sculpture.

Janet shook her head. "That's the wrong question to ask anyone. The most important opinion is your own. Did you achieve what you wanted?"

"I'd hoped for a smoother line here." She indicated where with her pinkie.

"Then you'll do better next time. Never leave yourself open to criticism. At this level people will pay you for your mistakes."

Elani laughed. "I never thought of that. Frederick was right. You're brilliant."

"Not quite," Janet said, but Elani didn't listen and didn't allow Janet to leave her side the rest of the evening. She introduced Janet to her agent, other acquaintances, pointed out the critics and a couple she'd done a commissioned work for then they talked about art until the event ended. Before leaving, Elani invited Janet and her aunt and uncle for lunch. They scheduled to meet later that week.

In the car on the way home, Mrs. Perry raved about how wonderful the event was. "And that Durand was nothing like you described in your emails, Janet. He was warm, considerate, and attentive."

"You met him?" Janet asked. "When?"

Her uncle looked at her through the rearview mirror. "He introduced himself to us."

"Sought us out," Mrs. Perry said evidently pleased.

"I wonder how he knew," Janet said hoping they hadn't embarrassed her in some way. Had their clothes or behavior given them away?

"He said he saw the family resemblance," Mrs. Perry said. She lifted her chin with pride. "He said the moment he saw me he thought he was looking at a prettier image of your mother."

Janet smothered a laugh by coughing; her uncle loudly cleared his throat.

"Naturally, he doesn't have the West Indian charm of Wilcox, but he's African and can't help that somewhat cool demeanor of his."

"You know about Wilcox?" Janet said.

"Of course, have you forgotten your emails to us?"

"Apparently," Janet said wishing she hadn't been so prodigious with her correspondence.

"I didn't find his demeanor cool," Dr. Perry said in Frederick's defense. "A bit reserved, but I didn't find it offensive at all."

His wife nodded. "True. He is handsome, not as handsome as Wilcox, but that's only because he doesn't smile as much or have Wilcox's pleasing manner."

Janet remembered the picture she'd sent of Russell with regret.

Mrs. Perry lowered her visor and looked in the mirror. "I'm glad you changed your mind about him, Janet. All evening I couldn't find one reason to dislike him as much as you do."

"Did," Janet corrected.

"And now we get to dine with a famous artist! What a treat!"

KAREN WAS happy the evening was over. She sat in her brother's rental car annoyed by how Janet had ruined her evening. She'd been able to convince Jeffrey that the announcement had been a mistake. Because he was quick to forgive, he instantly accepted her apology and decided to forget the incident. But Karen hadn't liked how Elani gushed to Frederick about Janet or how happy he was to hear her being praised by his beloved sister.

She looked at Tanya. "Did you notice that Janet was wearing the same dress she wore to Valerie's wedding?"

"No, I think—ow!" She cried when Karen pinched her. She rubbed her thigh. "I mean yes."

"You can tell it's old because it looks like she hemmed the sleeve. That's what happens when you wear old dresses."

"I thought she looked great," Jeffrey said.

Frederick and Elani ignored her. Disappointed, Karen remained silent all the way home.

~

"So how are things back at Hamsford?" Jeffrey asked Janet. The group sat in a private booth Frederick had reserved for lunch.

"Not much has changed. The most exciting thing in our lives was that Maxine and Trudy went away on a trip."

"What a pity," Karen said. "The men of Hamsford will miss them."

Janet ignored her remark.

"Of course the women in Hamsford must be suffering more after the departure of a certain Jamaican artist with a surname beginning with 'W'. Too bad no one was able to convince him to stay," Karen said in a cool tone. She sipped her drink, unaware of the true impact of her words. She didn't see Elani's face pale from distress or Frederick's darken. She didn't know about their dealings with Russell and had mentioned his name deliberately to remind everyone of Janet's crush.

To Janet's surprise Tanya came to her rescue—by design or accident, she didn't know—by mentioning the name of a different artist whose last name began with W who'd briefly visited the area. She announced how much she liked his work. Jeffrey jumped in referring to an architect with the same surname and Dr. Perry cheerfully shared that he'd also worked with a man with the exact surname. They all laughed at the coincidence.

To Karen's disappointment and Janet's triumph, the conversation went in a different direction than she had intended. Aside from that brief awkward moment everyone-excluding Karen— had an enjoyable time. When Dr. Perry expressed interest in doing some bird watching, Jeffrey, who was an avid bird watcher, invited them to join him the next day for a full-day excursion visiting a Montreal wetland area, known for having a wonderful variety of species, followed by dinner at their hotel.

Just as the conversation began to segue onto another topic, Dr. Perry received a call on his mobile and said that they had to go. Karen noticed the look of longing on Frederick's face as he watched Janet and her relatives leave and her sour mood worsened.

"Doesn't Janet look older to you, Tanya?" Tanya opened her mouth to reply, but Karen didn't let her finish. "It's amazing what a year can do. I don't know why she's considered one of the beauties of Hamsford I guess it's because the choice is so limited. Beverly is undisputedly beautiful but Janet is really just ordinary. Her face is too harsh. Her nose is too small, while her eyes are too big."

She glanced at Frederick hoping to elicit a response but he continued to focus on his meal. She continued determined to get him to notice her, even if it meant tearing up the character of a woman she knew he liked. "And then there's her mind. Everyone thinks she's so smart, just because she went to college, but we know that Hamsford's standards aren't very high." Karen laughed.

Jeffrey frowned. "Karen—"

She pointed at Frederick. "I'll never forget how you described her after that odious engagement party when everyone was praising Janet. You said, "If she's their definition of class and beauty then the entire lot had enough brain cells to fill a thimble." She laughed cheered that she'd remembered his insult so clearly.

Frederick set down his utensils in a sharp angry motion and stared at her with a piercing look that made her go cold. "Yes, I did say that. But now I think she's one of the most beautiful women I've ever known." He stood. "Excuse me," he said then left the table, leaving Karen to deal with the brief victory of getting him to notice her and the pain of having him break her heart.

The next day Karen feigned illness and begged Tanya to look

after her. She pleaded with Jeffrey to reschedule the outing he had planned because she didn't want to miss out on the fun. However, when her illness continued into the following two days, Frederick and Elani decided to treat Janet and her aunt and uncle to a fancy dinner cruise on the St. Lawrence River. They scheduled to pick them up early that evening.

Even though she knew Frederick didn't plan to stay, Mrs. Perry wanted to have everything ready for him. She went shopping for whatever food or drink he might request, just in case they stopped by the house after the cruise. She also asked her husband to go with her to buy several bottles of select wine. They left, but not before instructing Janet to make sure the house was spotless when he arrived. Janet was plumping up the pillows when the phone rang. She noticed the number and picked up. "Hello?"

"You need to come home immediately," Beverly said without preamble.

"Why?"

"Maxine's run away."

Janet gripped the phone. "What do you mean?"

"The day before she and Trudy were supposed to return from the school trip she disappeared. No one could account for her. At first we thought she must have been kidnapped but then Trudy told us the truth. Maxine's run off with Russell Wilcox."

Janet fell into the couch, shriveling inside. "What? How?"

"She slipped away at one of the rest stops. Trudy told us that Maxine has been emailing Wilcox for months. This is no coincidence. She told Trudy that they were eloping. I'd hoped it was a mistake, but a student on the trip admitted seeing them together before Maxine disappeared. We think that they have gone to Jamaica, but there's no sign that they're married."

"No," Janet said feeling her chest tighten. "That can't be."

"It's true. We've talked to people at the university and found out that his reputation was exactly as Durand said. I don't think he's going to marry her. Janet we have to find her. Daddy's gone to Jamaica to look." Beverly told her some more then said, "Please tell uncle to fly back with you as soon as you can. We need his help."

"I'll see if we can get on a red eye flight tonight."

"Good." Beverly hung up.

Janet sat staring at the wall. Maxine was ruined. The sound of the doorbell made her jump. She struggled to compose herself then answered.

"My God, what's wrong?" Frederick demanded when he saw her. He quickly softened his tone when she jerked back. "Sorry. I —you don't look well."

She didn't feel well. Thoughts of Ramani loomed in her mind: She saw Ramani after the attack, Ramani returning to the dorm drunk, Ramani with the 'Beast'. The room started to spin and her skin felt cold. She lifted a shaky hand. "Forgive me, but I can't—" She took a step forward and collapsed.

Frederick caught her before she hit the floor. He swept her up in his arms and carried her to the couch. He gently set her down then felt her forehead. "Where's your aunt or uncle?"

"They're out."

"Give me their number and I'll call them."

"No, I'm fine really." Her voice broke. "I can't tell them this over the phone." She started to sit up but he stopped her.

"Tell them what? What's wrong?"

Janet clasped her hands together to stop them from trembling. "It's Maxine," she started, but that was all she could manage before she was wracked with tears.

Frederick hesitated then drew her to him. She didn't resist. She cried as she hadn't since Ramani disappeared. She relived Mrs. Malik's despair and Mr. Malik's rage; her own mother's pain and her father's blame.

Finally her tears subsided and she leaned against him taking comfort in his quiet strength. "I'm sorry," she said embarrassed by the wet stain she'd left on his shirt.

"Tell me what happened."

Janet wiped her eyes. "I just got a call from Beverly. Maxine has run off with Wilcox to Jamaica. They aren't married. You know what he's like and you know what he'll do, if he hasn't already done it. There's no reason for him to marry her. She's lost to us forever." She pounded her thigh with her fist. "This is all my fault! Again I've brought disgrace. When I think of what I could have done to prevent this. I should have exposed him. I knew the type of man he was. You told me about his past behavior, and to beware of him, and I didn't tell anyone. I burned the evidence of his true nature! This is my failing as much as Maxine's."

Frederick turned away from her and said in a low voice. "Are you sure she's gone off with him?"

"Positive. When my uncle comes back, we have to go home right away."

"What's being done?"

"My father has gone to Jamaica, and Beverly hopes my uncle can help him search. They've spoken to people at The Art Institute in Michigan, trying to see if they could get a forwarding address, but didn't get one."

"Damn." Frederick stood when he heard a car drive up outside. "I'll tell Elani that you can't make it today."

Janet jumped to her feet. "Please don't tell her the reason."

He gazed down at her, his eyes dark. "I won't tell a soul."

Her shoulders slumped and she fell onto the couch, wishing his words could make her feel better. "Our shame will soon be exposed for all to see."

He knelt in front of her. "You have to be strong. This will not defeat you. Everything will work out. Do you hear me?"

She looked away.

He held her hands. "Janet?"

She faced him and looked into his tender gaze which mirrored the pain she felt. "Do you hear me?" he repeated.

Her voice was hoarse. "Yes."

He released her hand and turned when the front door opened. Her aunt and uncle stepped inside. "Durand, sorry we're late. Has—"

He walked towards the door. "I have to leave. Janet has something to tell you."

Mrs. Perry dropped her bags when she saw Janet's face and rushed to her. "Dear God who died?"

CHAPTER 37

"Si-gon-ya! Sigonya come quick!"

Sigonya heard her brother's shout from outside and rolled her eyes. "What is it now!" She went to the screen door then stopped at the sight of the man coming up the path. She rushed back inside and nudged her Aunty who was sewing by the window. "Aunty. He's back. Frederick's here."

For the first time in years, Hattie Seabright's eyes lit up. "He's here?"

Sigonya nodded.

Hattie ran to the door as if she was a young girl of sixteen instead of a woman past seventy and she felt the pain of the past melt away. Her life as the housekeeper for the Durands had been perfect before the gang attack. After that, everything changed. She knew no one blamed her, but she still felt guilty that she hadn't done more. Mrs. Durand had been like a sister to her and her institutionalization and death still hurt.

Hattie kept busy on the property and was comfortable with the work Frederick had given her relatives and he'd sent postcards, letters and emails about his travels and work, but they all paled to seeing him again.

For a moment she saw him as a boy of ten with a broken collar bone from falling out of a cocoa nut tree; at twelve sneaking food to a stray dog; at fifteen rushing off to play football with his friends. When Frederick reached the door Hattie hugged him as though he were still a little boy, although her head barely reached his shoulders.

"It's been too long."

"Big Mummy," he whispered, using his affection term for her.

"I'm sure he's had a long trip Aunty," Errol said. "Let him come inside."

Hattie brushed his suggestion aside. "In time." She looked up at Frederick, sensing something was wrong. "What brings you here?"

His face was grim. "Wilcox."

JANET RETURNED to a house in mourning. Her uncle had flown immediately to Jamaica to help with her father's search. Her aunt traveled to Hamsford with her. The weight of shame hit them the moment they entered. All the blinds were closed and no one spoke. They found Mrs. Barnett sitting motionless in the living room, staring at the wall. Beverly told them that she hadn't changed her clothes, bathed or left the house in days. She'd wailed the first two days after the news, but now she was too sad for tears.

When she saw the face of her sister, Mrs. Barnett fell on her knees and both women began to wail. After several minutes of weeping, Bernice spoke to her sister in hushed tones and was able to convince her to go upstairs and rest. Four days later Mr. Barnett returned home and—without a word—went straight to his study where he stayed the entire day into the next morning. He didn't need to come out. There was a half bath off his study, and he refused to eat. All they heard were his prayers, his cries and the sound of Elvis singing.

Before another day could pass, Janet decided to talk to her father. She went to the study and knocked then turned the knob. It wouldn't budge.

"Daddy?" she said. When he didn't respond she pounded on the door. "Daddy, please open up. It's Janet."

After a few moments she heard his footsteps and the door unlock, but it didn't open. She took a deep breath then stepped inside. What she saw made her want to weep. Her father looked as though years had been stripped away from him. His face was ashen, unshaven; his clothes in disarray; his eyes hollow and red from crying. He knelt on the floor like a beaten man. "Daddy, please get up."

"How can I rise to my feet when I must bow my head in shame?" he said. "Look at the shame your sister has brought on our house. For over twenty years I have struggled in dis country to build a good life for you and your sisters." He held up a finger. "And dis one act has ruined it all. Just wiped it away."

"Daddy we can—"

"We can do nothing. It is done. I didn't open the door because I want you to make me feel better. I know the weight of my choice. I feel it. This is all my fault. I should have listened to you."

Janet knelt in front of him. "Please don't—"

"Don't what? Feel the stain that is now on our name? Should I ignore the looks at the market? Forget the whispers I hear? I've been stripped of my deaconship and your mother of her position on the women's missionary board. We now have no church to go to. Even my business is suffering. Some of my clients have already withdrawn their accounts from mi."

Janet stiffened, indignant. "Then the shame should be theirs, not yours. You couldn't have know that Maxine would—"

"But *you* knew. The church's judgment of mi is right. If I cannot manage my own family, how can I manage their funds? How can I be a leader in the church?"

"Daddy this isn't right."

"There's nothing you can say, I accept my punishment."

"Punishment from whom? For what?"

"From God for my arrogance.... We'll have to move."

"I'm sure things will work out. They'll be found and things will be okay."

"Having a daughter live in sin, with a man, without marriage, how, tell me how, will *I* live this shame down?"

"By knowing it can't get worse."

BUT IT DID. Several days later Mrs. Perry sought out Janet who was helping Beverly in the kitchen.

"I just received a call from Godfrey. He told me that Maxine and Wilcox have been spotted."

"At least they're together," Beverly said. "Perhaps they are married and we don't know it."

"They aren't married and it's worse than we thought." She fell against the wall and her eyes welled with tears. "She's pregnant. The source said they'd seen her at a doctor's office and she's starting to show."

Beverly stumbled to a chair; Janet couldn't move.

Mrs. Perry covered her face. "My poor sister."

Beverly gripped the table. "And Daddy."

Janet wrung the dish towel in her hand. "How are we going to tell them?"

"Do we have to?" Beverly said.

"Better us than someone else," Mrs. Perry said.

Janet lay the towel down. "No one else must know. It's bad enough that she's run off with him, but this..." She couldn't finish.

Beverly raised her hands to the ceiling in a plea. "Dear God, have mercy on us!"

"This can only be kept secret for so long," Mrs. Perry said. "Godfrey assured me that the source won't tell anyone and Maxine and Wilcox are not in the same community where we grew up, so no one knows, but in time word will travel."

"Should we tell them together?" Beverly asked. "Perhaps we could bring them into the family room and give them something to eat. They haven't eaten well and some nourishment could make them stronger."

Janet shook her head. "Beverly, we can't make this any easier on them."

Mrs. Perry turned to the door. "All we can do is try."

THE MOMENT MRS. BARNETT heard the news she crumpled to the floor and began sobbing. Mr. Barnet burst from the room and ran out the back door and all they heard were his screams. Janet stood at the window and watched her father tear open his shirt and shake his fists at the sky. Tears fell as she saw him crawl on the ground and scrape up handfuls of dirt as though he wished to dig his own grave. And her heart cracked knowing there was nothing she could do, remembering the last time she'd seen him wail: The day after they'd buried her brother.

Crib death they called it, but her father didn't need a name. The light of his life had been snatched away. The son he'd hoped and dreamed for had been taken and that day too he asked God why, without a reply. They had spent their lives knowing of a name they couldn't mention, and a birthday they couldn't forget.

Janet turned from the sight of her father's anguish and she, Beverly and her aunt held each other and cried.

Mr. Barnett cried too. He knelt on the ground and rubbed dirt on his face and his clothes. "Dear God," he said, the weight of his sorrow making his voice hoarse. "Have I not been a good servant to you? Have I not tried to honor all your ways? I moved on when you took my son and now you've taken my daughter and my name away from me. What other punishment do you have for me? I live, but I'm dead inside." He ripped his shirt then collapsed to the ground.

Over the next week they did not receive any visitors. There was no music, no T.V., no radio. The house stood still. The elder Barnetts spent their days in fasting and prayer while the two younger sisters tried to make do. But they did not realize or understand the full scope of what was happening around them. Trudy sulked when their parents didn't eat with them for another night.

"They're avoiding me," she said.

"They're not avoiding you," Beverly said.

"I wish everyone wouldn't act like this is all my fault. Daddy won't even look at me, but I didn't do anything wrong."

You should have told us, Janet wanted to say, but she knew she was just as much to blame.

Francine spoke up. "It's a little exciting. Like we're heroines in a novel. God's given us this wonderful trial we should embrace. The ruination of our sister and our exile from the community forces us to turn to each other and will strengthen our family. Maxine's shame is a beautiful example of how dangerous men can be. In a book I read a woman killed herself after—"

Janet set her fork down. "Shut up, Francine."

"But—"

"You think you're smart, but you have no idea what you're saying. How can you read so much and know so little? You have books filled with knowledge." She tapped the side of her head. "But you haven't learned anything. This is not a story in a book, or a passage in the Bible meant for analysis. This is reality and it's not wonderful, beautiful or anything but a tragedy." She picked up her fork and they ended the meal in silence.

A day later, Mrs. Lind-Beecham came to help with some duties and the Barnetts welcomed her coming. But then an unwanted visitor showed up.

CHAPTER 38

Mother Shea arrived at the Barnett's house wearing her ostrich feather hat and purple high heels. Janet led her into the family room where Beverly, Trudy and Francine sat and asked that she forgive them but that her parents were indisposed and couldn't see her.

Mother Shea took a seat and sniffed. "As they should be. I knew something would come about. If they had listened to me last year none of this would have happened."

Janet stood. "I'm sorry, I haven't offered you any refreshments." She walked stiffly to the kitchen. When she didn't return, Beverly went to see what was keeping her and found Janet pouring salt in the pitcher of sorrel juice.

"What are you doing?" she asked.

"If she can put salt on our wound, I can put salt in her sorrel."

"No." Beverly emptied the pitcher in the sink. "I'll make tea and you wait. Remember she's a guest."

"A guest?" Janet clenched her teeth. "She's like the serpent in the Garden of Eden. I'd sooner welcome the devil's scorn than that woman's compassion."

"Janet," Beverly said in a harsh whisper.

"The sight of her makes me wonder. Who is this God we serve who mocks us in our misery? Sometimes—"

Beverly covered Janet's mouth and pinned her with a hard look. "Don't even think it. Wipe thoughts like that from your mind and stand firm in faith for *Though He slay me, yet I will trust in Him.* And if you cannot believe it then let me believe it for you. Okay?" Janet nodded and Beverly removed her hand. "Now I'll make tea."

"You were wrong when you said you were not strong." Janet leaned against the counter and folded her arms. "You are strong in all the right ways. I'm the weak one. My flaws glare out at me. My temper, my unruly tongue and so many other things. I hope He will reward your faithfulness. I know I will not be so fortunate because I have been foolish, proud and impulsive."

"His love for us never wavers, Janet. If I can love you with all your flaws He certainly can." She cupped Janet's face. "Oh little sister, you've grown and I'm so glad." She kissed her on both cheeks then set the tray.

When they returned to the family room, Janet tried to be civil as she sat and watched Mother Shea help herself to a handful of biscuits. "I knew this day would come," she said. "A cloud hung over this house for months. You welcomed that Wilcox fellow too quickly. Trusted him too fast."

Janet opened her mouth to argue, but Beverly's soft nudge stopped her.

"If you had done as God had appointed and Beverly had married Brother Jerome, none of this would have happened. God is punishing your family for disobedience. But I will pray with some of the sisters and elders from the church to ask God to forgive you all." After several minutes, and some more refreshments Mother Shea left feeling that she'd done her duty. Mrs. Lind-Beecham watched her go knowing that she had to do hers.

"Is it true?" Darika asked as they hid in Janet's car. She'd caught Janet's eye at the market and they'd secretly met there.

"Yes."

Darika swallowed and her eyes became moist. "You know that Ramani's dead, right?"

Hot tears filled Janet's eyes and she nodded, anguish searing her heart as she forced herself to face the truth she'd been trying to deny for years—that her friend had probably never made it to India and if she had, she hadn't been there long. Her friend had paid the ultimate price for her freedom. Ramani was dead, but somewhere out there her daughter lived.

Darika's voice broke. "There will never be any news and I didn't want to pretend anymore especially now."

"I know."

"She would have wanted you to have this. They threw out everything else but I managed to save it." She handed Janet Ramani's favorite red silk scarf.

"Thank you."

Darika squeezed Janet's hand then slipped out of the car.

Janet watched her go then wrapped the scarf around her neck, inhaling the faint scent of her friend, and wept.

MRS. LIND-BEECHAM HADN'T ATTENDED a church service in over fifteen years, but that Sunday she dressed with special care knowing that she had to present herself well. Her husband brushed her jacket and polished her shoes and she kissed him in thanks, grateful that Janet had brought such a wonderful man into her life.

"You're inviting trouble," he warned her as she prepared to leave.

"I don't care."

He smiled. "I'm glad," he said, then helped her with her coat. She arrived at the church just as Pastor Wainwright was about to start testimony service. She held up her hand, walked down the aisle and shouted, "Pardon me Pastor, but I must speak to the congregation."

"You can speak later," someone shouted out.

Mrs. Lind-Beecham stared at Pastor Wainwright. "No, I will speak now."

He nodded, then stepped aside. Mrs. Lind-Beecham approached the pulpit. "I have heard an' seen nastiness in dis community and most of it come from those of you sitting in these pews. You tink you so holy an' good dat you can treat the Barnetts the way you do. I expected it from some of you." Her gaze surveyed the group. "But when those of you wid influence." Her gaze fell on Mother Shea. "Felt too high an' mighty an' acted with arrogance, insteadda compassion, I knew mi haffi say someting. The Barnetts are good people. Who don't know dat Brother Barnett, as you used to call him, would give him shirt and feed anyone of you in need?

"Hasn't Mrs. Barnett done her duty as a Christian woman by helping di community, by volunteering and working hard on most of your church committees, in spite of the fact she hav five pickney fi raise? Even the holiest family has a prodigal son or daughter. Which of you is widout sin; let dem be the first to cast the stone."

Mrs. Lind-Beecham looked at one of the women. "Wasn't your husband di one I saw coming out of di bar di other day?" She looked at Brother Jeremiah and his wife Bessie. "Ask your husband who helped him wid his money troubles. 'Cause this big man of yours was too scared to tell you. I heard Mr. Barnett on de phone wid him."

She noticed Sister Gordon's daughter, Neta, in the crowd. "As fi you, most of all, wit all di dirty tings you're doing wit di boys, I know how you influenced dat Maxine. You tink I didn't see you. I was watching, just as God watches your every step.

"Most of you don't know me, because you don't care to know me." She tapped the pulpit to punctuate every word. "But. I. Know. You. I've been in most of your homes and cleaned and run errands and you never noticed me, but I noticed you. I may be dark and I may be poor, and to you I'm a sinner bound fi hell, but I believe in a God who is good and I pray Him don't send mi to heaven wid any of you."

The congregation gasped, Mrs. Lind-Beecham continued. "I am richer in spirit than anyone of you an' I'm happy I have never stepped in dis church before, because you can keep your Sista and Bredda titles. I have seen your treatment of one of your so call family and I'm glad mi not in it." She turned to Pastor Wainwright and nodded. "Thank you," she said then left leaving them in silence.

"Harder! Harder! Faster! Yes, that's it."

Russell groaned. He didn't like to be told what to do, but the girl arching herself into him could be bossy. Lucky for Maxine, she pleased him enough for him to forgive her. He kissed her between her breasts then down to her stomach. He paused at the slight swell. He'd been careless knocking her up, but every time she'd welcomed him between her legs he hadn't thought about protection. Not even thirty and he was getting sloppy. If he'd been more careful he wouldn't have lost his job at the Institute.

He looked down at her. She had about three more months before he'd completely lose interest. Pregnant women weren't a turn on. He teased her nipple with his thumb and she giggled. He had to admit she was lots of fun. He may make an exception, if she was willing to go down on him and put that bossy mouth of hers to good use. Or he'd get another woman to fulfill his needs when she couldn't. Feeling satisfied, Russell got out of bed and began to change.

Maxine watched him. "When are we going to get married?"

He zipped up his jeans. "Soon."

"I can't wait to show you off to my friends." She frowned. "Where are you going?" she asked as he put on his shoes.

Bossy and a nag. "Out." He shut the door behind him. He headed to the pub down the road. As he turned the corner, someone shoved him against the wall, fastening their hand around his neck. A knife glistened in the darkening light.

"I should have killed you that night."

Russell's gaze darted from the knife to Frederick's face. His fear fled. "But you didn't and you won't now. You have too much honor."

Frederick tightened his grip. "How much?"

"What are you talking about?"

His grip tightened more.

Fear shot through him, he clawed at Frederick's hand, fighting for breath. "I can't breathe."

"I know. How much?"

Russell wheezed out a number.

Frederick stared at him for a long moment then released him. Russell fell back gasping for air while Frederick retracted his knife. "You're going to take Maxine to this hotel." He handed him a card. "Her uncle is waiting there. You'll get married at the courthouse."

"And if I don't?"

Frederick held up his knife, his tone hard and ruthless. "I'll make sure that Maxine's child is the only one you ever father."

~

"I just received a call from your uncle," Mr. Barnett announced after he'd gathered his family together. "They've located Maxine. She's married."

The family burst into cheer, but Janet noticed her father wasn't as joyous as the others and wondered if he would ever be the same. He answered their questions about where the couple was found and when the marriage took place then said, "Janet, I want to speak to you," and left the room.

She followed him into his study and shut the door. "Yes?"

"I have a story fi you. I had this man in my home. I trusted him with my family and your uncle had to pay him to marry mi daughter."

"Pay him?"

"Yes. Your uncle wouldn't tell me the amount, but admitted that he had to settle some debts fi him before Wilcox would agree."

"Despicable man."

He released a heavy sigh. "And to think, now he is my son-in-law. Your uncle spent a lot of money I know I'll never be able to pay back. I sit here and I can see that my American Dream will never come true. There will be no more waiting. I will never be a wealthy man. I will never be respected. It's over."

Janet leaned forward desperate to break through his despair. "No, Daddy. Now that Maxine is married we can deal with the pregnancy. We can say that the baby was premature."

"People will know."

"But they won't say anything, because at least she's married now. You must see the blessing in this. This is not your sole debt to pay. I'll help you because it's my fault too."

"No, Janet. I—"

"You're the head of this family, but I carry your name too and I will always be proud of it, no matter what happens. You are not alone."

Large tears streamed down his face. "Then why do I feel alone?"

"Because you've locked yourself away in here for so long. You've not allowed anyone close. You can't hide anymore. You are a loved man. Think of what Uncle has done. He wouldn't have done it for a lesser man." Janet stood and came around the desk. "You give so much, but you have to learn how to receive." She wrapped her arms around him.

"Thank you," he whispered, accepting her strength because he had no more of his own, then he hung his head and cried.

A LOT HAPPENED over the next several days. Mrs. Perry returned home to Montreal, the church issued an apology to the Barnetts and reinstated them, and summer turned to autumn then winter. There were changes in the Barnett's house as well. Mr. Barnett placed new restrictions on Francine and Trudy, forcing Beverly and Janet to work longer hours in order to stay out of the house as much as possible.

In quiet moments Janet allowed herself to remember her visit to Montreal, although the memory always ended in regret.

"I wish I hadn't told Durand," Janet said to Beverly as they returned from the market. The sky was white above them while a cold wind from the Chesapeake Bay blew their scarves as they walked towards her car.

"About what?" Beverly asked.

"Maxine's behavior. Now that it's all over I wish he didn't know about it."

Beverly opened the trunk and placed their purchases inside. "Janet, you can't blame yourself. You had to talk to someone."

"I know," Janet said getting into the passenger seat. "But I cried all over him. I wonder what he thinks of us. Of me?"

Beverly was quiet a moment as she started the car then said, "It doesn't matter. You never cared what he thought before."

"I know," Janet said, unable to reveal her true feelings. "I used to be so certain of things, but now I'm not certain of anything—the future, the past, myself—they all seem a mystery to me. I don't know why I feel the way I do. I just wish he knew that everything worked out and that our family isn't as bad as he thinks."

Janet didn't have much time to worry about what Durand thought because the moment they entered the house Mrs. Barnett rushed up to them.

"I've heard such news! Jeffrey Farmer's coming back! He's going to settle some business in Michigan then return home to Hamsford to stay!"

"How do you know?" Janet asked.

"He's fixing up the property he bought."

"That doesn't mean anything."

"You don't furnish a house you plan to sell." Mrs. Barnett grabbed her coat. "I'm going to Sister Daniels to find out more." She dashed out the door.

Beverly sent Janet a look. "Don't say anything," she said, then headed for the kitchen.

Janet followed and began putting things away while watching her sister. "You don't seem too surprised."

"I'm not."

"You knew?"

"Yes."

"And you didn't tell me?" Janet grasped her chest as if she'd been shot. "I'm wounded."

Beverly laughed. "I didn't know how to tell you because I didn't want to get your hopes up again. He sent me a brief email —" She held up her hand before Janet could speak. "But he didn't mention anything specific. I've accepted that we're just very good friends."

Janet opened a cupboard and grinned. "For now."

THAT EVENING Mrs. Barnett shared her good news with the family at dinner. Jeffrey would be back in Hamsford before the spring. Janet's hopes increased when Charlotte told her that Jeffrey had hired her firm to decorate his house.

"Carte blanche!" Charlotte cried as she and Janet stood in Jeffrey's empty house. Her voice echoed down the halls. "I've never been so happy." She walked to a wall and pointed. "He wants a mosaic image here. He gave me a few suggestions." She handed a list to Janet. "Think you can manage?"

Janet looked at the wall then the list, images forming in her mind. "Definitely."

As soon as she got home Janet showed Beverly the list. "So which one should I do?" she asked spreading them out on the coffee table.

"Why are you asking me?"

"Because every day you may have to look at whatever mural I paint."

Beverly picked up a couch pillow and playfully threw it at her. "You're impossible."

"I know," she said, then both sisters laughed.

Over the next four weeks Janet worked day and night on the mural, while Charlotte and two other designers from her company took charge of decorating and furnishing the entire estate. The grand structure was bordered on the north and west by working farms, and from the east was a magnificent view of Hamsford and the nearest town could be seen in the distance. When Janet finally completed the mural she invited Beverly over to see it.

"I'm still not sure I should be here," Beverly said as Janet opened the door.

"We're not doing anything illegal and don't tell me you're not a little curious."

Beverly grinned. "More than a little."

"Good." Janet grabbed her sister's hand and took her inside. She led her directly to the mural located in what she and Charlotte called the grand room. Beverly stared astonished. She knew her sister was talented, but what she saw left her speechless.

Janet took her hand. "It's just the beginning."

"Are you sure we should do this?" Beverly asked as they went up the stairs.

"Of course. We have full reign of the house, you know Jeffrey, he doesn't mind."

Charlotte's design team had done an incredible job. The spacious interior was painted a neutral color scheme. The mansion boasted touches of European, Caribbean and North American elegance, yet had a down-home feel. It was impossible for them to see everything, but Janet couldn't help showing Beverly the master bedroom, with its light blue walls, and a tray ceiling with roped lighting to help soften the richness of the dark mahogany flooring. Off to the side was the master bath, a soothing, private retreat, with an oversized sunken spa, maple cabinetry and a marble sink and counter top.

Next Janet dragged Beverly towards the entrance. Beverly stopped on the landing and stared down at the double staircase and grand foyer amazed. "It's beautiful."

"Wait right there." Janet ran down the stairs then looked up at her. "Pretend you're the lady of the house."

"I can't."

"Just for a minute. It'll be fun. I'm coming to visit." Janet went outside then came back in. "Beverly! How nice to see you. I've just returned from Canada and I'm exhausted," she exclaimed, putting on an English accent.

Beverly nodded then lifted an imaginary train as though she was wearing a long gown. "I'll get Ms. Thomas to get you some refreshment." She slowly came down the steps. "Just leave your bags there and I'll show you to your room."

Janet set her imaginary bags down. "Thank you. How are the children?"

Beverly stopped at the bottom of the stairs and stared at her blank. "Children?"

"Yes," Janet said slowly, encouraging her to pretend. "Your children."

"Oh right. They're doing well. And yours?"

Janet laughed. "You know I don't have any." She stopped pretending and grabbed Beverly's hand. "There's one last thing I want you to see." She took Beverly around the corner and promptly crashed into Jeffrey.

Janet stumbled back and fell on her bottom; Beverly fell into a chair. Jeffrey stared at them. Janet hastily stood. "I'm sorry I didn't expect you back."

He flashed a shy grin. "Nobody did. I came under the cover of darkness." He looked at Beverly. "Hi."

She nodded unable to speak.

Janet cleared her throat. "I was just showing Beverly what we were working on. I hope you like it."

"I like it," he said his gaze still fixed on Beverly. "I like every-thing about it. Do you like it?"

Beverly finally found her voice. "Very much. I hope you'll be happy here."

"I will be if—if everything works out for me."

Janet took a step back feeling as though she'd interrupted an intimate moment, but Beverly stood. "We'd better go."

"Okay," he said. "but don't tell anyone you saw me. I'm only here for a few days and don't want to be bothered."

"Our lips are sealed," Janet said, and then hurried out the door.

Jeffrey took a step forward. "Beverly?"

She stopped and turned to him. "Yes?"

"I'm really glad you like the house."

Beverly smiled then left. She ran down the stairs, got in her car and started it as though a mad man was pursuing them. "I shouldn't have come."

"It was meant to be. He loves you."

"Janet I hope you're right because I love him too," Beverly said finally able to admit it.

Two WEEKS later Jeffrey officially arrived and the speculation about his plans circulated. To everyone's surprise he didn't have an open house, but instead invited the Barnetts over for dinner. It was a very marked gesture that a man of Jeffrey's stature and reputation would honor the family by making them the first guests in his home. And he did this not once, but three times.

These joyful events helped erase the Maxine incident permanently from the Barnett's name and they were finally seen in a new light. However, that light nearly dimmed again in late winter when Maxine returned.

CHAPTER 39

Maxine Wilcox returned to Hamsford with a husband, a baby and no shame. She waltzed into the Barnett's house proudly showing off her infant son.

"A boy!" she said holding the baby up for all her sisters to see as they sat in the family room. Russell sat beside her grinning and Mrs. Barnett grinned back. Her husband; however, did not. "Isn't it amazing Dee-dee!" she said. "I'm sure you want to hold him." She handed the sleeping child over to her mother.

"Yes," Mrs. Barnett said cradling the baby in her arms.

Maxine looked down at her ring. "I'm already a wife and a mother. By the time I'm your age Beverly I may be the mother of four. And Uncle Godfrey was so excited about Martin he set up a trust fund, in my name, so my little boy can get the very best education."

Mr. Barnett glanced at his watch. "When will dinner be ready?"

"At six."

He stood. "Call me then." He left.

Maxine frowned. "Daddy seems to be in a fussy mood."

"He has a lot of work," Janet said.

"Speaking of work, you should see some of the paintings Russell's working on. Can you believe that I'm the wife of an acclaimed artist? Aren't you proud of me Dee-dee?"

"Yes, my dear," Mrs. Barnett said, "but I think Martin needs to be changed."

Maxine vaguely motioned to the stairs, without showing any interest. "His things are upstairs. If you don't mind."

Mrs. Barnett stood. "No, I don't."

Maxine watched her mother leave then stared at her sisters. "I'd ask you what you've been up to, but I doubt any of you have done anything as exciting as I have."

Janet stood. "Let me go check on dinner." She went into the kitchen and walked straight out the back door. All the snow had melted, leaving the ground hard; the bare trees shivered as though chilled by the cold. But Janet didn't notice the cold. She paced in the garden then saw two weeds that had gone unnoticed in the summer and yanked them out of the ground.

"Am I disturbing you?" Russell said.

Janet straightened and turned. "No." She dropped the weeds and wiped her hands.

"I haven't had a chance to say hello."

"We said hello before Wilcox."

"We're family now. Call me Russell."

She wanted to call him a lot of things, but not Russell. "Hmm." Janet went back inside to the kitchen, letting the door close in his face.

Russell didn't take offense. He sat down at the kitchen table while Janet busied herself straightening cans in the cupboard. "Amazing how life works. We're now brother and sister."

"Yes."

"The heart can lead you in strange directions."

Janet glanced down at his trousers. "Is that what you call it?"

"What's gotten into you? You've changed."

Janet closed the cupboard then sat down in front of him. "Yes, I have, Bernard."

He swallowed, but his gaze never left hers.

"I can't pretend that I like you. In fact I won't. You will get smiles and kind words from my mother and my sisters." She narrowed her eyes. "But you won't get that from me. I'll never forget what you did to my family."

Janet stood, placed her hands on the table and leaned towards him, her voice filled with venom. "I'll tolerate you, only because I cannot kill you instead. But if you shame my family again, Durand's scar will look like a paper cut." Janet pointed to the door leading to the family room. "Go to your wife and son you have no business here."

Russell shrugged then sauntered away.

Janet fell back into her chair and covered her eyes.

"Where are the plantain chips?"

She looked up and saw Maxine. She pointed to the pantry.

"It feels like I've been away for ages. It's nice to be home. Everyone loves Russell and our life's so exciting. Our wedding was dull and boring. Hardly anyone was there. Just Uncle Godfrey and two other people whose names I can't remember and nobody smiled. Especially Durand, but he never smiles does he? Anyway I wore—"

Janet sat up. "Durand was at your wedding?"

"Yes, he—" Maxine covered her mouth. "Oh no, I forgot. I wasn't supposed to tell anyone. Forget I said anything. I don't want Russell to get mad."

Janet nodded unable to form words.

Her sister grabbed some plantain chips then skipped out of the room.

❀

"Durand was at Maxine's wedding?" Janet asked her Aunt Bernice the next evening. She'd emailed her to find a suitable time to call when everyone was asleep.

"You weren't supposed to know," Mrs. Perry said.

"Maxine doesn't know how to keep certain secrets. What happened?"

"I'm not sure—"

"Please Aunty."

"Durand was the 'source'. He'd found out about Maxine's pregnancy."

"How?"

"I don't know the details, it took me forever to get anything from your uncle, but this is what he said. Durand unexpectedly met your uncle at the hotel where he was staying in Jamaica and told him that he had found Maxine and Wilcox. He said he'd make sure they got marry."

"Did he say why?"

"He mentioned something about being responsible and that he would make everything right. Durand convinced Wilcox to marry Maxine. I know he paid him off, but Godfrey won't even tell me how much.

"He then secured a position for Wilcox at a state run boy's school where he likely won't get into trouble. Wilcox was not permitted to visit your family until after the baby's birth. He did all this but swore your uncle to secrecy. We don't know why."

"He hates to be thanked," she mumbled remembering Charlotte's words.

"What?"

"Nothing."

"He treated us to dinner a few weeks ago. He asked about your family, but I'm certain you were his main interest. I think he cares about you a lot. While you were in Montreal your uncle and I couldn't help noticing how he looked at you. I don't care that he's African I really like him. I just wish he would smile more—why must these wealthy Africans be so reserved?—but with enough practice and the firm hand of the right woman I'm sure he'll loosen up."

Janet made a noncommittal sound then said goodbye before hanging up the phone bewildered.

He'd traveled all the way to Jamaica just to save her family's reputation? Did he feel that responsible? Her heart wondered if he'd done it for another reason, then dismissed it. He was a man of honor and his sense of duty would be strong. Mrs. Amsted's words rung in her ear. *You don't know the man you've just rejected.* She didn't then, but she did now. Even if—dare she imagine it—he still had feelings for her, how could he ever think of being connected to a family whose daughter was basically sold? Not even purchased by the owner, but given away with payment. By him! How could he ever accept Russell as his brother-in-law? She knew it wouldn't happen.

They owed him so much and would never be able to repay him. He had offered their family the compassion that the town of Hamsford and their church had briefly taken away. He hadn't judged them and had restored Maxine's reputation and theirs. Yes, he was stubborn, but so was she and one day she hoped she would find a way to thank him.

THE NEXT DAY Janet looked through the sketches she did when she was at the lake house. She stared at the ones of Frederick, wishing she'd sketched his face. Now she could only see him in memory.

Beverly knocked on her door then peeked inside. "Come, Maxine and Wilcox are leaving."

Janet turned over another sketch. "Tell them I said goodbye."

Beverly grabbed Janet's arm and pulled her out of her seat. "Come on. It will be quick."

It wasn't. Maxine promised to keep in touch while Russell dramatically sent them his best wishes. After that he whispered to Janet, "It's clear that your feelings for Frederick have changed, but I wonder what he'll think of you when he sees your sketch."

His emotionless tone sent a wave of icy fear through her. "What are you talking about?"

"The sketch you did of me. I sent it to him. I know he's an art admirer and I thought he should see it." His gaze darkened with contempt. "And the next time you threaten me, think twice." He drew away and smiled broadly at the family then they were gone.

"A daughter married and a grandson," Mrs. Barnett said watching the car drive away. "What a blessing."

"What's wrong, Janet?" Francine asked seeing the stricken look on her sister's face.

"Nothing," Janet said then raced back inside to her room. She jumped on her bed and covered her eyes.

Moments later, Beverly entered. "What's wrong?"

Janet shook her head, her eyes still covered. "I've done something awful. I'm a fool. I thought I knew so much, but I don't know anything. Oh God what will he think of me?"

Beverly gently removed her hands. "Who? What have you done?"

Janet turned away unable to face her sister, her voice filled with despair. "I can't tell you. You'll be so ashamed of me. This has ruined any chance..." She picked up a pillow and hugged it. "Not that I ever had one. It's all over."

"Janet, I'm sure it will be okay whatever it is that's bothering you."

"It's not okay and I have no one to blame but myself." She buried her face in the pillow. "Please leave me alone, Bev. I am miserable and I deserve it."

"Janet—"

"Please."

Beverly left, but Janet didn't stay buried under the pillows. She went to her desk and started to write Frederick a letter then tore it up. *What could she say? Why would he care?* There was nothing she could do to fix this and she would have to suffer the consequences. Janet lay on her bed and stared up at her poster. "I wish Maxine and Wilcox had never come."

~

FORTUNATELY, a month later the Barnett's had an unexpected guest who they did welcome. Jeffrey smiled at them all and asked to speak to Mr. Barnett in private. Mrs. Barnett paced but Beverly was oddly composed. Janet asked her to join her in the kitchen then asked, "Do you know why he's here?"

A slow smile spread on her face then she nodded. "He asked me to marry him."

"He asked you *first*?" Janet said in disbelief.

"Yes, he wanted to make sure how I felt about him before he talked to Daddy. It's the way things are being done now. We've spent weeks trying to decide when to tell him."

"Weeks and you didn't tell me." Janet grinned. "You are sly."

"I didn't want you involved. I wanted to handle this on my own." Beverly looked a little unsure. "You don't think it was wrong to do, do you?"

"Of course not! He respected you by giving you a choice instead of dictating to you." Janet hugged her. "I'm so happy for you."

"I can't believe it. He told me he's loved me all this time and started making plans for us even after he'd heard about Maxine. He said nothing else mattered to him except marrying me and making a life here as his father had."

"That's wonderful."

"But we can't celebrate yet. Daddy hasn't said 'yes' yet."

"He will." Janet winked. "And if he doesn't Dee-dee will make sure he does."

"I'm so happy I can hardly breathe. This will mean so much to our family and then you can leave here and live with us."

"Don't think about me, Bev."

Some of her joy dimmed. "I can't be happy when you're not."

"I am happy. I'm over the moon that you're going to live the life that you deserve."

"Beverly!" Mr. Barnett called.

Beverly suddenly looked anxious. "Come with me."

"It will be okay."

"Please."

"Okay." Janet followed her and they both walked into the study. Jeffrey stood by the bookshelf, his expression grim.

hen Mr. Barnett saw Beverly holding Janet's hand he sniffed. "I see you've brought a supporter. Good because I want to understand something." He pointed to Jeffrey. "This man just told me that *he's* asked *you* to marry him and wants my blessing. He did not come here to ask *me* to tell *you* that he wants to marry you, as is the way it's supposed to be done. You've already made up your minds. What do you need me for? You might as well go off and marry yourselves."

Beverly hugged herself in dismay. "Daddy, that's not how it was, really. Your opinion does matter. We want you to be happy for us."

"But I'm not happy." He looked in Jeffrey's direction "I have nothing against you Jeffrey you're a decent man and I admired your father, but I have reservations."

"What reservations?" Janet said, knowing neither Jeffrey nor Beverly were bold enough to ask. "He's Jamaican, by background, he's rich and he's Christian."

"But he doesn't attend *our* church."

"At least he attends *a* church. Don't be petty."

Mr. Barnett kissed his teeth and muttered. "But I don't like this new way of getting engaged."

Janet took a step forward. "Would you prefer that she run off like Maxine?" His face darkened. Beverly gasped, but Janet didn't care. "Don't ruin this moment for them. Times are changing. Other churches have been doing it this way for decades."

Mr. Barnett threw up his hand. "Other churches do a lot of things I don't approve of."

"At least she's getting married to a man you can be proud of and the two of them respect you enough to ask you for your blessing. Valerie did it this way and others in our church have too. Please give them your blessing."

Mr. Barnett narrowed his eyes. "So you're going to tell me what to do?"

"Do you love your daughter?"

"How can you ask me that?"

"Do you love your wife? Or will your pride be the reason you say no?" Janet opened the door. "Go out there and tell Dee-dee you withheld your blessing because Jeffrey didn't ask you first."

"Shut the door." He kissed his teeth in disgust. "I don't know why God handed me a daughter like you." He looked at Jeffrey. "But Janet's right. You are a good, solid man." He held out his hand. "I give you my blessing *and my permission*. Treat my daughter well."

Jeffrey shook his hand, unable to contain his excitement. "I will."

Beverly came around the desk and hugged her father. "Thank you Daddy," then Beverly and Jeffrey held hands and dashed out to go tell Mrs. Barnett. Moments later Janet and her father heard a scream and a lot of commotion. They rushed into the family room to find Mrs. Barnett dancing madly in a fit of joy.

～

SEVERAL WEEKS later Jeffrey held their engagement party at his house in the glass-enclosed atrium, which accommodated their guests and a catered banquet. Outside, the enormous brick patio with built-in gazebos provided guests splendid views while inside the grand room, people danced to music provided by a DJ. The people of Old Hamsford were thrilled with the news of the upcoming marriage, although some were still annoyed to see the Original again. This time however, Jeffrey had a large group of friends and relatives from out of town who came so Frederick wasn't as out of place as before.

Janet saw him talking to a group of women and weaved her way through the group desperate to talk to him. When she reached him she realized the group was larger than she'd expected. A hot rush of jealousy knotted her stomach and made her more eager to speak to him. She circled around wondering the best way to get his attention. She cleared her throat, but nobody heard her then Frederick looked up and saw her. He said something to the women then walked over to her. He stopped a few feet away, but someone brushed past and he bumped into her. "Oops sorry," he said steadying her. "There are a lot of people here."

"Yes," she said breathless, soaking in the sight of him. He smelled wonderful and looked just as good.

"Sometimes I wish Jeffrey wasn't so popular."

"Yes," she said again, wishing she had something more riveting to say.

"So—"

"There she is!" Mother Shea's voice boomed. "This is the artist of that mural." She grabbed Janet's arm and dragged her away.

Janet looked back at Frederick helpless to stop the onslaught. "It's really no big deal," she said to Mother Shea.

"You don't have to thank me," Mother Shea said in a low

voice. "But I didn't want to see you stuck talking with that outsider."

"He's not—"

Mother Shea stopped in front of the mural and raised her voice again. "And now Sister Janet will tell us how she did it."

Janet shot Mother Shea a look then briefly explained her techniques to the small audience. Once she was finished she excused herself and again looked for Frederick. She saw him against the wall and headed towards him.

Her mother yanked her back. "Janet," she said. "There are *so* many men here who past the JCE test. Be on your best behavior."

Janet pushed down her frustration. "I am Dee-dee. Now I have to go."

"Why are you heading in that direction?" She turned Janet around. "Most of them are over there. Enjoy yourself."

Janet plastered on a smile and walked towards the location her mother indicated, but when she wasn't looking Janet darted out of sight. But when she looked for Frederick, she couldn't find him and her heart sank.

"I thought you'd be happy about this."

Janet turned and saw Abigail from the lake house. She gave her a fierce hug. "I am happy."

"Then how come you don't look it?"

Janet looked past her not ready to answer. "Where's Les."

"Stuffing his face somewhere. I'm glad to see you're all together again," Abigail said looking at Karen and Tanya then Beverly and Jeffrey. "I wasn't sure this day would come. Oh good Frederick's here too."

Janet heart lifted at the sight of him. "I haven't had a chance to really say hello."

"Jeffrey wasn't sure he would come," Abigail said.

Janet turned to her alarmed. "Why not?"

"He said Frederick's been a little lost without Milton."

"Why? What happened to him?"

"He sold him."

"He sold Milton? Did he say why?"

"No. You'd have to ask him." Abigail glanced up and saw Frederick heading for the door. "And you'd have to ask him now."

"Yes, I will." Janet pushed her way through the crowd then raced out the door. She reached Frederick before he got to his car.

"Durand!"

He turned.

"You promised never to sell Milton." She hated how accusatory her voice sounded so she softened her tone. "Abigail just told me. Why did you do it?"

"It was a price I had to pay."

"What price? Couldn't you have afforded it? Whatever it was?"

"No." He turned.

Janet jumped in front of him. "I know what you did for Maxine."

He walked past her. "It's okay."

Tears sprung to her eyes and her voice trembled. "You have every right to walk away from me, but I just have to know why you gave Milton away. I know it's none of my business, but I need to know. Then I'll never bother you again."

Frederick halted then slowly turned back to her. "I had to get Wilcox employed somewhere and a friend I know who could help me had one condition."

"You had to give him Milton."

"Exactly." Frederick released a weary sigh. "He's wanted Milton for a long time so I said yes. He promised to treat him well. You weren't supposed to know any of this."

"My uncle didn't break his promise. I just found out. I want you to accept our thanks. You've done so much for my family. You saved Beverly's life, saved Maxine's reputation and my father's name. You got me a wonderful job with Charlotte and now this." She gestured to the house and the sound of festivities. "It's because of you. Everyone should know."

"I don't want them to." He began to turn. "Now I have to go."

Janet grabbed his sleeve. "It wasn't what you think," she said in a rush.

He stopped. "What?"

"The drawing Wilcox sent you... It's not—It didn't mean anything." She wrung her hands. "I don't blame you for what you must be thinking of me. I've thought worse of myself. He doesn't mean anything to me. That sketch was a mistake and he sent it to you to punish me."

"No, Janet," he said with a sad smile. "He sent it to punish me."

Janet's temper flared. "It's not fair that you've had to give up so much because of him."

Frederick shook his head. "I didn't give up Milton for him or for Maxine or for your family." He briefly closed his eyes as if gathering courage. "I did it for you."

Janet looked up at him with hope. "Then you forgive me?"

Frederick hung his head. "Janet, I can't do this. I can't—" He searched for words then shook his head again, spun away and marched to his car.

Janet again blocked his path. "Please don't go."

"I have to."

"Why?"

His patience snapped and he seized her shoulders with his careless strength, his voice hoarse with emotion. "Because I promised last spring that I'd never bring up a certain subject again and God help me I want to but—"

"Yes."

He paused. "I'm sorry?"

"Yes, the answer is yes." She rested a hand on his chest where she could feel his heart racing. "I will marry you, Frederick."

He dropped his hands to his side, his voice barely a whisper. "Say my name again."

"Frederick."

His face broke into a smile and he lifted her up and spun her around, with such joy that Janet burst out laughing. "My dear, wonderful Janet." He kissed her then cradled her face in his hands. "I've waited so long to hear you say it."

"And I could say it a million times and never tire of it because now my love has a name and it's Frederick. Frederick. Frederick."

His mouth covered hers again with a sweet tantalizing kiss that coursed through her veins. Janet met his ardor with her own, relishing in the sensation of her burning hunger and desire for him, amazed at how it was heightened by her love. Once art had consumed every bit of her heart, but now he was her new passion. She'd never known that a man's lips could taste as juicy as honeydew yet call to something so deep and intimate inside her; that his arms could make her feel both safe and reckless; or that his gaze could settle the inner longings of her heart.

Frederick drew away and studied her face in wonder. 'I'm afraid to let you go."

"Then don't." Janet took his hand and led him to the side of the house. Together they stared at the purple and blue sky and the melting sun as it cast its orange glow on the trees and the town. It made the church spire shine like gold.

When Janet turned from the sight to look at him his expression was pensive. She squeezed his hand concerned. "What's wrong?"

"When I stood at this spot almost two years ago, I was a different man. After what had happened in Jamaica it's as if something inside me died. I did what I was supposed to do and took care of my obligations. I even volunteered and donated to charity but I didn't feel anything." He looked down at her with tenderness. "Until I met you. You made me want to live again. To enjoy life and then when you rejected me—"

Janet covered her eyes and cringed. "Please don't talk about it. I was so brutal."

"No, it was good for me. It made me angry, furious really, but it forced me to feel again. You're not alive unless you feel some pain. You made me face my arrogance and pride and even, I hate to admit it, my selfishness. I wanted to prove myself to you *and* to myself. You made me want to be a better man.

"Jeffrey said that Hamsford would change my life, but he was wrong." He brushed his lips against her forehead. "You did."

Janet closed her eyes reveling in the sensations he awoke in her. "You changed mine. I didn't know myself before." She opened her eyes then cupped his face, knowing that she'd never be able to gaze at it enough. "I didn't realize that I sketched people in my mind just as I did on paper. It was an ugly truth you forced me to see." She wrapped her arms around him and rested her head against him. "My dear, Frederick. I'm so happy." She suddenly stiffened.

"What is it?"

"I just realized something."

"What?"

She looked at him terrified. "You have to ask my father."

Trudy and Francine sat at the top of the stairs, while Janet and Beverly sat on the bottom steps, waiting for Frederick to emerge from their father's study. While they couldn't make out what was being said, they heard their father's booming voice, which wasn't a good sign. Moments later Frederick came out, shut the door behind him and looked at Janet. "He said no."

Janet jumped to her feet stunned. "He didn't mean it."

"I did mean it," Mr. Barnett said coming out of his study. He looked at Frederick and shook his hand. "I'm sure you're a nice fellow, but that doesn't change my answer." He walked into the family room.

Janet followed him. "We're not asking for your permission."

"I know you're trying to pull that Jeffrey/Beverly stunt with me, but it won't work this time."

"It's not a stunt."

He sat and turned on the TV.

"Why won't you give us permission?"

He turned up the volume.

Janet knelt by her father's side and tried to reason with him. "I know he's not Jamaican, but he spent a lot of time there as a child and still owns property there."

Mr. Barnett shot her a look. "I don't care if he owns half the country! He's not one of us."

"Daddy, be quiet he might hear you."

"Let him hear me! Let everyone hear me! I can talk anyway I like *in my house*. I will be the one who will make the decision who my daughter marries. And you will not marry him. He comes from the land of polygamy. How do you know he doesn't have three or four wives at home?"

Janet stood horrified by her father's accusation. "He doesn't."

"We know nothing about him. His ways are too different from ours."

"They're not that different he—"

Her father cut her off mid sentence with a motion of his hand. "I cannot sanction this union. My answer is no and it's final. Tell him to go."

"Daddy."

"Tell. Him. To. Go." When she didn't move, her father stood. "I will."

Janet stopped him. "Don't. I'll do it."

~

"I TRIED TO REASON WITH HIM," Frederick said as he and Janet walked to his car. "but he wouldn't listen. I don't want to come between you and your family." He stopped in front of his car and looked at her with regret. "I'm sorry."

"I shouldn't have told you to ask him," Janet said in a hoarse whisper.

"It's not your fault."

Mrs. Amsted's words came back to her with force. *You don't know the man you've just rejected.* "Let me tell him about you," she said her voice tense in desperation. "He has to know all that you've done."

"He's a proud man, Janet. It will make things worse."

"But he's forcing me to choose."

Frederick turned to his car. "I'll accept your decision."

She knew he would. He wouldn't force her or pressure her. He wouldn't judge her or berate her. He would simply disappear from her life and never bother her again. "Frederick?"

He turned to her his eyes dark. She'd once thought they were cold, harsh, distant, but now she saw they were guarded. He was guarded. He had to be. He was used to pain, betrayal and disappointment.

"I lied."

She felt him grow still.

"The first moment I saw you I thought you were amazing. I think so even more now. You can doubt a lot of things, but never doubt how much I love you." She wrapped her arms around his neck. "I've made my choice." She toyed with the curls at the base of his neck. "And I choose you." She kissed him.

He deepened the kiss, pulling her close to him and for a long moment they found solace in each other.

"It won't be easy, love," he whispered, his breath warm against her ear.

Janet closed her eyes, reveling in his solid strength, her heart beating wildly. "I don't care. I want to be with you."

They held each other as if nothing else mattered, but their feelings for each other.

"I have to go," he said.

"I know." She didn't move.

"I'm not going to disappear."

She reluctantly released him.

Frederick studied her face, a muscle twitched at his jaw. 'I hate leaving you." He looked at the house and narrowed his eyes. "I could go back in and—"

"No, I don't want you to go back in there. You've done enough. I'll talk to him. I know how to deal with my father."

Frederick hesitated then sighed resigned. He got into his car then lowered the window. "Call me."

"I will."

"Tonight."

"I know."

"I won't sleep until you do."

A faint smile touched her lips. "I promise. Now go."

He sent her one last searching look then started the car. Janet watched him drive away and whispered. "No matter what happens, I am yours."

Daddy I hate you! I hate you. I hate you. The words bubbled up in her throat, but she didn't let them out. Janet couldn't move or speak. She felt like someone had scraped out her insides leaving her hollow.

Beverly came outside. "Janet, come inside."

Janet turned and looked at the house. For the first time the sight repulsed her. It wasn't a home; it was her father's kingdom. It was his domain and he could rule it anyway he wanted. He controlled their lives, as though they were chess pieces on a board without feeling or thought. And for the first time Janet realized that no matter how good she'd been, no matter how many times she'd stood by his side, he wouldn't bend. Unlike Beverly and Maxine, she'd been foolish enough to ask for his permission and his blessing, and he'd refused her. Her love for him wasn't enough.

"I can't go back in there."

"It's going to be okay. Daddy has calmed down."

A rush of fury engulfed her. "Calmed down? All that matters now is how *he* feels, how *he* thinks, what *he* wants, but what about me! What about what I want? No I won't calm down. I'm furious. I'm furious that no matter what, I'm never good enough for him." Janet swallowed hard as tears fell down her face. "I didn't ask for him to care about my grades, my degree, or my job. But I was the one who told Frederick to go to him and ask for my hand because I respected him as my father and this is how he treats me and Frederick, a man more wonderful than you know." She vigorously shook her head. "No, I can't go back in there."

Beverly held her hands together pleading. "You have to. Please, Janet."

"What's the use of being good? I never hiked up my skirts or dresses when he wasn't looking like other girls did, I never snuck out with boys. I stroked his ego, listened to his fears, always believed in him and tried to be a good daughter. Why isn't it ever enough for him to trust us?"

"Give him time, Janet. You can't leave like this. Think of Dee-dee. Think of us."

"I am." Janet took a deep breath and walked into the house. She passed by her mother and sisters, who were still sitting on the stairs and stormed into her bedroom. She stood on her bed, ripped the poster off the ceiling and then grabbed her suitcase from the closet. She opened her drawers and began to pack.

Mrs. Barnett came into the room. "Janet, don't be hasty."

She continued packing.

"Your father will come round. Just know that he's thinking of you. We really don't know this Durand person. We didn't even know you liked him. We all know him to be arrogant and—"

"He has his faults. So do I, but I more than like him. I love him and I want to be with him. He's amazing. If only I could tell you all that he's done. But this isn't about Dur-Frederick. This is about you trusting me. Do you trust me?"

"Janet—"

"Do you!"

"I don't know," Mrs. Barnett said helpless. "Sometimes I don't know you. I don't know who you are. You are my daughter but the way you think is so foreign to me."

"Is it really that foreign? Isn't this what you wanted? That I move from my father's house into my husband's?"

"Yes, but—"

"But what? I could've left months ago and lived on my own, but I stayed because you'd both suffered so much. Now I follow your rules and it's still not enough. It will never be enough. I'll never measure up to his—your standards. I've found a man I love and I will marry him."

"But he's not Jamaican."

"No, he's not." Janet snapped her suitcase closed. "But Wilcox is." She moved towards the door. "You can be proud of him."

Mrs. Barnett stopped her, but didn't know what to say. Janet kissed her mother's cheek. "I love you Dee-dee," she said in a soft voice.

Her mother stared at her with fear. "Where will you go?"

"I don't know. I have some savings."

"Please stay," her mother whispered. "If people were to find out..."

"If anyone asks, tell them I'm traveling."

"But it's not safe out there. Who will protect you? You could get murdered."

"It doesn't matter," Janet said. "In this house I'm already dead." Janet left the room and raced down the steps, past her sisters, who still hadn't moved, and grabbed her coat from the hall closet.

"Where are you going?" her father demanded.

She didn't turn to him. "I'm leaving," she said then opened the front door.

He rushed in front of her and slammed it closed. "No, you're not."

Janet stared at him with defiance. "Yes, I am."

Mr. Barnett raised his voice. "If you leave this house you will fall into sin and find yourself cast into hell. You will find yourself drawn into all sorts of abominations."

"No I won't. God will watch over me."

"But I—"

"You. Are. Not. God."

Janet heard a collective gasp from her sisters and even she couldn't believe the words that had escaped her, but somehow they freed her. She finally saw her father clearly, as though a film had been removed from her eyes. Yes, that was it. All her life he'd been like a god—a supernatural force to be obeyed and feared, but now she saw that he was just a man: A man who would turn to dust just as she would. That made them equal. And just as she had flaws he had them too and she could forgive him for that. At that moment, Janet let her feelings of hatred melt away.

"I love you, Daddy, but I can't live with you anymore." She pushed past him and walked out the door closing it firmly behind her.

Mr. Barnett stared at the closed door shocked. *She was gone.* He hadn't been able to hold onto her, she'd slipped out of his grasp. An outsider had stolen her from him. No, that couldn't be. Janet wouldn't do this to him after all he'd done for her. He waited for the door to open. For Janet to reappear and apologize, but she didn't. His face darkened with anger and his heart hardened. Let her go then! The world could have her. He turned to his wife and daughters. "There will not be one tear shed for her," he said in a quiet voice filled with anger. "Not one. Understood?"

They nodded.

"I'll change the locks tomorrow."

Mrs. Barnett stared at her husband as if he'd gone mad. "Winston."

"If she doesn't want to be part of this family then she won't be."

His words pierced her soul and she feared the irreparable damage his actions would do. She looked at her daughters. "Go get your dinner," she said then she turned to her husband. "Winston, come here." She walked into the family room.

Mr. Barnett followed his wife at a leisurely pace and when he saw her take a seat, said, "Speak fast woman, I want to get mi dinner too."

Mrs. Barnett spoke slowly gathering her courage. She'd never confronted her husband before. That wasn't her role. With the necklace incident she'd kept silent, with Brother Jerome she'd followed his will, but now things had changed. She didn't understand Janet but she understood love and when her daughter talked about the Original she saw her face glow. Mrs. Barnett couldn't allow her husband to diminish that. Tonight her daughter mattered more than her fear.

"You are not going to lock my daughter out."

He pointed to the door outraged. "Did you see how she spoke to me? Her *fadda?*"

Mrs. Barnett flinched at his tone, but kept her voice low. "Because she was provoked." She held up a hand. "I'm not saying it was right, but we must honor her request. You must. I know that he is not Jamaican," she said quickly. "But his friend is and we can trust Jeffrey. He is careful in his choice of friends and as shrewd as his father was." She waved her hand when he opened his mouth again. "I know he is Anglican, but like Jeffrey he attends church and he's a wealthy man."

Mr. Barnett sniffed. "I knew it. You're just thinking about his money. His money won't save her soul or make her happy. I know—"

"You don't know your daughter!"

Mr. Barnett stared at her.

"You run this house from your study and you love your children, but you don't know them. You haven't taken time to."

"I do know them."

"Then why can't you see that Janet is just like you? Remember how your family didn't approve of me? They thought you could have done better and your mother told me so. But you married me anyway. I am not going to watch another child of mine run away from us. Yes, I know about our rules and our ways. But we can't hold on so tight, Winston. We have raised them. Now we must let them go. *You* must let them go. Especially now, or it won't get better with the other two."

Mr. Barnett held his hands out imploring her to understand. "A man must stand on solid ground or drown. Do you want me to drown? I am not inflexible. I gave shelter to that Wilcox fellow in my house although I despise him. I endured listening to Jeffrey and Beverly *telling me* they were getting married. But this is too much. Our daughters don't marry outsiders. That is our tradition."

"She loves him."

His hands fell to his sides. "How far must a man bend before he breaks?"

"When it comes to your children, you will bend as far as you need to," Mrs. Barnett said in a soft voice. "Janet wants to leave the house of her father to live in her husband's and you are going to bless them." She stood and picked up the phone.

Mr. Barnett tightened his mouth. "I will—"

Tears threatened, but Mrs. Barnett refused to cry. "Call your daughter and tell her to come home."

"I don't know where she is."

Mrs. Barnett held the phone out. "You have her mobile number."

"I'll call her later."

"Call her now."

He raised his brows in surprise. "So now my word means nothing to you too? You have no respect for me?"

"I will always respect you. You are my husband and the father of my children. You are a deacon in the church. A successful businessman and you are also wrong. Call our child home."

Mr. Barnett snatched the phone away from his wife then angrily dialed. When Janet's voice came on the line he stood paralyzed, his heart twisting with an unrecognizable pain. He remembered bringing her home from the hospital, teaching her to ride a bike, posting her first painting on the refrigerator, and helping her recite her first prayer. He had raised her to womanhood and now he had to let her go.

Mr. Barnett tasted the salt of his tears as he thought of his son buried in the ground, Maxine away in Florida and his father's own harsh words regarding his choice of a wife and knew he did not want to give his daughter that kind of lingering pain. "Janet, I'm sorry." His voice cracked, but he didn't care. "You have my permission and my blessing. Please, daughter, come home so that I can give you away."

CHAPTER 42

Mrs. Barnett was the happiest woman in Hamsford the day Beverly and Janet got married in a double wedding. They decided to coordinate their color choice and wore simple white satin wedding gowns, with matching gloves, a pearl-crusted wedding headdress with a shoulder length veil, and small pearl necklaces. Jeffrey wore a light-blue tuxedo, while Frederick decided on a contemporary dark brown one. Valerie was Janet's matron of honor, while Beverly selected Francine, who treasured her role for years to come. Elani, Trudy and Tanya were brides-maids each wearing knee-high ruffled crepe dresses.

Mrs. Barnett beamed proudly wearing a stunning silver-blue designer outfit and matching hat her daughters had purchased for her. Mr. Barnett sat solemn beside her, choosing to wear an old suit he'd had in his closet for years. Mother Shea looked just as solemn as Mr. Barnett, but few noticed her facial expression, instead they were distracted by the floor-length yellow gown she wore, with matching shoes, clutch purse and three foot high ostrich feathered hat. Mrs. Amstead sat in the front pew and forgave Janet. Karen sat in the back and did not; and in the middle, Hattie Seabright wiped away tears of joy.

Three months later, Frederick, Janet and Elani flew the Barnetts, the Perrys, and Aunt Thelma to Frederick's West African hometown to meet his family. After Frederick showed them the three hotels, local radio station, movie production company and twenty bedroom mansion he owned, he and Janet prepared for their second wedding ceremony – in accordance with the native law and customs in that region of the country.

Janet arrived at Frederick's family compound in a horse drawn carriage, with a solemn Mr. Barnett sitting stiffly besides her. While the 'official' marriage was a simple exchange of a bottle of palm wine and three Kola nuts (one for prosperity, one for fertility, and one for a long and blessed union) word had gotten out in the community, and hundreds of people filled the streets outside the residence stretching to the end of the block. Several large speakers were erected, in anticipation of the crowd, to allow the exchange to be heard and experienced by all. Once Frederick's senior uncle accepted Janet, on behalf of the family, the newlyweds drank wine from a large decorative gourd, and then they were off to the reception. Janet, Frederick and selected guests flew in a private plane to a small airport where three limousines picked them up and drove them to the hotel.

The ballroom, located in one of the grandest hotel in the nation's capitol, had fifty-five round tables covered with stiff white linen table cloths, and attired with fine Wedgewood china plates and 24 carat gold utensils. Sculpted crystal wine glasses, engraved with the family emblem sat alongside large glass canters filled with ginger beer. In the middle of each table, a single etched glass covering was placed over six small round bowls with floating candles. Brightly colored handmade napkins, made by traditional artisans, were shaped in the form of the Saki Bird, a native and beloved bird of the area, thought to bring good luck to married couples. At the head table, Janet and Frederick, now wearing regional outfits, sat alongside Frederick's family including his uncle, his mother's sister, Elani, Mr. & Mrs. Barnett, Mr. & Mrs. Perry, and Aunt Thelma.

Once the many honors, toasts, and blessings were finished, the guests were treated to a banquet of food. As was the custom, several large cows were slaughtered and prepared for the sumptuous feast- *avocats aux crevettes* (avocado-shrimp appetizer), roasted and curried goat, apricot glazed meat pie, beef pot roast, sugar snap pea salad, fish rolls, jollof rice (similar to jambalaya), doh doh (fried plantain), grilled salmon, curry rice, pounded yam, vegetable stew, and pepper pot soup. For dessert, guests dined on baked banana pudding, pineapple milk sherbet, Chin-Chin (a sweet pastry), ginger beer and orange spice tea. (Of course traditional wine and beer was available for those who requested them). An over-sized 7-layered white cream wedding cake decorated as an exact miniature replica of the bride and groom, including a photo image of the two, sat on an elaborate table off to the side, guarded by a trio of young men, who stood admiring the female guests.

The women, including Janet, looked like members of a royal court. Their outfits sparkled from the delicate lace to the extravagant headdresses made out of stiff damask that would have made Mother Shea's hat look demure. Each woman tried to out-do the other both with the cost of the material and the complexity of each design. Janet's outfit, and those of her female family members, as was the custom, were all made of the same material. Handmade gold-lace bodice tops, trimmed with precious stones. Their ankle length wrap skirts, made out of a dazzling orange silk, hugged their hips, and complemented their form. Frederick and the men of the family wore knee-length tunics and matching trousers all made from one dark green silk trimmed with 24 carat gold piping. The children were dressed in their finest – the girls in formal party dresses; the boys in tailored suites dashed to and fro among the guests.

Following Janet and Frederick's first dance as a married couple, the crowd descended onto the dance floor where the live DJ and six giant speakers kept the music pulsating throughout the night into the early morning. The ceremony was covered by local and national media and was featured on the popular worldwide cable channel African Horizons, so that it could be seen all over the world by their relatives living in the US, England, Canada and the Caribbean.

Upon arriving back home in the States, Mrs. Barnett's joy could not be contained. She'd accomplished marrying off three daughters in the space of one year, which solidified her belief in God and renewed her efforts with the church.

Mr. Barnett missed Janet but soon grew used to her absence. In time he became a frequent visitor to their home and grew to admire and respect Frederick. His admiration increased when Frederick taught him about the power of investing.

Francine went on to the university and became a Women's Studies major. Trudy decided not to go to college and took Beverly's old job.

Beverly took joy in being a wife and helped Jeffrey expand Hamsford, to the thrill of some and the horror of others, and stood by his side when he ran for mayor and won.

Janet moved to Frederick's home in Delaware, where their days were filled with laughter and their nights filled with pleasure. Sometimes Janet would lie awake unable to sleep, marveling at her good fortune—her large art studio where Frederick had hung her degree, the commissioned work that would keep her busy for years, and her ability to travel the world. On their honeymoon Frederick had assured her that she could return to Hamsford as often as she liked, afraid that she may get homesick and miss her old life, but she knew she never would.

Janet looked over at him now as they lay in bed. It was mid-afternoon but neither cared. She studied him. He made a marvelous model and she'd spend the rest of her life capturing him in every medium she could think of.

"Frederick?" she said, knowing he wasn't asleep although his eyes were closed.

"Hmm."

"What do you think about hanging a mirror on the ceiling?"

Frederick opened one eye and stared at her with affection. "I was right." His mouth curved into a slow, intimate smile. "You do have a dirty mind."

Janet laughed and slipped her arms around him feeling blissfully free and truly alive. He gathered her close and she rested her head against his chest and closed her eyes. Everything was perfect. At last she was home.

ABOUT THE AUTHOR

Dara Girard, an award winning, national bestselling author of more than forty novels, began her writing career at the age of six with a ball point pen and her mother's diary. Fortunately, her mother loved the story so much her daughter escaped punishment. Writing on the walls, however, got her grounded. Born to a British mother with Jamaican heritage and a Nigerian father Dara loves to travel, eat French pastries and hear from readers.

You can write her at:
    contactdara@daragirard.com
    or
    P.O. Box 10345
    Silver Spring, MD 20914
    If you'd like to receive a reply, please send a self-addressed stamped envelope.

Visit her website to sign up for her newsletter and get sneak peeks, monthly updates on new releases, and special offers.

For more information visit
www.daragirard.com